We'd   ass
merc

reac   e'd
Only   ent.
Over   ise.
Dorr   ing.
let it   hen
the   ned

weren't protected by our coded armor be   that

ped the tracker open on his wrist and watched the grenade's route. None of the other teams reported any contact. That meant that none of the rooms or quarters were occupied between here and the bridge.

My gut started to coil. "They're lying in wait," I said, just as the ceiling panels slid aside and fire rained down . . .

ACCLAIM FOR *WARCHILD*

"WARCHILD is a riveting, edgy thriller that packs an emotional punch like a tactical nuke . . . brilliantly realized alien culture, complex politics both human and alien, and action that crackles with reality . . . solid in conception and execution. Lowachee conveys uncomfortably well the mental and emotional fragility and strength that come out of war zones." —**Elizabeth Moon, author of *Against the Odds***

more . . .

"A magnificent first novel. Characters you'll never forget. An exciting tale of civilizations colliding, and a boy caught between loyalties."

—**David Feintuch,** author of *Children of Hope* and *Midshipman's Hope*

"A vivid, darkly powerful novel of a youth coming to terms with the universe and with his past."

—**David Drake,** author of *Lt. Leary Commanding*

WARCHILD

KARIN LOWACHEE

ASPECT®

WARNER BOOKS

An AOL Time Warner Company

WARNER BOOKS EDITION

Cover design by Shasti O'Leary/Don Puckey
Cover illustration by Matt Stawicki
Book design by Charles Sutherland

Warner Books, Inc.
1271 Avenue of the Americas
New York, NY 10020

Visit our Web site at www.twbookmark.com.

An AOL Time Warner Company

Printed in the United States of America

First Printing: April 2002

10 9 8 7 6 5 4 3 2

To Winifred Wong & Yukiko Kawakami
For sushi, sanity, and safe harbor

ACKNOWLEDGMENTS

Many people contributed to the various stages of this novel's life, directly or indirectly. I wish to thank (in alphabetical order):

— The critiquers from the old DROWW, who saw part of the baby draft

— Carole Dzerigian, for character psychoanalysis

— My family and friends who put up with my panics, for advice, support, and logistics (Yo, Ghetto Lamp Photography, "It's all good.")

— The F.O.G.ians: James Allison, Cecilia Dart-Thornton, and Charles Coleman Finlay (also a Sock Monkey, who suggested I submit to the contest and sent me the info)

— Sue Glantz, for unwavering belief

— Jaime Levine and Betsy Mitchell, for editorial insight and making this first foray such a positive experience

— Tim Powers, for seeing potential

— The Sock Monkeys (one of the best crit groups and bunch of writers): Keri Arthur, Jan Corso, Caroline Heske, Steve Nagy, Sensei Steve K.S. Perry—whose willingness to share his experiences of things both martial and military deserves special mention, but all the SNAFUs outside of dramatic extrapolation are mine; Marsha Sisolak and Jason Venter

— The Sporks (the other best crit group and bunch of writers): Angela Boord and her Boyz, Jennifer de Guzman, Mike Dumas, Roger "Jack" Eichorn, Elizabeth Glover, Meredith L. Patterson, Nancy Proctor, Keby Thompson, and Helen Vorster

— Meinwen Tsui, for all those discussions on Arctic weekends that fueled my muse

— The wonderful people I taught, worked with, and learned from in Kangiqliniq. Qujannamiik nanurmit.

And, finally, on behalf of Mustard, thanks to Ketchup.

PART I

I.

You didn't see their faces from where you hid behind the maintenance grate. Smoke worked its fingers through the tiny holes and stroked under your nose and over your eyes, forcing you to stifle breaths, to blink, and to cry. Footsteps followed everywhere that smoke went on the deck—heavy, violent footsteps—and everywhere they went, shouts went with them. Screams. Pulse fire.

You hardly knew what to listen for, where that one voice you wanted to hear so badly could be among all the other voices that rose and fell on the other side of your screen. Your shelter. Your cowardice.

But your parents had told you to hide if something like this happened. There'd been drills, even in the middle of your sleepshift, so you knew when the klaxon wailed and Daddy and Mama went for their guns and ushered you into the secret compartment in the floor that you were doing what was right, what you were told to do. Pirates or aliens or the Warboy could attack *Mukudori* and you had to stay hidden, just in case, just like you practiced. Daddy and Mama would come back and get you when the klaxon stopped and they'd say you did good, Jos. Daddy would call you his brave soldier boy, and you would believe it. When they lifted you out of that hiding place and smiled at you so proud, you didn't feel like an eight-year-old at all.

But they hadn't come back to the secret compartment. The little yellow light in there winked as if something was wrong with it, on-off, on-off, until you shut your eyes and just listened. But you were under the skin of the ship, like Daddy said, and it was quiet. You didn't hear outside, and outside couldn't hear you. It kept you safe. It was too dark so you opened your eyes and looked up, touched the light, touched the rough walls, but time went away with every yellow blink and nobody came. It got too warm, as if somebody had shut the air vents.

You waited until your legs were numb from sitting in that small space and Mama and Daddy didn't come back. Everywhere was silence and you were too scared to move your fingers and unhook the latch that would open a way into the bedroom. But eventually you had to. Eventually you had to find out why Daddy and Mama hadn't come back like they always did at the end of drills. They never forgot. Daddy would brush off your bottom and ruffle your hair while Mama locked the guns back in the cabinet. They thought you didn't know how to open it. But you did. You thought of that cabinet as you finally crept out of the compartment and made a run for the other side of your bed. You peeked above the rumpled covers but there wasn't anybody in the room and you couldn't hear anybody in the outer room either. So you climbed over your bed and then over your parents' and ran to the outer room so you could take the comp chair and use it to get to the cabinet. Quick before somebody came in.

You stood on the chair and poked the right numbers that you'd seen Daddy and Mama use, then the green button, and waited. The cabinet comp beeped, then the lights behind the buttons glowed green and you grabbed the handle and tugged. A rack of guns. You couldn't remember exactly how to use them but you probably could figure it out. You'd seen

Daddy and Mama use them on the firing range. Daddy and Mama were good with guns, even though they were engineers. Everybody old enough had to be good with guns, Daddy said, because of the war. Nobody could predict aliens or the symps like the Warboy, and merchants like *Mukudori* could get caught between some Hub battleship and a strit one, you just never knew. And pirates were worse. Pirates liked to take hostages.

Never can be too safe, Mama said, when she locked away the guns after a drill.

You took the smallest one in the cabinet and looked at it all over, where the activation was, where the safety was, where the kill release was. Your friend Evan was older and he'd explained all the parts before, even though he never let you touch one. But now you could protect *Mukudori* like Daddy and Mama did, if you had a gun. You hopped down and ran to the hatch to put your ear against it like when you played hide-and-seek with Evan and Derek.

Now you heard the noise, muffled, and smelled smoke very faintly. You didn't want to go out, it was better to hide in the room and wait. But what if something was wrong with the ship and you had to evac? What if something was wrong with the intercom so you couldn't hear the captain telling you to go? What if Daddy and Mama got hung up somewhere and couldn't come back for you? Strits or pirates attacked merchants, Mama said, because the Hub warred with the strits and the pirates were greedy. What if they were out there now? You knew you were breaking regs by opening that hatch but you couldn't sit and wait when it had been so long without anybody coming to tell you anything. You had a gun. You could help.

So you opened the hatch. It took a lot of tugging, and the noise got worse. You crept down the corridor, twitching at every sound. Voices around the corner screamed words

Daddy had told you never to repeat. The sound of pulse shots bounced toward you. Someone fell into view. Derek. Just this past goldshift you'd played with Derek in the gym and there he was on the deck, looking at you, but he wasn't looking at you. He was bleeding from his head. He didn't move. The screaming kept on but it wasn't the klaxon, it was Derek's mother. Even distorted you recognized her Martian accent.

Then she went quiet and a suited form walked around the corner. You didn't see the face. It wore a helmet with no markings on it, not like *Mukudori* helmets, and thin armor. You stared.

You stared. It came toward you like a creature from the vids, black and sleek, scarred on its reflective face, carrying a big gun. Rifle. It took its time. It said, "Kid," in a hollow voice that didn't seem to come from anywhere near where the mouth should have been. It walked toward you like you were no threat, walked over Derek where he lay still and staring. It tracked blood across the deck and that would've made Cap very, very mad.

You went deaf.

You raised your gun and shot the creature directly in the chest. Somehow your fingers had found the release and the trigger and the small gun went *pop pop* in your hand, spitting out two bright red pulses that burned the creature through its armor and cast it to the deck.

Two more came around the corner, faster.

Your hand spasmed again, raining red on the creatures so they scattered. Then you turned and ran because suddenly space became noisy again. Now you weren't deaf. Footsteps chased you. The creatures chased you. You knew all the towersteps and you took them, holding the rails, hooking your ankles and sliding down the way you'd done a hundred times, playing.

But somewhere along the line you'd dropped the gun. Going down the stairs.

Stupid, stupid Jos. They shouted above you on crew deck, below you from engineering deck. Now you were on the command deck where Cap should have been. You pounded away from corridor mains and into corners you knew from years of exploring. You remembered the best hiding place in the galaxy. You squeezed into that maintenance shaft and shrank back in the shadows, hoping the ship would not lose gravity, violently, and send the loosened grate across the deckplates. You smelled smoke and tried not to breathe.

Mukudori was dying. The steady low thrum of her atmospheric controls whined to a halt. You knew the word "die." You'd seen it now. Somewhere Simone shouted "No!" You heard Hasao screaming for Johann, you heard all the silences after, silence creeping toward you from all over the ship, deck by deck, until nothing remained but your own breathing.

Dead in space.

You lost the gun. You lost the gun and now you had no defense. Were you going to sit and wait for the creatures to leave the ship and shoot it from wherever they'd come from? Mama said that was what pirates did. What aliens did too, because they didn't like to take prisoners. Were you going to go out and look for Cap, for friends, for family? Daddy and Mama didn't know where you were. You shouldn't have left the secret compartment. You shouldn't have gone so far because now if they were looking for you they would never find you. You were in the best hiding place in the galaxy.

You couldn't breathe. The shaft was filling with smoke. You shut your eyes and covered your mouth with the bottom of your sweater but it didn't help. You coughed, big wracking coughs as if your lungs were going to fall out your mouth and onto your lap.

The grate opened and a thick, gloved hand reached in and dragged you into the blinking red lights that meant the ship needed help. You couldn't stop coughing, even when the hands pinched and felt you all over in places nobody was ever supposed to touch—Daddy had said so when you'd gone on stations and into playdens with other kids. But these hands poked and Daddy wasn't anywhere to hear your voice. You kicked and swung fists but the hands hit you then. The creatures kicked you and yelled at you to stop it or they'd shoot you. The violence of it shocked you motionless.

"He ain't armed," one of the creatures said.

"He was. This is the one killed Martine."

They hit you again. You stared at their boots. The deck was cold against your cheek. Above your head, far up against the lights the creatures carried on their distant, hollow conversation. You blinked and your eyes ran. Something red made a film over your sight.

"He'll be good. He's strong."

"Pretty."

"He'll grow. What does he look like, six?"

"Hey, kid, how old're you?" Something prodded your back. You couldn't answer.

"Look at his tag."

The gloved hand came back, smacked you when you tried to roll away. Your head spun and you couldn't see clearly. The hand reached in your sweater and yanked out the chained disk from around your neck. The reflective helmet that gave no features came close, looking at your face on the tag and all the basic information it held in case you were lost on station and something had happened to your parents or the ship. Something had happened. But these were the wrong people. They wouldn't help you.

In the helmet you saw your own eyes. They were black holes.

"Eight. Small for eight."

"Can use a P-90 well enough."

"Yeah, Falcone will wanna see him." The hand let your tag drop, lifted up your head by the hair and turned your face this way and that, then pried open your mouth and looked in. You bit. The creature slapped you again. Hard.

"Gonna have to beat the attitude out," was the last thing you heard.

II.

Deep nausea from a deep leap through space pushed you awake. But you were blind.

Then lights hit you in the face. Stinging. Somebody screamed. Shadows formed out of the light and there Adalia reached for you as a man dragged her out a hatch before you could even sit up. The hatch slammed in with the speed of a chopping knife and darkness swallowed you whole. Whimpers bled from the corners of the room, all around you.

Little Adalia. Four-year-old Adalia.

"What's happening?"

Your voice was not your voice. It sounded small and it echoed in the black room. You were cold and the air smelled metallic and rank. The darkness sat thick and solid around you. But maybe a senior was in here with you. Maybe someone who knew things.

"Pirates," someone said.

"Evan?" You sat up wiping your eyes, feeling stickiness, sniffing. "Evan, where are you?"

"I'm here. C'mere, Jos."

Evan and his brother Shane stayed with you when your parents and their parents got together off-duty. Evan used to bully you sometimes, dump food on your clothes and make you jump to get toys he'd hold over his head. But now Evan kept talking to you in a soft voice until you found his leg and then his arm and hugged him there to not let go. Evan was twelve. Not grown-up yet. But he was strong and he could protect you if that man came back.

"Where did they take Adalia?"

"I don't know." Evan paused. "We're on their ship."

"It's pirates? Not aliens?" Your voice sounded shrill. Evan kept patting your hair and back.

"Yeah."

Others came to Evan. They were all younger than twelve. You recognized the voices. Tammy, Whelan, Sano, Paul, Indira, Kaspar, Masayo . . . all crowded around Evan and you, touching for comfort, shivering as you shivered, sniffling and crying. Scared.

Now that you weren't alone you were more afraid. Everyone else's fear added to your own and your heart trembled, all your insides shook, and you dared not ask where Daddy and Mama were. Evan usually had a big mouth and tousled you rough in gym sometimes, but now he was silent in a way he'd never been silent in all of your life. What had he seen? What had happened to *Mukudori*? But you couldn't ask. Evan patted you and didn't speak unless you asked a question.

But no more questions. You huddled with everybody else, all who might have been left, and tried for hours to sleep.

III.

In the dream you were home. Mama was tucking you into bed and whispering "my starling," like she'd call Daddy her darling, but playing on the name of the ship. *Mukudori* meant starling, she said. My starling. You fell asleep like you always did to the hum of *Mukudori*'s drives, and it was a song that brought with it the sounds of your parents talking softly to each other when they thought you weren't awake. Sometimes Mama sat with you, rubbing your back with her hands, which felt dry and rough even though her touch was light and made you drowsy real fast. Sometimes Daddy sang to you. Daddy's voice wasn't so great and sometimes you fell asleep to their laughter and Mama saying, "You'll make the boy deaf."

You dreamed.

But light woke you hard again. The man had returned with Adalia, whom he threw to the floor beside you. Her jumper was torn and her face smudged with tears. You tried to touch her but the man stepped in and grabbed you up, hit Evan when Evan refused to let go. Evan fell back with a bruised eye. You screamed and kicked but the man yanked you out anyway. The hatch slammed shut, silencing the cries behind you. The man swore, dragged you by the arm so hard you thought your bones would snap. With satisfaction you noticed bright red welts on his arm where you'd dug your nails.

He bodily lifted you down the corridor. Dirty, dank corridors, not like *Mukudori*'s. Dull red stains painted the gray bulkheads. Pulse-beam scars cut angular designs through yellow deck numbers and doors. The lev whined and grated, smelling of steel and sweat. He dragged you into a small room, bare and brightly lit, and left you there. You rubbed your arm and leaned into the corner, looking around. But there was nothing to look at. It wasn't home. It was a nightmare you couldn't wake up from.

Then another man entered. Tall, with spiky silver hair, a smooth face, and smooth blue eyes that didn't blink as they looked at you for one long minute. He came to the corner and took your hair, rubbed it between his fingers like you'd seen Mama do with silks on station promenades. He said, "Lovely color. Like sable."

You couldn't retreat. The bulkhead stood behind you like a guard. The man touched your cheek and rubbed like he had with your hair, took you by the ears and looked into your eyes, his own unblinking, they hadn't blinked once. The blue irises were like welding flames. He looked into your ears and ruffled through your hair, made you open your mouth like the first creatures had done, and put his fingers in and pressed your gums. You coughed, tried not to gag, eyes watering because you knew if you bit down this man might kill you. He forced your chin back and looked at your throat, then lifted your hands and inspected your fingers, your nails, your knuckles. Then he stepped back.

"Take off your clothes."

It was cold and you shook. You shook from more than the cold. You couldn't move.

He reached into a cargo pocket on his jacket and pulled out a cigret. "Take off your clothes."

While he struck the end of the cigret with the silver band of his finger lighter, occupied, you moved obediently. Fear filled your mouth, tasting like ashes. You stared at the floor and stood there naked, goose-bumped, holding your pants and sweater and underwear in your hands. Your tag lay cold against your chest.

He took away the clothes and tossed them across the room.

You tried to cover yourself. He bit his cigret between his

teeth and grabbed your wrists, turned you around and raised your arms, turned you again and again like the mannequins you'd seen in shop windows on station. His eyes went everywhere on you and his hands followed, pressing and prodding and lifting. You were too scared and embarrassed even to cry. It was hard to breathe.

Then he let your arms drop and walked to your clothes, picked them up and tossed them back.

"Dress."

The smoke from the cigret stank like rotten vegetables. He watched as you pulled on your clothes. You knew he watched even though you couldn't raise your head. It was a fight just to keep your whole body from shaking violently.

He came forward again and lifted out your tag, looked at it front and back, then longer at the front where the image was.

"Joslyn Aaron Musey. What kind of sissy name is that?"

Did he want an answer? You couldn't speak anyway. Your throat closed. You couldn't raise your head and now you did want to cry. You had to cry but—no. No. No.

"I asked you a question, Joslyn Aaron Musey."

You whispered, "Jos."

"What?"

Loud voice. A voice that sounded full of bad smoke.

"Jos," you repeated. "M-my family calls me Jos."

"Your f-family?" Mocking. "Shit. You know your family's dead, don't you?"

You stared into that face. The tears pushed behind your eyes but you forced yourself to stare into that unlined, mocking face, and you didn't breathe when it blew smoke toward your nose. You stared. And you memorized. You memorized like Daddy had always told you to do if bad people ever approached you.

The man was laughing without sound. Straight white teeth.

"You have fight. That's good, you'll last." The eyes raked over you head to toe. "And you're a good-looking kid. That'll be a bonus. You seem healthy. And smart. So you know that defiance at this point is a waste of my time. I'll get rid of the kids who cause me trouble. Copy?"

He smoked. He looked down at you as if he'd just asked your birthday.

You remembered a name you'd heard. "Falcone." You were never going to forget it.

Falcone smiled again. "Smart boy. Maybe I'll keep you for myself."

You stared at the floor again, but this time so he wouldn't see the hate in your eyes. It might have made him angry. You didn't fight when he got another man to take you back to the room where Evan and the others waited. You walked calmly. You saw how it was going to be: silence unless asked a question. Thoughts in your head that would never reach your eyes or out your mouth. Waiting.

Waiting without feeling. *Don't think back. Don't dream.*

IV.

Eventually they took everybody out, one by one, and brought them back again. Some returned bruised. Others crying. Others silent. Evan came back with all his hair cut off. Evan had long blond hair that he always used to wear in a tail, like his older brother Shane who made stationers stare when he walked on their decks. But Evan came back with his head shaved and a large bruise on his cheek, a cut on his lip and a breakable look in his eyes. He sat in the corner and didn't want anybody to touch him. You tried to and he shoved you away. You didn't think, then, they were treating everybody the same. The place that was left, this small room with the only people you knew, was already destroyed. They'd taken your leader. Evan couldn't protect you if he couldn't protect himself.

Like Mama and Daddy. Your heart hurt.

Sano said, "I heard one of them. When they took me. We're going to Slavepoint."

"You're lying," Tammy said. "Slavepoint's a bogeyman tale."

"It's not! I heard!"

"You're only seven. What do you know?"

"I heard! They're gonna sell us to bad ships and we're gonna have to scrub decks and eat old food our whole lives!"

You knew the stories. Parents said sometimes when they were mad at you that they'd dump you off at Slavepoint. The senior kids like Shane said the pirates met there with nice merchant ship kids that they'd taken in some raid, or they captured goody Universalist ship kids and traded them at Slavepoint for drugs and guns and money, and you had to serve the pirates in all sorts of nasty ways that might mean cleaning out their refuse cans—but if you were really bad they dumped you on the strits. And everybody knew aliens were worse than pirates because aliens ate you.

You found it hard to believe aliens could be worse than what you'd met.

"Shut up!" Evan's voice, out of the dark. "Just shut up, all of you."

Evan's parents were dead too, probably. And Shane. Maybe they'd died together, protecting engineering.

All those bad thoughts floated in your head and you just wanted them to stop.

All those thoughts stank like the room. You'd seen a toilet and a sink when the hatch had opened, but it was hard for the boys to aim in the dark. You hadn't eaten in more than a shift, probably, because you didn't want to use the dirty toilet.

You sat with your arms around your knees and rocked to pass the time. Every now and again Sano would call, "Jos?" And you'd answer, "Yeah." So they knew you were alive.

Then one shift you woke up to silence. You'd slept hard, harder than normal, like that time a couple years ago when Daddy gave you an injet after you fell off the bed and knocked your chin. That injet had made you sleep hard too, and took away the pain. Now you were starving and couldn't even hear breathing.

"Evan?" Darkness and silence. "Tammy? Sano?" One by one you called their names but nobody answered. You felt something building inside that went far beyond fear. A scream that would never be loud enough.

"EVAN! TAMMY! SANO! ADALIA! MASAYO! WHELAN! PAUL! KASPAR! INDIRA!"

At the top of your lungs. A plea. A chant. Until you had no voice left, until their names became desperate whispers on the verge of dying.

V.

Was there ever a time you didn't feel afraid? You couldn't remember. You had to eat. When the bread and soup came you ate. You used the dirty toilet. You no longer smelled the stink. Mama and Daddy were dead. They'd left you in this place and all the crying in the universe didn't change a thing. You got used to the drives of this ship, the higher

whine than *Mukudori*'s. You learned the cadence of the
thumps and screeches that was the sound of this ship moving through space. Sometimes in your sleep you thought you
heard voices. Sometimes light appeared behind your eyes.
But you knew it was a lie. You knew your world was only
darkness.

VI.

The hatch opened when you were sitting on the toilet.
The man there laughed and swore and waved his hand in
front of his face.

"Wipe your ass. Let's go."

You washed your hands slowly because you didn't want
to go with this pierced, pale man. The light in the corridor
blinded you. He grabbed your arm because you couldn't
walk steady.

The corridors looked the same as the last time you'd seen
them. Ugly. Battle worn. Were you the only kid here? Probably. If not, they were probably all in small rooms like the
one you lived in.

The man took you up the loud, rattling lev and in front of
a hatch with a strange red emblem on it, then hit the comm-
panel there. A voice you recognized said, "Enter."

The man dragged you in and left you there with Falcone.

It was a small room. A gray desk, a narrow bed, and webbing for storage. Two cabinets high on the wall. Falcone sat
on the bed with a slate in his hand. He looked at you with
the flame-blue eyes you remembered, that you were never
going to forget.

"Joslyn Aaron Musey." He smoked. He flicked ashes into

a small tray beside him on the blankets. "Looking worse for wear."

You didn't know if you had a voice. You weren't sure how long it had been since the others were taken or since you'd last spoken. It seemed many shifts. But it didn't matter; you didn't want to talk to this man.

"I suppose you're wondering where your friends are."

You stared at a pockmark in the floor.

"Yes? You want to know where your friends are?" Impatient.

So you said, quietly, in a hoarse voice, "Yes."

"I sold them. They're gone. Poof. On other ships. Maybe dead by now. They got me a good deal. *Mukudori* knew how to raise kids, I give them that. And they were a little challenge to take—for a merchant."

You said nothing. It wasn't anything you hadn't figured out already.

"Want to know why I didn't sell you?"

Say what he wanted to hear. "Yes."

"Come here."

No. In your head you said no. You couldn't move. You said no.

"Come here, Jos." He stubbed out the cigret.

You moved. Don't feel. Don't think back. Don't.

He took your arm, looked at it.

"Have you been eating?"

"Yes."

"Are you afraid?"

". . . Yes." What would be the point of lying?

"Afraid of me?"

You stared at his leg. Then you looked up into his face. No feeling. Shouldn't feel.

He smiled. "You're a tough one. What I thought." The smile widened and he put his hand in your hair and rubbed.

"Go take a shower, Jos. Right there." He pointed to a narrow door you hadn't noticed because of the webbing on it. "Go on." He let go of your hair and patted your bottom. Like Daddy used to do.

You hit him. Both fists and as much as you could before he snatched your wrists and backhanded you across the face. The floor came up. He grabbed you by the neck and hit you again and you cried. All the tears came that you thought you'd stopped forever.

Where were Daddy and Mama? Why did they have to be gone?

"Stop sniveling." He took a knife from his boot and sliced off all your clothes, so expert he didn't touch skin despite your struggling. Then he put you in the bathroom, pried open the shower door, and shoved you in. Cold air then cold water hit. It shocked you into silence. "Get your breath," he said. "Breathe." He waved the water to warm. You couldn't move. The water stung your eyes until he told you to blink and to keep blinking. Then he scrubbed you head to toe, everywhere, and mocked things about you that you couldn't help. He laughed because you were eight years old. Then he cut the water and waved on the body dryer, left it on until you felt wind stung.

He gave you clothes. A big sweater that was meant for an older kid and pants you had to roll up. Then he put you in his bed and that made the sick, nervous feeling worse. Daddy and Mama used to cuddle you in their bed sometimes when you had a nightmare, but you didn't want to cuddle with Falcone. He couldn't take away your nightmares. Other things you knew about in a vague way from watching vids with Evan and his friends—things like that happened in bed too, things you thought your parents did that had to do with loving each other . . . but you didn't love Falcone. There was nowhere to go because you were against the wall and he was looking at you with that smooth, mocking smile.

"Go to sleep, Jos. And don't be afraid—well, not too much. You're mine now."

He left you there. You didn't sleep. You shivered wide-eyed, under the heavy blankets that smelled like him, and in the big clothes, and watched the door.

VII.

Sometime later you heard a short beep from the walls. Soon after Falcone came back and went into the bathroom. The shower cycled. Then he came out naked and went to his webbing and pulled out and on dark gray coveralls, leaving the top unzipped and hanging from his hips. He had a tattoo of a bloody four-armed woman on the left side of his chest. On his right wrist, you saw now, was a detail of her dark face. But the one over his heart held weapons and danced, and around her waist hung severed hands. It was a monster from a nightmare. She moved when he moved. He stuck his feet in boots and went to his desk and sat, propped his foot on the edge of the bed and looked at his slate. He hadn't once looked at you. Maybe he thought you were asleep. Only your eyes showed above the blankets.

He smoked as he worked on his slate. You looked at him, trying to avoid that tattoo. His hair was gray but he didn't look as old as Cap. He had the same shape as Daddy, not soft like Jules in engineering, who sometimes worked with only cutoffs on so you saw his arms jiggle when he lifted things.

You looked down at the boot on the end of the bed. Inside had been a knife. Was it there now?

"Did you sleep well?"

Your heart jumped. He was still reading his slate but when you didn't answer he looked at you.

He reached inside his desk, brought out a bag of flavored crackers, and tossed it on the bed.

"Eat something. You look pale." A can of cold caff followed.

He expected you to eat so you sat up, pushed down the blankets, and opened the bag of crackers. You weren't hungry but you popped the can and set it precariously on the mattress after a few sips. The too-sweet taste made your sick feeling worse but he was still looking at you so you ate more crackers.

"You didn't sleep," he said.

"No."

"Well, you better learn. I'm going to want you alert."

You filled your mouth with crackers so you wouldn't have to talk.

"You're going to have to start speaking. But not too much. Just enough to impress."

You found yourself chewing harder than needed. Impress who?

"I'm going to teach you. And you're going to learn. Copy that, Jos? Because if I don't think you're learning then I have no use for you and I'll sell you to some ship that won't treat you as nice. Copy that, Jos?"

"Yes." Was this nice?

"Smile. You know, you're cute. Smile."

It meant nothing. It was muscles in your face. It was staying alive. You smiled, only your mouth.

He laughed. "You merchant kids are so smart."

You thought about that knife in his boot, about the first of them you'd shot and killed.

He came over to the bed and sat. Without thinking you pulled your feet away under the blankets and grabbed the can before it fell over, but he didn't seem to notice. He leaned a hand behind your back, on the bed, and ruffled your hair with his other hand.

You sat very still. He smelled strongly of soap, but not like the kind Daddy used.

Falcone said Daddy was dead.

You bit the inside of your cheek, or else you were going to cry.

"Jos," Falcone said, in a heavy voice, like a teacher. "War is a horrible thing, isn't it?"

You glanced up at him, but couldn't look for long. He was too close. His breath tickled the top of your hair.

"In this war," he said, "there are things we do that other people might not think appropriate or right. Do you know what I mean?"

Your mind raced. You shook your head, because you didn't think it smart to fake understanding. Your teachers on *Mukudori* would frown, but this man might hit.

"Well," he said, "take opportunists, for example. Do you know what an opportunist is?"

It sounded like a trick. He kept looking at you, waiting.

So you said, "No."

"You should." He tugged your hair playfully. You flinched. "Your ship was an opportunist ship. Just like mine."

You looked at him. Now he was lying and you'd caught him at it. *Mukudori* wasn't a pirate.

"It's true," he said. "Merchants are opportunists. Some merchants ferry information and supplies for the military, because it's war. The war gives merchants the opportunity to work for the military, against the strits and their symp allies. The war gives me the opportunity to get what I want when merchants are running around for the military, trying to avoid strits. We're all out here trying to do our best in a bad situation. Do you understand?"

He didn't wait for you to answer this time.

"Some merchants don't want to get too involved in the war, so they look down on those merchant ships that do. They say those merchant ships that work for the military are wrong. Do you think they're wrong?"

Your head felt hot. What did he want you to say?

"Do you think they're wrong, Jos, to work for the military?"

The bag of crackers crumpled in your fist. "No."

He smiled again. You didn't let go of the bag. He said, "That's right. Some people might say those merchants are wrong, but then other people say those merchants have the right. They're opportunists and they have the *right* to work for the military."

He paused but you didn't say anything. You weren't getting it and if he knew so he might hurt you.

"So this ship, here"—he patted the bunk—"my ship *Genghis Khan* is also an opportunist ship. And some people might say we're wrong for taking the things that we do, and doing what we want, but I say we have the right to it. While EarthHub is running around waging war against aliens, we're just taking the opportunity that's in our way—to make a living. Just a living. Now could that be wrong, Jos?"

All the words swirled in your head. He kept rubbing the back of your hair and down your neck, but it didn't make you relax like when Daddy or Mama did it.

He waited for an answer. So you said, "No," just like before.

"No what, Jos?"

"No, it's not wrong," you said quietly.

"That's right. It's not wrong. Nothing we do here is wrong. Look at me."

You missed Daddy and Mama. You missed them so much your eyes hurt as bad as your heart.

But you looked at Falcone.

"You are so smart," he said, staring at your face, not in your eyes. He looked at your mouth for some reason, and touched it lightly. "Smart kid," he said.

The silence was the loudest sound you'd ever heard. It buzzed above your heartbeat.

The silence was louder even than voices.

He leaned over to the side-table drawer and took out a pack of cards. They looked well used. "Do you know how to play?"

Your drink had spilled and the bag had fallen on the deck, but he didn't seem to care. You moved the wet piece of blanket. "I know asteroids and comets."

"Shit. Not kids' games. Poker?"

"No."

"Watch."

He showed you new games. He said these were important. When your mind wandered he hit you, so you concentrated. He said you had to learn so he could take you on stations and win people over, that if you won people over he'd do even nicer things for you, more than giving you clothes, food, and a place to sleep. He said to control your face and that was how you won. He rubbed your hair and smiled when you showed you understood, but it wasn't the same kind of smile Daddy gave you when you did something well.

Falcone never said what people he meant—it was just *my people*, or *some people*, or *the people you will meet*. You didn't ask, but you knew he wasn't talking about people who could've been friends of *Mukudori*. This wasn't *Mukudori*.

You stared at the worn cards and felt him sitting so near, and it was nothing like *Mukudori*.

He played the games with you until you couldn't keep your eyes open. Then he commed someone to come get you and take you to your room.

"You learn quick," he said in parting. "See you next shift, Jos."

You looked at him until the hatch shut. You thought you were going back to the dark room, but the guard forced you next door to a small quarters, smaller than Falcone's, but clean and designed the same. He left and the lock outside beeped. It was still a jail but now you had light.

You crawled under the blankets and curled up. At least these didn't smell like him.

VIII.

A woman guard pulled you out of bed, threw you in the shower, and made you wash. Then she put you in the same too-big clothes you'd worn the previous shift, took you back to Falcone, and left you with him. He was setting up a small-screen vid. He sat you on the bed facing the vid and put in a cube.

"This is it. No mystery."

A picture ran. It was of people doing things to each other. You couldn't blink. You weren't sure what you were looking at or what it meant. But you knew it wasn't something people normally looked at except with a lot of whispering and giggling, like Evan did when both of you and his friends watched stolen vids and your parents were away in the lounge. "You're too young," he'd say.

But those vids hadn't been quite like this one. This one was almost funny, all the noises and faces. Almost.

You stared and shifted. You didn't really want to look at

it but Falcone was looking at you as you looked at the vid and more than anything you didn't want to meet those eyes. You sat on your hands on the bed and watched for all the minutes it ran, showing different people doing different things to each other. It wasn't just between daddies and mamas. Afterward you felt like you needed another shower.

Falcone said, "You'll get over it."

He put the cube away in his drawer and took your face in his hand. His thumb moved over your cheek but you couldn't hit him. He'd just hit you back. Or do worse. You had the feeling there was worse.

"Did you understand what you just saw?"

". . . No." No matter how hard you tried to forget, those images burned behind your eyes.

"When you're older you will. People will want you like that because you're nice to look at. But you'll know it's just a way you can get to them. You'll be able to get things from them if that's all they want. Stupid rich people will fall over themselves for your face. Your mama always called you her handsome boy, didn't she?"

"No." My starling. You didn't want to remember because you might cry.

"Well, it doesn't matter. You're my handsome boy now."

You didn't want him to touch you. You didn't want to know about any people. You didn't want to feel like no matter how hard you scrubbed in the shower, you wouldn't get rid of his soap smell. It filled your head, even when you weren't near him.

"Here. Read something. You can read, right?"

"Yes."

He handed you a smaller slate, a child's slate. It was like the primer you'd had in your room long ago, the one with lots of stories and animation in it.

"You know how to use one?"

"Yes."

"Good. Someone will bring breakfast. Be good now, Jos, and maybe you'll get a reward."

You didn't look up. He messed up your hair and left. You wanted to throw the slate across the room.

Instead you poked the button to activate it.

IX.

"Manners, Jos. They do love good manners."

Your fingers hurt from holding the knife and fork just so. You sat on the other side of his desk, he across from you as if you were at a table in a restaurant. He'd laid out place settings and even a napkin that he said went on your lap. He gave you "good" food to eat: little bits of steak, shell things, and fish. All but the steak tasted funny and felt worse in your mouth. He said the steak was real meat. It wasn't bad but it didn't sit as well as the burgers you were used to.

You knew food like this cost money, because it was always a treat when you ate it on station with your parents. But you didn't want to eat like this because the creds it took to buy it all could have been Evan's life.

Falcone said to forget *Mukudori*.

He talked more about them. His people. His people that you were going to impress with how nice you looked and how well mannered you were, and how that was going to make his business dealings easier and that was going to make him happy and he'd give you anything you wanted.

You wanted to go home, but he didn't mean that.

After eating he made you brush your teeth because, he said, you had a pretty smile and he wouldn't have it rot. You didn't see why he was so careful about your teeth but let his ship look so bad, but then one shift in a lunch session he said how his crew wasn't supposed to be comfortable, that comfort brought laziness and inattention. And all the scars in the ship reminded them of that fact.

You didn't see anybody on *Genghis Khan* other than Falcone and the people he called to escort you to your quarters when shift was over. His crew always looked at you like they either wished they were in Falcone's shoes or they wished they could dump you off and forget about you. They took you to quarters, took you to Falcone, back and forth for many, many shifts. You'd learned the beeping that came from the walls was the ship's way of signaling shift change. At your goldshift you went to Falcone's quarters and stayed there learning what he wanted: reading, reciting, eating, dressing, math, and science—until he sent you to sleep or made you sleep in his bunk. He assigned physical exercises for you to do in quarters and made your guard watch until you'd finished them.

He spent a lot of time on you. It seemed you pleased him, because he never talked about selling you.

Sometimes he hit you to get a point across, or if your mind wandered, or if something had happened on the ship or at a port they'd docked in that bothered him. You never knew what ports you hit, or how far you'd traveled since *Mukudori*. You never heard or read the Send so you didn't know what really had happened to Daddy and Mama. Maybe they weren't dead. You dreamed that they weren't, but you knew not to ask.

Once after a port call he sat you down for breakfast in his quarters, as usual, and talked the whole time. But he wasn't talking to you. He gestured with his knife as if he wanted to slice somebody up.

"EarthHub," he said, "is weak."

You sat still.

"They're going to lose this war and the damn Joint Chiefs are going to wonder why, when all along they were told, *by me*, that the only way to win is to get rid of the strits entirely. But blowhards like Ashrafi prefer to take a *humane* approach to everything. Humane. When we're dealing with fucking aliens. You know how to win a war, Jos?"

He didn't wait for an answer. He was angry about something that had nothing to do with you, for a change.

"You know how to win *anything*? To get what you want? You go right for it without hesitation, without remorse, without quarter. Never regret and never second-guess. These glaze-eyed new captains parade around the Hub with a shit-load of artillery coming out of their asses, and still the Warboy's fleet is blowing Hub stations and killing Hub citizens. Bloody Hub deserves to lose. They waste time patrolling us when they should use everything against the strits and the symps. That's how you win."

You remembered that Falcone wasn't just a pirate. He was a captain too. He'd mentioned once in passing that he used to be a Hub captain, but that could've meant anything—in the military or a merchant group or even a passenger line, though you thought he seemed most like a soldier. Sometimes he talked about the Warboy, the human sympathizer captain of the alien fleet, as if he admired him. You thought maybe Falcone was a symp too, but then sometimes he talked about mister-this and senator-that in the Hub that he knew, that he was going to show you off to, and he'd swear at the strits and symps like he wanted to beat them all on his own.

"That's how you win," he said again, but only to himself.

You didn't move. He looked at you anyway, seeing you now, and said, "Winners get the prize."

Falcone had moods. When he was in a good mood he smiled a lot and brought you presents. When he was in a bad

mood all the crew seemed to hold their breaths and the ship
was a whole lot quieter, and he yelled at you more. When the
guard took you to his quarters in that routine you were used
to, you could tell if Falcone was going to be nice or not in
the first glance.

"What're you good for?" was a frequent question when
things didn't seem to be going right for Falcone, when either
the Hub fleet or the strits were harassing him somehow.
Sometimes he shoved you or flicked his fingers on your
chest because he knew it bothered you, or if he was in a
nasty mood he put his hand in your hair and caressed it because he knew that bothered you the most. It made the blood
swim in your ears and all under your skin so you felt it. You
hated it when he touched you. You hated it so much you
thought about blood and Falcone, Falcone covered in blood,
the ship blowing up, and all kinds of things you couldn't
make happen because you were still a kid—even though you
dressed grown-up, and learned to talk well and eat neatly,
and follow orders like one of the crew.

Falcone's pet. That was what the guards called you. They
made animal noises and looked at you sometimes . . . sometimes one or two of the guards looked at you like they
wanted to ask you questions. Or do more than ask.

When that happened you never slept. Because they had
the code to get into your room.

Falcone's pet. What're you good for?

"I know what you're good for," the guard sometimes
said, and stuck out his tongue in a way that wasn't telling
you to get lost.

It seemed you grew but you couldn't be sure since Falcone gave you new clothes when you did something well,
and these clothes weren't two sizes too big.

He'd taken away your tag a long time ago.

One shift he came and got you himself, waited while you

showered and handed you the clothes he wanted you to wear: a blue sweater and smooth black pants. He liked you in blue because your hair was dark and it also matched your eyes, he said.

"Congratulations. You lived to be nine."

"Thank you, sir." He liked to be called "sir."

"Since you've excelled so admirably you get a gift. We're going on station. Put your boots on."

You sat on the bed to do so. Going on station where pollies were—excitement made your stomach flip, until you wondered if you were going to finally meet one of his business-people. You really hoped not. Not if they were like the guards. Or like Falcone.

When you stood he came up close to you and put his hands on your shoulders. You didn't flinch much anymore when he did that. He didn't like it when you flinched.

"I'm proud of you, Jos. You've turned out to be a good investment. So far."

"Thank you, sir."

"If you do anything to jeopardize me, I'll shoot you—right on the dock if necessary. Copy?"

"Yes, sir."

He smiled into your eyes and touched your cheek. Then he took your hand. "Let's go."

It was the first time in a year that you saw more of the ship than the one corridor your quarters were in. He took you down the lev and through more corridors that looked the same as the one you saw every shift: stark and battered, with low ceilings that made the lights seem up close and more dirty. Here his crew walked around, some of them bare-armed. They weren't in any uniforms. They talked loudly, laughed, and stared at you. Many called out "sir" to Falcone as you passed. They all made way for him as you neared the airlock.

A station. Pollies were on station. Your parents had said if ever you were lost and couldn't find *Mukudori* or crew from friendly ships, you had to go to the station pollies.

Guns weren't allowed on station but it wasn't really enforced—EarthHub was at war, after all. You knew Falcone had a gun somewhere or else he would not have made the threat. He crushed your hand in his as he strode down the lock ramp toward the customs officer. The woman there looked you over and took the small cards Falcone handed to her. You knew they were passports and merchant licenses and the information encoded was a lie. You stared at the woman, hoping she would look at you. She did, but all she seemed to see was a ship brat. You wanted to shout: *It's a pirate ship, can't you see that? Why can't you see that?* But the grip on your hand numbed you all the way to your tongue.

She scanned the passports, her pen beeped, and she waved you on.

Falcone led you around the high, wide dockring to the main doors. You read on the walls, between ship locks: Chaos Station.

You almost stopped walking. You kept staring even when you had to turn your neck. From the starmaps he'd made you memorize you knew that Chaos was in the Dragons—where stations were few and far between, but military space-carriers were not. Deep space. You knew from school on *Mukudori* that Hubcentral was closest to Earth. Then came the worlds and stations of the Spokes, then the Rim, which had been *Mukudori*'s main trading sector. The Dragons saw most of the war with the strits, because the strit homeworld was in deep space. *Mukudori* had never been in the Dragons. Most of it was unchartered.

Falcone had to be crazy. A pirate on a station where spacecarriers docked? You looked up at the ship listings as you neared the doors that led to the inner station. Lit on the boards were ship names like *Yeti* and *Shiva*—merchants you didn't recognize. But there were other names that gave hope, the ones with the endings of EHV and a registry number— EarthHub Vessel. Spacecarriers.

Next to pollies they were the best things if you needed help on station. They had soljets who could protect you, who were sworn to protect EarthHub and its citizens. You knew soljets by the black uniforms they wore and the patches on their arms that bragged their homeships. Or you saw the tattoos on their wrists. That was proof when even uniforms could be faked, because nobody did the tattoos like their own shipboard artists who coded the designs somehow.

Your parents had told you this long ago. You looked at those military names with hope. *Archangel. Macedon. Archangel* was scheduled to undock in five minutes. The station comm blared it. Falcone took you off the dock and onto the concourse. You glanced up and saw him smiling, the face of someone doing a dare and having fun with it. But his hand gripped even tighter as you moved into the stream of people.

With two carriers in dock and a handful of merchants, the concourse was busy. Even so you saw the dinginess of this deep-space station—nothing like Basquenal, a Rim Guard station that boasted high-end dens and cybetoriums for kids. You didn't notice many children here. The paint on the walls looked covered in ashes. Some of the walls were even blast-scarred with signs plastered over the holes, warning of open power cables. The bazaar tables displayed cheap trinkets and bold items that mostly soldiers would like, and were manned by tired-looking, gaudily dressed men and women. Food scents from a dozen different cultures warred with one another in your nose, making you hold your breath. Your stomach clenched.

All around you black uniforms walked, yet you couldn't speak to any of them.

Falcone tugged you toward a glass-fronted restaurant, out of place compared to the other bland entrances. People watched you—you, not Falcone—but most of them seemed no more dangerous than who you were with already.

Falcone sat you down and went to take his own seat when the station gave a great boom.

You twitched and saw people running. That sudden. As if you'd blinked and awakened in a different place. Funnels of black poured by the glass windows. The station boomed again, louder this time, and the glass shook. The spice bottles on the table fell over. Falcone reached to grab your arm.

On the table was a fork. You had it in your hand now. You slammed the prongs into Falcone's fingers.

He yelled. People dashed from their seats and out the restaurant. You dived among them, small and lost in the trample of legs. Voices talked over the station comm. Another voice yelled louder behind you, but it was swallowed in the noise the station made. Fires leaped up inside the walls. Larger bodies shoved you along. A black arm brushed close and you grabbed it.

"Sir—"

The arm knocked you back and kept running. Most of the activity headed toward the dockring's main access. By force you ran there too, following where you saw black.

"Help—sirs—"

One of the soljets hauled you along, then shoved you out of the way toward one of the merchant ships. She didn't even look.

"Get off the dock, kid!"

"Wait!"

She ran off. Black uniforms poured up carrier ramps. Soon the dockring would be clear and someone from Falcone's ship, or Falcone himself, would catch you. You tried to grab another uniform sleeve but suddenly the station shuddered again, knocking you off your feet. You fell hard on your elbow and yelped, but nobody heard. All above you men and women scattered. A soljet said to his comrade as he ran, "They're docking!"

Way down the dockring, almost out of sight from the curve of the walls, a small explosion went off at one of the locks. You hauled yourself up, moving slow in the rush. Your head pounded and smoke stung your eyes. You held your arm and tried to veer toward one of the carrier ramps.

Then new faces poured out of that blown lock.

They weren't human. They were tattooed, with skin in colors you'd never seen before on a face except as a mask. They shot at the soljets, sharp bright pulses. The soljets stopped boarding, knelt behind cargo bins, loaders, and ramps, shooting back in stiff streamers of bright red. It was a noisy station festival, full of light and color, except people were dying. Merchants and Chaos citizens caught in the cross fire fell.

You froze. You had never before seen an alien. They came closer around the dockring, moving with the precision of skill and focused aim. They wore long outer robes that fluttered behind them, as if they were flying. None of the soljets paid attention to you now.

Someone grabbed you over the face. You recognized the smell of the hand.

You bit. He released you and you ran straight into the platoon of soljets ahead of you.

"Drop that gun!" one of the jets yelled.

Falcone might've been chasing you. You didn't look. You ran as fast as you could. People screamed at you to stop and get out of the way. An alien face looked at you from across

the decreasing distance of jet-occupied dock. The eyes were
completely black.

A fist slammed into your back and threw you to the deck.
The last word you heard wasn't one you understood.

X.

That was all I remembered about Falcone. It was enough.

PART II

I.

When I woke up it was a different ship. I could tell by the whining pitch and the rhythmic *thud-thud* of its drives. I was in a small room with only a flat black mat on the floor, which I lay on, stomach down. Naked. Covered in a blanket and bandaged around my chest and back. I felt the soft fabric. My body hurt. It was an effort just to blink and I wanted to sleep. For a long time. Maybe forever.

Deep breaths pulled in warm air, not cold like on Falcone's ship. My stomach coiled. If not *Genghis Khan*, then where?

The walls were bare, clean, and painted pale yellow, with broken red lines running around just below the ceiling. Stenciled every now and then beneath the lines were small curving shapes, like the thorny flowers my mother used to keep by her bedside in skinny bottles. The lights in the bolted ceiling were square and bright. At least I had lights.

It didn't smell like a pirate ship, all cold and musk. It didn't look like any merchant I'd ever seen.

I was facing the hatch. The lock release chimed and an alien walked in.

For a second the shadowed head gave a scary silhouette before I realized he wore some sort of cloth wrap that covered his scalp and draped down around his shoulders. His clothing wasn't like anything I knew. It coiled around his body in wide strips, covering him completely from ankles to throat, deep gray. Draped over that was a loose black robe with those same thorny markings running up from hem to collar on the right side. For some reason he was barefoot. That was strange on a ship that could get cold or get blown. Blue tattoos dotted his toes and feet, disappearing into the strips around his legs.

I blinked, forcing breaths out, and made a small sound, I didn't know what. Help. Go away. All the stories about strits came to mind in a rush. How they would eat you—

He crouched smoothly and the shadows fell away.

It wasn't an alien.

His face seemed to shift between human and the strit ones I'd seen before passing out on Chaos—the odd skin tones and black eyes. His eyes were dark around the pupil but not all black like the aliens'. He had a twisting, dark tattoo that crept up one wide slanted cheekbone, around the outer part of his right eye, and dipped like a tail to the middle of his forehead. It kind of resembled the flower designs on the wall.

He was human but I didn't see a human expression on his face, not even a mocking smile like I was used to with Falcone. He just stared at me steadily like some kind of animal, the kinds I'd seen in my primer. The ones that ate meat. Crouching there on the balls of his feet, hands folded in front of his knees, he looked ready to pounce.

I couldn't move. He touched my back. My hands clenched but there wasn't anywhere to go, nothing to do. The room was too small and my breathing too loud.

His fingers were feather light and they didn't stray. I couldn't see what exactly he did, but I felt him fold the blanket down and check the dressing. Just lifting the bandage.

My skin pulled and I hissed, tears squeezing out the corners of my eyes. He gave no sign that he heard. After he was finished he folded his hands again and looked into my eyes as if he had never moved. All his gestures seemed lazy because they were slow, but I knew they were just deliberate. Not wasted.

"Your name, what." He used a soft voice. His accent was heavy but I didn't recognize it. The way he said the words didn't seem like a question.

"Jos Musey." To my own ears I sounded terrified. He smelled different. Not like cigret smoke or sweat or steel, or food just eaten. Not like any perfume. It could have been body oil and some sort of spice. The air of the ship smelled of it, I had smelled it before he came in. It swam around my head, totally different from Falcone.

But that didn't mean a thing.

"Jos Musey," he repeated awkwardly. His hand brushed against his leg and suddenly he held an injet.

Injets. Drugs. Falcone sometimes threatened with them.

"No—wait."

He ignored me. The narrow, flat point of the injet pressed my skin. Then came the sudden click of the release.

"It is necessary," he said before my eyes shut.

II.

When I next awoke it wasn't on any ship. Around me was silence, like the deep inside of a station den, where the gulping sound of energy towers couldn't even get through. The ceiling was lacy white and divided by large eight-sided shapes, high above my head. I lay flat on my back on a firm mat on the floor. My back didn't hurt anymore and that was a relief, though my limbs felt heavy and achy. The room had a tall window and sunlight bled through the hole-filled curtains, making designs on the rich red rug.

I had never seen sunlight like that, an intense hot yellow, not even on stations that rotated to face the sun. Maybe this station was just really close to the local star, like Siqiniq in the Rim. I had never been in a room like this either, more expensive-looking than any den I had ever stayed in with my parents. Nothing about it seemed out of place. The red shapes on the walls looked like the knotted design I remembered from the ship and that strange man's face—hugging thorns that seemed to connect the four corners of the room and touch every piece of reddish-black furniture. A shiny black screen stood loosely unfolded by the far wall. Painted on it in white were more swirls that might have been an alien with arms outstretched as if to fly. All the furniture was low to the ground, as if you were supposed to sit everywhere—a table, a smooth box with drawers and a mirror above it, all shiny like the screen. Not used up like things on Falcone's ship.

I remembered Falcone's people, the people he wanted me to meet. Rich people I was supposed to impress and look pretty for.

I rolled over to push myself up and caught a shadow as it lay across the rug. Someone was sitting in the corner by the window, watching me.

I had on clothes at least, a belted blue robe that reached my ankles. I got to my knees and looked at the corner.

It was the same man from the ship. The human that seemed alien. He didn't look as old as I'd first thought. His hair hung to his shoulders, dark brown and a little wavy, instead of tied up in that scarf. It made his face seem less cold. He sat on his haunches staring at me, wearing the same wrapped clothing as before, but pure white. He didn't move.

I shifted away, to see if that made him do anything. He just blinked. I touched my back, the soft robe, pressed my spine. It didn't hurt at all. He must have used bot-knitters on me but I didn't remember feeling the itches. I didn't remember anything except waking up that one time. He could've done anything while I was asleep.

My insides twisted, burned.

The air seemed thin and my movements a couple seconds too late. How long had I been out?

You weren't supposed to speak unless asked a question. So I didn't ask.

Since the man in the corner didn't do anything, I looked at the curtained window, at the sunlight making art on the floor. Slowly I stood and went toward it.

"No," he said.

I stopped and looked at him.

"You are not strong," he said, in that accent that made me have to work to understand him. His eyes grabbed on to me.

I folded my arms against myself. He was talking. Maybe he wouldn't mind if I talked too. "What did you do to me? I was shot."

"High set paralysis pulse from a Trenton PE sidearm," he said, with what sounded like distaste. "You are small. It burns you badly, nearly to death if I don't fix."

"Why did you help me?"

He didn't answer. He rose smoothly. I backed up a pace. He took one step to the window and touched the wall by the curtain edge. A screen came down behind the curtains, shutting out the sun. Lights in the ceiling opened automatically. I stepped back again when he looked at me. He wasn't as tall as Falcone but I didn't like the slow way he moved. I didn't like this room and its silence.

He said eventually, "The man that shoots you, who." His voice rose and fell in all the wrong places.

I tucked my forearms into opposite sleeves. So he didn't know Falcone. Or made like he didn't, for some reason. "A pirate."

"A pirate, who."

His focused face made my hands cold. I tried to keep looking at him, the way Falcone liked it, but his stare was worse than Falcone's. I couldn't see anything in it, what he wanted or expected.

"The captain of *Genghis Khan*," I said. "Falcone."

This didn't seem to affect him either. "He shoots you, why."

"Because I ran away."

"You are with Falcone, why."

"I'm not with him." Slowly I moved to the other side of the mat away from this man.

"He wants you, why."

"He's a pirate." I tried not to sound afraid or rebellious. This man hadn't moved from the window but I remembered the injet he'd somehow slid from those clothes with no pockets. I glanced at the door. It wasn't marked by anything except the division in the wall. It had a slide latch and a narrow gap near the floor, not like ship hatches.

"You run from him, why."

The large room was shrinking. It got harder to breathe.

"He—he's a pirate." I didn't want to say anything else.

"You are with him, how much time."

"How long? I—I don't know. A year, standard? I don't know. He had me . . . he kept me locked up most of the time."

Where was Falcone now? Did he know where I was? Where was I?

"What do you want?" I asked carefully.

The man stepped toward me. I backed up quick and he stopped.

"You are with Falcone, how. Falcone has you, how. Why."

"I'm not with him, I ran away."

His eyes tightened. He said more slowly, "You *were* with Falcone. How. Why."

"He just took me. He just attacked my homeship and took me."

"Your ship, where."

"It's dead. *Mukudori.* He told me it was dead." I looked into the dark eyes. "Do you know it?"

I didn't want to hope. But maybe this man had information. Maybe I could get it from him. Somehow.

"I do not know your ship," he said. "Yet. Your age, what."

"Nine. Falcone said nine. EarthHub Standard." Which didn't mean much to kids in deep space, Falcone said. Because life was harder than in Hubcentral, he said.

Maybe on pirate ships.

"Only nine," this man said, and for the first time his gaze slid away, to the wall.

He gave no clues. Why didn't he just tell me what he wanted? Games. It was always these grown-up games.

While he looked at the wall I stared at the tattoo on his face. It was strange, and he smelled strange, and this room was strange, with its silence and all of its straight, perfect black and red furniture and thorn designs. I didn't like it any more than what was on the *Khan.*

I looked at the door again. If I bolted, I bet this slow-moving man would move a lot faster. And there'd be a fight and he'd probably hit me. So I didn't move. Eventually his eyes found their way back to me, but I still couldn't read them. If they were interested they didn't show it.

Maybe he was going to sell me anyway.

"*Mukudori*," he said suddenly, as if he just remembered, stumbling around the name. "That means what."

I rubbed my nose. "Starling."

His eyes narrowed. "Small star, yes."

"No, a bird. A starling. An animal that flies?" We'd all learned the origin of the ship's name by the time we could read. His eyes didn't change so I wasn't sure if he understood. "How come you don't get my language?"

"I don't speak it first."

"Are you strit?"

His eyes flared. It was the only sign of anger, but it was enough. "That is an insult."

I didn't understand. He wore what looked like an alien tattoo. And I had a sick feeling about where we were. I was pretty sure we weren't near Earth. He would never have been allowed near Earth looking like that. "You're a symp, aren't you? Not a strit, a symp?"

He frowned. "You say striviirc-na, not strit. You don't say symp."

"Why not?" Everybody called them strits and symps, not striviirc-na and sympathizers.

"It is rude," he said, and took a few wandering steps around the room, over the red rug, which landed him closer to me. "I call you Hub scum, yes. Pirate bastard, yes. Same thing."

I moved away again. "Oh."

"You do that, why."

"Do what?"

"Step back."

"Because." I shifted, scratched at my arm. The robe was slippery against my skin and for some reason it made the cold spread through me. "I don't know what you want."

"I want you not to be afraid."

I'd heard that before, enough times to know it was a lie. "I don't know you and you're a symp."

That should've got me hit. But he didn't move.

"And you know about sympathizers, what," he said instead. His eyes widened a bit and he shrugged slightly, a gesture I couldn't read. He gave weird signals.

I didn't answer. It was probably a lead-in for some blame and abuse.

He kept looking at me. And waited. So I said reluctantly, "You started the war."

"How."

He didn't tell me the answers like Falcone. Maybe he really wanted to know what I thought, but I doubted it.

I didn't say anything.

"Jos Musey-na," he said. "You can speak all right. I hope to know what you know."

"Why?"

"You are here," he answered, which wasn't a real answer. All this time his voice hadn't risen. He stayed far back from me.

If all he wanted were answers, then maybe this wasn't going to be so bad. If.

"We're at war because you took the alien side. Against EarthHub. Even though the aliens wouldn't share their stuff from that moon. I forget the name of the moon."

"Qinitle-na, in my language. Plymouth, in yours."

"Yeah. Plymouth. We needed that stuff and they wouldn't trade or anything. You helped the aliens kill humans and steal Hub ships and tech to protect the moon, and you're human. So you're traitors."

"He tells you this, the pirate."

I shrugged. "Everybody knows." It was always on the Send, and sometimes my parents had talked about it. And Falcone talked about it.

"There is always a wider view," this man said.

Then he just walked out.

I stared after him, at the door. He didn't come back. Maybe it wasn't a trick. Or maybe he went to get his people because I'd answered wrong. My stomach hadn't unknotted yet. I went to the door and tried it. Locked from the outside. I wasn't surprised.

I sat on the floor mat, near the wall, and wrapped my arms around my knees. I just had to wait. Sooner or later he'd come back, or somebody would, and maybe they'd take me out of this expensive, quiet room and show me what they wanted. Take me back to Falcone maybe. Or sell me to somebody else.

Stupid. I wiped a cuff across my eyes. I'd been so close to those soljets but they hadn't even looked. Or cared. It shouldn't have been a shock. Bad luck like that happened. Like with my parents, who hadn't come back. I hadn't thought about them in a long time, but now they came up in my head and walked around, in *Mukudori* red and gray coveralls, what they wore for work. Just like that they came out, but they were dead so what was the point. They weren't here and couldn't help me and soon Falcone was going to get me back and it would just be like how it had been for the last year.

Maybe that was better than being with a symp who just looked at you with his serious face, like he wanted to own what was inside your head.

I rubbed my face, got up, walked around to give myself something to do. The rug was soft and thick between my toes. Rich thing, like the clothes Falcone had made me wear. It was just a matter of time with that symp. He might be slow about it but he was still a symp, a traitor, and that couldn't be better than a pirate, no matter what he said.

It was better not to think about it, so I explored this jail instead, running my fingers along the smooth walls. The designs on it weren't painted, but stuck there, raised from the surface. The edges of the walls brought me to the painted black screen, so I peeked behind it. A geometric toilet that looked basically like the ones I was used to, and a sink and a tub. The tub would take me a while to figure out; it had no showerhead above it and I couldn't see where the water would come from.

I looked down at my robe. I didn't smell, which meant somebody had cleaned me while I was asleep.

I folded my arms and looked away from the tub, listened. Nothing, so I quickly used the toilet and washed my hands. You always had to be clean because nobody liked dirty kids.

Above the sink was a mirror. I tried to ignore it but it was close and big. I caught two eyes like red-rimmed gunshot wounds, and messy hair, the color Falcone liked—sable, he'd said.

I felt his fingers in it, sliding through.

I went back around the screen and pushed at it so it hid everything behind from view.

III.

I slept awhile and woke up and was still alone. Little sounds marred the silence, coming from behind the curtains. Things I'd never heard before. Squeaks and whistles that didn't sound like any machinery.

I went to the window, slapped the wall panel as I'd seen my jailer do. The screen folded up. Small shadows fluttered away from the other side of the curtains. Through the lace patterns showed large white shapes. I pulled the cloth aside and immediately stepped back.

I expected space. Wanted space, like you wanted good dreams. Just the view from a station.

But here a world fell away at my feet. The room, the building I was in, seemed to be slammed into a mountainside. I knew the word "mountain" from my primer. They were rough monsters coughed up on the surface of planets. I caught glimpses of jagged gray slanting away beneath the window and more flat-topped buildings descending like large steps stuck into the rock. I saw green, then a bright blue sky, before I yanked the curtains shut. My head throbbed and I couldn't breathe.

I'd never seen sky except from space. Or in holos, in a cybetorium. On a vid maybe. Always separated by the fact of my feet on a station or a ship deck.

A hand landed on my shoulder, steered me to the mat, and set me down. The sunlight disappeared with the sound of the screen unfolding. When I blinked the man crouched in front of me, held my shoulder again.

"You are not strong." He watched me as if what I had done told him something interesting.

I tried to pull away from his grip. "Where am I? Who are you?"

He held on a beat too long, just enough to make me stop struggling. "Do not fight me. You will lose." He let go.

His alien scent wrapped around me. I edged farther back, still feeling his hand on my shoulder even though he kept it to himself now. He gestured to a tray on the floor, near the mat. He must have brought it back with him. What I smelled wasn't all him, he'd brought me food in a round red box and a white cup full of water. My stomach made noises at the sight of it, despite the memory of that sky. I couldn't remember the last time I'd eaten.

"For you," he said.

I crawled over and picked up the warm box, glanced back

at him. He stayed where he was. Maybe it was drugged but I was too hungry to care. The food looked like rice except it was twice as long, pale yellow, and tasted like peas. Draped overtop were strips of green leaves, strongly salted, and ringed around were balls of meat I had never tasted before. They were spicy and burned my mouth. I was so hungry I swallowed most of it whole, shoveling it all into my mouth.

I watched him to make sure he didn't do anything fast, but he kept his distance and just let me look. The closer I looked, the younger he seemed. A lot younger than Falcone. His skin was pale brown but his eyes and hair were very dark. I couldn't look away from his facial tattoo—deep blue and in some places it seemed black. It twisted and turned into itself but never broke the smooth curving line around his right eye, framing it like a sentence bracket. Some of the points repeated exactly in angles. Maybe it was some kind of writing. That would be strange. But everything about him was strange. Uncomfortable. Too silent.

Faint shapes showed beneath the wrapped white strips of clothing, following the lines of his muscles. One shape on his forearm looked like a blade. Another longer one sat on his shin. I thought of Falcone with the knife in his boot.

The man's gaze moved to my eyes from the wall designs, where he'd been concentrating. For a second he stared, as if daring me to stretch and touch him.

I didn't move.

He said, "You have questions, what."

I didn't answer.

"Ask them now or never."

It sounded like an order. "Where am I?"

The dark eyes drilled into my own. "Aaian-na."

The alien world.

I had felt it but hearing it was another thing. This was far beyond Chaos Station. This was—lost.

"Why?" Now even the thought of safety seemed impossible. On Falcone's ship I'd dreamed of it and when the chance had come I'd taken it. Here there would be no chance. Here I didn't exist.

"He shoots you. They think you're dead. You are a pirate—no. You are a good liar—I think no. I am curious. So . . . now we have you."

"I don't want to be on a planet." Especially not this planet. My hands shook. I set the food box down.

"Your ship is dead."

It wasn't news but it still stung. "I don't know if it's dead, I never saw. He just said so and he could've lied. I want to go home."

"There is no home, Jos Musey-na."

"I didn't see them shoot my ship!"

He stared at me steadily. "Your starling is dead."

"How do you know? For all I know you could be with the pirates, you're an alien. What happened to Chaos? Did you blow it up?"

"Not entirely." His eyes wrinkled with a hint of amusement. At what I didn't know.

"Why'd you attack it?"

The amusement grew, a slight twist of his lips. "We are at war."

"Who are you?"

"You leak with questions."

"You asked! Look, I want to go back. If you aren't going to kill me, or sell me, then put me back."

"With Falcone, you go."

That almost shut me up. Until I realized it was a question. "On a station," I said. "I don't care. On Chaos if you didn't blow it up."

"On Chaos I went to rescue my brother, a prisoner there."

Probably he'd gone just to wreck something. Strit ships

attacked Hub ones all the time and they hit stations too, and who cared who was in the middle. "You're just like the pirates."

"That—is wrong." His finger poked between my collarbone.

I moved away fast, blinked, and rubbed at my eyes. "What're you going to do with me?"

"You think, what. Don't cry."

I thought suddenly of Evan, holding toys above my head. I forced the memory out. "I'm not crying."

"Think."

"What—to dress me up and teach me manners?"

"No."

"Then what?"

He stood. "I want only what you want."

"I don't want to be here!"

As if what I wanted ever mattered.

"There is only here," he said gently.

IV.

When next I awoke he stood near the door holding clothes. I sat up and slid to the wall. Sleep made my head heavy but I watched him, tense. He didn't approach, just tossed the clothes at my feet from where he stood. The pants and shirt were black, loose, and looked new and soft. I gathered them together, glanced up at him. He still watched me but after a moment his eyes widened slightly and he turned his shoulder, looking away.

My hands shook as I changed. The clothes spread out from my body like wings. Maybe I hadn't upset him with all my rebellion before, since he gave me new things now.

Without warning he started to talk to me but not in a language I had ever heard.

I stared at his back, arms folded against my chest. After a moment he turned around to face me, still talking. He had to know I didn't understand a word. Then I noticed he was repeating the same phrase in a steady way, so clear I was able to pick out individual words by the way he breathed. His voice rose and fell in a definite rhythm, the beat of sentences, and seemed lighter than the voice he used when he spoke my language. The lilts, slurs, and long sounds were almost musical. I didn't understand any of it but the first short part.

"*Oa ngali* Nikolas-dan."

A human name in the middle of the alien words. He watched my eyes and made a gesture over his mouth, repeating *Nikolas-dan*. He said it *Nee-ko-las*.

"That's your name," I said finally, grudgingly. My words sounded foreign in the room.

"*Enh.*"

I took that as a yes. He chattered on, a flood of different words, and pulled a slate reader from one of the black drawers near the wall, held it out to me. Still looking at me as if he could read my genetic code. As if I should understand what he was about. I had no idea. But it wasn't something I could figure out unless he wanted me to, so I took the reader and activated it.

Symbols blurted across the screen, mixed with words I recognized, some of them broken up by short lines and spelled out. Translations. The angular symbols, so much like the wall and tattoo designs, were their written language. I stared at the strit writing, not knowing what to do with it. I didn't want anything to do with it.

"Alien," I said, remembering his reaction to the word "strit." "Why do you want me to learn alien?"

He said something sharply. Somewhere in there I heard "alien" and saw the heat in his eyes. So alien was off-limits too.

Too much like Falcone's lessons, except these weren't even in my own language.

It was stupid, but my eyes started to burn. I brushed at them angrily and held the slate out to him.

"I don't get it."

He put his hand on it and gently pushed it back toward me, making me still hold on or else it would drop. "The answers are in here." Said in my language.

"Answers to what?"

I was hungry. I was tired and at this point I was too far away from any kind of rescue to think obedience could get me back—

Not home. But somewhere I could go where hands didn't yank me around.

"*Mukudori lo'oran,*" he said.

That was dirty, to say that. I gripped the reader. "What?"

"*Mukudori lo'oran. Falcone lo'oran.*" He pointed to the slate.

"What does that mean? What do you know about my homeship? What about Falcone?"

I still wasn't convinced he didn't plan on selling me back at some point. Pirates ransomed prisoners. Why wouldn't strits?

He took the reader, poked at it, then handed it back. It showed a different screen. Staring out at me was the four-armed woman of Falcone's tattoo and below it the word "Kali," then a long paragraph of strit symbols.

"What does this mean?" Frustration spilled out of me like blood. I glared up into his dark, direct gaze.

"*Haa ta lo'oran.* There the answers. Jos-na. *Kaa-n sa'o-ran ne.* You want them, how much."

The roll of understandable and alien words together seemed as threatening somehow as the face of the many-armed woman scowling at me from the reader. On her belt hung severed hands; it brought up the image of people walking around with bleeding stumps that made it impossible for them to touch or hold anything.

He wanted me to grow hands, like Falcone had wanted. But not my hands.

I held the reader and didn't look up. The symbols made no sense, no matter how long or hard I stared.

My fingers turned white. This place, this strit. Symp. Why didn't he send me back to space? I just wanted to go back. On a ship, not a planet. What would I have to do to get back?

I rubbed my cheek. It was damp.

Nikolas-dan touched the reader lightly and scrolled back to the first screen. He pointed to one strit symbol among five rows of symbols, and then to three other thorny shapes from other places in the rows. "Jos," he said. Then his finger moved, very slowly, over nine more symbols from the same group. "Nikolas." He touched them all again and they lit bright yellow, while the others stayed green. Yellow like the alien sun outside.

I understood finally. Like birth, or an identity, you first began with a name.

V.

I learned new words from Nikolas-dan and the reader, like "day," which is when we had lessons, and "night," which was when I was supposed to sleep. The planet had natural shifts, Nikolas-dan said, which were dictated by its rotation. He said "dictated" and explained what it meant, and "rotation," which I knew already because stations rotated; so did the cores of the old Hurricane-class merchant ships that we used to sometimes meet on layovers.

He didn't teach me these things in my own language. It was all in strit.

I never left the room, not once for a planet month, which Nikolas-dan said was twenty-seven *days and nights.* I didn't know what that would be in EarthHub Standard, so I didn't know what the date was and how long I had been gone from home. Or from Falcone. Nikolas-dan didn't let me leave the room, just like Falcone those first few days. He said I wasn't ready and since I'd grown up on a ship it shouldn't bother me so much. It didn't, at first.

It took a month just to get used to the fancy room, to realize that other people weren't going to just walk in and out. Only Nikolas-dan came at the same time every day. In the *morning.* So I got used to him coming and going in his silent way. He was a lot quieter than Falcone.

Sometimes at night I opened my eyes to the total darkness and thought I was back on *Genghis Khan,* except there was no sound, none that made any sense. Busy noises sometimes came through the glass. Nikolas-dan said they were animals, birds, and insects. They were outside because on planets you could breathe outside of buildings, it wasn't like on ships. The noises were small and high, sometimes, in regular beats that made it hard to fall asleep. Others were loud and long, like someone moaning. Nikolas-dan said I didn't have to be afraid. The animals couldn't get inside unless I opened the window. But I didn't even fold up the screen.

The animals came anyway, into my dreams. Shadows with pointed faces, like the pictures in my primer long ago. They sat beside Falcone. All around us a woman danced with hands hanging from her belt. Sometimes I dreamed that

I yelled at Falcone in strit and he laughed because it was babble. Once I dreamed of my parents and they didn't understand me either. So I had to leave them. Had to.

Sometimes Nikolas-dan was there in my dreams, but he didn't laugh and he didn't let me leave. And he never left me.

I knew all the corners of my room now. Nikolas-dan helped me roll up the rug and stand my pallet against the wall, then made me clean the glossy brown floor with a big brush and water. But it wasn't so bad because once it was washed it smelled like the fruits he brought for dessert when I learned all my lessons for the day.

In the mornings he brought me food and clean clothing and took out my dirty ones. We spent hours on the floor going through screens of basic strit words and sentences like "My name is Jos-na." When I asked him about Kali or *Mukudori* he'd point to the screen with the information but I couldn't yet understand anything but simple words here and there that didn't add up to much. He'd locked out the reader so it wouldn't listen to any command to translate, and looking up words in the dictionary took too long. He refused to just tell me. I had to work for all of it.

He wouldn't answer my questions unless I asked them in strit, and it was a hard language. He said Ki'hade wasn't even the only language he knew from this planet but it was the one they mainly spoke on this side of the *continent*. I hoped he wouldn't make me learn the others. I had to listen really close because they sang a lot of their words and if you didn't sing them right nobody would know if you were talking about something in the past or future or right now and it would get confusing. There were so many different ways to say the same thing, and some of their symbols looked exactly alike except for one line or curve that made the word "war" turn into "one," or something.

I was sure if I had to actually speak to a strit I would be absolutely confused and probably insulting. Nikolas outright laughed at me once when I wearily said, "You ate me for breakfast," instead of, "Will we have breakfast?" In one lesson, when I'd had enough of parsing sentences, he made me write my name in strit and the meaning, which according to him was "playful" or "merry." He thought that was funny too, since mostly I was serious. He found my mistakes amusing and wasn't shy about showing it. In an odd way it got me to work harder—not to please him, but to shut him up. Maybe he knew this.

"So what does your name mean?" I asked, not in strit, while we ate our midday meal. "I bet I know—nasty teacher, right?"

"*Ke* Nikolas-dan *ke u'itlan sastara.*"

He said it quickly and all I caught was the word "people."

He handed me the reader, on the vocabulary screen. I sighed and put aside my bowl, licked my sweet-sauce-tasting fingers and wiped my hands on my pants, which made him frown. I poked at the screen to bring up the input bar. "So spell it, Nikolas-dan."

"*Enh?*"

He always gave me that straight-ahead look when I got lazy and didn't speak Ki'hade. He knew I knew the word for "please."

"Nikolas-dan, *tori.*"

Very nicely he spelled the unfamiliar words. I added the translations to my list of slowly growing vocabulary, like he told me to do.

"*U'itlan sastara* . . . victory of people?"

"Nikolas," he said. "In your words—the people's victory."

That sounded pretty full of it. I scowled. He smiled at my face. It made him look human, and young.

More than once I daydreamed during lessons, my head full of symbols and words and sounds, and found myself staring at the tattoo on his cheek and how it curled around his dark eye like the arm of a spiral galaxy. It didn't matter his features were human—he walked, talked, dressed, and for all I knew pissed like a strit (however it was that strits pissed). And despite myself I was curious to know how he got that way, and why he didn't mind.

His history wasn't at the top of my curriculum. The lessons revolved around things like geography of the planet, concepts like "house" and "forest" and "ocean." Weather was a big thing too. I discovered that up close when I first experienced rain pounding on my walls and window. I didn't sleep the entire night. He said it was summer, though, and there wasn't usually a lot of rain.

Once was a lot, I told him.

Every time I thought of the world falling away from the window I felt sick. So the screen stayed folded down. He never asked about it. Still, I wondered what was outside of this room, in the rest of the house, and when I could see it. Anything, just to get away from these lessons.

It was nearly night and the evening birds began to talk. The sharp, sweet smell outside bled through the window. Nikolas-dan told me it came from a clinging plant on the outer walls. It only smelled strong when the sun went down. At first it had made me sick but now I almost liked it. It helped me dream less, though now I almost always dreamed in strit. So he made me work even with my eyes shut.

He said he wasn't a pirate, but he made me work like Falcone had. And even Falcone let me watch vids sometimes, when I was good. This room had no hologames or vid.

"It's been over a month," he said, in Ki'hade. "You still want to go back?"

"I don't want to go back to Falcone but I don't want to

learn any more stupid strit." I slapped the reader down on the mat. I had to say "stupid" in my own language because he hadn't taught me the word in strit.

I always said strit in my head, but never to his face. Except now.

He looked like he wanted to hit me, for a second, but then it passed and he just looked. He looked for a long time until I started to feel stupid for making noise. Even when I yelled, he never hit me or yelled back. I tested him a few times, but he never touched me.

"You're tired," Nikolas-dan said.

"This stuff is hard." I folded my arms. "I can't even get away from it in my sleep."

"Do you see Falcone too? Or your parents?"

I didn't say anything or look up. But he wasn't like a human. He never filled silent spaces with conversation. So his question hung in the air for a long time, rattling around in my head.

I wished he hadn't mentioned my parents. Sitting in this room, on a planet, the thought of them unrolled with a sting, like the black insects I sometimes saw in the corner of my room, hard little things that bit your finger if you poked them.

"You're not my parents," I mumbled. "So stop asking."

After a moment he said, "I'm sorry, Jos-na."

Weird adult. He always said things like he meant them, as if he had a reason to be honest with me. Now he sat across from me, elbows on his knees, all calm good feelings. I got used to seeing him this up close, so I noticed every line on the tight bands of cloth that wrapped him up and all over. I noticed the dark blue tattoos on the backs of his hands, circles and swirls. His eyes seemed older than the rest of him. But I still couldn't read them. He never let me that close.

"Am I going to stay here forever?" I asked. In this room, on this planet. Unsold.

"No."

Usually I had to pry answers out of him. The quick reply made my stomach sick. So he was going to sell me after all.

But he said, "You're not going back to Falcone."

I looked up at him. "Probably not unless the price is good."

His face was very still. "I have said it, Jos-na. You won't go back." As if he meant it.

I didn't know exactly what he was, other than a symp, but after a month I thought he was somebody important. He'd brought me here and took care of me, and nobody seemed to mind because I never heard yelling. But I knew better. Nikolas-dan owned me now because he'd taken me off Chaos, even though he never said so. He owned this room when he was in it and when he left this room he probably owned the planet.

But he wasn't as bad as Falcone. So far.

"What does '*dan*' mean, in your name?"

As long as I asked questions he wouldn't make me write exercises. And he would stop asking me questions.

"It's the short form of the word '*ka'redan.*' "

"What does '*ka'redan*' mean?"

"Assassin-priest." He said it in my language, then switched back again to strit. "That is as close as I can translate. It's not wholly accurate. *Ka'redan* is my place. It's where I belong."

"This is a striviirc-na thing, isn't it?"

For some reason that made him smile, briefly. "Yes."

"So you're a priest?" That was kind of funny. The Universalist priests I'd met long ago on stations didn't look or act like him.

"I help bring peace to the confused. Order in our society.

Ka'redane search for our place in our training and our duties. Therefore I'm an example."

He could say that without arrogance. It just confused me more.

I pointed to the shapes beneath his clothing. "You're an assassin." I knew that word. The Send had reports about strit and symp assassins who went on stations and killed people, usually govies.

Somehow it didn't surprise me he was like that.

"Yes."

"Why haven't you killed me?"

He didn't answer right away. Then, "I think you've stood enough in the place of death. For now."

Did that mean he was going to kill me sometime in the future?

I couldn't find the words to ask him. I didn't know if I wanted the answer. Maybe he would kill me if I didn't do well, like Falcone had always said. Or keep me locked up forever, just learning his lessons and eating his food. He was better than Falcone, but whatever stopped him from taking what he wanted once and for all was going to end, and then all the silence and softness he showed would disappear.

They were both slavers, after all.

VI.

One late afternoon, during a break from lessons, he said out of nowhere, "Do you like it here?"

Falcone had played this game with me—tried to make me grateful.

"It's all right. What I've seen of it."

He acted nice and sometimes smiled at me over meals

and lessons, but at the end of it was a locked door. I always slept facing the door.

"You fight," he said. "But I think out of survival. Habit. Perhaps for something you're afraid to lose. But I've treated you well."

"So did Falcone."

"Did he?"

"Yeah, he did." But we both knew who was lying.

Maybe he knew in some weird alien way about the dreams I had lately. I barely remembered them in detail now, but they always felt bad when the morning came.

"You want answers, Jos-na. But here you have to earn them. How can we trust you?"

"*You* trust *me*? I'm the prisoner." I stood, as if there was someplace I could actually go.

He made me do exercises in the morning that stretched my muscles and taught me a different way of breathing. Sometimes they helped when I lost myself staring at the walls and their designs. He said the designs were there to meditate upon, even though they didn't say anything specific. But sometimes nothing helped, not even jumping around the floor until I was so tired I couldn't move.

Nikolas-dan said, "You think only in terms of prisoner and not prisoner. This is a place in-between. This is where you are until you wish to leave your prison."

"Leave?" I almost laughed. "With the door locked?"

"You need only ask, Jos-na, and I would open it for you."

"Right."

"Why don't you believe me?"

I'd learned that when he asked a question he really did want your answer, not something that would just make him happy.

"Why should I believe you, Nikolas-dan? You're going to change."

"I will?"

"I don't know why you act this way. Why don't you just get to the point?"

"Act this way?"

I folded my arms and looked around, not to really look, just to avoid him. He still sat on the mat, looking up at me. He was always so calm. I walked to the wall and leaned against it.

"Jos-na," he said, "I've watched you pace this room for the last week. You want to leave. But you stopped asking."

"Because you said no."

"So you give up?"

"You said no."

"You weren't ready before. Before, you only wanted to leave because you wanted to run, but there isn't anywhere to run to on Aaian-na. Now . . . now you want to leave, but not just to run. Now it's because you're ready. Do I speak true?"

"I don't know."

He unfolded to his feet. "Don't you?"

"I don't know! The only thing I know is a bunch of strit stuff, and I don't know what good that is."

"If you leave this room, Jos-na, you are going to meet striviirc-na. Sooner or later. If you can't speak Ki'hade, how will you talk to them?"

"Maybe I'll avoid them. I don't want to meet any aliens."

"What about the reports in your slate about Kali and *Mukudori*? They are in Ki'hade."

"You can tell me just as easy, but you don't because you like to play games."

"That is Falcone in your head, speaking through your mouth."

I looked up at him quickly, then down again at the floor. He had never said anything like that before. His voice was hard, but it didn't sound directed at me. I knew enough Ki'hade to hear the meaning behind his words.

"Jos-na, the things you want to know are better if you're ready to know them."

"And you decide when I'm ready?"

"Things have happened too soon for you. I think you need to slow down."

I stared at the floor so hard my eyes began to hurt. "Nikolas-dan, what do you want me for?"

The silence between my question and his answer felt as large as a planet.

He didn't touch me, not with his hands. "I saw an injured child on a deck, injured maybe because of something I had done—or not done. I brought him here so he can grow— away from the war, for a while. I teach him things so he can know the striviirc-na, because he is on their world. They are not beasts that will eat you. I want this child to live. I think he wants to live. But it's easy to live and harder to trust. Do I speak true?"

The pain behind my eyes spread to my head and down my throat, to my chest. It was hard to breathe.

"Jos-na," he said. My name in his voice, in a way I'd never heard it. And still he didn't get too close because he knew I'd just move away. He didn't try.

I couldn't understand why he never tried. He attacked stations and killed people, like Falcone.

He said, "I am not Falcone," reading my thoughts somehow.

The wall was hard against my back. "Nikolas-dan, will you open the door?"

He didn't answer right away. He waited for me to look up into his eyes and ask it again with my own. So I couldn't lie.

Then he said simply, "Yes."

VII.

He let me step out first, into an empty, quiet hallway with dark blue carpeting down the center. The color of the walls shone pale gold, beribboned with thorny shapes, just like my room. Left and right both led directly to two more doors, paneled like mine, full of fancy design.

"This way, Jos-na," he said, and pointed down my right.

So I walked. Open-eyed globes of light cast moon circles on the thick carpet. The edges of the floor were shiny white tiles. Just the one hall looked like a high-end station den, full of color and priceless materials. Earthly things. Planet things that weren't found on merchant ships—or pirate ones.

Nikolas-dan stopped at the next paneled door and slid it aside, motioning for me to go first. I stepped just inside, thinking of aliens. But I didn't see a strit, just a woman. And my heart made a fist and started to pound.

The woman raised an unnaturally white hand and motioned me forward.

"Come," she said, in my language. EarthHub language.

I took another step, but that was all. She didn't look EarthHub. Her face was totally white, the color of *Mukudori*'s corridors, except for the twin tattoos that curved around the outer edges of her eyes—dark blue tattoos like Nikolas-dan's, like a mask or a face of some Earth bird. She could have been an alien except her features were small, soft, not like the sharp bold angles I'd seen on Chaos Station. She was human, like Nikolas-dan was human. It was far from my kind of human. Far from the Hub.

I was far from the Hub. It didn't seem more obvious than now, facing this white-faced stranger. She sat motionless at one of their low black tables, in this room that had all the vid-familiar comforts of a house on Earth but none of the human touches. The air was cooler here than in my room, the colors all black and white and pale gold, with some small shapes of red. I glanced over it all, avoiding the strange woman's face and her sharp gray eyes. I looked at the tall black screens in the corner, the white paintings flowing across them in ways that made pictures of man-shapes and tree-shapes, so detailed it was almost like the animation in my primer. The shelves and thin carved objects, all shining shades of red, were the types of things I could never touch in my quarters on *Mukudori* because they belonged to Mama or Daddy and sat high above my head where I couldn't reach them.

These little sculptures were low on the ground, like all the drawers, like the bed in the corner with its black frame and curving legs in the shape of feathers. A wide bed, neatly blanketed in red.

I pulled my hands up inside my sleeves and shifted.

The white-faced woman sat at the table, in the center of the room on a thick black and gold carpet, watching me. Letting me look and looking at me. Nikolas-dan still stood behind me in the doorway.

"Come," the woman said, this time in strit. In Ki'hade, so I understood. Her voice was lighter than Nikolas-dan's. Her hair was blacker, longer, straight down her shoulders. Her eyes were the color of the gun I'd used to kill that pirate long ago. Her gaze narrowed slightly. "Do you understand me?"

"*Enh*," I said, one word in the alien language that I couldn't screw up.

"Come here," she repeated, stronger.

A hand touched my back. Nikolas-dan. I flinched away, took a step. The woman kept staring, bright silver eyes in that wide, white face. She didn't look real. She could have been painted or sculpted or sprung from a dream. She wore strips of cloth, like Nikolas-dan, but pure black and pure gray, all wrapped together and around her body. Her arms showed the smooth curves of muscle, more slender than Nikolas-dan.

An assassin-priest, *ka'redan*. She had to be one too.

"Is the boy wither-brained?" She smiled a little, looking above my head.

"No, *ki'redan*," Nikolas-dan replied. "Just afraid."

My hands curled tight. My feet felt weighted by too much gravity.

"Sit, it will be all right," the assassin-priest said, pointing to a flat cushion on one side of the triangular table. The back of her hand had the same circular patterns as Nikolas-dan's, the skin underneath just as white as her face. Only her fingernails were pale pink.

I approached and sat, put my hands in my lap. They were still clenched, so I eased my fingers loose. Nikolas-dan knelt and sat back on his heels on the third side of the table.

"*Oa-nadan ngali* Enas S'tlian-dan," the woman said formally.

The name was sort of familiar but I couldn't remember from where. Maybe Nikolas-dan had mentioned it in one of his long lessons.

"*Oa ngali* Jos Musey-na," I answered quietly. It was easy to say your name. It was all I could handle right now. Most of the striviirc-na vocabulary and forms Nikolas-dan had pounded into my head fled like criminals.

It seemed we sat staring at each other for a long time. I looked at her fully, the way Nikolas-dan always looked at me. The striviirc-na way, he said. Except nobody in this room was an alien. The features beneath the ultra-white face resembled my teacher's. The high cheekbones, the vaguely almond shape of the eyes, the curve of the mouth. But female.

A sister? Or mother?

For some reason I'd never thought Nikolas-dan would have relatives. I couldn't imagine him in a family.

Nikolas-dan poured what was now a familiar hot drink into three handleless cups placed at the center of the table. He'd explained that you should never let a guest's mouth go dry. Over the weeks I'd gotten used to *yenn*—red root tea. I swallowed without breathing and it didn't seem to taste so much like very sour apples. We took our first polite sips, then Enas S'tlian set her cup down and moved her eyes over my face and body. I knew better than to twitch when someone looked at me like that. I stared at the tabletop, at my blurry reflection in it with black shadows where my eyes should have been.

"How are you, Jos-na?"

I glanced at Nikolas-dan, then back to Enas-dan. They both stared at me, but not quite like pirates. Just curious and patient, waiting for me to tell them something they wanted to know.

Still, my heart didn't slow down. "I'm all right."

"You look well. Better than when Niko first brought you. My son tells me you learn quickly."

Niko. Son.

Nikolas-dan sipped his tea, silent. It was his mother's turn, then.

I shrugged, but not in the way symps did to emphasize a question. "I thought I had to learn or else."

"Or else?"

I shrugged again. On the table by Enas-dan's elbow was a slate. She saw me look at it.

"You want to know about your ship," she said, not a question.

I had to think of the alien words now, just because I thought of *Mukudori*. It nudged my striv-mind out of place.

Always a bad sign. To know a language, Nikolas-dan said, you had to stand inside of it.

"Enh." Simple was best.

Enas-dan poked the slate lightly, then slid it across the table toward me.

Just like that.

On the screen was the emblem of my homeship, a white bird-shape on a circular red background, in flight.

"If you have any questions," she said, "perhaps words you don't understand, you may ask. But the translation restriction isn't in force on this slate."

She knew about my lessons. I looked at Nikolas-dan, but his composed expression wasn't any explanation. So I looked back at the slate, at that symbol.

The words beneath it were in Ki'hade. For a moment I couldn't touch the screen, but out of the thorny shapes formed words I recognized, so I reached and scrolled and read.

About my homeship. About how on the merchant route between Austro and Siqiniq stations, a Universalist ship called *Ascension* discovered the remains of *Mukudori*. I read about how the Austro Salvage Authority and the Merchants Protection Commission investigated the wreckage and concluded that my homeship was attacked by a pirate, possibly two.

Simple distant words for a stifled, tangled thing.

I read how the MPC got a tip that *Genghis Khan*, a Komodo-class ship captained by former EarthHub officer Vincenzo Falcone, was responsible. But no ransom demands were made, nobody could do anything but catalogue the dead and missing and inform the living relatives. The *Khan* evaded the Rim Guard.

It was a report made over a year ago—September 30, 2183, it said, more than a week after my eighth birthday—

with no follow-up. Nobody had discovered anything else. We had all just disappeared among the stars and nobody knew where. Unfortunate but maybe inevitable, because of the increased pirate activity in the Rim, it said. The slate gave translations when I asked, told me the short meanings for those long words, in perfect EarthHub lettering.

It was a small report for something that sat big in my throat, like a stone I couldn't quite swallow. I read it all until I felt like choking.

But I didn't cry. It all just sparked in my head, jerked and writhed like live wires cut loose and dangerous.

"Falcone was an EarthHub Armed Forces captain?" I asked Enas-dan. This assassin. And her son, who was my teacher.

"Yes," Nikolas-dan answered. "Long ago."

"Jos-na," Enas-dan said. "Do you remember if you have family that weren't on your Starling?"

I kept scrolling the report in the slate. Soon the many-armed woman came up, with the word "Kali."

"Jos-na?"

"No. I don't know." Maybe an aunt, but I didn't remember her name or if she was a real aunt and not just a friend of my parents. "*Kali*, this was Falcone's EarthHub ship?"

"Yes," Nikolas-dan said, looking once at his mother. "It was a deep-space carrier."

"What happened to it?" My eyes hurt. I didn't want to read from the slate.

"He decided to chase my husband," Enas-dan said. "And he lost."

I blinked. "Your husband?"

"Drink your tea, Jos-na," she said. And sipped her own.

I picked up the cup. It felt heavy. I drank and the liquid seemed to eat through my stomach.

Enas-dan said, in my language, "Falcone was a carrier

captain for EarthHub twenty years ago EHSD. His ship was the *Kali*. He was a very good striv killer. He still is, when he bothers to be. When he isn't raiding merchants and Rim Guardians for theft and ransom."

Striv was okay to say, it was just an abbreviation. But I was surprised that she didn't speak Ki'hade now. She didn't even have an accent, like Nikolas-dan.

And she knew Falcone. She wasn't going to hide it from me.

"I never met the man," she continued. "But my husband Markalan did, ship to ship in the Battle of Ghenseti. Long before your time. Ghenseti was a military outpost, a double leap from Chaos. A major resupply base for the deep-space carriers. Markalan chose to attack it."

"Why?" I said, before I thought. "Why do you—symps and stuff—why do you fight for the strivs? Against humans?"

Enas-dan picked up a thin piece of green root from a small plate on the table, rested an elbow on her bent knee, and chewed. A minty scent threaded through the air. "Falcone, he attacked your Starling, yes?"

It always came back to that. But I thought there was more to the question, so I just nodded and waited.

"Falcone takes things that don't belong to him. He doesn't care that it's wrong to attack merchants and steal children. He thinks merchants are fair game in this war. I suspect he thinks this. I've read some things about him. He was the same way as a captain. He did what he wanted no matter what the Hub said, or what was right. Pirates are like that. If you don't freely give them things, they take them anyway. So it is with the Hub."

"How can you say that? My ship—" *Was a Hub merchant.*

She poured more tea. "Long ago, when I was younger

even than Niko, Markalan and I went on a mission to deep
space as part of an expeditionary force for the Hub. Have
you heard of the *Plymouth*?"

"It's the moon where the strits—where the striviirc-na
were."

She didn't say anything about my mistake. Neither did
Nikolas-dan. "Even before that. The *Plymouth* was the ship
I worked on. We found the moon with the striviirc-na scientists. Qinitle-na. The moon had a lot of materials that the
Hub needed—elemental compounds that we use to make
transsteel. Transsteel is the thing we build ships and stations
with."

I knew that from science classes on *Mukudori*, and hearing my parents talk. And Falcone's lessons. For deep-space
development, transsteel was the most important thing next
to quantum teleportation of light, for communications. Falcone liked to attack shipments of transsteel.

"So," Enas-dan said, not sounding like a symp at all now
that she wasn't speaking the alien language. "*Plymouth*'s
captain tried to open communications. The language was
difficult—as you well know—but not impossible to learn. It
took a couple years but we established a rapport. Conversation. Just enough to find out that the striviirc-na wouldn't
share their moon."

"Why not? It's because of them this war—"

The EarthHub language fooled me. As if I now had a
right to speak to them this way.

But they didn't tell me to shut up. Nikolas-dan watched
me with the same calm, unreadable face. And Enas-dan just
shrugged a bit.

"Is it because of them? Why did they need to give a reason? They were clearly first on the moon and had been there
for a few years. Yet when they said no, *Plymouth*'s captain

decided to take over the mines anyway. Many strivs were killed."

This wasn't how they taught it in school, or what I remembered from the Send. "So that captain was like a pirate?"

"Yes," Enas-dan said. "Human technology was more advanced. The striviirc-na hadn't the ability to leap or travel faster than light. Their scientists had taken a ten-year trip to reach that moon. And they wanted it for themselves because we weren't part of their system, we didn't understand that when their scientists study something, they believe there is an almost spiritual link between the observer and the observed, that each has their place and it shouldn't be interrupted lightly. *We* are the aliens to them. We **had** no *na*, to their thinking. Do you know what *na* is?"

Na. Place. The first principle of striviirc-na belief. Nikolas-dan had taught me. So I nodded.

Enas-dan said, "The strivs don't have gods, they don't worship a higher power. But they respect *na*. It's the center of their beliefs. Or . . . I ought to say it's the center of Nan'hade beliefs. Not all strivs on Aaian-na believe the same things, and not all sympathizers are allowed everywhere on this planet."

"Then why do you stay? Why do you live here with them?"

She didn't hesitate. "Because I helped them repel the *Plymouth* from that moon. Me, Markalan, and half of the crew. I made my decision long ago not to side with pirates. In whatever shape or form."

She sat there with her alien skin color and tattoos, in alien dress, in an alien room, and I believed her. But just because she didn't see herself as a pirate didn't mean it wasn't true. In school you learned that the first symps stole weapons and tech and gave it all to the strits, training them so they could fight us and kill us, which made the war really bad. But I remembered the fast way the teachers covered the starmaps, and where EarthHub's borders were, and how we successfully kept the strits at bay. We didn't want to destroy them, we just wanted them to stay in their place. What was bad about that?

Nobody ever mentioned that the war started when striviircna were killed in the first place because the Hub was greedy.

"I know this is a lot right now," Enas-dan said. "And you might not believe us. I hope you will make up your own mind about us, now that you're here."

Enas S'tlian. Markalan S'tlian. The names clicked in my memory. Not S'tlian, but Gray and Maida. They had started the war, everybody said. My parents had said so when they talked with Evan's parents sometimes. Markalan Maida and Enas Gray.

And their son the Warboy.

Terrorist, killer, strit-lover. Those were the meanings of the Warboy that the Hub hated and Falcone half admired. Because Falcone said the Warboy was the best kind of pirate. He hit fast and disappeared, keeping the enemy off balance.

But that had come from a pirate.

But *Mukudori* hadn't liked symps either.

But this was Nikolas-dan. My teacher. Who never once touched me and never raised his voice.

"Why—" The tea was a sour taste at the back of my throat. "Why do you care what I think about you?"

They looked at me, gray eyes and dark, from the two other sides of the table.

Nikolas-dan said, "We want you to be happy here, Josna."

I found myself staring at my cup and the deep red flakes of tea at the bottom of it, like dry bits of blood.

"Did Niko teach you what Aaian-na means in Ki'hade?" Enas-dan asked.

I shrugged, remembered they read that as a question, so shook my head.

"Aaian-na," she said. "The place on which we stand. Striviirc-na: those who live inside the place. Jos-na: Jos who stands in his place. You see the subtle differences? There are places that are sacred—*hiaviirc-na*. The *place* where we find ourselves. Our *place* in relation to others. Our place in society. Our place—here." She tapped her heart. "Where is your place, Jos-na?"

She spoke so softly yet it made my head hurt. It made everything inside of me twist and ache. I couldn't look up. "I guess my place is wherever you put me."

Nikolas-dan said, "Another word, Jos-na. *Buntla-na*. The displaced ones. Orphans. Criminals. It's not a desired state."

"I didn't ask to be orphaned."

"No. But here is where you are. On Aaian-na. *Place* is a changeable state, Jos-na. It can be altered."

I turned the cup slowly on the table. I got away from Falcone. Is that what he meant?

Enas-dan said in my language, "The most elusive of places is not where we are, but where we can be."

I looked deep into those gray eyes, searching for truth.

I knew Nan'hade was ruled by groups—castes. *Nae*. Places, again. The ruling *na* was the *ka'redan-na*. I read something about how the country used to war a lot until the *ka'redane* made order and taught their students how to make order through "righteous killing." *Oka'redan*. That was what Nikolas-dan called it. And everyone was born into a societal *na*, but you could change your *na* if that was where your spiritual *na* led you.

Did they want me to be in their place? Their *na*? A symp

on this world? Was that going to make me happy, learning what they said was important?

Buntla-na. So I learned a new word, another way to say what I was. Another small word for a meaning so large it filled my head and spilled into my dreams, and never left me. My parents were gone but this new meaning stayed. I was going to be *buntla-na* for the rest of my life, because a report said my ship was dead and everybody was lost or killed. And that was all. That was all and everything.

I didn't know if I'd ever be anything like happy—here or elsewhere.

Maybe they knew this, because they didn't ask again.

VIII.

Nikolas-dan walked me back to my room. Our steps made no sound on the thick carpet. I couldn't relax with him at my back. Once inside I faced him, arms folded, ready for a talk about how I'd conducted myself in the meeting with his mother. The knot hadn't left my chest. It pulled tighter.

But he stayed in the doorway and just said, "I'll bring you something to eat." He moved to slide the door in, then stopped, giving me a second look.

I stepped back a pace, glanced at the wall.

"Do you want to come to the kitchen?" he said, as if it was something he asked me all the time.

That surprised me and I shrugged to hide it.

"No? Yes?" He imitated my shrug but for a different reason.

"Nikolas-dan, what's going to happen to me?"

"Whatever you want, Jos-na."

"Stop lying!"

His brows went up. "Why am I lying?"

"You teach me strit, make me meet your mother, and you tell me you want me to be happy because you felt sorry for me or something when I was shot. So what am I supposed to do for you?"

"Nothing."

"Why can't you just tell me?"

"There is nothing to tell." He stared at me as if something was wrong with me but it wasn't my fault. Like you'd stare at a crippled person in the dark corners of stations. "Jos-na, listen to me. Falcone killed your ship—"

"I don't want to go over that again."

That report and its big, blunt words.

"He killed your ship and took you and it was no place to be, Jos-na, with a pirate. I understand."

"No you don't. Just leave me alone, okay?"

"He's with you still, even though he isn't here."

I looked at the symp. Hard. "So what are you? Why should I believe you? You're going to a lot of trouble to make me feel good about being here. So what am I supposed to think?"

"Maybe that if your parents were in my place and found an orphan, they would do the same thing. For no other reason than it was right."

I heard my breaths. We both did.

"You never knew them, you don't know what happened!"

Why was it that bad things stayed longer in your memory and good things faded? Their faces were beginning to gray around the edges, even when I shut my eyes. The longer I stayed on this planet, talking strit, talking with symps, the quicker they faded. Everything I knew was fading, except the bad things.

"I know what pirates do," Nikolas-dan said. "I've killed my share."

He didn't say it proudly, like Falcone did when he talked about Hub ships. My teacher's calm face hardly smiled, but then it never twisted in rage either. "Warboy" didn't seem to suit him, until you saw the way he moved and those blade shapes beneath his clothing. Until you talked to him and knew everything he said was more than just the words.

"Where is your life now, Jos-na? On *Mukudori*, with Falcone, or here? How many times have you divided yourself? When are you going to collect your pieces? I've provided a place but you fight it all day."

There was no running from this place. Whatever they did to you, you'd just have to put it away. It might have started out with language learning, but it was just another card game. You had to learn the new rules and deal it.

At least Nikolas-dan left me alone at night.

He stood by the door, waiting on me. But if this was his game, I didn't have to just lie back and play. He wasn't as bad a teacher as Falcone, so maybe I could get something out of this. Maybe I could show him—maybe it would be different this time.

I was on a planet. Time to move, Jos.

So I went to my window. It was different this time. It was more than a month removed and after the truth of my ship, written in a slate. *Don't think back. Don't dream.*

I pressed the panel to raise the screen. It folded up, spilling in moonlight. Slowly I leaned toward the clear glass and gazed out, down the slope at the shining, shadowed rooftops stuck in the rock, and out over the dark green trees, farther than I'd looked the first time. In the distance was an odd silver shimmer on the horizon and the bright high moon in two places, the lower of the two less clear and rippling. A mirror reflection. Stars lay scattered around the moon and across the sky, close and brilliant. Maybe because it was night I didn't feel the dizziness I had the first time. I knew the stars. They'd once been my home.

All the while I looked, Nikolas-dan said nothing. He didn't try to tell me what I was looking at, as Falcone would've done. He had already taught me the words for everything I saw.

IX.

The house was full of moonlight. I curled my hands at my sides and walked forward through the quiet rooms. Nikolas-dan padded behind me, soft steps at a distance. Never crowding as I walked from wide room to wide room—a common area, a kitchen, a dining area with walls of windows that looked on large entwined trees outside, dark and thick. The rooms were separated by sliding doors and filled with low furniture, black and red, like my room and Enas-dan's room except decorated in even more detail, in those thorny shapes. Like a maze on everything you touched. Some of the doors we didn't go through.

The hallways between the common rooms curved like the garden path my parents had taken me to, once, in Austro Station's arboretum. Except here the floor was smooth dark wood. Objects in alien designs sat on tables, in corners, some that I thought were supposed to be animals. Birds. Trees. People with swords and strange combinations of people and trees like some kind of genetic accident. Striviirc-na art.

We ended up in a west-facing room with a window open to the cluster of trees outside. Night insects and birds talked. The scent of the sweet vine was everywhere. A whistle breeze moved the curtains around and made the trees shiver.

"Won't things come in?" I asked Nikolas-dan. He stood near one of the black screens, watching me.

"We have guards," he said.

I'd meant animals and bugs.

"Where's your father?" I asked him. The house was quiet, not like a ship full of people on duty.

He didn't answer for a moment, but when he did he didn't let me look away. "He's dead, Jos-na. From a Hub battle three years ago."

For the seconds it took him to tell me, the usually composed expression on his face slid a little sideways. I almost heard the thoughts behind his eyes. They echoed in my own head.

"Doesn't that make you mad?"

He shrugged. "How will that change things? I need only move ahead."

"I guess it's easy for you." He was older.

"No, Jos-na. Never easy. Only necessary." Then he quickly moved to the door and turned up the lights a little from a tiny pad on the wall. "Sit. I'll bring the food." And disappeared.

So his father was dead too. Maybe he did understand me, just a little. Of course he'd never lived with pirates and he was a symp.

I found a cushion, with my back to one of the screens, and sank down. Beside my foot, on the dark wood floor, a fingernail spider crawled. Its little black body skittered and stopped in jerks, as if it couldn't decide where it wanted to go. I watched with a mix of disgust and fascination. When it came too close I pulled away.

"They aren't poisonous," a throaty voice said.

I looked up, startled. A man stood in the doorway, tall. He had a normal skin tone and for a moment I thought it was my teacher—they had the same tattoo around their right eyes and a definite resemblance—but something about the way he stood, I knew it wasn't Nikolas-dan in the next second.

Nikolas-dan said he found me on Chaos Station, where he'd gone to rescue his brother, a prisoner there. So he hadn't been lying. At least he did have a brother. It was obvious in this man's face and his gray eyes, darker than Enas-dan's, but shaped the same.

"Don't be frightened," the man said, in Ki'hade. "The poisonous spiders, *eja*, they aren't in this area." He approached, a slender figure in assassin-priest white robes, barefoot on the floor and soundless. All of them, they moved around like ghosts. Before I could say anything or slip away, he crouched and picked up the spider between his thumb and forefinger, and mashed it.

I swallowed, dry-mouthed, and got caught looking in his eyes. How could he do that bare-handed?

He smiled. It wasn't my teacher's quick, crooked expression. This one wrinkled the corners of his eyes, like a path often used. Tired. "You're not scared of this little thing, are you? Never mind, it won't hurt you now." He stood and went to one of the tables, removed a single square of red cloth from the small pile there, and wiped his hand. "So you're Niko's student? *Eja*, we were beginning to wonder when he'd choose one. I admit I hadn't thought it would be an orphan from the Hub."

Silence followed his words. He wanted a reaction from me and glanced my way, folding the cloth neatly once he was done with it.

"What does *eja* mean?" I said, because I didn't want to talk about the Hub.

"*Eja*. What do you say in your Hub language? Like"—he waved his fingers a bit—"um? Hmm? Ah? You know?"

He sounded like he was teasing me, and smiled again. Falcone had smiled a lot when it suited him too.

"How do you like it here so far?" he said, sitting on one of the chairs and stretching out his legs. He reached behind his neck and drew his long hair into a knot. All loose, casual movements that put me on edge. I didn't know why, but he acted too familiar. Or too much unlike the symps I'd met.

"It's okay."

"Your accent isn't bad. Still too much of the Hub in it, though."

He didn't say it meanly, but it made me frown. "I've only been here a couple months."

"Yes. We quite admire you for getting away from Falcone."

I picked at my pants leg. Did everybody know?

"You're one of the lucky few. I hear he guards his prisoners like a mother with a child."

Except my mother. That little thought crept in and I flushed, guilty. She'd tried and so had my father. Did he know that too? He sounded like he admired me, but like my teacher I felt an added weight behind the words.

Except he wasn't my teacher. "So you know Falcone? Had dinner with him?" Maybe it wasn't smart to be mouthy with one of them, but I couldn't help it.

"I don't know him personally. He's notorious. Surely you're aware."

"Nobody seemed to know him on Chaos."

"Maybe they did, but didn't care." His smile showed teeth.

"Why wouldn't they care? Two carriers were docked there."

"Maybe the carriers are bad."

I looked at him for a long second, but it didn't help. I couldn't guess what he was after any more than with the rest of them. "The carriers can't be bad."

He hesitated, then laughed. "*Eja*, you're right in this case.

Those two carriers weren't the kind you can bribe. *Sraga*." And he smirked.

"*Sraga?*"

"Niko didn't teach you that word? It means 'fuck.' Or something like. *Eja*, it's rather more rude in Ki'hade."

He liked to talk, but not like a teacher. I stared until it made him laugh again, and then I couldn't look at him.

"So how could Falcone go on Chaos and nobody know?" I asked before Nikolas-dan came in.

"His notoriety forces him to change his appearance." He sounded bored now, and shifted in his seat. "*Eja*, I suppose Niko hasn't started your combat lessons yet?"

A shadow appeared in the doorway.

"I hadn't mentioned them yet, Ash-dan," Nikolas-dan said, sounding a little annoyed. He brought in a tray of food and set it in front of me on the floor. "*Jos-na*, this is my younger brother."

I said, "Combat lessons, Nikolas-dan?"

"I'm sorry," Ash-dan said. "I assumed you would've started the meditations at least."

Suddenly it seemed like I wasn't in the room at all.

"Not quite yet," my teacher said. He didn't sit beside me like he usually did when he brought me meals. Instead he stayed standing, facing his brother. "Have you spoken to Tkata yet?"

"Just now. She's on ship already."

"Yes, and the supplies?"

"On schedule. *Eja*, I'll have all the information for you tomorrow morning."

Nikolas-dan glanced down at me. "Then I'll speak with you later, Ash."

Ash-dan looked at me and he didn't smile. "The Hub will miss you, Niko. Are you sure it's wise to teach one of its pups all the arts of the *ka'redane*?"

Nikolas-dan gestured in a way I couldn't read, and something in it made Ash-dan laugh, though it sounded a bit forced.

"I do what I please," Nikolas-dan said, "and in a minute it will please me to hit you." But he wasn't serious. Ash-dan stood and nudged his brother's arm as he walked by to the door. My teacher did something fast with his elbow that nearly pitched Ash-dan into the wall. But Ash-dan kept his balance and just laughed, not looking back.

"How did he get on Chaos?" I said, once the door slid shut.

Nikolas-dan sat across from me and opened the dishes of food. "When I am on planet, Ash-dan co-captains *Turundrlar*—my ship."

I worked out the parts in my head. *Turundrlar. Death-strike.*

Nikolas-dan continued, "He was in one of our fighters, on a rendezvous mission, when a Hub convoy jumped him."

"But you're both here now."

"He had to take some time, and so did I."

A prisoner on Chaos, I remembered. A symp on a Hub station. And Nikolas-dan had rescued him. And me.

"How long was he on Chaos?"

The answer was short. "Weeks." He sipped his tea. "He's going off-planet soon, again. I will stay here."

With me. I looked down at the food and speared a vegetable with my double-pronged fork.

"Now that it's out," Nikolas-dan said, "would you like to learn how to fight like a *ka'redan*?"

"You'd teach a pup from the Hub?" I had to ask.

"My brother and I differ on some things, but I choose my student and Ash has no voice in it. I choose you and you are no longer in the Hub. So tell me."

If I learned how to fight, nobody could ever take me

again. I looked into his eyes, human eyes, and that contradicting tattoo on his face. The Warboy, whom all the Hub feared.

"I'd like that very much, Nikolas-dan."

X.

Before fighting, I had to learn how to breathe. For this he took me to a new room at the other end of the blue and gold hall where our bedrooms were, set apart from the rest of the house—for privacy, Nikolas-dan said. It was early morning and already the house started to look different. Now the paneled doors at either end of the hall weren't walls to my exploration, but windows.

"*Inidrla-na*," Nikolas-dan said. "The place of learning."

He led me into a wide, echoing room. I took one step inside and stopped.

An entire wall was glass or some other transparent material. It let in the dawn—faint stars and a sky streaked with color. I couldn't move, faced by that largeness, larger even than the view from my bedroom window. The water below the sky looked like the gems my mother had sometimes worn on her dresses for special events, winking and moving. Light made the world a banner, full of colors I didn't even know the names of, rippling in the breeze, teasing my lazy eyes. I couldn't seem to capture them all at once.

I edged farther into the room, up against the glass. The world fell away from the other side of a long balcony. More buildings retreated below the edge, shadowed white steps in a staircase that seemed made for giants. All of them looked similar, flat and squarish and broad. Figures stood on some of the other balconies, but too far for me to tell if they were human or striviirc-na. The roofs were patterned in those swirls, but they weren't all the same. The deep green trees sprouted like hair among them, growing from the gray and brown mountain rock.

I had to remember to breathe.

"Come," Nikolas-dan said, from behind me. "Stand with me."

He taught me how to breathe. Facing each other on opposite sides of a small white circle embedded in the gloss-dark floor, he made me sit, stand, sometimes move my arms in and out, timed with my breaths. After a couple weeks he put weights in my hands or made me move in strict hands-and-feet gestures that tested my balance. I caught on quickly, he said, and he seemed pleased. I didn't let him see how the praise affected me, but sometimes when he left me alone to practice I'd smile as I performed the movements. These weren't Falcone's military-styled exercises, and no guard stood over me to make sure I finished them. When Nikolas-dan stayed he kept out of my space and corrected me with a soft voice and by example.

The point of these movements, he said, was for me to become so grounded in my place that nothing touched me. Not even my thoughts, my pain, or my hunger. It was useful. I could disconnect so well I lost awareness of time. I lost myself in those minutes.

The days began this way, just breathing, instead of with my head in a slate. The new words I learned had to do with the new world I had entered, the one within Nan'hade. The ruling world. Nikolas-dan's world.

Ka'redan meant assassin-priest. *Ki'redan*, First Master assassin-priest. *Kii'redan*, Second Master assassin-priest.

Ash-dan, long gone off-planet to fight the Hub in his brother's place, was a *kii'redan*. Enas-dan, who sometimes joined her son and me during meals to see how I was doing, was a *ki'redan*. Enas S'tlian, whose adopted striviirc-na last name meant "first among us." But she hadn't been born on Aaian-na, like her sons.

My teacher was *kia'redan bae*: no other. Without comparison. The strivs had created a word for him because no other sympathizer had ever earned such a rank in the *ka'redan-na*. He was second only to the Caste Master and had never taken a student before me. Enas-dan said I was special, and lucky, and her son talked about me all the time, about how proud he was of the progress I made.

At night, before I fell asleep, I turned the words around in my mind and let them catch the light. No matter how hard I looked I couldn't see flaws in them. Like the sweet-smelling vine outside my window, they brought good dreams.

XI.

After a few weeks of learning breathing exercises and memorizing different *denie*—the stylized gestures—Nikolas-dan met me in the *inidrla-na*, as usual, and disappeared behind one of the two unfolded black screens near the east wall. The screens were carved white in what was now a familiar style of striv figures and scenes of battle. Not with guns, but swords, like the hologames I used to play with Evan. Lined on the opposite wall were those same swords, the tallest in the middle set in an upright position, blade ceilingward. It was twice as long as my arm. Beside it on both sides were smaller and smaller swords in a line until they became daggers. They reminded me of the stories from striv history about caste assassinations and bloody betrayals that made EarthHub's war seem distant and mechanical. I'd read that the older homes of the Caste Masters were built with the enemy's blood rubbed into the wood. I looked down. The floor was smooth, polished, deep brown almost to black, with faint lines of red in the grain. I wondered.

My eyes kept drifting to the weapons. They were mysterious, dangerous, and beautiful. Dark silver with grips of carved black and white. Bone?

Nikolas-dan emerged from behind the screen, carrying a smooth-edged sword made of black wood. He put the practice weapon in my right hand, then fixed my left hand below on the hilt. It was the size to fit a child's grip.

Who used swords now? It was fascinating but a gun might've been more useful. I had never heard of striviirc-na attacking soljets with swords.

Nikolas-dan went to the wall and dislodged the largest sword. He stood directly opposite me about two meters away, holding the weapon by his thigh with the blade point in my direction.

I wanted to step back, but didn't.

"*Jii*," he said. "The blade. *Jii-ko*. The blade style." He walked up to me and rested the point of his sword against my forehead. It took all of my will not to run while a snake of discomfort writhed in my stomach. He said, "*Jii-klala*. The blade mind. These three things you will learn first."

The level of my learning had just stepped up. I saw it on his face. Behind it he asked a question. Was I ready?

The weapon felt awkward in my hand. Nikolas-dan moved back to give himself room, then stamped forward and swept his sword down with a cry. The breeze of its passing lifted a lock of my hair. I gripped my small blade, heart thudding. He demonstrated again. One easy movement. Easy until I tried it.

There had been a hologame that spread like rumor aboard *Mukudori*, a fighting game using ancient weapons that played into the imaginations of kids raised on battles between ships and guns. *Knights of Fire* it was called, where men and women fought in single combat using swords of all shapes and sizes with the skill of their human controllers. I had adapted quickly to the game. My knight had racked up kill points like an "unrepentant crusader," my father used to say—flashing sword moves that had made my shipmates laugh in amazement.

This was nothing like that game.

I slashed with my wooden black blade, one step forward in that downward stroke, then back again to start over. Just that one move, step and slash, while he called out words in Ki'hade, making me repeat them. Numbers. Counting. He told me to visualize the movement in my mind as I did it, to listen to the sound of the blade slicing through the air, the sound of his voice, the slap of my foot on the floor as I stamped forward. I felt the muscles in my body move. He told me to slash harder after every step back into the rest position. He spoke to me until I couldn't hear any more, until it all became a rhythm as deep as my own heartbeat.

I didn't know how long he kept me at it, but by the end I knew the weight and song of that sword. I stood inside of it. It was like another form of meditation, except I knew I could kill with this skill.

Something in me began to open.

"Before the dagger you must learn the long sword. When you can fight at a distance from your opponent, then you may learn to fight *yta'n okaara*. Heart to heart."

Like the slashing movement, his words buried deep until I felt them, until I didn't have to think about them for them to be there.

The four different *jiie-ko*, or blade styles, he taught me included a dictionary full of new vocabulary that he drilled just as hard as the martial forms. Once I'd mastered the very basic movements—drawing, parrying, cutting, and returning the sword to rest—Nikolas-dan taught me the styles. A third of a full day was spent doing the moves from my *jii-na*: the place of my sword, which was basically the center of an invisible circle around my body that I was supposed to protect. If I kept the enemy on the outside of that circle I would be able to defend myself better in a combat situation—unarmed or against weapons like blades. Obviously I wouldn't be able to defend myself against a gun using that method. Only guns could fight guns, unless the shooter got inside my circle. Nikolas-dan said the gun training came later.

Older, I thought he meant.

My *jii-klala*, or blade mind, had to be inside the eight essential forms of striking before I could step out further in my training. This was the *ki'ya* of the *ki'jii-ko*—the first principle of the first blade style. Without knowing those eight forms I would never advance.

Nikolas-dan demonstrated the eight forms himself. He brought his own *jii* into the *inidrla-na*, a beautiful sword about the length of his shoulder to his fingertips. The hilt shone black, carved with those familiar swirling patterns that he'd told me were meant for meditation, just like the patterns on the walls of the house. The guard was round, engraved, the shape of an open flower, the color of bronze. The blade itself was pale silver. His movements with it reminded me of hours I'd spent watching raindrops run like tiny rivers down the windowpane in my room. Peace despite the violence of a storm. I saw it on his face. It was a dance only for him and the *jii* and the air they moved through in silence.

He showed me at half speed so I could see exactly where the sword was in relation to his body and the invisible opponent. Then he showed me in combat speed and I could barely see where the blade went. It hung at rest by his thigh, blurred, then hung at rest again. The air around him sang the movements. To me it was perfection. He was perfection.

Once the physical training part of the day was over, he sat with me for a light midday meal of seafood and soft vegetables, and talked. He told me about the animals on the planet, about sailing and snow and stories from the past, when Caste Masters were challenged and both the accusers and the accused had to stand before the First Masters and be judged right or wrong. He said in the old times both parties didn't even bother the First Masters—they settled things themselves, the way assassins did. The other seven castes even hired the *ka'redane* to settle *their* fights sometimes, which always caused a scandal because the *ka'redane* weren't supposed to be mercenaries. He said there was less of that now, especially since the sympathizers had been integrated into Nan'hade. The Caste Master had strict laws about how sympathizers were treated.

I dreamed in striviirc-na, dreamed of the planet and nothing else. I didn't see, speak, or think anything but the language that was around me, that I saw in those rooms and over the balcony, in the lines on Nikolas-dan's face, in his eyes and the eyes of his mother when she visited. They were all Aaian-na.

The war and Falcone got further away, became only words on a screen that I could shut off. In the Tree Room, where I'd first met Ash-dan, Nikolas-dan let me read Send reports stolen from Hubside, translated into Ki'hade by a sympathizer. It didn't matter what language they were in, the meaning was the same. With every passing month, Hub carriers tried to trespass farther through the demilitarized zone—the three-dimensional buffer between Hub space and striviirc-na space, which Markalan S'tlian had set up with Hub officials when he'd been a ship captain leading the striv fleet years ago. No colonization or satellite operations were

supposed to exist in the DMZ. Ideally the buffer was all that
kept EarthHub from pushing through to Aaian-na, but that
was changing.

At the time of the agreement, Enas-dan said, EarthHub
hadn't wanted to own Aaian-na. But opinions were changing. One faction of the space government, with support from
some of Earth's more powerful countries, wanted to "eradi-
cate the strit threat once and for all." As if the striviirc-na
had any intention to invade Earth or even its Spoke colonies.
If they encroached in the Rim, it was only to retrieve prisoners or attack military outposts that helped fuel the carriers
and battleships that kept invading the DMZ.

The people's victory, Nikolas-dan's name meant. I understood it now. The Warboy was his father's successor in
space, against EarthHub, and the only thing stopping the
Hub from invading all the way to the planet, like they had
done with Qinitle-na and a handful of other moons and pre-
viously claimed striviirc-na territories since then. The Hub
called Nikolas-dan a terrorist, but he only did enough to
keep the Hub at bay. If he wanted to fully attack, it would
escalate the war and double the casualties. He and Enas-dan
both told me so. Nobody on Aaian-na—striviirc-na or
human—wanted that, despite what the Send said.

Enas-dan was the leader of the sympathizers in
Nan'hade, which was the strongest of the three countries
that allowed humans to live with strivs. She worked directly
with the Nan'hade assassin-priest Caste Master—the
ki'redan-na. They helped the humans and striviirc-na live in
peace.

In addition to my physical training in the *inidrla-na*,
Nikolas-dan made me learn all about how Nan'hade operated
(these lessons were usually in my room or the Tree Room),
about the eight castes and their colors and symbols. The
swirling circle was the symbol of Nikolas-dan's caste, the

assassin-priests, who didn't go around just killing people, he told me with a crooked smile. They kept the other castes in line, not through fear, but respect. There had been caste wars years and years ago, and the *ka'redane* had ended them through force. But then they'd made the laws that made the other castes redefine their places in society, and everybody's *na* became less about status and more about your own progression toward *hiaviirc-na*. The sacred place.

Out of conflict you found your *na*, but nobody in Nan'hade believed now that physical conflict was the way to find it. Societal conflicts weren't desired now. The focus was on the emotional *na*, and the emotional conflict. Though everything was intertwined like the designs on their walls and the tattoos on their bodies, each line and curve could still be separately tracked, like you tracked a string of words that made up sentences in a paragraph. So all your principle *nae* were intertwined yet separate.

These were the slate explanations, but when I dug through Nan'hade history, I found stories about Caste Masters that abused their power, and the bloody conflicts that followed. Still, always at the end, they assassinated the bad Caste Masters and someone better took his or her place. For a time.

When I wasn't learning the arts of the *ka'redane*, Nikolasdan let me paint. It was something to do besides read and train, something totally different, and I enjoyed the quiet moments in the *inidrla-na*, looking out at the sea and trying to copy it on rolls of canvas. It was somewhere to put my mind that had nothing to do with where I was or where I'd been. Only colors and shapes mattered. Sometimes Nikolasdan joined me, both of us choosing a part of the landscape to interpret through paints, and he taught me in that too.

It was comfortable to sit with him because he didn't interrogate me. We could sit for hours together without a word between us. At the end of it sometimes he smiled, as if our nonconversation had amused him. And then sometimes he frowned, as if he remembered something that bothered him. He told me that it was sympathizer business and nothing that I needed to worry about. I should only concentrate on my studies and my training.

Sometimes I looked at his profile when he painted, at his tattoo, and thought someday I was going to get one too. I'd be a *ka'redan*, not *buntla-na* anymore.

One morning during breakfast he told me to start my exercises on my own, he had to check on something before our lessons began. In the *inidrla-na* alone I did my breathing under the glare of sunlight in the room, but it was too hot so I went to the glass wall to open one panel, let in a breeze. I liked to do the drills with the scent of the sea and trees around me. There was a latch on one side of the glass and I pulled. Birdsong greeted me, riding on the warm breeze. A little rainbow-feathered bird perched on the balcony. It tilted its head at me and didn't fly away, like they usually did.

I stepped out onto the balcony, my feet instantly warming on the baked tiles. There wasn't any barrier between me and the outside air and the rolling-down landscape below me. It always gave me a moment of slight dizziness, if I wasn't careful.

The balcony stretched the length of the window, about a meter out from the building. The sun was brighter out here, hotter. It seemed to prick through my skin and squeeze around my throat. I went cautiously to the bird but as soon as I held out my hand it peeped and leaped away, dropping like a dart toward the trees below, then alighting on a branch. I held the top of the balcony for security, leaned a bit to watch. The rail was at the level of my shoulders so at least I couldn't slip and pitch over the side.

All the roofs below me were flat and white, but shadowed in those swirling designs. The walls were brightly painted in rust reds, blues, golds. Lips curved down from the edges of the roofs, making a little shade over the balconies. The breeze brushed over the side of the mountain and through my hair. Water winked in the distance, a blue deeper than the sky, but I couldn't hear it. Only the trees whispered, answering the wind. I'd heard wind before outside my window, but here it was as clear as the glass that usually separated me from feeling it.

Below me on my left, on another balcony of another building about five meters away, stood a slender figure I had never seen before. That balcony was always empty. Branches partly covered it but it leaned over, extended one long arm, and cast something down the slant of the mountainside, in the direction of the sea.

The object floated, got jerked by the breeze, and danced upward for a bit, then spun and flipped toward the lower roofs. The flight reminded me of the paper ships we used to fold and fling off the upper ramparts in main engineering, when Jules allowed us. We'd watch them soar and dive, flying through the air totally unlike how our ship cut through space.

I rested my chin on the rail and squinted at the figure. It wore tight clothing, almost like the white coils I'd seen on Nikolas-dan and his mother, except the white arms and sides were bare—gaps in the fabric all down the legs. Something about the movements reminded me of my teacher, the slow deliberate gestures. But something was off. They were too smooth.

The figure had long white hair, white like Enas S'tlian's face was white. The skin was the same. As it tilted its chin to look up at the sky and stringy clouds, I saw a flash of black eyes.

Completely black eyes. A striviirc-na.

I shrank down until only my eyes showed above the balcony. I couldn't tell if it was male or female. It had a face
that made the S'tlians' seem friendly by comparison. It
looked carved from stone, as if someone had a general idea
of human features without bothering to put in fine details
like lines beneath the eyes or at the corners of the mouth, or
the little indentations where nose met cheeks. The nose was
oddly small compared to the boldness of the rest of the face,
the lips just as white as the rest of its skin. But its skin shone,
as if polished like their black screens. The tattoos around its
eyes and down the edges of its cheekbones were dark silver
swirls and points, more complicated even than Nikolas-
dan's, shining slightly under the sun. For some reason it reminded me of the white pictures on the black screens.

Long neck, broad shoulders, slender torso . . . I took
them all in, rising farther above my hiding place.

Maybe it saw me in the corner of its eyes—or sensed me
in some alien way I had no way of knowing. But it turned
then and looked at me square on.

I saw nothing friendly in that face. I saw nothing at all.
Against the white of its skin, the large upswept black eyes
pinned me with the pointed authority of a gun barrel.

The striviirc-na moved suddenly, without sound, grabbed
one of the thick branches of the tree brushing against the
balcony, and vaulted up onto it. Diamond points danced
below its raised arm. I thought it was a trick of the sunlight
before I recognized the thin skin of a small wing fluttering
free from the gap in its coiled bindings. It sparkled like raindrops on a windowpane, a wide flexible arc from the wrist
to the waist.

Before the striv landed firmly on the branch, he (or she—
though something told me it was a he) flung himself to another branch, and another, all around that tree until he was
in leaping distance of my balcony.

In one uncoiled jump he landed right in front of me, a soft slap of bare feet on the balcony tiles. He straightened as if one long muscle ran through his body and looked down at me as I backed up.

My shoulders hit the window panel of the *inidrla-na*. My heart thudded inside my head, an echo from where it had dropped into my stomach.

His body looked like a human's, except for the see-through wings that folded softly against his sides now that his arms were down. Two legs, two arms, all in basic human proportion though the limbs seemed a bit too long. He was smaller in height than Nikolas-dan. The way he moved was not human. He approached me with soundless steps, face fixed, more graceful than my teacher. This one was born with it.

His white hand—completely covered on the back by silver tattoos—reached out and grasped the top of my hair, but not violently. I gasped. Or squeaked. It wasn't a caress or even a possessive touch like Falcone used to do. Instead it seemed curious, as if he wanted only to know if I were real. The touch let me know that he was real, that I wasn't dreaming it, that maybe he wasn't going to hurt me. It was gentle.

Then he released me. One long sculpted arm pointed toward the sea.

"You saw me release my *klal'tloric*," he said, in Ki'hade. The words came from deep in his throat, but were as clear as birdsong. He paused and said in my language, "Mind enemy." Then he switched back to Ki'hade. "This is what many *ka'redane* do. Do you like this world?"

I got asked that question a lot. They wanted me to like it. Of course they did, it was my home now. Before, I hadn't seen a sunset or stood outside and felt the heat on my skin. I hadn't held a *jii* in my hand. But now was different.

"Yeah. I do."

"You have language," he said. "And thought. Now you need strength. Do you like the *kia'redan bae*?"

I rubbed the end of my nose and glanced up at the expressionless white face. My heart had stopped running. He smelled like the sweet vine, and despite his alienness, I knew he wouldn't hurt me.

"Nikolas-dan teaches me a lot. I'm learning a lot."

What did an alien mean when he said "like"?

The breeze made his long white hair lift off his shoulders. Up close I saw lines in the wings, fine as thread and just as silver as his tattoos. I wanted to touch it but didn't dare.

"I am pleased," he said, then sprang onto the balcony railing in one light move. He turned, standing on that narrow bar with no show of fear, even though he was a hairbreadth from a tumble to the rocks. His toes were long, curling around the rail.

Before I could discover more details on his body, he leaped off the balcony onto a branch, walked around and under the shadowy arms of the tree, and landed lightly back on his own balcony. Without stopping he disappeared inside. I stared after him but he didn't come back.

I leaned my chin on the railing and peered over the rooftops toward the sea in the distance. My heart drummed in my head, louder even than the breeze. Not out of fear. I couldn't see where his *klal'tloric* had landed, but I stared at its flight path until my teacher arrived to begin the day.

XII.

I didn't tell Nikolas-dan about my conversation with the alien. I spent hours with my teacher every day but the brief meeting with the white and silver striv was something I kept to myself and only opened up when I was alone. It felt rare, unusual, and I didn't want to ruin it with talk. It was enough just to hold it in memory, and wonder.

The leaves outside the Tree Room turned all shades of red, gold, and lavender. The hot days began to die and the sunlight went away faster. Outside, the morning sun rose reluctant and low. We had more of these kinds of days, now that summer was gone. The insect noises had gone away too and the sweet vine began to die, taking with it the scent that gave me good dreams. But I didn't need it now. At the end of a rigorous day doing sword and *denie* work, I slept soundly. The vine would bloom again when the weather turned back warm, Niko said. But for now it would die.

In my head I started calling him Niko, like Enas-dan did.

Fighting Niko took all of my concentration. He read me easily and if I only blinked too long he had me on the floor. We used wooden *jii*, in length just like the real ones but lighter and blunt. They still hurt when they hit with the force of a cutting blow but wouldn't draw blood. The *inidrla-na* rang with the connection of our blades as Niko attacked my *jii-na* and I desperately tried to keep him at bay. He barked advice at me when he saw me getting desperate. A desperate mind was not a blade mind. Usually his voice, so familiar to me now, could bring me out of myself and into the place I was supposed to be: in this case, inside the blade.

But I fell out of that place when the alien I'd met on the balcony suddenly walked into the *inidrla-na*, from the door.

Niko whacked me on the shoulder with his blade and threw me to the floor.

I yelped and held the bruised area, wincing. My teacher stood above me, glaring down.

"There is more where that came from, if you don't concentrate."

I didn't answer, knowing there was none, and looked toward the doorway where the striv stood. He was still there, silent, serious, and impressive. My secret.

Niko said, "Stand, Jos-na."

I levered to my feet and pushed the wooden blade through my belt out of respect. The striv came forward. Even though I was aware Niko stared at me, I couldn't take my eyes from the alien. I met his black gaze in the way that was proper greeting.

His voice was just as musical as I remembered. "Orphan of the Starling. Is Niko beating you up enough?"

I tried to hide my surprise at the question. "He's trying," I answered politely.

"Succeeding," Niko corrected.

There was an animal on this planet that Niko had shown me in vidstills and I had seen blurs of at night, high and deep in the trees—a burly creature about the size of a small man, all black fur and wide black eyes. *Uurao* were nocturnal tree-dwellers and nonviolent unless provoked. One picture showed the eyes illuminated by the flash of a cam. This striv's dark eyes reminded me of that—fixed on me, curious and large.

"You can outsmart the *kia'redan bae*," he said.

"I think so. Niko says I'm smart." I smiled, then realized I'd used the short form.

Niko said, "Sometimes, but not recently."

"Enh," the striv agreed, too quickly for my liking. But I knew the tone they used. Niko had taken it with his brother. *"Kia'redan bae,"* the striv continued, then spoke a string of words in a dialect I didn't know.

Niko gestured easily and said something back. Neither of them looked at me. The striv fluttered a wing, the lilts and slurs in his words so perfect that Niko's human voice seemed rough against it.

The striv glanced at me once more, then turned and left the room. I watched him go. "Are they always that abrupt?"

"Yes. What's done doesn't need to be lingered over." Then Niko thumped me on the head with the hilt of his wooden blade, not very hard but hard enough, and moved to take up a sparring stance once more.

I rubbed my head. "What was that for?"

"Because you looked, *ritla*."

"Of course I looked. You people come in and out like ghosts."

"You people?"

"Who is he? What were you talking about?"

"We were talking business, Jos-na. As for who he is, can't you guess? He is *ki'redan-na* D'antan o Anil. The Caste Master."

XIII.

The next morning after breakfast in the Tree Room, Niko said, "Let's go to the roof. There is a garden my mother says you will like."

That meant going outside, something I hadn't done except on the balcony. For the past few months my life had been only work, with the occasional afternoon spent painting or drawing. It felt good to be busy, to learn from him without pressure, to not have to worry about anything.

Now he led me through a door I had always found locked from the *inidrla-na* hallway, up narrow, tiled stairs winding on the outside of the building, and onto the flat roof. The edges and eaves were bordered in blue and red designs, but the central area was hard and grainy. I looked around for plants or flowers and saw none.

"Where's the garden?"

"Wait," he said. "Sit here."

I sank down beside him on the border of the roof, facing inward. Ridges on the flat top, five to ten centimeters high, made patterns in some places. In heavy rains the buildings made waterfalls. With their curved eaves the water built up and flowed over, like stacked glasses I'd seen once at a wedding on *Mukudori*.

Here the rain poured over the balconies, all the way down to the beach and the sea. Niko had told me about the crevices and tubes along the mountainside, which redirected a lot of the debris that built up during storms. Otherwise in heavy rainfall the houses sat buried in mud. People used to die under piles of mud and fallen trees. Once I'd figured out the house wouldn't collapse no matter how much rain fell or lightning struck, the noise of the storms started to sound like a weird kind of music. Like the drives of a ship.

Planets were scary sometimes, but no more than space.

We sat in silence as the sun crawled higher in the sky. Niko could stay quiet for hours. I looked up at him, followed his squinting gaze toward the heavy trees and their clothing of bright leaves. Some of the leaves had already started to drift down or got caught in the breeze and landed on the roofs. Birds called to one another and once in a while the branches shook from the scampering weight of a small reptile or mammal. I remembered the Caste Master walking on the branches, perfectly balanced.

Minutes passed and I noticed the patterns had changed on the rooftop. The early afternoon light made the ridges cast shadows that brought the roof to life. Slowly I stood and stared down at the perfect design that bracketed Niko's face, copied here on the roof in sharp darkness, in a circular shape. It resembled a complex dragon with its tail in its mouth. But it wasn't a dragon; it represented the *jii-na*—the place of the sword, the combat circle of every assassin-priest. The circle of your *na*.

The tattoo reflected his status. The more complicated it was, the higher your status in the caste. The color of your skin marked the caste—white was the *ka'redan-na*. Sympathizers didn't have to undergo the altered pigmentation, but some of them did—like Enas-dan. I wondered, when the time came, if I'd choose that way too.

"It's a shadow garden," he said. "Depending on the sun, the pattern changes slightly."

"I like it."

"You know it's your birthday," he said, abrupt as a striv.

"It is?" I hadn't kept track of the months in the Send reports, and EarthHub Standard Dates just didn't apply on this planet.

"You're ten." He glanced up at me, squinting. I stood with my back to the sun. "By the Hub's reckoning."

I felt older. I knew about young crews and old time, how you found them the deeper you went into space away from Earth and its stations and colonies, even with leap points to shorten the distances. My mother had explained about why people looked so much older on stations even though to me we saw them only a few months apart. Maybe I felt older because I was stationary. Or maybe just because in my head I *was* older.

"In the Hub, when it's your birthday, you get gifts." I smiled at my teacher, rubbed the sole of my foot over the warm pebbles.

"So I've heard," he said. "Ash-dan is due back in a couple months. When he does return, you'll be ready to spar with him. That will be your gift."

"A spar?" That wasn't much of a present, but he was a symp and an assassin-priest. Spars would have to do. "You always beat me. How am I supposed to fight him?"

"With open eyes." He returned my smile now.

I scowled. "Why Ash? I've only talked to him once."

"You need to face somebody you don't know. It will be a public spar. After that you'll begin training with peers."

That would be fun, being with other kids my age. Although I didn't specifically miss it. Niko and I got along well enough. "But I don't want to fight in public."

"Why? How do more eyes make a difference to your skill?"

"What if I mess up?"

"You won't. You are the student of the *kia'redan bae*, though sometimes you are *ritla*."

"What's that mean?"

"Unworthy student." He couldn't stop smiling now.

I hit his shoulder playfully. The contact shouldn't have surprised us, but it did. His eyes widened slightly. We necessarily touched each other in unarmed spars, but this wasn't a spar.

I thought about apologizing, but thankfully he just said, "*Ritla*. Put your weight behind it next time."

XIV.

Two months later, as Niko said, Ash-dan returned in the middle of the night when I was asleep. I heard the transport land outside the house but was too tired to bother waking up fully. I saw him the next morning when I went to the kitchen to forage for breakfast. He stood in front of the heatplate, his back to the door and stirring a pot of what smelled like candy-bark soup. That was one of my favorite things so I approached his elbow.

"Is it almost done, Ash-dan?"

He jerked in surprise and a hot spoonful of soup splashed my cheek. I winced and wiped quickly with my sleeve. For a moment he stared at me, as if trying to figure out who I was.

"Jos Musey-na," he said finally. "*Eja*, you startled me."

I was shocked myself, now that he faced me. His gray eyes had shadow crescents beneath them, the corners of his mouth deeply lined. But his eyes didn't blink or move from my face. I went to the far counter and dislodged a cup from the rack, just to give myself something to do. He'd opened out the little window in the corner and a cool morning breeze washed in, chilling my hands.

"You look well," he said. "Maybe even a little taller."

For some reason even his compliments sounded like insults. Even though I knew I *had* grown.

"So Niko hasn't yet got tired of you," he continued, turning back to the pot and stirring again.

It didn't sound like a tease. I turned the cup in my hands. "I'm learning really fast."

"I suppose you would. *Eja*, you had advance training with Falcone."

He said it so calmly, thrown off his tongue. Mine felt like stone.

"That was a long time ago." I couldn't remember the last time I'd thought of Falcone, but now it didn't matter. It all came back like a sudden leap from a long, deep point.

"Only a year," Ash-dan said. "Or so. *Eja*, you might want to know that he's still out there. Evading justice."

"So?"

"Maybe one day you'll meet him again."

"I don't want to meet him again."

"No? Not even when you're a *ka'redan*? I knew Niko's work would be wasted on a Hub orphan. *Eja*, I thought vengeance would be the peak on your mountain." He yawned.

Why was he saying these things? I looked at the steam rising from the pot. "I'm not going back to space, so how would I meet him?"

"Oh, yes, you're right." He stirred at a steady rate. "Niko's going back, though. I suppose you'll miss him terribly."

"He's going back?" Of course he would, now that his brother was here. But somewhere in my mind I'd hoped Ash-dan would leave again when the time came. My training wasn't finished.

"You must know he has to return. His *na* is in space, not with a *buntla-na ke taga ke go*."

"What?"

He smiled down at me. "Pirate-trained orphan. Here." He held out the spoon to me, filled by the pale red soup. "Taste it and tell me if it's finished."

My stomach was upset now. "No thanks."

"*Eja*, didn't you want to know?"

I glanced into his eyes, but saw nothing there. It wasn't the habitual guarded expression in Niko's or Enas-dan's faces. With Ash-dan, there was simply nothing there. I hadn't seen that since my time with Falcone.

What was it like in space now, that it made him into this?

I didn't want Niko to get like it. Quite suddenly I needed to be around my teacher. I set down the empty cup, backed up, and headed for the door.

"Jos-na," Ash-dan said.

He was a *kii'redan*. I was a student. I turned and looked politely at his hollow face, while the blood flowed cold through my limbs.

"I look forward to the spar," he said.

XV.

That day I managed all right in the warm-ups and drills—my individual kicks, punches, blocks, and weapons work—but I failed miserably as soon as Niko reviewed the sparring. After the tenth time landing hard on the mat, and even once rolling right off onto the floor, Niko stepped back and motioned me to stand.

"You meet Ash-dan at the end of the week," he said.

"I know. I'm sorry." I folded my arms.

"Are you nervous? You know it shouldn't be a factor."

It wasn't nerves. After days of meditation training, I knew I could handle nerves. He knew it too.

"Why didn't you tell me you're going back to space?"

Something flickered behind his eyes. "Who said so?"

"Ash-dan. He thought I knew."

"I was going to tell you after the spar. I have to go back. It will be fine, Jos-na. You will be in a class. Enas-dan and my brother will be your teachers."

I wasn't reassured. "Both of them?" I didn't mind his mother.

"Ash-dan will be teaching you comp work."

Irritation clawed the back of my throat. "Why?"

"Because it's not my area of expertise."

"You don't know how to use a comp?"

He breathed out. "I know how to use one, but not in the way I want you to know."

I walked away, two strides. "Why?"

"Jos-na." He stepped toward me and stopped.

I glared at him. "I didn't think comp work had anything to do with being a *ka'redan*." And I didn't want Ash-dan to show me.

"It doesn't, necessarily. But I think it's something you

should know. Now stop questioning your teacher. You knew one day I'd have to return to my ship."

"Why can't I go with you?"

"Because you haven't finished your training."

"Then stay and finish it!"

I went too far. His face shut down, the way it got when he wanted to remind me that he was the *kia'redan bae*.

I looked toward the wide window, at the balcony. The day was overcast.

He didn't say a thing. He let me hear those last words until the echo left the *inidrla-na*. I tucked my hands up into my sleeves.

"Jos-na," he said finally, "I'm sorry but I have to go."

I watched the trees outside sway in a gusting wind. "What would happen to me if you got killed?"

"My family cares for you."

I didn't want to sound like a child. So I pressed my lips tight.

"My mother would take care of you."

She was busy a lot. And her white face reminded me too much of the Caste Master. Too much like the paintings on their screens and the scrolls of art on the walls. Something to look at but never touch. Something made by a foreign hand.

I wanted him to tell me that he wouldn't get killed, even though it would be a lie. I wanted just to hear it from him, because I would believe that lie if he said it.

But he didn't say it.

"I have to go back," he repeated instead.

"Why? It's not like the war's going anywhere."

"One of us has to change that."

I looked up at him. "Change it?"

"Too many sons have lost their fathers, Jos-na."

My throat started to hurt. I swallowed. "That won't

change. Besides, you're the Warboy. Who would listen to you?"

He walked off the sparring mat.

I managed to steady my voice. "Are we finished for the day, Nikolas-dan?"

He said gently, when I expected hardness, "No, Jos-na. I won't waste your company with anger. Now let's work on your *han* strikes."

My *hane*, daggers, sat in a corner wrapped in their ritual bindings. Silence followed me as I went to retrieve them. When I stood again before my teacher, holding them in preparation for a lesson, he inspected my grip with first his eyes and then his hands. He only touched me when it was necessary to teach.

"You must not hold them too tightly," he said.

I knew this. But instinct made me think that I would lose them if I didn't.

XVI.

The morning of the spar, Enas-dan came to take me to the *inija-na*, where it was going to happen. I'd thought Niko would take me, but she said he was already there. I bathed quickly and dressed in my standard black, quilted and loose, pulled on soft boots because we were going far, she said, and met her in the Tree Room. I ran my hands through my hair to put it in order—I never knew how it looked since I never used mirrors. Enas-dan wore a head cloth, wrapped around her hair like the rest of her clothing wrapped her body. It was all white, blending into her skin.

She led me out the main doors, onto a wide flagstone porch, covered, the roof supported by polished black

columns, carved with symbols. The trees were thinned
around the immediate area, cleared entirely in one spot directly in front of the porch. On that landing pad sat a small
humpbacked ship, probably unable to seat more than ten
people, like the launches some merchant ships used for out-
riding. It was black, with a nub nose and a sleek, pointed
tail, and rested on splayed landing struts, humming. Underneath its thick belly poked two maneuverable, cone-shaped
jets. The transport looked like it belonged in the water but
sounded like the insects outside my window in summer,
thousands of them.

Enas-dan yanked open the sliding door and lifted me up
and in as if I weighed nothing, then followed. Inside sat the
Caste Master.

"Jos-na," he said, as if we'd just spoken yesterday.

"*Ki'redan-na,*" I said, sitting in the cushioned seat beside
him, near one of the small, clear windows. Enas-dan echoed
my greeting and sat on his other side. He waved a hand at
me that I knew was their way of acknowledging people, then
he and Enas-dan started talking in some dialect I didn't
know.

The little ship lifted off with a vertical thrust, smoother
than I anticipated. I looked out my window. All around was
a muted humming as we skidded above the thick treetops,
going up the mountainside. The landscape moved. It started
to make me dizzy so I glanced back at the adults.

The Caste Master looked very much the same as the last
time I'd seen him. He wore all white, his hair and face the
same pearly color I remembered, his silver facial tattoo shining in the soft yellow light of the cabin. His strangely unlined face and the backswept angles of his jaw and
cheekbones made him look unfinished. An artist's interpre-
tation of a man-sculpture he didn't have time to detail. The
large black eyes flickered around the cabin, as if out of ner-

vousness, but I didn't think the *ki'redan-na* had to be nervous, especially here.

A fold of the small, transparent wing rested against my arm. I looked at its tiny lines. He smelled like wildflowers, as if he'd spent the morning outdoors. When he looked down at me I made a point not to turn away.

"*Inija-na,*" he said. "The place of testing."

"Yes, Caste Master." I didn't know if it was the flight, but my stomach rolled uneasily. The flight, the spar, this alien talking.

The black eyes blinked once and the bold head tilted. The gesture reminded me of something but I couldn't think of it. "What has Nikolas-dan taught you?" he asked.

"*Ki'redan-na* . . . Nikolas-dan has taught me a lot. What exactly would you like to know?"

"What would you like to tell me?"

His eyes didn't leave my face. He was strange but not like in the old vids that made aliens seem so horrible. Not even like on the Send, which often showed flashes of eyes and their little pointed teeth. He resembled humans just enough to totally fascinate me, and the differences only made the similarities more obvious.

"*Ki'redan-na,* I've learned the structure of the castes." Start basic.

"Yes?"

My ears popped. When I glanced out the window near Enas-dan all I saw was a deep blue sky.

I'd memorized the information back when my days were filled mostly by reading. "I learned that the *ka'redan-na* is the first of the eight castes in Nan'hade. The *ka'redane* embody the central beliefs of the striviirc-na—"

"Which are?"

I was in the *inija-na,* being tested, here in this ship.

"Conflict—whether in society or in self—assists in coming

to the place of your ultimate self. The *ka'redan-na* teaches this thought through the martial forms. They also provide the best conditions in which you can achieve *hiaviirc-na bae*. The *ka'redan-na* provides structure and peace in society. Which is a paradox since you're by nature both creators of conflict and catalysts for peace in which the spiritual *na* may be cultivated." Slate answer.

The Nan'hade striviirc-na, who made up most of the spacefaring crew in the Warboy's fleet, had no gods. The "godless strits" was a common term in EarthHub.

Their philosophy and caste system, which was a loose translation to begin with, intertwined and branched into different areas of their lives like trees in a forest, a thornbush, or the symbols you found everywhere you looked in this country.

I couldn't tell if he was satisfied by my answer. He said, "What is *na*?"

"Place. Caste, when in relation to the hierarchy of societal *na*."

"One more question. What are the principal *nae*?"

"Physical—body or environment; emotional—including your mental state; societal—your role or occupation in society; spiritual—all forms refined to achieve *hiaviirc-na bae*."

Enas-dan watched me from her corner.

"Do you believe what you say?" she asked.

"*Ki'redan,*" I said. "I include it in my training."

The Caste Master's eyes narrowed. "That is a bad answer," he said bluntly. "But perhaps to be expected."

I clasped my hands in my lap, suddenly cold. They didn't speak to me for the rest of the ride. Eventually the ship touched down and the engines whined to a halt.

Enas-dan yanked back the door to reveal a sprawling, colorful building and the enormous vista around it. She jumped out, followed by the Caste Master (who flowed more than leaped from the hatch), then reached back to take my arm since my eyes were fixed on the sight. Bristling mountain peaks jutted all around us, taller than the one we stood on, with a sliver of sea far off in the distance, so dark and calm it looked more like a land horizon. The cold air blew through me as soon as I left the inner warmth of the ship, tugging my clothing and tossing my hair into my eyes.

I walked beside Enas-dan and followed the Caste Master toward the *inija-na*. It was fancy compared to the other buildings I was used to around the S'tlian house, and seemed older, some of the paint chipped and faded in places. The eaves were carved, deep red and gold. The walls were also engraved, blue and gold, showing battle scenes in what looked like one continuous panel around the outside of the building. Wide stone steps led up to a veranda. The roof was supported by sculpted three-meter-tall striviirc-na forms, their heads touching the roof and their hands holding swords, blades upward: a column of stone assassin-priests with fierce black eyes.

Standing on either side of the quadruple doorway were two more guards, but they weren't made of stone. They didn't acknowledge my stare as we passed, but they looked directly at the Caste Master, a brief, intense recognition. I peered up at their tall, wrapped forms, looked back even as we crossed the threshold into the *inija-na*. Warm air reached out to draw us inside the heavily carved inner portico where more assassin-priests greeted us, guarding another quadruple doorway. The tiled floor, all in the *ka'redan-na* patterns, echoed our steps.

Then we entered the *vas'tatlar*—proving ground. Not a place of testing, which to them implied learning; this large, high room was the place where you established yourself. It spanned about a hundred meters with a smooth, dark wooden floor, rimmed by white and gold tiles where assassin-priests and other castemembers stood, talking quietly to one another. An attack of alien faces and language came at me as I walked close to Enas-dan's side. I understood snatches here and there, this one discussing his son, that one her job.

Caste colors flowed over my sight, like looking on a garden of flowers. Some of the people were robed, some not. The assassin-priests wore the coiled clothing, other castes in loose tunics and pants, larger versions of my own outfit. Some wrapped their hair in those long cloth headdresses. Tattoos in many different patterns decorated faces of all colors. Though the dominant skin tone in the crowd was *ka'redan* white, I noticed pale blue, lavender, black, blood-red, ocher, gold, deep sunset orange, and leaf green—their natural skin color. Most of those were children who hadn't been formally accepted into a caste. They stood in the front rows, serious wide faces in miniature to the adults.

Enas-dan walked me along the outer edge of the crowd. The Caste Master had disappeared. As I glanced around I met the gazes of other humans—sympathizers. The faces were shocking in their familiarity: eyes with colored irises, lined skin, earth-tone hair. But all were tattooed. All belonged to one caste or another.

My shoulder grazed one of the long silk banners that hung from the ceiling down the wall. We stopped by a plain wooden door. She scratched it briefly and Ash-dan opened it.

I forced myself not to step back as his eyes impaled me, even though he smiled. The glow of all the new surroundings quickly faded.

"*Eja*," he said, "isn't this exciting, Jos-na?"

His tone was like someone talking to a kid that needed to be amused. I said, "It's new, Ash-dan."

"Don't worry." He laughed. "I won't hurt you too badly."

"Stop trying to intimidate him," Enas-dan said with mock anger, putting a hand on my back to guide me inside. "Before your brother takes issue with you."

I went by Ash-dan, trying not to touch him.

"*Eja*, now that would be a spar," Ash-dan replied, then raised his voice. "Niko, that knocking we heard, it was your student's knees."

Enas-dan sucked her teeth in disapproval, but laughed.

Niko stood in the middle of the small paneled chamber, half-naked and rubbing some sort of cream on his hands.

I tried to make my mind blank against the teasing.

"Thank you for bringing him, *ki'redan*," Niko said to his mother. "Now please leave us alone, both of you."

"*Eja*, take a breath, Jos-na," Ash-dan said in parting. "All *ka'redane* do this."

How was I acting that he thought I needed reassurance?

"*Enh,*" Enas-dan agreed, and patted my shoulder lightly. I was glad when they left, though the room suddenly seemed much larger and Niko stood far away. I tucked my hands up inside my sleeves.

"How do you feel?" he asked.

"Sick," I said. "Do I really have to spar today?"

"Ignore Ash-dan. He only tries to rattle you."

"I know." I looked away from his eyes. He wore only the coils about his legs, to the top of his thighs, and shorts of the same white that made it all look like one continuous length of cloth. I had never seen him so uncovered. His chest was bare, without tattoos, and as smooth as polished shell, the color of pale brown stone. A couple small scars cut across his ribs, but that was all. He held a rolled length of the same white cloth and stood barefoot. "Why are you getting dressed here?"

"For the same reason you will." He tilted his head at me, then held out the rolled cloth. "Take this."

I stepped close enough to do that. He said, "Pay attention. Now you're going to learn the ritual wrapping of the *ae-da*—the chest guard." He held his arms up and away from his body. "Start at my right waist and wrap around the stomach first, then the back and around again."

I did as he instructed. He talked me through it, how many coils exactly to go around his torso and how to tuck the end securely between his shoulder blades. I didn't like to touch him and be that close to him. I had never been that close to him, so close that I felt the warmth of his skin.

He told me how to wrap the *enie-da*—the arm guards—then finally to wrap him over the shoulders, crisscrossing beneath his armpits from around and behind his neck . . . a process that took me a half hour and a chair to stand on before he pronounced it complete. In all of it I finally got to see the slender molded sheath strapped to his inner left forearm, where a slim blade was housed. As I wrapped his arm he told me to leave a sliver of a gap in the coils, and demonstrated once I'd completed it how he could swiftly pull the blade from its oiled sheath in one move, almost like sleight of hand.

Standing on the chair, I could look at him eye to eye. "Do you do this every time you get dressed?"

"Only before a spar," he answered.

"Do I really have to fight Ash-dan in front of all those people?"

"You know all testing is done in the *inija-na*. Don't fear it. It's a time of celebration. Witnesses are expected, especially those already in one's chosen caste."

"I'm going to lose. I'm nowhere as good as Ash-dan."

"The point isn't to beat him. What have I taught you, *ritla*?"

"'It's in the struggle that we discover our ability.' I know." I couldn't argue with him.

"What's really troubling you, Jos-na?"

I shrugged. "Why does Ash-dan say those things to me?"

"He is only teasing."

"He calls me a pirate-trained orphan."

The mildness went out of his eyes. "Does he?"

Now I felt like a snitch. So I shrugged, the human way.

"What else does he say to you?"

The conversation in the kitchen now seemed distant. Something in Niko's face bordered on intolerance. But not toward me.

I didn't want to cause trouble. "He just teases me. I should just block it out."

My teacher didn't say anything.

"I know Ash-dan doesn't mean it, right?"

"Jos-na," Niko said. "My brother had a difficult time on Chaos. And he was close to our father. He is a good captain and a good *ka'redan*, but he hasn't yet cast off his *klal'tloric*. Do you understand? There are some things he can't disregard."

"Like what?"

"Like the Hub and everything in it." He paused. "But don't let that stop you from fighting him."

"It won't." I wasn't in the Hub anymore. I'd show Ash-dan.

"Good." Niko lifted me off the chair and set me on the floor.

"So are you going to fight Ash-dan too?"

"No. I will fight the Caste Master."

I looked up at him. He was smiling.

"Don't worry," he said.

"I'm not worried."

"I won't get hurt, Jos-na."

I didn't answer. Niko smoothed the fabric on my shoulders, a sudden affectionate touch that made me freeze.

"Let me show you what it's like to no longer be afraid."

XVII.

As the Caste Master and Niko took their beginning stances in the middle of the sparring space, everyone sat on the floor. I found the S'tlians after a quick dodge through the crowd and squeezed in front of Enas-dan with the other kids. Nobody sat in front of me.

The spar was shockingly brief. A *ka'redan* stood at one corner of the open floor and began the match with a command. In a blur Niko pounced. He kicked high, his knife suddenly in one hand. *Enihan'jaro* attack. The blade slashed down and diagonal as he landed. But the kick hadn't connected. As if it were orchestrated the Caste Master crouched fluidly to avoid the first attack, then rolled to dodge the slashing blade. Niko leaped again, without a break in the flowing line of his arm. *Saj'deni* strike. But Anil-dan was already on his feet. I blinked and saw the *han* flip through the air. In another blink the Caste Master engaged Niko's arm with his left, his small wing wrapping around Niko's wrist, surprisingly elastic. The heel of his right hand shot upward. Niko's head snapped back, then the rest of him followed. His body landed with a thud on the wooden floor. The side of Anil-dan's hand slashed down, the transparent wing flaring wide, but he stopped just short of Niko's throat.

I didn't breathe. The entire fight had been in silence—both from the crowd and the opponents. I couldn't believe it was over so quickly. I had identified all the moves, knew the defenses and counteroffenses for them—Niko had taught me. And yet he was beaten—by speed alone?

Enas-dan said behind me, as if she read my mind, "At such levels the fights are never long."

I remembered Niko's words from training. The objective was to fell your opponent with the least number of moves—

preferably one, as the swordmasters did. They were assassin-priests, after all. They didn't train only for show.

The fact Niko had gotten in as many moves as he had against the Caste Master, instead of being taken down in the first second, said enough about his skill.

As I stared, Niko rose without any injury or stiffness and crossed an arm with the Caste Master before stepping back. The Caste Master walked off the sparring space without a backward glance. A few people began to leave. Was that it?

Niko retrieved his *han* from the floor and disappeared back into his room. A group of striviirc-na children swarmed over the open space and began sparring, some of them against two or more opponents. Some were smaller than me but moved with incredible skill and precision, all in silence except for the slap of bare feet on the floor and the soft thuds of limbs colliding.

I looked back at Ash-dan. He pointed to the room in the corner.

I walked on concrete feet.

Niko met me inside the door. "Come." He smiled. "Give me the honor of performing the ritual wrapping on my first student."

I looked up. My cold hands began to warm.

"Hold your arms out," he said.

I did. For a flash of a moment I remembered my father pulling me out of the secret compartment after a drill, right into his arms for a hug and a pat. I blinked to clear it.

Niko held my sleeves lightly and tugged, peeling off my shirt.

He was my teacher and I tried not to shiver.

"It will be all right, *s'yta-na*," he said softly.

I didn't know what that word meant and for some reason I didn't ask. I just nodded and fixed my gaze to a point on the floor.

He wrapped me up like a mummy, in silence. I stood as still as he had when I'd performed the ritual on him. I thought about tossing Ash-dan on his ass. I imagined it since it probably wasn't going to happen. When Niko finished he set me in front of a narrow mirror on the wall at the back of the room, standing behind me with his hands on my shoulders so I couldn't dodge away.

"Look up, Jos-na."

"I don't need to. Let's just go."

"Your teacher is asking. Look up."

It was the first time in over a year that I saw myself in a mirror. Maybe he knew.

My eyes weren't as dark as I remembered. Against the black wrappings they showed a bright blue-gray. My face had lost a lot of its baby fat and my hair hung over my ears, dark and straight. I looked up into Niko's reflection. He watched mine. Me in striviirc-na assassin-priest clothes.

I didn't think of Falcone except in the realization that I wasn't thinking of him at all. Even though Niko stood behind me as Falcone used to do, with hands on my shoulders. The weight was different. Niko's hands were hardly any pressure at all.

I wondered if my parents would have recognized me.

"Now you are ready," Niko said.

XVIII.

Ash-dan waited for me in the center of the sparring space; he had shooed the children to the sides. They watched as I approached, tree green, solemn-faced sprites with the skill to kill a body with their bare hands. Some of the adults, maybe their parents, stood behind them. They watched too, just as serious and silent. Niko veered to the side to stand by his mother—and the Caste Master, who stood like a piece of art, or an animal breathing in his surroundings.

As I faced Ash-dan across that small gap of three meters, I felt his pointed humor lance through me like a laser bolt. As if all of this amused him in some dark way. I had no idea why. Some things were unknowable, like why Falcone had chosen my ship to attack, and why he'd kept me after he'd killed or sold the others. Like why Niko kept me but treated me better—he a symp, the Warboy, a murderer of merchant ships himself, if you believed the Send.

I saw myself meeting Ash-dan's smoke-gray eyes. Some part of me stood with the other sympathizers and striviirc-na—maybe because I'd faced it so many times already in my sleep, or maybe because I had learned it was good some-times to take yourself away.

As Niko took a step out onto the sparring floor I moved slowly into the ready position of the *hante'sajie-na*, the place of swiftness and silent blades, my choice of fighting style here. I balanced with my hands up to defend, like all the spars I'd done against Niko in the house. I didn't have blades, but Ash-dan would. That was part of the test. I came back inside myself, inside my circle. A cold ball rolled in my gut and went hard. I watched Ash-dan's eyes. I watched for when the light would change behind them.

Niko commanded, "Begin."

I leaped back immediately to avoid Ash-dan's attack. I knew he'd be faster than me off the mark. If I wanted to at-tempt a hit I had to first get out of his way so he wouldn't take me down with one swipe, like I knew he could. He may have been a Second Master compared to Niko's Incompa-rable status—what I was accustomed to sparring against—but at that moment it made no difference.

Ash-dan prowled me for a second, then attacked again, kicking at the level of my chest. I sprang back and felt the breeze of its passing. He followed up with advancing kicks. I stayed just out of range, so the attempts grazed by. In his eyes I read his annoyance: He wanted me to engage.

But I knew the moment I did I was beaten.

He pressed his attack, which I kept avoiding—running from. It wasn't pretty or neat or even brave. But Niko had said my advantage was in my swiftness—I was smaller and moved quickly. This seemed to frustrate Ash-dan. His face tightened. He wanted to be done with me in one blow. That was the weakness in my enemy that I could exploit. I was no match for his technical skills.

Finally I allowed him to come closer—it was all over at that point. As soon as I let him into my combat circle he took me down. He didn't try to be fancy about it. Like lightning his left leg shot around mine. His left hand grabbed my shoulder, the other free to block my punch. But I didn't punch. I seized his forearm where I felt the hilt of his blade in its wrist sheath and yanked it free as I went down. I didn't fight gravity or the force of his move. On my back I slashed with his blade across his chest.

I counted on his agility. If he didn't move I would bleed him.

He danced back and I misjudged him. He wasn't so in shock at my maneuver. Before I had time to roll away his foot shot out and kicked the blade from my hand. My wrist snapped. I yelled.

Through pain-filled vision I saw Niko take a step and stop, staring at me fiercely. Tears squeezed from my eyes. The *vas'tatlar* was dead silent. They waited for me to get up. It was only my wrist. My legs could still move. Courtesy demanded I get up, even though the fight was over. At my level it was over with the first injury or surrender.

Ash-dan watched me, just out of strike range.

My breaths echoed raggedly in my head as I struggled to my feet. Fire lanced up my right arm and down the entire right side of my body. I faced Ash-dan. Slowly I approached. The arm that I was supposed to cross with Ash-dan's, in that form of respect after a spar, was the injured one. I grit my teeth and held it up, elbow bent. I stared into Ash-dan's eyes, hating him. He was good enough to stop his blows for the sake of a spar.

He crossed arms briefly, jarring my broken wrist. I made a sound; it echoed in the silent room. Then he said quietly, so only I heard: "You should never have pulled the blade."

I was sweating. I said, "Next time I won't."

From his eyes I knew he heard the double meaning. I could have stabbed him with it, instead of slashing. He knew it.

Maybe it wasn't smart to threaten a *ka'redan*. But I was in such pain I didn't care.

He whispered to me, "Falcone would be proud." Then he brushed my hair back, as if in apology for breaking my wrist.

I couldn't breathe. He smiled into my eyes, then walked from the sparring space, picking up his blade as he went. Niko approached and lightly held my good arm.

Nausea rolled in my chest. The world seemed to cave in.

"Niko," I said. I tried to be brave. But now it was just myself and my teacher, and even to my own ears I sounded like a child.

XIX.

In the empty *vas'tatlar*, Niko bandaged my wrist with the open aidbox beside him. The numb-out he'd injetted killed the pain, but as the tiny bot-knitters worked on my bones they itched like a dozen insects scurrying under my skin, and I couldn't scratch. After three weeks they would crawl out the tiny tube in my arm and "die." Which meant I wasn't going to spar again anytime soon, or go to any new class.

Except the comp work with Ash-dan.

"He didn't have to do that, Niko. He could've stopped before."

My teacher frowned, smoothed the bandage, and sat back on his heels. "I know."

"Are you still going to leave me with him?"

Niko breathed out. "This was a reckless moment. I'm going to talk to him."

"He mentions Falcone like he wants me to remember. I don't like him, Niko." I wiped my eyes, couldn't help it. Drugs always messed up my emotions, even numb-out.

"He mentions Falcone."

"Yeah. And I don't want him to teach me anything. I don't see why I have to know comp stuff. I mean, I already know how to use one. Just let me take that class with Enas-dan, Niko."

"You need to know the comps, Jos-na. The *ka'redane* can't only depend on the scientists and engineers to help us. EarthHub has advanced technology. All of us need to keep up with it."

"Then why aren't you?"

"I said it's not my area of expertise, but I'm not unfamiliar. Ash-dan is an expert. You learn from the experts."

"He doesn't like me."

"I will talk to him. And you won't be alone. My mother will be here too."

"I don't care."

He stood. "Let's go home, Jos-na."

Home. My home was going back to the stars.

XX.

Usually strivs and symps made no fanfare when they left and returned. They hadn't with Ash-dan, at least. But I still hoped Niko would give me some warning before he went back to his ship.

Two nights after my spar with Ash-dan, while I was lying on my pallet in the dark trying to ignore the nastiness going on beneath my bandage, my door slid aside.

"Jos-na," Niko said, a shadow in the doorway with a soft voice.

I sat up, hugging the blanket around my shoulders with one hand.

"May I come in?" he asked.

I nodded before I realized he couldn't see me in the dark. "Okay."

He stepped in and slid the door shut, then turned up the lights to a comfortable glow. He was dressed in his coiled clothing and a long robe. The one I'd first seen him in, when I'd awakened on his ship after Chaos.

I held my injured wrist. He approached and knelt across from me, not too close.

"Jos-na, I expect you to do well for *ki'redan* Enas. And for Ash-dan."

I couldn't speak.

"If he says anything inappropriate, I want you to tell Enas-dan. Do you understand?"

He was the Warboy. He had to go.

"I'm trusting you to still be my student, even in my absence. The student of the *kia'redan bae*. I am already so proud of you, Jos-na." He searched my face.

"I don't want you to go." I barely said it. "You won't come back."

"I plan to."

"You're going to get killed."

"Jos-na . . ." He took a breath. "Believe that your teacher will try his hardest to return."

"That doesn't matter!" My arm was aching and itching. I wanted to rip off the bandage and my skin while I was at it. "Just go then. I don't care."

"I know that's not true."

"I don't care!" I shouted it into his face. "You all just leave anyway. Except the people I want to leave. They always stay."

"Striviirc-na don't usually say good-bye. But I wished to see you. I'm going to miss you, Jos-na, even though you're a stubborn, sulky *ritla*."

He never pitied me. That was all it took. I was a kid and my arm was killing me and the snake in my chest kept coiling tighter until it smothered my breath and squeezed the tears from my eyes.

I stared at my pallet as if it would transform before my sight.

I didn't move, not even when I felt his hand on my head. It was uniquely his touch, the way he ran his fingers through my hair like I was something worth remembering. Or just something of worth. It was nothing more than that. It had never been more than that.

But then it was gone.

XXI.

When I woke up, Ash-dan was in the room. I sat up and slid my back to the wall.

"Let's not waste time, Jos-na, now that Niko is gone. *Eja*, since you can't spar in Enas-dan's class, we'd best get started with the comps."

He held a comp, stood looming in my door like a tree. I rubbed my injured arm and climbed out of the blankets.

"Can I eat first?" My head was still foggy from sleep and I needed another injet. How did he expect me to work?

"Be quick. I've other duties."

I went to the door but he didn't move away. I looked up at him. "If I'm such a chore, then don't bother."

"My brother has asked me. I think it's a waste of time but who am I to question the *kia'redan bae*?" He stretched an arm and blocked me further from leaving the room, leaning on the door frame. "You are a smart little one. *Eja*, I regret breaking your wrist. It was instinct only."

I stared up at him, didn't answer. People like him didn't care what you said.

"I will teach you these comps. And what we talk about will stay between us, yes? You are my student in this. Students and teachers don't report on each other."

I looked at his robed arm. I couldn't see an outline of a sheath, but I knew it was there.

"Nikolas-dan is my teacher, *kii'redan*." I tried to duck under him but he was fast and lowered his arm, put his other hand on my shoulder.

I stepped back against the opposite side of the door frame, but his fingers gripped.

"Jos-na. Nikolas-dan isn't here. Enas-dan is going on an excursion to the northern province with the *ki'redan-na* until you are healed and class can begin. It will be you and I in this house. Let's be wise."

I could've fought him. The anger rose in my throat like bile.

But he was right. Niko wasn't here.

I looked up at him without raising my chin. "Let me go, Ash-dan."

He smiled and straightened, opening a way for me into the hall. "Come back here when you're finished eating. We have much work to do."

XXII.

"Now, Jos-na, I want you to think of the *hante'sajie-na*."

I sat on my pallet, in my room, like all those mornings I'd spent with Niko learning the language over a year ago. Dull light filtered through my curtains. The days were shorter, colder. It would never snow a lot here, but the winds came down from the mountaintops and shook the houses.

"The *hante'*?"

"Yes." Ash-dan opened his black comp case. "Any facet of it you wish. Perhaps one of the *jii* strikes."

I pictured a single *han* set on a wall, blade upward in the respectful manner. Then I imagined myself taking it down and swinging it in the first form.

"Do you have the image?"

"Yes."

"That will be your symbol then, your image of protection and identification. Your symself."

I frowned. "For what?"

"For when you learn to step inside of a comp."

He didn't just mean figuratively, as the striviirc-na used the phrase for knowing something thoroughly and without doubt. He meant literally.

He turned his comp toward me and told me to spend some minutes manually exploring the system. It was much more complicated than the compslate I was used to, and the primer, with many more access points and even light teleportation satellite hookup. I didn't understand what I needed these for, and told him so.

"I'm going to teach you communications and comp infiltration, of course," he said bluntly.

I stared at him. "Why?"

"Because your teacher wishes you to learn, *buntla-na*. Stop asking questions you know the answers to. You will irritate me."

"But why do I *need* to know this? Comp infiltration—do you mean burndiving?" That was illegal in EarthHub. People still did it, though. Evan's brother Shane had dabbled in it. But what was illegal for a symp? Nothing, of course.

"*Eja*, I don't know that word, 'burndiving.' But you need to know this because Niko says so. Now shut your mouth and listen." He dislodged a small case from the side of the comp and handed it over. "Put these on your eyes. They are optical holopoint receptors."

I opened the case. Tiny, vaguely red lenses floated in a clear liquid. I knew they were used for holoaccess to comp systems, but I had never touched them before. Even the games we used to play on *Mukudori* or in cybetoriums used an eyeband instead, just because they were cheaper.

"Put them in," Ash-dan said impatiently.

It was awkward and took me a few minutes, but I did it. A slight red tint covered my sight. Ash-dan leaned over and tapped something on my comp. Suddenly the 2-D list of files erupted into tall corridors, with me in the center of it, looking up. Except it wasn't me. A vague red shape hovered where I thought I should be.

"Now," he said. "You will learn how to build your symself."

It took hours of disciplined concentration, like my *jii* training, to memorize the strings of code that would activate my symbol once I'd let loose the ID packet in the system. Moving my symself through the virtual world of communication and information was similar to the mental part of martial training I'd already begun. The *jii-klala*, blade mind, fit comp work too.

Sometimes Ash-dan joined me in the false world of the comps. I felt his dark humor rising off him like body scent. When he burndived with me inside the pyramids of programs it was like having an assassin at your back in real time. I almost heard him laughing, even in the comp. Nervous that he'd somehow lock me in the matrices, I always tried to keep him near my symself. His image was a flowing white shape, a bird of some kind, and he moved swiftly. The forum of a comp seemed no different to him than the *vas'-tatlar*.

"Are you ready to spar me?" he asked a week into the training, while he showed me how to deke out a comp's systematic security patrols. He didn't say it aloud, but the words appeared at the edges of my field of vision, in the progging shorthand he'd had me memorize on the first day.

My symself flickered and I had to stop, pinned against a wall of yellow files.

"Concentrate," he said. I saw lines of security probes snaking through the comp corridors from the direction of the files I was supposed to break through. "Pay attention, *buntla-na*."

Then his symself blinked away—gone.

"Ash-dan!"

It was a city grid, and my shout was like a siren going off. He'd left me to be gobbled by the polisyms. I had nowhere to run, or nowhere I knew to run to—every alley sprouted a security probe, a hard blue comet of polisym. I wondered if I died in the comp if I would die on the outside.

I tried to pull down the pocketed code for an exit but I

couldn't find it. Instead I found purposeful white traces of Ash-dan's footsteps. He'd broken through my security tabs and stolen my code before leaving. I hadn't even felt it. I had no way out.

"Ash-dan!" I said out loud as the polisyms came toward me down an alleyway of protected files.

He appeared again on my left and opened up an exit, a round red ring that he chased my symself toward, a mental shove. I blinked and dumped the exit code in a flurry. The holopoints disconnected and I saw his face across from me, my room around us, sparking with the ghost lines of the comp. It was cold and my eyes burned.

"It's no place for children," he said, and I wasn't sure if he meant the comp or the room or the planet.

I'm not a child, I wanted to say. But I didn't, because he wouldn't believe me. He wanted to step on me, like adults did with kids they hated having underfoot.

XXIII.

A week and a half since Niko left, a week and a half into comp training with Ash-dan, I got sick. Headaches plagued me, my stomach refused food, and all my muscles ached like I'd spent a nonstop day doing nothing but drills. Ash-dan said sometimes the headaches happened at first because you were getting used to the world of the comps. The other sick feelings, he said, were just my weaknesses.

"*Sraga,*" I told him. He didn't even have the decency to make me soup. I dragged myself to the kitchen twice a day to force liquids down my throat before I got sicker. Enas-dan commed twice and seemed genuinely concerned about me, but she was still tied up in some sort of meeting in the north. She said she'd be home in a week.

I stayed out of Ash-dan's way and he mostly ignored me, told me only to tell him when I was ready to get back to work.

The days passed and I was alone. I sketched, sometimes painted. Ugly misshapened faces, melting eyes and open mouths in streaks of black and red. Not pretty like the striviirc-na paintings. I drew segmented arches like the bulkhead skeletons of some ships, yellow spots in the corners like old lights, little white points like stars. Stars that never changed and didn't care. After, I threw all the pictures in the garbage.

I went to the *inidrla-na* when Ash-dan wasn't in it, stood on the balcony wrapped in blankets and breathing sharp, salty air. A spatter of people dotted balconies below but they were too far to see clearly. Clouds huddled in the sky. When they got that dark it meant rain.

I thought about flying right over the balcony and down the mountainside. What did you toss when your mind enemy refused to let go?

When the storm hit I watched it from inside the *inidrla-na*. Water beat at the long windowpanes. The world outside seemed to melt into a gray mass of nothing, broken only by white claws of lightning raking the sky. A big noisy beast. Its cries shook the room. My nerves jumped, wouldn't settle. Not even when I retreated to my room, on my pallet, under the blankets.

A flash of lightning tore around the edges of the screen on my window. I jerked awake, not sure when I'd even fallen asleep.

"Jos-na," someone said, and a shadow crouched by my side.

"Niko?"

He leaned forward and his face caught the bar of light pouring in from the hall. It wasn't Niko. Blue eyes shone from the shadow, hot as welding flames.

I struggled to sit, back away.

But Falcone had me by the arm, my bad arm, and the pain made me kick and scream. No training in me. I fought like a netted fish against the anchor of his hold, managed to scramble off the pallet, across the smooth floor to the far wall.

"Jos-na!"

I cradled my arm and pulled in breaths. My skin was wet. Sparks went off in my sight, then a flash of light that didn't go away.

My room. Feet approached and I looked up against the ceiling lights, saw Ash-dan staring at me. Confused gray eyes.

I put my head down, numb from my arm upward. Numb from the inside out.

XXIV.

After that nightmare, Ash-dan was more attentive. He fixed my bandage, gave me more injets for the pain, and cooked me candy-bark soup. He said I was lucky I wasn't sicker, being from space, even though Niko had probably inoculated me before I'd even landed. I said I didn't remember, I hadn't been awake at the time.

I didn't want to talk about Niko with Ash-dan. I didn't want to do anything but sleep.

I was better by the time Enas-dan returned, but when she saw me in the Tree Room fooling around manually in my comp, she wanted to know if I had slept since Niko had left.

"I still have a little bit of the flu, *ki'redan*. But it's not so bad."

"Where is my son?" she asked, and she didn't mean Niko.

"I don't know, *ki'redan*."

She approached closer, crouched to where I sat on my cushion, and put her hand on my head, running it over my hair and down my cheek. I didn't move. She didn't linger, but stood quickly and strode from the room.

I was too tired to follow, though I would've liked to have heard that conversation.

Later, somewhere in the house I heard a door slide shut. In minutes Ash-dan came in. "You seem to be better." He didn't pause, but came right up and knelt and put his hand behind my neck. "What did I say before, Jos-na? Do you remember?"

"Don't touch me." I tried to wrench my head away, but he held on. So I grasped his forearm with the good intention of shoving him on his ass.

But he put his other hand on my chest, not quite gripping the front of my shirt. His fingers seemed to burn through my clothing.

My uninjured hand shot up toward his chin but he dodged it, slid his hand under my armpit, and squeezed. Hard.

"Sshh," he said.

"Let me go!" I brought my knee up and jabbed an elbow.

He slammed me onto my back and shoved his knee in my gut. It knocked out my wind. "If you can't fight me properly, you'll never last. I think you know this. If every time something happens you feel the need to run to Enas-dan, or my brother, what sort of *ka'redan* will you make? You are a Hub orphan. *Eja*, I have little hope for you."

I couldn't breathe. I lashed out, caught him in the face

with a fist, and rolled quickly when he leaned back, letting up the pressure.

"Good," he said. "Very good."

"Ki sraga!"

"Go on. Run to my mother. She is meditating in her room. Go and disturb her, tell her what I just did. Explain to her about your nightmares, how everywhere you look there is nothing but Falcone—"

"That's not true!"

It wasn't. It never was the truth until he made it so.

He shrugged. "Isn't it? Such a pretty boy you are. Pretty like a girl."

"Shut up!"

He laughed and unfolded to his feet, loose white robes brushing his body in layers. Hiding his weapons. "Niko isn't coming back for a long time. *Eja*, you know this? He might not be back for years, as this planet reckons time. There are things going on, larger than one *buntla-na ke taga ke go*. Even if that *buntla-na* has such beautiful blue eyes. My brother is immune."

The cold cloud in me began to grow, whispering through my head and heart like smoke.

"You take him away from what he truly should be doing—destroying the rude place that you come from. In you he thinks he sees all the sweet innocence of the Hub. But I know you, Jos-na. You are a pirate's whore, though you sit there in striviirc-na clothes. And here I am forced to waste my time with a whore."

He walked by me to the door.

"Go ahead, Jos-na. Run to my mother. Turn that face and all your tears to her. Use it like how Falcone trained you."

When he left I didn't hear it. I barely saw it. I didn't move. Words flailed in my head, wild fists that battered me and left me bruised.

XXV.

I told Enas-dan nothing, and Ash-dan acted as if nothing had been said between us. So I kept to myself when I could and tried to put it out of my mind. In a week the bot-knitters crawled out the narrow tube in my arm and died in ashes on my bandage. I clenched a fist-sized exercise ball every few hours to strengthen my arm. There wasn't even a scar, a mark to show what had happened in the *vas'tatlar*. A month since Niko left, my class began.

Enas-dan held it in the *inidrla-na*. Two other students showed up, both of them striviirc-na. They spoke together in a dialect I didn't know, but I listened for a second just outside the door. When I walked into the room they both stopped and stared at me, big black eyes in broad, greenish-brown faces. Uncasted faces, no pigmentation. They were both taller than me, their feather-textured hair tied back and flowing down their necks. They didn't look much like the Caste Master.

I moved to the center of the room and began my breathing exercises. Enas-dan wasn't there yet and my head felt clouded, my body stiff.

"Your name?" one of the strivs asked in Ki'hade, stepping up to my right side. I stood still, kept my arms in. His companion drifted to my left. A female striv. It was obvious even with her loose black pants and shirt, which was open at the sides to allow her transparent wings to move.

"Jos Musey-na," I answered.

"Jos Musey," he said. "What name is that?"

"A human one. What's yours?"

"Mra o Hadu-na. I am Ash-dan's student. This is Yli aon Ter'tlo-na, Enas-dan's student. You're the student of the *ki-a'redan bae*."

"*Enh.* He's my teacher."

I couldn't read their faces but they didn't stand too close. They weren't trying to intimidate me—yet.

"Will you be going to space after you're fully casted?" the girl asked. Her voice trilled much more than Hadu's.

"No. Why would I? Are you?"

"You're human," the boy said. "You could serve the fleet in space, maybe even across the buffer on a Hub sympathizer ship. We can't."

"I want to go to space," Ter'tlo said, "and serve on *Bae* S'tlian's ship. Not stay here and wait for the Hub to invade."

"Enas-dan will prepare us," Hadu said. "We heard you're *from* space."

"Who told you?"

Enas-dan strode into the room. "I did. Jos-na, your classmates are curious. They have never met anyone so recently from the Hub."

"I've been on Aaian-na for over a year." I wished everyone would stop reminding me where I was born.

"You speak well," Ter'tlo said, but it sounded like a joke. Her pointed teeth bared just a little.

"Maybe you fight as well as the *se'latbe-na* too," Hadu put in.

Se'latbe-na. The engineer caste, which knew as much about fighting as an assassin-priest did about building a house.

I followed Hadu with my eyes as he positioned himself on the floor in a crouch, to begin his respects to the first *ki'redane-na.* Ter'tlo did the same. I was last, and clasped my hands firmly in that gesture that honored the dead.

Enas-dan looked us over. "*Eja*, let's begin."

XXVI.

The class was much like the individual training, with the same proportion of minutes spent on warm-ups (about half the class time), compared to the drills of kicking, punching, and blocking that followed. I quickly learned that Ter'tlo was the senior student, so Enas-dan demonstrated many of the new moves with the female striv before letting Hadu and me attempt it together.

Hadu had the innate grace of his species, and didn't hesitate to tell me that he had been training with his teacher since he was five years old. He also never hesitated to tell me how he was going to get himself to space in order to fight the Hub. I never answered him on those claims. He wasn't truly against me, but we sparred well together. It showed better control if you stopped your strikes before contact, but I accidentally made full force contact once, in a kick that caused a large orange bruise on his arm for days.

Once the class finished and I helped Hadu clean up the *inidrla-na*, I retreated to my room. If I stayed too long about the house, Ash-dan always found me, even when we weren't doing comp work. He didn't speak to me outside of the training time, but I didn't want to be around him unless I had to. Luckily Enas-dan was so busy with her sympathizer work and training us, she never commented.

But she visited me one evening as I sat in my room reading another Send update. I hoped in a way one of the updates would mention Niko so I'd know what he was doing, but then I never wanted it to be a death report.

"Enas-dan, how often does Niko contact you?"

She folded down next to my pallet. "Once a month if he can, but it depends on if it's safe to transmit. I just received his first message. He asks how you are."

I tilted the slate at her. "Safer than he is, I guess. This

says there're more debates going on in Hubcentral about how to end 'the strit threat.' What would happen if they decide to attack Aaian-na space?"

She always answered me directly, since the first time I'd met her. "Many of the people on the planet who are training, like you, would have to actually fight. But we don't want it to get to that. Nan'hade, Vran, and Isuitan are the only countries truly together against the Hub. The rest of Aaian-na are divided and do not always look to the stars." She took the slate from me and shut it off. "Jos-na, Niko is up there with the hope that the war will end. But it's a difficult thing to try and stop a war when the other side has little interest to do so."

"Why doesn't Niko just—raise a white flag or something?"

Enas-dan sighed. "Because the Hub hates him. They wouldn't listen. There have been so many deaths, over these many years, that people are just too angry to stop."

I thought of Ash-dan. "But even if it did stop, how could you trust the Hub?"

"That's what we don't know. There hasn't been a summit between our worlds since the accord that set up the demilitarized zone. And you see how that's disintegrated. People in the Hub still want to own us."

I poked at my blanket.

"Jos-na. Niko asks how you are. What should I tell him?"

"Can't I write to him?"

"No, I'm sorry. Our communiqués are limited in length. But tell me what you would like to say and I will pass along the gist." Her eyes bore into my face.

"Tell him I'm fine, I guess."

"How are your lessons with Ash-dan?"

"Fine. He says I learn quickly." Among other things.

"You keep to this room a lot, Jos-na. You know you can walk down to the shore when you please, or go to the roof."

"I know."

She pursed her lips briefly, patted the slate, then handed it back to me. "Next week we begin training on guns. Niko told me you had asked him about them." She smiled.

"Enas-dan, when's he coming back?"

Her smile faded. Her white face and twin tattoos were a mask I couldn't see behind. "When he can, Jos-na. Truthfully, I don't know." She stood and pressed my hair lightly. "In the meantime, try to leave this room. Ask Ter'tlo-na and Hadu-na to show you around the mountainside. They know it well. You can take your sketchbook."

"Maybe I will."

I had no desire to ask them. I only thought that Niko had left me here, like my parents had left me, and any day now I would know for certain that he was dead.

XXVII.

"Eyes," Ash-dan ordered, and I obediently popped in my holopoint receptors. This, my daily dose of comp training, here in my room that the *kii'redan* invaded with his disapproving presence. I tolerated his brisk instruction because I had to, meanwhile marking in my slate all the days Niko was off-planet. The dates had accumulated to nearly ninety. They felt like a year.

I activated the comp with a glance and the three-dimensional, citylike grid display of the comp-ops blinked into view across my entire sight. "Communications," Ash-dan said. I flickered up to the icon and accessed. After waiting a few moments for the simulated satellites to bounce the quantum light around, I passively traced the coded netline until I came to the fail-safes of the simulated Chaos Station commgrid. Ash-dan had constructed a full sim of Earth-Hub's communications grid in the Dragons—at least the part of the Dragons they regularly patrolled. Deep space was too large to outfit entirely. The grid was pretty complicated and if I didn't know better I would've thought it was the real thing.

The restricted access wall loomed high and bright. It was supposed to be a deep insertion retrieval mission: Get in, get out, leave no footprints on either end of the link. Ash-dan didn't follow me in this time, but I was aware in that height-ened way burndiving gave you, aware of his gaze outside of my symbol self, looking for my mistakes.

I inspected all the facets of that wall despite Ash-dan telling me I was on a time limit. One wrong flicker and the polisyms would launch. So I gave the code a good look over, then followed one particular seam where I thought I could insert an interrupt without too much notice—hopefully none at all if I was quick enough. But as soon as I constructed the crank to get me through the wall of code, my symself alerted the spatial awareness part of me—somebody was crawling up my butt. When I flickered that way I saw the bright blue globes of military polisyms.

Bastard, I thought fleetingly, and beat a hasty retreat, triggering alarms on my heels in a firepath. I cast a false sig in my wake for the polisyms to devour. Most of them de-scended on the code, tearing it apart for content. Others kept the track. I saw my out, a circle of red hyped to my sight alone, and dived through. I blinked out of the main system ops, breathing hard as if I'd actually run, and glared through the afterimage hologrid at Ash-dan.

"Why so panicked?" he asked blandly.

"Those were EarthHub military tracers! Is this real-time?"

"What if?"

"I almost got marked!"

"Yes." He frowned. "Not much grace in that tail-turning."

"Is this real?" If they'd caught me they would have trapped my symself, restricted me from blinking out. I didn't want to know the consequences of that.

"You adapt well to comps. I thought to challenge you."

Assassin-priests were smooth liars. I stared, then finally popped out the receptors.

Ash-dan said, "You're going to have to learn not to run from military traces. You should diffuse them instead."

I busied myself putting the receptors back in their liquid-filled cases.

"And you definitely must learn not to set off alarms."

"Next time I'll tiptoe." I snapped the cases shut. "Does all of this mean that once I'm casted I'll be assigned to satcomm security or something? I didn't think ka'redane did that."

"That will be up to Niko," he said shortly, and rose to his feet. My lesson was over.

I wondered if I killed Ash-dan out on a walk or something, how the Caste Master would prove that I'd done it.

I asked Hadu-na as we practiced on the gun range, a narrow room set apart from the rest of the house with human-shaped sim targets and a collection of weaponry. Enas-dan was working with Ter'tlo-na a few meters away, showing her how to handle a rifle.

"Say I killed somebody, Hadu-na. How would the Caste Master deal with that?"

He gave me a direct look. "Do you plan on killing somebody, Jos-na?"

"No. I'm just asking."

He fired a couple shots from his striviirc-na-altered LP-

150. They landed a bit wide of the mark. One of his wings flicked sharply. "It would depend on who you killed. *Eja*, in the later proceedings. Early on, the Caste Masters of all involved would hear all sides involved. Then they would decide who was right and who was wrong. If you were wrong to kill, then the *ki'redan-na* would send a *ka'redan* to equalize the event—if the person you had killed was not someone with high status in their caste. If the victim was of high status, then the justice would be public."

"He'd have me killed in public?"

"Yes, of course. You would deserve to be disgraced and confronted directly. But this is for murder, Jos-na. We aren't so strict for lesser crimes."

"You know, you aren't all that different from the Hub. They have capital punishment too."

Hadu turned to me and set his rifle down on the sim controls, hard. "Don't say that."

"What?"

"Aaian-na is nothing like the Hub." His wings fluttered as he brushed by me, toward Ter'tlo.

I looked down at the rifle. A modified EarthHub one, not very bulky even with the sniper scope attachment. It fit my smaller than man-size frame and reach. I picked it up, set the pulse width, and aimed like Enas-dan had shown me.

My human target died a perforated death.

XXVIII.

I wrote comms to Niko even though nobody sent them. I marked off the days since he'd left. Three more months passed.

Three years fled the same. Three years of training with
Hadu-na and Ter'tlo-na, growing taller—though I was still
only 157 centimeters at nearly fourteen years old, biologically, which was a whole head shorter and only a year
younger than Hadu-na. Enas-dan told me I shouldn't compare myself because they were striviirc-na. Naturally. And it
was true, in the spars it never mattered.

I worked with Ash-dan in comp simulations of complicated Hub satcomm grids, in scenarios that included retrieval and transmission, interception and ghosting. When I
would ever use this knowledge, I didn't know, but sometimes I dreamed of codes and symbols, constructing com-
mands even half-awake. I buried myself in my room, diving
problems Ash-dan set on me, and even enjoying it. When I
was in the comp, I was alone and nearly unstoppable. I had
an affinity for it, in the same way I had for shooting. I was
faceless and skilled, and sometimes I even beat Ash-dan at
his own game, in those sims.

I ignored Ash-dan's dark jokes and reminders about Falcone. When I was in the comp, or on the gun range, or in
class practicing my *denie*, all of them became white noise.
Enas-dan called it focus. For me it was peace. It was the
place I could go where nothing mattered.

My classmates chattered to me about the possibility of
serving in space, an obsession they had, and every time they
mentioned it I thought of Niko. Who knew how long it was
for Niko? Maybe he didn't feel the distance or the time.
Maybe he asked Enas-dan about me just to be polite because
he was my teacher. Maybe one day Enas-dan would come to
my room, eat breakfast with me, then tell me that some Hub
ship out in the deep had finally got the Warboy. I half expected it every morning I awoke. But the word never came.

Niko's face began to gray around the edges, like my parents'. Maybe one day I would serve on a striv ship and meet

him out in the deep. I tried to think what I would say to him, but nothing came to mind.

Then I thought my classmates could have space, if they wanted it.

Whenever she was around, Enas-dan took me to art shows and life-sized puppet theaters, martial and seasonal festivals, and boat excursions in the summer. I played in snow. Sometimes *ki'redan-na* D'antan o Anil accompanied us. He introduced me to artists and athletes, scientists and teachers, both striviirc-na and sympathizer, who always ended up talking about the war effort—and especially how difficult it was to sustain the conflict. Discussions about the war weren't just relegated to the Hub Sends. Here on Aaian-na it was on everybody's tongues. What was the *kia'redan bae* waiting for? He ought to push a peace, some said, and others said he ought to deliver a harder blow to the Hub to make them step back.

In private, the Caste Master told me that a new space government had been elected in Hubcentral, and this one advocated a stronger, more decisive stance against Aaian-na. They were talking about eradicating Aaian-na's spacefaring ability altogether. The fringe factions were now in control.

My vocabulary list grew exponentially, and so did my dread for the future.

I even picked up a few phrases in different dialects, though my classmates still teased me about my accent. So many days spent traveling and seeing new things, yet I knew they were just a pocketful of experiences compared to what Aaian-na offered. Sometimes I hardly believed how big the planet was and how much of it was simply unknowable.

Whenever I wasn't training, I painted and drew. I spent a month trying to capture the perfection of snowflakes. My room became stacked with canvases and scrolls, though I always threw out the artwork inspired by my darker moods.

My fourteenth birthday fell on the first day of the Festival of Stars—*Sh'aieda*. It was a nationwide, four-day celebration of the first striviirc-na flight into space, some hundred fifty years ago. Now it was also an irony, since their few colonies had been razed by EarthHub forces and all striviirc-na who weren't in the Warboy's fleet were forced to live on Aaian-na. They would have explored more except the war got in the way. Planet resources went to that.

The festival was held every eight years; it had followed this pattern since humans were discovered nearly forty years ago. Enas-dan told me that was because their soldiers served eight-year tours, so the interval commemorated their war dead and their current soldiers, those who could not return to the planet. This wasn't an unusual striviirc-na trait, to celebrate and mourn at the same time. They accepted the conflict in the idea.

Ter'tlo, Hadu, and I sat on the roof by the shadow garden, which was completely shadowed now, at night. Golden lights twinkled on all the houses up and down the mountain, striv imitation of the stars overhead. Every once in a while we saw a light arc and fall toward the sea, burning out far above the water and the tops of the trees . . . someone remembering a dead soldier. Falling stars made of paper and flame.

Inside, Enas-dan and Ash-dan entertained the Caste Master and other high-ranking castemembers. I'd stood around and talked for as long as I could bear it, surrounded by striv faces and voices and the smell of food. The week before, Ter'tlo had been officially made a member of the *ka'redanna*. She was no longer just a student. The strivs inside made much of it, while Hadu and I wished our time would come soon. Ter'tlo-na's indigo tattoo adorned her newly pigmented pearl-white forehead in intricate swirls, seeming to make her black eyes glow, though it was probably just her pride. Enas-dan had ritually wrapped Ter'tlo-na and presented her before *ki'redan-na* D'antan o Anil. Many high-ranking assassin-priests had attended in the *inija-na*. Yli aon Ter'tlo had been resplendent in pure white and indigo and she'd performed her *jiie-ko* dance with perfection.

Tonight I escaped at dusk to watch the stars above and below. The two strivs followed me, once the talk turned to the war.

I dangled my legs over the roof edge. "Ter'tlo-na, when will you find out your duties in the caste?"

"The Caste Master said after the festival." She sat beside me and fluttered her wings. I'd learned that many of their emotions showed in how they flicked their diamond-specked wings. The easy wave now meant she was relaxed and happy.

Hadu-na stood and looked toward the dark sea. His olive skin shone slightly under the moon. For night duties they smeared paint or wore a mask. On exercises I'd seen Hadu in black from head to toe. Even his eyes disappeared in the night. They crept quieter through the trees than the leaf-eating *uurao*. Sometimes I pitied those people who jeopardized the order of things. Though assassin-priests rarely dispatched people permanently, they still policed the population. Criminals were never noisily brought to justice if they could be taken in silence—unless of course you wronged a high-ranking castemember.

I understood now why Hub ships feared being boarded by the striviirc-na.

Hadu said, "Let's go for a walk among the trees."

Ter'tlo trilled an assent and we climbed to our feet.

"I'd like you to come back inside," Enas-dan said.

I was startled by her voice, but the other two weren't. She walked as softly as they did, I hadn't even heard her approach, but strivs had better hearing.

I said, without much hope and not a little sarcasm, "Are they gone yet?" All those chattering guests.

She frowned. "Jos-na. Just come."

I sighed and trailed her back down the stairs and into the house, with my classmates trailing me. A walk would have been nice.

I wove through the slender striv bodies in their iridescent festival garb and the scented human ones similarly dressed but without the rippling of wings. They were mostly strangers. I spied the *ki'redan-na* in a corner of the Tree Room, by the wide open window, in a wash of gold and silver lights strung on the great sunset tree outside. He wore gold and white robes with open arms and sides and he'd dusted gold specks on his wings that gently flew around his body when he flicked them.

Beside him stood Niko.

My walk through the crowd slowed to a dead stop.

My teacher wore layered white robes, gilded around the collar. His hair was tied back in a way I'd never seen it, longer than I remembered, bound in a tail at the base of his neck with gold string. The perfect angles of his facial tattoo showed dark against his skin. He spoke with the Caste Master and held a delicate tube of drink in his hand.

I was looking across time, into the future where too much had changed.

"The *kia'redan bae*," Ter'tlo-na said in a hushed voice. She had never met him. "Jos-na, introduce me to your teacher."

"Not now," I said, then walked around the bodies that stood in my way, leaving Ter'tlo and Hadu behind. Quiet striviirc-na reed music threaded through the voices and smothered my footsteps.

But Niko and the Caste Master had excellent peripheral vision. They both noticed me before I was five meters from them. They both turned to watch my approach, but I met only Niko's eyes.

I couldn't read them. They were as dark and impenetrable as the first time I'd met him.

I stopped an arm-length from their corner and looked directly at *ki'redan-na* Anil. I greeted him out of formality and he returned it. Then I looked at Niko, up close. Despite the immaculate appearance, he seemed tired.

He said, "Jos-na. You grew."

"Nikolas-dan. Kids do that."

Only then did my heart start to pound, deafening me. I couldn't bring myself to call him by the familiar name. And he didn't offer it.

I wished all these people would clear out and leave us alone. And then in the next second I wished I hadn't followed Enas-dan back to the party.

Every little sound hammered in my head. My eyes built up pressure.

"Your eye has improved," Niko said, turning away slightly.

I followed his gaze toward one of my paintings that Enas-dan had displayed on the wall. It was one of the mountains from the vantage of sea level, done in a black-brush technique I'd seen ancient striv artists use. Harshly outlined but blended toward the center of objects, with white and gray highlights. I'd detailed a lone striv standing on a lower balcony in the foreground, an arm outstretched as if he'd just tossed something into the air. The wing flared.

"I experimented with the Oran era style, *kia'redan bae*."

"I would like one of your paintings for my house, Josna," the Caste Master said.

I remembered Niko and me sitting on the balcony, drawing together. I blinked. "By all means, Anil-dan."

"You must not be too hard on your teacher for being gone so long," he continued. "He does my work."

I carefully didn't look at Niko. "Of course, Anil-dan. I understand that."

I hadn't been aware I had shown any resentment, even though in silent moments I more than felt it. I wondered, not for the first time, if striviirc-na had any telepathic ability. Hadu said no, but it could have been one of those things humans weren't supposed to know. Especially an uncasted human.

I said, "I won't be hard on him at all, Anil-dan. I'll challenge him to a spar."

The Caste Master found that funny. His wings waved briefly.

Niko said, "Perhaps I can speak with my student in the *inidrla-na*, after which he then can fight me."

I met his stare, and his humor. "I'd like that."

Niko set his glass down on one of the low tables and cut through the crowd without a further word. I followed. His robes billowed behind him like a banner, caught in a cool breeze swept in from the open window.

I captured my classmates' stares as I passed. Farther in the corner Ash-dan stood. His eyes were smoked glass, hard and sharp.

None of them stopped us. The hallway leading to the *inidrla-na* was off-limits to the party. As soon as I shut the door behind us, a quiet landed on our shoulders. Niko turned under the moon-glow of the ceiling lights and looked down at me with a different expression in his eyes. A softer one. For a long moment he just stared. He never needed to speak just to fill the silence.

I schooled my face. I thought I did well. I'd had four years of practice.

He said finally, "I had to be away, Jos-na. I'm sorry."

I didn't answer.

"I didn't plan to be," he said.

I shrugged. "Didn't you?"

"I didn't plan to be gone that long. But organizing defenses—" He stopped. Maybe he saw something in my expression. "How have you been? Tell me the truth."

"Your brother and Enas-dan are good teachers. They are my teachers, right? They've been my teachers for nearly four years. You were only my teacher for one."

Now he was silent.

"I didn't expect you to come back," I said. "And now that you are—" I shrugged again. "How have I been? I'm fine. I've learned everything you wanted me to learn. In fact I'm really good. But Enas-dan probably told you that in one of her reports."

"I can see that you're really good," he said mildly. "With words. I understand them."

"I knew you would." I headed for my room. No need to linger over things.

"Jos-na."

I stopped at my door and looked at him. "Yes, Nikolas-dan?"

"It hasn't been four years for me. But it's still good to see you, s'yta-na."

I slid my door open. "I'm glad my face pleases you." I went inside and shut the door behind me. I didn't turn up the lights.

XXIX.

I went to bed early and lay staring at the dark ceiling, unable to sleep. The window screen was up and the glass open, revealing the span of stars and the sound of drumming in the distance, mingled with that curious wailing flute that was classical striviirc-na music. The festivities would go on for another three days. Flaming lights descended from houses above us, fallen soldiers extinguished in midair.

An hour before dawn a shadow passed outside my door; I saw the movement in the narrow gap near the floor. The door slid aside and a silhouette stood there.

"Jos-na, may I come in?"

During my language lessons he'd never asked. But now he did. Somehow he knew I wasn't asleep.

"Yes." Even to my own ears I sounded restrained. I slowly released the bunched sheet in my fists and climbed to my feet out of respect.

He stepped farther into the room, shutting the door behind him, but didn't call up the lights. Fading moonlight spilled at his feet. He approached and brought with him the scent I always associated with the first time I'd awakened aboard his ship, when I was still healing from Falcone's shot. Faint oil and some sort of spice. I thought he was going to stop in front of me but instead he went to the window and looked out for a moment. I held my hands behind my back.

"Look," he said.

I walked over slowly until I stood by his shoulder. He seemed smaller. The top of my head reached his chin now instead of the middle of his chest. I looked up to search for the familiar facial tattoo. In the white moonlight it showed clearly, as did his eyes. Lines had appeared beneath them where none had been before.

"Look, Jos-na." He pointed to the sky.

I saw stars. Then I noticed a brighter shape in the night, pinned there like a diamond brooch.

"*Turundrlar?*"

"Yes. It's docked at our repair station. We had—casualties."

I fingered the back of my sleepshirt.

He looked at me and held out his hand. On his palm was a small, silk-wrapped object.

"What's that?" I didn't take it.

"For your birthday. In the Hub, you said, gifts are given."

I didn't think he'd remember, or bother. I barely remembered.

"It's not an explanation," he said quietly. "Just a gift."

I took it. It was light, the silk white and soft. I unknotted the ends and a round silver object spilled into my hand.

My parents' faces looked up at me, inlaid in a chained disk ID, like the one I'd once had. Young faces. They'd been young.

My sight blurred so suddenly I couldn't stop it. Something invisible folded around my shoulders like heavy arms.

"Where—" But the words stuck.

"*Mukudori*'s homeport was Siqiniq. I had a contact there forward me part of the archived crew files. Then I had this made. Look on the reverse."

I turned it over with clumsy fingers. My homeship's bird-in-flight symbol was engraved there. I couldn't breathe. "Why'd you go and do this?"

He sounded concerned and a little distressed. "Does it bother you so much? I'm sorry, Jos-na. I thought you'd want it."

I wanted it. I closed my fist around it. I wanted it so badly, so suddenly, it was impossible to shut out. To shut him out.

"When are you leaving again?" I couldn't look up.

"When you're ready to come with me."

The words released the grip in my chest. But I couldn't believe them.

"I want you to return to space with me, Jos-na. Do you want to go back on a ship?"

"I want to go with you." It fell out of my mouth the way truth did, without thought or adornment. I felt my face flood red.

He said, "Do you have a flamelight?"

Clarity in his question, like fresh air. I went to my drawers and pulled out the light and the paper ships that everyone had made before the Festival of Stars.

He took one of the ships from me and walked out of the room, to the *inidrla-na*. I followed, barefoot across the wooden floor, onto the balcony. Boats shone in the distance, on the moon-jeweled sea. The horizon was a strip of blood-red, the first glance of the sun. Without looking at me he lit his paper ship; it was powdered and caught fire with a puff, giving off faint blue tendrils of smoke. He held it burning in his hand for a long moment, then cast it into the air. It danced on the faint breeze, a wild meteor, before the planet's breath swallowed it into ashes.

I lit my own and thought of *Mukudori*. My family hadn't been soldiers but they were what I wanted most to remember. The silver disk was a warm imprint in my free hand. I remembered Evan and his shorn hair, his bruised face. I remembered Adalia crying.

I flung the burning ship into the dawn.

For a long time we stood there, saying nothing. I looped the ID disk around my neck and held the top of the balcony, watching the dark sea curl under the face of the moon. My heart settled but my hands were cold.

At length I said, "Up there, in the war—is it bad?"

Very quietly he answered, "Yes."

The silence walked a marathon between us. He didn't

look at me, he didn't move closer. Eventually I went back to my room, heavy with fatigue. Even then he followed and stood by my window until the sun rose, and stayed awake while I slept.

PART III

PART III

I.

I must have heard the sound of *Turundrlar*'s drives change pitch in my sleep, because I awoke just before Niko's voice came over shipwide comm, informing the crew we were out of leap velocity. I lay on my pallet, momentarily disoriented; it had been this way for the last two weeks, silent running toward the DMZ. The first leap halfway through those weeks had made me sick for the entire shift. I hadn't been on a ship in leap in five biological years. Instead of just quietly blacking out for a few seconds, I went under for five minutes and awoke with nausea. My body still expected to feel the natural rhythms of a planet, not the artificiality of a ship's drives, lights, air, and hours. And leaps. Some part of me felt it all familiar, but most of me wished I could wake up to sunshine, if only because it was gentle.

"Lights, fifty."

They came up halfway, a dull bronze glow. The tiny cubicle in the corner seemed far away, but I climbed out of my blankets to the sink and washed the sleep from my mouth and eyes. The water on ship tasted slightly bitter, not sweet like I was used to on planet.

We'd spent a month on Aaian-na after Niko's return. It wasn't much of a training period, but more like a vacation. I had even less to do with Ash-dan, which I enjoyed, and a couple weeks into it Hadu-na and I were formally accepted into the *ka'redan-na*. Niko ritually wrapped me in assassin-priest whites. I had never seen him so solemn or so pleased. I was a little disappointed that he didn't tattoo me, but if I was possibly going to work for him on the Hub side, like Hadu had predicted and Niko confirmed, I couldn't wear a striviirc-na mark on my face.

Hadu-na envied my position on *Turundrlar* with the *kia' redan bae*, but he got assigned to another ship that *kii'redan* Ash-dan had recommended him to. I eventually introduced Ter'tlo-na to Niko. I didn't know what she told him, but *Turundrlar* became her assignment too. For me, being a human on his ship meant sometimes he'd send me away to reconnaissance or drop information on Hub stations—that was part of the sympathizer network—but the risk was worth it because I always had him to back me up and bring me home.

And it was home, despite the initial displacement. My quarters were beside Niko's, we took meals together like we did on planet, we trained and sometimes sparred in the ship's *inidrla-na*, and instead of sitting together on the balcony we found moments to look at the stars from the view window in the main crew lounge. All of the striv fleet ships were based on stolen Hub designs. A little exploration brought back memories of *Mukudori*'s decks. And *Genghis Khan*'s.

But *Turundrlar* wasn't anything like a pirate ship. It was brightly lit, inherently striviirc-na in decoration, and the sounds of passing crew as I opened my hatch were all the lilts and long vowels of Aaian-na languages. And the scent was Niko's scent.

I headed down the corridor to the mess. I usually met Niko there for breakfast. One thing I missed from the planet was the wide variety of foods.

In typical striviirc-na fashion, nobody said farewell on my last night on planet, but they made a colorful dinner of all my favorite foods, at least. Enas-dan didn't shed any tears, but she trimmed my hair because, she said, I was starting to look like an *uurao*, all uncombed. Then Caste Master Anil-dan came to the house to speak to Niko privately, saw me in the Tree Room, and said he knew I'd serve Aaian-na well. That lit something inside me.

Ash-dan said nothing to me. He acted polite once Niko was back. Maybe his distaste of everything EarthHub had cooled. I no longer cared. He was on planet now and I wasn't. Everything he'd taught me I would put to use for Niko, and the rest I could forget. Ash-dan didn't matter anymore; Niko had me trained in comps because he always intended for me to serve aboard *Turundrlar* with him and help the sympathizers in space—help *him* gather and send information to his contacts. Ter'tlo had been right; it was much better than waiting on Aaian-na for the Hub to invade. Niko needed me here, on ship.

The deckplates dully echoed back my footsteps. Not a spot of dirt on the Warboy's ship, though its corridors and common rooms showed more than a little travel wear. The ivory walls weren't as glossed as they probably had been right out of the shipyard. The quiet, grim nature of its crew was testimony enough of the ship's long-established purpose and all those who had died in service to it. Intricate designs I'd first noticed then became familiar with on Aaian-na decorated every bulkhead on *Turundrlar*—symbols of meditation, Niko said once. They directed your thoughts to home.

Now he sat at a far table in the sparsely occupied mess, absently eating and staring at the patterns on the bulkhead. I walked into his sight line and he pulled himself out of whatever thoughts were occupying him, gestured to an untouched box of food on the table.

"Thanks." I sat and dragged the box closer to my side. We ate in silence for a few minutes until my curiosity won over. "Niko, why didn't you tell me at first that this was going to be my assignment after I was casted?"

He peeled a piece of fruit and stayed silent for a moment. "I wasn't sure I wanted you on ship, Jos-na, when it was all said and done."

I set my cup down, tasting the sour tang of tea at the back of my throat. "Why not?"

"Because you're safer on Aaian-na."

"Yeah, but for how long? If I can do more here, with you, then—"

"Do you mean that?" His gaze fixed on me.

"Of course I mean it." But I was confused by his sudden doubts.

"You've been reading the Send updates, yes? EarthHub's pushing more aggressively through the DMZ. Our fleet is spread thin just fighting them back. I even suspect pirates are trying to use parts of the DMZ as sinkholes. I can't allow that. But I don't know enough about the Hub's deep spacers to know the best way to approach them. Or defeat them." His eyes didn't leave my face.

"Your contacts in the Hub—?"

"The spacecarriers are what we meet out here. They are the ones really fighting this war. They are the ones who truly know why they hate us, because we've met in battle."

Like Falcone and Markalan S'tlian.

"But they're also the most impenetrable. The carriers recruit their own crew and decide which orders they're going to obey from the Hub. Do you understand, Jos-na? Some people in the *Hub* are afraid of those crews, or at the very least they're suspicious of them. The link back to Hub-central from the Rim and the Dragons is farther than our link to Aaian-na. And their captains are rather more independent."

Falcone had been a carrier captain. Now he was a pirate. Was it that far of a leap?

My food sat cold on my plate.

Pirates were encroaching toward Aaian-na too?

"Niko, have you met Falcone out here?" I'd not read about his death in all the Send updates. And I'd never cared to ask my teacher until I found myself back in space. It was just easier to forget instead of know about him.

"No," Niko said. Then somewhat wryly, "I haven't had the privilege. We suspect he's gone into hiding because he hasn't been harassing the Hub at all. At least not directly."

I played with the handle of my fork. EarthHub, pirates— Niko wanted to stave them all off. But if he couldn't . . . Instinct told me he had more to say. This was all leading to something that made him hesitate.

"I didn't tell you about coming with me on *Turundrlar*," he said, "because I didn't know if I could ask you—I didn't plan on not wanting—" He stopped.

I looked up in surprise. Never before had he stumbled on himself like this. His eyes were steady and unusually bright.

"I need you to do something for me, Jos-na."

I didn't say anything. He knew my answer. I was here.

"These carriers," he said slowly, "are an enigma to me. Their captains and their crews. One captain and one crew in particular. This captain has a father in the EarthHub Joint Chiefs of Staff. This captain's also given me the most trouble over the years. I need to know more about him. I need to know if peace is even possible with people like him, and if not—I need to know their weaknesses. From the inside."

Nothing moved within me.

"Jos-na, I need you to be my eyes on this deep-space carrier."

I couldn't move my hands, or my gaze from his face. His steady face, so controlled, asking me this thing even though his voice stayed low, so low as if any louder would make it break.

But it wasn't his voice breaking. It was a little place inside of me.

"Is this what you trained me for all along?"

He didn't answer. I wasn't going to let him get away with that silence, not now.

"You trained me so you could get rid of me?"

"No," he said, immediate and hard. "I saved your life and gave you a home. I thought you loved it."

"I do. And now you want me to leave it."

"Jos-na, you know you're on this ship to help me, to help the sympathizer network in the Hub. As a *ka'redan*."

"I'm here because I—" Wanted to be with you. *My teacher*. But I didn't say it. "What if I don't want to?" I said instead.

"Would you listen to me before you made up your mind?"

"So you can justify throwing me away?"

"I won't throw you away."

I ached from the skin inward. "We have a different meaning for those words, Nikolas-dan. Spying on a Hub carrier wouldn't take just a week or two, like a drop-off on Austro or a meeting on Chaos. Those carriers only hit ports once every couple months, and only insystem once every few years."

"Yes," he said. "But I would never trust anyone else to do this for me, to be gone that long, to be that qualified, and to be in direct regular contact with me or Ash-dan. You know the satellite codes to Aaian-na. You know Ki'hade. You know the Hub. And you're the right age and background to get on that carrier. They actively recruit orphans."

"So you did your research. Did you know all this when you saved my life?"

That hurt him. He didn't try to hide it. He sat back and clenched his jaw.

At the moment I didn't give a damn. My eyes flooded. I pushed back my chair and left the mess.

II.

Everywhere I walked looked the same. It was *Genghis Khan* and Falcone was taking me through her corridors, holding my hand, telling me that I could get things from people if all they wanted was my pretty face.

But it wasn't worth it. Not when the things you wanted came tarnished.

Not when you were tarnished.

III.

Niko wasn't Falcone. He came to my quarters and asked for entrance, then stood just inside the hatch and watched me where I sat on my pallet. Like the first time, except I remembered a different pallet in a different room, one with sunlight. I remembered a different room, with beds and a compartment in the floor. I remembered faces because I had them now on a disk around my neck. Faces Niko had given back to me, when they were disappearing.

He'd given me a lot, and asked only for one thing. Why had I thought you could get so much for nothing?

"*S'yta-na*," he said.

I knew that word now. I pieced it together. *First place of the heart*, literally. *Dear one*.

I couldn't hold any words. They all danced around in my head like jittery young birds, fluttering in random flight.

He crouched in front of me. "You know I wouldn't have asked if it weren't important to me. If I didn't trust you."

I looked at him. He was close but didn't touch. "I can get killed and that doesn't bother you."

"Of course it bothers me. As it bothered you when I went away. But I still had to go, and I still came back. We can't get around the fact of this war, Jos-na. *Ka'redane* cannot."

"So it's my duty."

"I won't force you. There would be no point in that."

"We're heading toward Hub space now, no matter what I say."

He sighed slightly. "Yes. But I'm taking my time."

"So you assume I'll go."

"I hope. Half that you will and—half that you won't. But my hope isn't what I need. Or what Aaian-na needs."

Some things are bigger than you, Jos. That was what he meant. He was the Warboy and some of his reputation was rightly earned. But why should I care about the war? Maybe what I needed was to stay alive.

Except that wasn't all I needed, now. I cared. I'd been trained to care. Or maybe that was something nobody could avoid. And maybe you cared more the harder you tried to avoid it.

My thoughts were threads, tied up in knots.

I stared at Niko's hands because I couldn't look at the pain in his eyes. I couldn't look at my reflection in them.

I said, "What do I need to know, Nikolas-dan?"

IV.

He de-stritified me. By layers and over slow weeks as we headed through the DMZ, he peeled away the world he'd introduced me to in the last five years. He left me bare in the aftermath, half myself and half transparent.

I had to lose my Ki'hade inflections, which had bled even into some of my EarthHub words, so I wouldn't get shot the moment I opened my mouth. I had to learn the Austroan way of talking, because Austro Station was going to be my refuge after Chaos, to replace Aaian-na. I watched a lot of vids of actors and politicians from Austro and mimicked them constantly. Niko was my teacher again, in this, as he gave me file after file of information, and tested me on it.

I had to pass for a station-raised orphan. Niko prepped me completely about Austro history of the last six years, especially its social and child welfare services. I studied maps of its molecular-looking modules, which included business facilities, port and station offices, and residencies. Some of it brought back vague memories of childhood spent in the station's junior cybetoriums and dens on layovers.

I read about *Macedon* EHV-4229, the carrier I was supposed to infiltrate, and its Captain Cairo Azarcon, what little information was available on the man. His past was so tightly sealed not even a burndive into military records produced anything but the standard profile, which only included his accomplishments from the Navy Space Corps Academy and onward. I could've dived deeper, maybe, but that would have taken more time and energy than I had before my transfer, and more risk. Military polisyms and barriers were rampant in high-level files and nearly impossible to deconstruct or break, even for an expert like Ash-dan. Or one of his students.

Azarcon's adoptive father was an admiral. That could've

explained the bristling security. The other explanation, of course, was that Azarcon hunted the enemy with regular success. EarthHub didn't want his past to be easily accessible, especially to spies.

Which was why Niko wanted me to do what I'd agreed to do. Except nothing in me made me feel like it had really been my choice. The person who'd agreed to go wasn't the person who prepared to leave. Everything I learned about the Hub threatened to push out the last five years, until I almost expected to meet myself when I turned a corner. Except it would be a stranger looking back.

I cut my hair in the short style currently popular on Austro among boys my age. Niko had acquired an old military duffel and Hub-style station wear: nondescript coveralls, a sweater or two, and worn manufiber pants. Trying them on was like slipping into someone else's skin.

Niko came to see me at the last shift before my transfer to his Hub contact. I was packing that old duffel for the fifth time and reciting Austroan history to myself, with an Austroan accent.

At least he didn't ask how I felt.

"I think that bag is as ready as it will ever be," he said, leaning against the bulkhead near the table where the duffel rested.

"I'm glad one of us is."

He put his hand on the bag, forcing me to stop fussing with it.

I breathed out. "I'm not ready, Niko."

"Would you ever be?"

"Maybe." I'd never be ready because I'd never want to go.

"What you're doing is important to me. I want you to know that, Jos-na."

"Important to you or the war?"

"Is there a difference? We are in this war."

I said quietly, "It makes a difference to me."

He paused for only a moment. "You're the difference in everything I've done since you were nine years old."

You always saved the things in your head until they were forced to come out. And sometimes it was too late, even then.

I glanced up at him, at the corner. Gripped the bag. "How am I supposed to fight on an EarthHub carrier when I'll be fighting your fleet?"

"You'll do as you must."

"Kill striviirc-na?"

"You are a *ka'redan*, Jos-na. All the training, while it focuses the mind, is at heart a killing art."

"I don't know, Niko. What if *Macedon* meets *Turundrlar*?"

"We can't grow our worries from what-ifs, Jos-na."

I held the duffel ties because my hands were shaking. He saw that, then looked into my face. Very slowly he put his hand over both of mine, and steadied them.

"You know all that I can teach you, *s'yta-na*."

"It's not enough." I didn't mean for this task alone.

His hand was something solid, warm, and without threat. I didn't want it to go. But he said, "Aaian-na was your *inidrla-na*. EarthHub will be your *vas'tatlar*."

And he released me.

V.

Captain Racine of the small merchant ship *Cervantes* let me sit on the bridge as we headed deeper into EarthHub territory. It was a legal, registered ship whose homeport was Austro. It was also a sympathizer ship. The captain said she'd known Niko for years. She called him Bae S'tlian. I sat on the worn seat at the back of the cramped bridge with my duffel bag at my feet, half listening to the crew chattering softly to one another and the tapping of the captain's fingers on her chair-comp. She wanted me where she could see me—not that she didn't trust me, but simply because you could never be too careful. Posting a guard on me was somewhat too obvious.

I'd fallen asleep those last hours aboard *Turundrlar*, because I knew I'd need it. Niko stayed, like I knew he would. Later, at the airlock, he kissed me on both sides of my face where my tattoos would have been if I'd been allowed to have them, and held me a long time. A crushingly long time, without regard for Captain Racine who stood in plain sight. He didn't give any last advice or tell me good-bye, only the embrace. My head filled with his scent and my ribs felt his arms. We left each other dry-eyed. I didn't look back and he didn't wait to watch me go.

Any words I might have spoken to Captain Racine lodged in my throat and stayed there. After a couple idle questions that went unanswered, she left me alone in my silence. I fingered the silver disk around my neck. Even now I felt Niko's fingers in my hair, the pressure of his hand on my head in that comforting way that had replaced all the unwanted touches Falcone had given me.

I thought of all the things Niko had given me. And all the things he never had and now never would.

VI.

I had two fake IDs. One to show Customs upon disembarking *Cervantes*, which I would immediately burn up, and another to show *Macedon* that verified my falsified past as an orphan raised through Austro Child Welfare Services and the EarthHub War Orphan Program, Austro Division. My supposed caseworker was actually a caseworker in the ACWS—and a sympathizer. These weren't Aaian-na symps like Niko, raised on Aaian-na and completely stritified. They were Hub symps, Hub citizens who disagreed with the government's stance on the war and found more sympathy with the "enemy."

Not everybody felt the Hub had a right to dictate how far the strivs traveled toward Hub space and which moons and sectors they had to relinquish because the Hub needed the resources. Some were unconvinced by the steady Send reports and features that cycled propaganda about how badly the strits treated human POWs, how the only thing strits wanted was the destruction of human bases, stations, and ships, how the symps were traitors who were no longer even human. Some Hub citizens knew that the only thing stopping the Hub from taking over Aaian-na entirely was the Warboy, and they agreed with him. The Caste Master and the S'tlians had more than one spy in the enemy camp. But none on *Macedon*, yet.

I was going to meet the caseworker briefly—it wouldn't take more than that since we'd both been briefed thoroughly on our "common history." Niko had timed it well, through updates from his operatives in the Hub, so that *Cervantes* arrived in Austro port a stationday after *Macedon*. Deep-space carriers only went insystem for major resupply every five sy (or stationyears). During these runs into the Rim they usually recruited, as crew were lost during skirmishes and battles. Austro had a permanent recruiting center for all branches of the armed forces, though the Navy Space Corps was by far the busiest. This was my in. Biologically I was fourteen years old; you were a legal adult at sixteen. In wartime, orphans no matter how old could enlist on any ship

that would take them—most became scrub kids. But the
deep spacers took anybody they deemed fit and willing to
fight, and put them in gear.

I shouldered my old duffel like a crewman prepared to
spend a few days in a den, stepped by the Customs Officer
after he approved my ID, and eventually integrated myself
into the stream of activity on the merchant dockside. The
carriers always docked at military designated locks, so the
only uniforms here were maintenance and loader crews and
a few merchants who used formal unis. Colors and patches
of a dozen different ships swept by me as I threaded my way
to the dockring's inner doors, where my contact stood.

The caseworker was a towering, grizzled old man, old
like station cits got old, displaying his standard age on every
line of his face. No time dilation deception for his sedentary
self. Mr. Grish Mankar was eightyish sy and looked it despite suspended aging treatments. The washed-out appearance of his dark skin and slight yellowing of his eyes said
he'd had more than one SAT. He squeezed my shoulder tight
enough, though, placing his other hand on my back to guide
me away from the docks, toward the concourse. I tried not
to automatically shove off his touch.

"The recruiting office is on the tenth level," he said as we
walked.

"I know." I'd memorized the station map. Austro was
made up of ten modules, which roughly resembled flattish
molecules, stacked in a basic tower design with splayed
legs. It made station additions easy but to get from one leg
to the other took a quick ride on a podway or a longer ride
on a pedway. The legs were the docks. The offices were in
the central modules with the residencies.

I walked tense. Mankar said, "Relax," more than once,
which didn't help. Austro, a commercial Rimstation, was the
largest station this side of the Spokes (Pax Terra near Earth,

in Hubcentral, was comparable) and that much humanity—teeming, colorful, and loud—was more than I'd had to deal with in five years. You simply couldn't walk without someone brushing by you or outright bumping into you. Storefronts noisy with ads, corridor merchants and their kiosks trying to steal sales from the stores, the ever-present scents from eateries and restaurants, and the mix of civilian, polly, and military uniforms everywhere. You couldn't alight on any one thing; it was all just a mass of sensory bombardment. Everyone walked through your personal space with no regard whatsoever. I couldn't relax. Levs spilled and swallowed bodies up at an alarming regular rate, sending people to and from the many offices, residencies, and dens that populated the station.

Not one striviirc-na, of course, unless you counted the recruitment holo-ad showing a handsome soljet with one foot on a fallen alien, or the cycled Send reports blaring from wallvids with updates on the war. Every once in a while a striv face flashed across the screen, a POW or a dead "war criminal." You might have believed EarthHub was doing fine, here where the war had yet to really touch. Nothing mentioned about the stations in the Dragons, like Chaos, or other Rimstations that had suffered in blitz raids. Nothing about the ships that had lost skirmishes in the deep.

My eyes flickered to the second tier of the concourse, the balcony and steel columns where snipers could hide. I wasn't entirely positive someone wouldn't see me for what I was and decide to take a potshot.

Mankar guided me finally into one of the levs, squashed between an executive of some sort and a polly. I ignored the secured gun and nightstick at the polly's hip, even though it pressed against my arm. She glanced idly at my plain gray clothing, my duffel bag, and my guardian, then looked up at the chiming numbers. Mankar and I had to squeeze and ex-

cuse ourselves off the lev when our stop came up. It was a
relief to walk into the cool, mostly empty corridor of the Social Services, Child Welfare wing. He led me through narrow blank hallways and past working people who hardly
glanced up, into his office—a small, bare space that reminded me of a ship cabin. I glanced at the comp, the
deskcomm, the shelves stuffed with holocube boxes and the
occasional hardprint folder. A life spent behind a desk, under
white light. A station cit's life.

I sat my duffel on one of the faded chairs and opened it
up, tugging out a sweater. Best to change clothes in case
anybody I talked to later on *Macedon* had glanced at me
leaving *Cervantes*. Mankar went behind his comp and
tapped away at something while I changed. At least he was
that polite. I set the first ID on his desk. He took it and
dropped it into a rubbish bin beside his seat, then pulled out
a small vial of liquid and poured it on. The ID fizzled and
smoked slightly, melted and disappeared into a vague lumpy
mass.

I popped in my optic holopoint receptors, the only way I
was going to get the burntech onto *Macedon*. They completely scanned all belongings and your own person—so the
plan was to wear the ware. With no connection to a comp the
lenses created a slight ruby film over my sight, undetectable
from the outside looking in, and didn't impair it too much.
Niko had told me *Macedon*'s comps had the same holoaccess optional component, though obviously more sophisticated than the average domestic comp. I'd trained on
military models, specifically EHV carrier-class Navy ware,
though I hadn't known it at the time.

I pulled off the image disk from around my neck and
tucked it into a pocket in the bag (if they couldn't see it, it
was one less thing for them to ask about), then rummaged
through my belongings once more, quadruple checking that

I had nothing incriminating in my possession. Nothing but a very few changes of clothing, typical of a station-bred orphan, a pad of paper and pencils, station-bought, since there was nothing wrong with an interest in art—supposedly a gift from Mankar, though they were from Niko. I had no weapons (they would just be confiscated), no tools other than the holopoints. Whatever else I required would have to be found on the ship somehow or dug from memory. Most everything I needed was in my head—contact codes, contact lists, report codes, satellite codes, and ship schedules.

I looked up to find Mankar staring at me. I snapped the duffel shut, tied it off, and hefted it over my shoulder. "Anything else?"

He seemed hesitant, even a bit amused in a sad sort of way. "You're younger than I thought you would be."

I went to the door and palmed it open. "No, I'm not."

"Good luck, then."

I kept one hand in my pocket, on my Austro citizen ID, and retraced my way back to the lev, then up to the tenth level from dockmain. Nobody spared me a glance. There were advantages to large stations; people tended to blur faces, as if their survival in such crowded confines depended upon it. I thought I might have some trouble finding the recruitment rooms in the network of corridors (despite my memorization) but as I got on the coreward part of the level, a trail of holo-ads hung ghostly near the ceiling, directing you toward "your future in the EarthHub Armed Forces."

I followed the ads, right along with a few other fools, bypassing the open doors of planetside and station army, Rim Guard, insystem Navy and Marines—straight to the room that stood separate: deep-space carrier recruitment. It wasn't as crowded as the others. The military reps weren't stiff-looking, shiny officers like in the other branches. Here the black-uniformed soljets from *Macedon*, *Wesakechak*, and

Archangel (the three deep spacers in dock) sat around hurling insults at one another and telling all the prospectives to go "be fruitful and multiply"—as one of the *Macedon* jets put it. They looked bored. Apparently most of the potential recruits weren't even worth a scan.

But I'd read a bit about *Macedon*, public records and some that weren't. I strode to the jet's desk, where she sat rocking back on a chair, and plopped my duffel on top. She was the one sitting so I figured she was the official recruitment officer; another *Macedon* patch loitered in the room, but he was flirting with an *Archangel* jet.

The sergeant—Hartman, her breast patch said—gave me a pointed, blue-eyed stare. Despite her short, mussed hair that made her look like some sort of demented pixie, her gaze was confrontational and vaguely annoyed.

"What you want, sprig?"

"I want on *Macedon*," I said, in my Austroan accent.

"I'm sure you do." She kept rocking back on the chair, fingers laced over her stomach. Her uniform sleeves were pushed up. As she lifted her hand to scratch her head I saw the *Macedon* tattoo emblazoned on her inner right wrist—a blond man's profile in the ancient Greek style, against a sixteen-pointed black star. Nanocoded in the colors was her *Macedon* service number, something that couldn't be faked. If you bore that tat and weren't crew, you had to hope you never bumped into someone who knew better. It was a misdemeanor by law and a death warrant if you were caught by any of the real crew.

"So where do I sign?" I kept my gaze on her face. She was a surprisingly slight build, with large eyes and equally large lips. And a scathing grin.

"You wanna sign," she said, as if I'd just asked to be shot. "Hey, Madi, this sprig here wants to sign on *Mac*."

The other *Macedon* soljet looked at me from the *Archangel* desk he was sitting on, and laughed.

"Tell him to come back once his balls have dropped."

Sergeant Hartman said in all solemnity, "Sorry, sprig, you're gonna have to come back once your balls've dropped."

I looked at her, looked at the comp open on the desk, and grabbed it, swinging it around so I could see the screen. Her chair tilted forward with a smack and her hand shot out, grabbed my wrist in a crushing grip.

"Hey, mano, you don't touch my ware."

"I just wanted to see the form." And get your attention.

She stood and shoved me back. "It don't say nothin' but 'Casualty Information.' "

"Your ship so bad your people die on you?"

I had her complete attention now. I had the whole room's attention. Her teeth showed. "Only the ones we vent."

I smiled. She smiled back, giving me a second, hard look.

"I think I hear one of 'em droppin' now," Madi said, cupping a hand to his ear. "Small ping, but audible."

"Bigger ping than yours, blondie."

The jets from all three ships catcalled and gestured. Madi started to laugh. Hartman didn't.

"Let's see your shit."

My heart beat fast. I kept it separate from my expression and handed her my Austro citizen ID. She looked at it, then ran it through her comp, which was turned back facing her so I couldn't see the screen.

"Joslyn Aaron Musey. Orphan. Fourteen years old, Austro stationyears." The blue eyes came back to me and looked me up and down. I carefully kept my face blank and she eventually looked back at the screen. "Dead ship *Mukudori*. Never heard of it."

"It was—"

"Six years ago. Yah, I see."

I became aware of the other *Macedon* jet, who'd slid off
the *Archangel* desk and now stood close behind me. He was
tall and I felt his breath blowing over the top of my hair. I
kept still, facing Hartman. She read my fake file, silent, and
something in it made her eyes change slightly.

"Well," she drawled finally, "seein' as you got at least
one ball, I suppose we can have a second look. Private
Madison will take you aboard."

I was surprised they allowed me on ship so easily. "That
it?"

Now she laughed. "Nah, sprig. That the beginning."

VII.

Madi frisked me right there in the room, thoroughly,
while the other jets looked on and teased. It was all I could
do not to knock him on his ass. Then he did an initial search
through my duffel, appropriated it afterward, and pointed
out of the room.

"Go west, young man."

I was beginning to think jets were all a little crazy.

"Be gentle with him, Madi," Hartman called as we left.

We headed to the module's dockmain, down the lev and
through the crowded, noisy concourse again. We passed
more than one jet from *Macedon* who yelled at Madi or gestured in hand signs I didn't understand. Madi didn't talk to
me, but he chattered at people he recognized, making me
wait beside him like an appendage. Just before we hit the tall
double doors that led out dockside, Madi grabbed my sleeve
to stop me and flagged down a figure by one of the kiosks.
I saw a gray-clad, nonuniformed back and a long blond

ponytail. For an instant I thought, *Evan*, and had a picture of him and his older brother Shane strolling station decks. Evan before the pirates had shorn his hair and bruised his face.

Madi called, "Dorr!"

The figure turned, sighted us, and grinned. He was young, no more than twenty maybe. Or at least that was how he looked, which wasn't exactly reliable in deep-space crew. He flipped whatever he was holding at the kiosk merchant and strolled over.

"Yo, mano." Grayish-green eyes flickered to me briefly. "Ain't this one a bit young for you, Madi?"

I wanted to scowl, but didn't. I knew he was watching me from the corners of his eyes.

Madi snorted. "Sarge's pick. Stavros actually let you out?"

"Good behavior," Dorr said, smiling like it was a joke. His short sleeves showed off his ship tat and another one half-hidden on his upper right bicep.

"The power of dimples," Madi said, and Dorr laughed, showing them there high on his cheeks. They belied the actual smile, which looked like he was up to something. "O'Neil's been looking for you," Madi went on.

A spark of interest lit Dorr's eyes. "Yah? Where is he?"

"I saw him last by Abacus."

That was a club and den. Not a pricey one.

Dorr headed off with a backhanded wave. "Thanks."

Madi gave me a little shove and we continued on our way with no more voluntary interruptions. The dockring was about three times larger than the one on Chaos Station, cavernous, cold, and once we got to the military ships, restricted; it took us a while to get to *Macedon*'s lock. We passed the other carriers' locks, evident by two jets standing guard on each. *Macedon*'s was no different. They were fully armed with LP-150 rifles, standard sidearms, and comm-studs. They didn't joke with Madi; they barely glanced at us. One of them simply cycled the lock open when we approached up the ramp, our booted steps echoing slightly.

Inside the carrier wasn't much of a surprise. They weren't so far removed from pirate ships. We walked down scuffed, pale gray corridors—clean, but still utilitarian. Overhead, above the lines of lights, the pipe guts and grated innards of the ship lay exposed and occasionally marked with paint in a code I didn't understand. The null-g handholds running the length of the bulkheads were chipped and in some cases missing entirely, showing tiny holes where bolts should have been. Deck levels were painted in yellow by stairwells and lev doors, but no signs directed you to major centers like galley, jetdeck, bridge, or flight deck. This wasn't an accommodating merchant ship. You saw it in the crew that strolled by, most in black fatigues, some in dark and pale gray coveralls, all of them visibly armed, not just the officers, negotiating the narrow corridors and fellow passing crew with unthinking ease.

Clean recycled air wafted through the decks, marred only by people's lingering cologne or soap scent.

I tried not to think about how easy it would be just to run.

I had no idea where Madi was taking me and he didn't volunteer the information. We rode the noisy lev up and he followed me out. The new corridor was less scarred and quieter. Most everyone we passed bore an officer's rank. Madi didn't salute any of them but I caught the difference in the number of stripes and pins. Most of them wore black battle fatigues. If you weren't looking you'd think them all jets.

We stopped outside a hatch marked simply CAPTAIN.

By now my heart thudded in my ears. I hadn't thought they'd make me confront the man so early in the game, but maybe this was normal procedure. Madi palmed the entrance light, which gave a brief buzz and stayed red for a moment, then blinked green. Madi opened the hatch and I stepped in first at his look. He didn't follow.

"Joslyn Aaron Musey, sir," Madi told the man behind the black desk, as if he'd been expecting me. I realized that he probably had and the distracting route to the ship had not been accidental.

"Thank you, Private."

Madi left with my duffel bag, which I knew would be thoroughly scanned in my absence. I heard the hatch shut behind me and remained standing, taut and staring at the person sitting casually back in his seat.

Information about the inner workings of *Macedon* was decidedly slim, and that was all due to the fact of its captain, who was even more of an enigma and seemed to purposely keep it that way. Most of the info I'd studied about the ship had been public record and statistical; some had not been, but had still been short on knowledge of specific ship culture—which was a salient feature on all deep-space carriers, and completely individual. The man who ran the ship was just as individual and probably more dangerous than the average inner system carrier captain. They still felt the long arm of the Hubcentral-based EarthHub Joint Chiefs. Deep-space carriers were so far from regular channels of communication that many in EarthHub considered them border rogue. Still, as long as they brought down striviirc-na, nobody complained too loudly.

Captain Cairo Azarcon's basic file stated that he was the adopted son of EHJC Admiral Omar Ashrafi. He was thirty-eight EarthHub Standard years, had started out as a hunter-killer pilot but quickly moved up the ranks due to an impressive battle record and aggressive leadership skills. As captain of *Macedon* he'd brought down at least five striviirc-na battleships (which I knew were *ki-na* ranked destroyers) and countless lesser-classed vessels. The man had a reputation for ruthlessness and a complete disregard for public opinion.

Sitting back, one hand on the chair arm and the other casually on his desk, he looked me up and down with brief movements of his dark, slightly angular eyes. He looked barely older than ponytailed Dorr and dressed no different from Private Madison. His apparent youth shocked me, even knowing how the passage of time was so relative. He hadn't looked this young in his service picture, but then he'd been in full dress uniform, capped and somewhat shadowed. Nothing at all distinguished him now as captain of this ship, other than the practically camouflaged four black stripes on his black-uniformed arms. His skin was pale like most people who spent their lives on a ship. His hair was black and roughly combed out of his eyes, making them seem all the more stark. They bored into my own with the authority of someone that had power over life and death.

"Musey," he said, in a deceptively quiet voice. "Fourteen and ready to join a war?"

"Yes, sir."

"Why?"

I had no idea what to expect from this man. His eyes never left my face.

"I don't want to spend the rest of my life scrabbling for a living on Austro, sir." I kept my gaze fixed on a point just above Azarcon's head, on the bare gray wall. The entire office was bare, clean, and right angles, utilitarian except for one holopic protruding from the desk, angled mostly away from me. I couldn't see the image.

"Better rushing for a living than dying in space," he said, in that same relaxed tone.

"Sergeant Hartman said nobody dies on *Macedon* unless they're vented, sir."

"Did she?" Amused. "Well, that's true. But once you're off *Mac*, say on a mission somewhere, then you're fair game for all the strits and pirates."

"Yes, sir," I said, because he seemed to want an answer.

"Tell me why I ought to consider signing you when you're stupid enough to want off a relatively safe station and onto a carrier that doesn't see civilization but once every five years."

"Because I'm good, sir."

"Good at what? Looking pretty?"

"Good at whatever you want me to do. Sir."

He breathed out in a fast, mocking laugh. "Oh, I can see what you'd be good at. Orphan?"

His comp sat open in front of him. Hartman must have transferred my file.

"Yes, sir."

"Made your living—how? In the tunnels or in bed? Or both?"

"In hard work, in odd jobs, wherever they'd pay me legal, sir."

"I have no need for a kiosk clerk."

"I learn fast, sir."

"I'm sure you do. But I still have no need for a cred counter."

If I couldn't get on this ship it was all blown. "Sir, I want to fight the strits. I want off this damn station and back on a ship. I was born on one and it's what I want, sir."

"Military's different from merchant. Sun to moon. Why don't you hire onto another merchant? Or go religious and join a Universalist crew."

I hardened my voice. "Because I want to fight and I'm not religious. Sir."

"You might be if you survive your first battle."

I looked him in the eyes. "I already did, sir, which I'm sure you're well aware. My ship was *Mukudori*."

He didn't blink. "Yes, I am aware. I remember when that hit the Send. How did you escape Falcone? It was Falcone blew your ship, wasn't it?"

He knew so, and I realized he must have known more about Falcone than I did, since Falcone was a former Earth-Hub captain.

"He took me onto Chaos. The strits attacked and I escaped in the . . . chaos."

"I remember that too. By the dates it seems you were aboard his ship for about a year."

"Yes, sir."

He studied my face for an unexpectedly long time. Then he reached and touched a button on his desk. The hatch clanged open and Madi stepped in.

"Private Madison, let Musey loose on the dock for a gauntlet run."

"Yes, Captain."

Azarcon's black eyes fixed on me. "Do you know what the gauntlet is, Musey?"

It was one aspect of deep-space carrier culture that I did know about. And dreaded. "I run, jets chase me, if I survive intact then I'm on the ship."

Azarcon smiled coolly. "If you survive intact, then I consider letting you on ship. Since very few do, I'll say my good-byes and good luck now."

"I'll see you soon, Captain."

I'd read him right. The smile widened, but it wasn't friendly. "Hopefully you'll live long enough to regret it." He nodded perfunctorily at Madison and returned to his comp as if I'd never been there. I followed Madi's example and saluted, despite the fact Azarcon didn't even look up, and left.

Madison clapped me on the back. "He must like you. Now he wants us to kill you. It ain't too late to back out, you know." His grin baited me. He looked like a vapid, smiley blond but his eyes were ice.

"Where's my stuff?"

"Oh, we're castin' lots for it down in jetdeck."

I wouldn't put it past this crew. As we headed back to the main airlock, more and more jets started to collect in our wake until they trailed behind me like a pack of silent wolves. Azarcon must have commed them. My nerves twitched, then began to harden. I listened to their booted steps behind me. I didn't speak to Madi, or any of them. Once the airlock opened I darted out and down the ramp in a dead run.

They followed, swift as black smoke.

VIII.

The pounding steps behind me resounded like pulse fire all around the half-empty dock. Jets from the other two carriers watched impassively as I raced toward the unrestricted sectors of the ring. The jets behind me didn't make a sound. Nothing but their bootsteps, gaining.

I burst from the military sector doors and rammed into a blue uniform. She yelled. We both tumbled to the deck, her hand shoving against my cheek. I rolled and scrambled to my feet. A jumble of faces seemed to freeze in my sight. Someone mouthed, "Damn jets!"

I couldn't hear the words over the rise of shouts.

I darted through the crowd, ducking low.

"You can't do that here!" someone yelled from behind, not to me.

"File it!" came the reply.

I glanced over my shoulder. Merchants and dockworkers clogged the jets, protesting. It didn't last. Not much could hold back a squad of running jets. They bled through the objections like black oil. All they had to do was flash their ship tats.

I headed straight for the concourse, among people and noise and more than a dozen different corridors branching to different sections in this module. I could get lost. No appealing to pollies in a situation like this. Not for me and not for the cits caught in the middle. People tried, but deep-space carrier crews—strit killers and war heroes—had good lawyers and bad reputations.

I darted behind a trinket kiosk to catch my breath and peered out toward the wide central corridor, eateries across the way and the diverting flow of traffic to the levs and ped-ways. The upper levels held a continuous ramble of people going in and out of shops and entertainment services.

The jets spread out for a systematic search. There were only a dozen of them, but they asked the people. They ze-roed in on tunnel kids who had no reason to lie or dislike jets that shared a similar contempt for station authority. One kid gestured toward my kiosk.

I ducked out and ran toward the nearest connecting cor-ridor, over to the main shopping district.

One of them must have anticipated me. I felt the swiping passage of a hand near my shoulder before I plunged into the streaming traffic of people and wheelrunners. I kept low and knifed through the shocked crowd, impolite, brutal with my elbows, crashing when I couldn't bounce. Swearing and yelling from innocent bystanders chased me. Word of the gauntlet spread out from my flight like a fan; soon the crowd thinned in front of me. I swore at them. The jets now had a clear line of sight.

I veered into one of the clothing stores. The holo greeting barely got out a word before a flow of black uniforms cut through it behind me. I turned quickly and breasted through the racks and displays, knocking some down, heading for the supplier access behind the checkout.

"Hey!"

I ignored the clerk and shouldered my way through to the back, past inventory and compdesks, straight out the rear door.

Three jets ran toward me from the alley leftward. They'd rounded me. I spun the opposite direction and saw two more jets turn the corner from the main throughway. I looked up and jumped, grabbed the neighboring store's marquee overhang and hauled myself up, legs swinging. One knee found the narrow ledge while I scraped for a decent hold on the pitted plas-molding of the building wall. These places had no roofs, extending instead into the station ceiling, but they had windows. I levered myself standing and edged along to the half-open plexpane to my left. It was just within arm's reach.

The jets stopped below me like frustrated dogs. One drew her gun and fired.

The paralysis pulse burst a half meter from my shoulder, scarring the wall. I clung, fingers digging. An intentional miss.

"Come down," that jet said.

So I could get beat to a pulp? I freed one hand long enough to give the woman my nonverbal answer. They didn't want to shoot me down—too easy for them.

"Go upstairs," the jet said to a couple of her comrades, who promptly disappeared. That left three. I'd had similar odds more than once in the *vas'tatlar*. I looked down and jumped.

They hadn't expected that. I dropped on one of them,

throwing him to the deck, and rolled quickly before he could grab me. The other two pounced immediately but I had already gained my feet. I kicked out and followed through with a roundhouse. The woman landed on her ass. The third came in closer and more cautious. He deflected my combination punch attack and tried to wrap my ankle. I jammed my fist under his chin. He fell back. The other two climbed to their feet, despite the blows.

The woman had dropped her gun when I dropped her. I dived for it. Boots slammed down and I rolled and tripped one of them. He landed half on my legs but my fingers already found the weapon. I shot him. I kicked him off me and aimed at the other two back and forth, fast.

"Get back!" It was set on high paralysis. The jet I'd downed would wake up with splitting pain and nausea.

The other jets came through the back door and around the corner, totaling twelve, including the two that had gone to the window where they'd thought I would try to escape.

Madi crowed, stepping forward. "The sprig's got spit!"

I stood swiftly and kept my back to the wall, aiming.

He held up his hands in a gesture of surrender, but nothing in his eyes said he believed it. "That won't earn you any favors, mano."

"It'll earn you on the deck."

"Look up first."

It could have been a ploy, but the two were in the window. I couldn't keep them and the others in sight. I fired up just as one jumped down toward me. I dodged. He missed. I didn't. It was all the distraction Madison needed. I got off one more shot that downed a third jet before Madi ducked in close enough to seize my wrist and force it up. I punched at his spleen. He sidestepped and my blow merely grazed. I had to restrain myself from fighting too hard or else they would get suspicious. I allowed another jet to grab my legs

out from under me. They took me down on my back and
Madi knelt on my chest, wresting the gun from my fingers.
I gasped from the pressure of his knee and struggled violently, but each of them had a limb while Madi held down
my torso.

"Bad business," he said conversationally, "takin' a jet's
piece."

"She shouldn't have dropped it."

"Nah, she shouldn't've." Madi looked toward the female
jet. "Sarge is gonna rail you, Nguyen."

"I'll shoot him now," Nguyen said as Madi handed over
her gun.

"Nah. We want him awake." He grinned at me. "You actually shot three of us. Kinda impressive, but it lands you
square in our bad books." He stood and stepped back. "Get
him up."

Two jets let go my legs while the other two hauled me to
my feet. Their grips threatened to stop blood flow through
my arms. I considered kicking them but the looks on their
faces dissuaded me. They'd shoot me. If it came down to it,
they might decide not to use paralysis.

"Madi!" a voice called.

The jets parted. The blond, ponytailed man named Dorr
strolled toward us from the concourse. Trailing him was a
slightly shorter man with cropped light brown hair. Dorr was
still dressed in civilian clothes and grinned impishly, all
angel-faced dimpled and without compassion.

"Yo, mano," Madison said in greeting. "O'Neil—" To the
other man. Then to both: "Say 'lo to our fem."

Dorr came right up, eyed the three still-paralyzed bodies
on the deck, and looked at me. His eyes raked me over, slow.
"Whew. You right, Madi. Fresh meat."

O'Neil rubbed the back of his neck, surveying the scene.
I saw the ship tat on his inner right wrist, a sword with wings

flared behind it. *Archangel*. "You *Mac* jets're rusty. Look at the mess this sprig made." He had a clear Martian accent and a small scar by his right eye. He grinned broadly.

Dorr dry-sniped him, one pointed glare.

My arms were going numb. I used the distraction of the exchange and wrenched away enough to kick the jet at my right straight in the knee. He staggered, but the other grabbed me in a headlock. I moved to slam him back against the wall but Dorr suddenly stood in front of me. He smiled and gutted me with a gun I hadn't seen him pull.

I grunted and kicked toward Dorr's shin but the jet holding me threw me to the deck. Dorr pistol-whipped me when I tried to get up. I lay momentarily stunned and a boot slammed into my side. Others quickly joined, rapid hits, rapid seconds of biting pain. Then they retreated just as quickly, leaving me curled and gasping.

"Haul him up," I heard Dorr say.

They wrenched me to my feet. My vision blackened. I tasted blood trickling out the side of my mouth.

"You gonna fight still?" Dorr asked. My sight slowly cleared. He was obviously a higher rank than anybody here because they all seemed to defer to him. Or maybe he was just the most dangerous.

"Erret," the *Archangel* crewman said. But not to stop him.

"Yah, comm me," Dorr said offhandedly, without turning his eyes from me. O'Neil strolled off. This wasn't his crew and he couldn't care less if they beat me to death.

"What's his name?" Erret Dorr asked Madison.

"Joslyn Aaron Musey."

"Cute. Better get him to Cap."

"Should we?"

"He downed three of us, didn't he? He's bloody fem. Toss him to Cap." Dorr pulled a cigret case from his pants pocket and slid out a stick. He sparked the end with his finger-band lighter and took a drag, smiling at me all the while. In my pain-ridden state I thought vaguely of Falcone and spat blood at his feet.

He said, "Spunky." His stare was invasive.

I didn't know how serious he was, but I chilled to the bone.

Dorr laughed, looking into my face. "Take him to Cap, Madi. Before he hypes himself."

They dragged me bleeding and bruised back to *Macedon*—taking the long route, I suspected, just so I'd have to walk with the pain. Station cits and various ship crew stared but didn't stop us or offer help. The pollies stood by the walls, hands on their sidearms and nightsticks, watching silently. They hardly ever tangled with deep-space jets. The cleanup afterward just wouldn't be worth it.

I glared at them as I went, flanked by lawbreakers.

As we entered the lock all the jets but Madi fell away, disappearing down the corridors like ghosts. I shuffled beside Madison, one arm across my gut where I'd been kicked the most while he held my other arm in a crushing grip, as if I were in any condition to fight or run. I licked the side of my mouth where it stung.

"Bruised some ribs, prolly," Madi said brightly. "You got off easy. Nguyen wanted to kill you."

I didn't answer.

"She shouldn't have let go her gun, though. And Sanchez, Ricci, and Bucher are gonna want your hide for puttin' them out. Whooee, you gonna have to watch your six real close."

"That mean I passed?"

"Nah." He propelled me into the lev. "Command deck. Whether you make it on or not, they gonna come for you."

I stared absently at the grated lev door, listening to the

hydraulics clank and growl until we jarred to a stop. I felt it in my teeth and marrow. He walked me out. If I'd had anywhere to run to on this damn station, I would have tried for it despite the pain. I didn't want to be on this ship, with these people, and that pirate of a captain who condoned murder under the guise of recruitment. EarthHub claimed they were more civilized than the striviirc-na, but at least the strivs I knew weren't sadists. If they took you out they did it without malicious abuse.

Madi set me in front the captain's hatch and buzzed. It lit green almost immediately and Madi put me inside. Azarcon watched me from behind his desk, expressionless. He nodded at Madison, who promptly left. I stood alone in front of the man, whose black eyes assessed me like a slave trader's.

"Where did you learn to fight?" he asked without preamble, and somehow I wasn't at all surprised he knew the details of the gauntlet run. Dorr hadn't come back to the ship with us.

"The orphanage had classes, sir." It had, given by volunteers—and symps—in the community. Supposedly I'd been an avid participant since I was nine years old. "That and . . . outside of the orphanage."

"The gun handling?"

My ribs ached, chomping fire. "Outside of the orphanage, sir. Fell in with a bad crowd. Once upon a time, sir. They taught me."

"No arrests."

"A smart crowd, sir."

"So it wasn't all legal jobs—hard work, decent pay—was it?"

"I never killed anybody, if that's what you're asking, sir."

"That's not what I'm asking. What other skills might you have that aren't in this record? That Mr. Mankar might not know?"

So he'd spoken to the caseworker. Or somebody in his crew had.

"None, sir."

"None?" He shifted in his seat, folded his hands on the desk, and looked at me. A deceptively young face. How many others had taken that face for granted? "What did you do for a year on *Genghis Khan*?"

I blinked, shifted my weight. I desperately needed to sit down but he didn't offer. "What do you mean, sir?"

"I think it was a clear enough question, Musey."

I wiped at the blood on my chin. "He taught me to play poker. To eat nice. To talk properly."

"To fire a weapon? To fight?"

I had overplayed it. "No, sir. I was only eight."

"What else, Musey? Because Falcone wouldn't have kept you for a year if all he did was socialize you. What else did he do?"

"Nothing, sir."

"Did he rape you?"

I stared. I didn't breathe. The corners of my sight started to black out. Azarcon didn't blink. He waited.

"No. Sir." I didn't know what that had to do with anything, besides this man's own prurient interests. I would have launched across the desk and killed him if I didn't think he had a gun somewhere beside him or on his person.

"Are you going to collapse on me, Musey? Because if you do you'll wake up on dockside."

"I won't, sir."

"So you don't remember what else went on when you were in Falcone's custody."

"Nothing else went on, sir."

"Would you like to sit down, Musey?"

It wasn't an offer. The longer I stood under his stare, the worse I felt. "Yes, sir, I would like to sit down."

"Well, you may sit once you've answered my questions. I might even send you to my medbay. Where did you learn to fight?"

"Sir, on station. In classes the orphanage offered. And among other orphans."

"Yes, I spoke to the instructor. She quite remembers you. Mr. Mankar was very clear about monitoring your progress through the years. I myself find it truly impressive you fought off a dozen of my jets, paralyzing three of them no less."

"It was a matter of survival, sir. On station as well as with your jets."

"Yes . . . it was. Not unlike *Mukudori* and *Khan*. Are you a survivor, Musey?"

I blinked sweat from my eyes. "I like to think so, sir."

"How did you survive a year on Falcone's ship?"

What was this man's agenda, other than testing me when I had physical distractions? Had he known Falcone personally, to be so interested?

"Sir, I did what he wanted and when I saw my chance I ran."

"They teach rather well for free classes. I must recommend them to my jet instructors."

I didn't answer. He didn't speak for a long time.

"We'll talk some more later, Musey. Right now you better get those ribs checked. And that blood cleaned up before you stain my deck."

"Yes, sir. Am I in, sir?"

He stood, resting hands on his desk in a manner that managed to seem both casual and intimidating. He was a tall man. The long eyes stared blackly into my own.

"Did I say you were in, Musey?"

"No, sir."

He touched his desk and the hatch opened behind me. His gaze shifted over my shoulder.

"Take him to medbay, Private Madison. Once he's fit, put him in the brig."

IX.

Madison laughed at me all the way to medical. "Cap must really find you interestin' if he's botherin' to keep you in the brig."

"I'd rather he bother to let me go."

Madi laughed a lot but I wasn't deceived. He propelled me through heavy double-plex doors that opened into a wide, white trauma room. A bank of beds lined the far wall with curtain dividers. Gunmetal-gray, mobile examination equipment stood at silent attention in one corner. The overhead scans were folded up toward the ceiling, their grips rubbed raw from use. Locked cupboards, windowed private rooms, labs, and offices ran around the main area like satellites around a station, broken only by the lines of shut doors. The place smelled of sterility and clean air. Crew clad in pale gray BDUs, immaculately smooth, attended to a few griping patients on flat examination tables in the center of the room.

A tall, white-haired man approached us. On his arms were black commander chevrons and the twin snakes patch that marked him Chief Medical Officer. The name badge said Mercurio. His gray eyes pinned me like a specimen under a scope.

"New victim, Doc," Madi said.

"Put him on exam three."

Madi obeyed the man's brisk tone and almost shoved me

to the table. Wincing, I climbed up and sat, sagging from the relief of finally being stationary. Mercurio tilted my head and looked me over face to chest with almost rough competency. Then he lifted an injet from a mobile tray by the table and loaded it with a capsule.

"What's that?" My arms tightened around my body protectively.

"Lie back."

"What's in that?"

But Madi took hold of my shoulder and pushed me back. I had no choice. I held my ribs and stared up at the flat round lights high in the ceiling. Mercurio shoved my arms away and pulled up my sweater.

My heart jumped, then the injet kicked in, right in my stomach. An intense heat spread out from my gut to my extremities, dissipating in sharpness as it went. I took deep, painful breaths and tried to stop my heart from racing. Mercurio pulled over a portable scanner, gripped the wide handles with his eye pressed to the scope, and bent over my chest. The instrument hummed as he ran it up and down my body and over my arms and legs. The liquid he'd injetted highlighted all my innards. It was a standard procedure, now that I realized what it was.

His head was close and the hair was dark at the roots. His hands weren't as old as that white hair suggested. His forehead was only vaguely lined. I had to clench my fists to stop myself from shoving him away.

Finally he straightened and pulled a slate from his gray lab coat, tapped at it briskly. Everything about him was that brisk, as if he had better things to do. He looked at me with cool eyes.

"You've broken your wrist before."

"Yes, sir." I pulled my sweater down and tried to sit up without aggravating my ribs. Impossible.

He held my head in one hand. "Close your eyes."

I did, not liking it. He sprayed my face with something that smelled strongly of astringent and burned the cut on my mouth the same. I clenched my teeth and he dabbed at my face and sprayed something else that left a metallic taste on my tongue. My lip tingled like tiny legs were crawling over it. Bot-knitters closing the cut. He wiped my face roughly after a couple minutes and I saw the minuscule dead bots speckled on the cloth like ashes. For some reason my stomach lurched and I felt the blood drain from my face. I took several deep breaths. Mercurio gazed at me until I got over it, then he finally injetted the painkiller. Welcome relief, though Madi stared and some of the other patients in the room stared all through it, recognizing me for a stranger.

"Put him to lie down," Mercurio said to Madison. He wasn't going to do anything about the bruises on the rest of my body. Maybe that was on the captain's orders. And to me, with a detached kind of concern: "Give the ribs a rest. The painkiller has a healing agent as well; it's best if you're stationary."

I wanted to tell him that was up to the jets who'd stomped on me, but one of them stood beside me. The doctor walked off and a medic came up to fix the tray of tools. I slid down, pressing gingerly at my side, and walked where Madison directed. Quite suddenly I wanted to sleep. Maybe they'd let me in the brig. At this point I didn't care where.

"You're a quiet one, ain't you," Madi commented as we walked. "Or is it because you're plotting?"

"Take your pick."

He laughed. He took me down a couple levels, to a part of the ship that seemed completely removed from any other area. Unmarked hatches lined the blank corridors. It was so quiet I couldn't hear anything but the silence itself. With the ship in dock, not even the drives hummed. This was so deep

in the innards you could probably yell all you wanted and
nobody would know. Which was the point.

Madison directed me through a triple reinforced hatch.
The brig bulkheads were scarred from laser bolts and the
temperature decidedly lower than where we'd just been. Ten
cells stood in an L shape around one half of the room, each
large enough to hold about twenty men standing, though
there were only two sets of bunks in each. On the right was
the security station console, presently unattended. Madi put
me in the nearest cell to the hatch. The lock beeped when he
shut the gate.

"Enjoy," he said, cut the lights, and walked out.

X.

I sat in the dark, unmoving.

Sometime later I realized my head was nodding, so I lay
back on a lower bunk, under the blankets where it was
warmer. The black bled into my sight until it filled my head.
The only light came from the tiny red glow on the lock. I
shut my eyes because it made no difference. No matter
where I looked I saw Falcone.

The dark was his ship, where ten of us had sat huddled,
where I'd wormed into the protection of Evan's arm. I tried
to remember their names but only recalled Evan and Adalia
and Tammy. The dull pain from my ribs numbed my
thoughts. The painkiller made things bleed together. Or inconstant memory made traitors of survivors. Where were
they now? Probably dead.

Niko was a dream. Maybe I'd dreamed it all on that
planet, with the sea and the trees and the strange, deadly
creatures with white faces and black eyes. Niko was a cruel

dream, the kind that made you want to stay forever, made your reality even worse when you awoke. I wanted to doubt that he'd cared anything for me. He'd put me here, this far away and in this kind of specific danger that he must have known would be just like after *Mukudori* had died.

But I couldn't doubt him. Instead like a masochist I ran the memories through my mind. The way he'd held me before sending me away.

The thoughts made my eyes ache, but that was all. I knew how to step out of myself.

I wanted to take out the optic receptors. I could feel them like a layer of skin over my corneas. They hadn't done a thorough security scan of my body yet. The receptors were water and silicon based. They shouldn't show up on anything but a direct intensive examination. That was what Niko said. If *Macedon*'s crew caught them on me I would be lost in this brig forever.

But maybe I was lost already and they just refused to tell me.

XI.

"Lights, one hundred."

They came up, burning through my lids. I blinked and squinted toward the brig hatch. Out of the blur materialized Erret Dorr. He came toward my gate and leaned a shoulder against it. I didn't know how long I'd slept but my eyes felt gummy and my ribs stiff and sore. The painkiller was beginning to wear off. I forced myself to sit up, slightly bent over so my head wouldn't bang the top bunk. All my muscles and bruises protested any sort of movement. I raised my eyes to meet Dorr's, felt them water to combat the dryness.

The cold air in the brig sucked moisture. I wrapped the blanket around my shoulders.

He studied me silently, dressed in uniform. Black from neck to boots, battle dress, and a holstered sidearm, with corporal stripes on his arms above a fierce lion insignia shield. He looked like a lion himself, hair untied, long loose waves just past his shoulders, pale and bright. Everything about him put me ill at ease. I couldn't stop thinking of Evan when I looked at him, and Evan was dead.

And Dorr had beat me down on station. I didn't forget that.

He let the silence carry for quite a few minutes, then laughed that devil's laugh, despite the angel's face.

"You don't speak, do you? Everyone else who gets in this brig either swears to the solitary stars or pleads like a man with a monster hard-on."

I had nothing to say to that.

"How're the ribs?"

A direct question. His eyes, despite the mockery, were laser-pointed.

"Fine."

"Did Merc work his voodoo on you?"

I shrugged and studied him. He seemed unperturbed.

"Witch doctor Mercurio. He worse than us jets."

He talked like a tunnel rat with a deceptive, lilting accent, but nothing was said casually.

"You a cute fem." His dimples showed deep.

I was glad of the gate between us. "What do you mean 'fem'?" It was an insult, of course, and I had my suspicions.

He surprised me by answering straight. "The acronym. FFM. Fresh fuckin' meat. Fem." He smiled. "Femme."

"Spell "acronym," Dorr."

He laughed and looked at me twice. "Musey. Muse. You're past cute and on to entertaining."

"I'm more entertaining with a gun."

"A brain. Whoa mano."

"Where're the rest of you—raping and pillaging?"

"Nothin' to pillage on this damn station." Big grin.

I wished I'd kept my mouth shut.

"So you grew up on Austro, did you?" he continued.

Sent by Azarcon, I was sure of it. "Yeah."

"What was it like? I mean, after a ship."

I shrugged. "I was young on my ship."

"Austro is big. It can swallow even *Mac*."

"Stations are just big ships that don't move."

He found this extremely funny. He said, "And planets are big stations with oceans and mountains?"

I was surprised he knew those words. Most crews, and jets especially, were very shipcentric.

"Yeah."

He loved that thought. He leaned his cheek on the bars and kept grinning at me. I thought then that he wasn't much older than me, that maybe he really was his apparent age. "You ever been on a planet?" he asked.

"No. You?"

"Nah. Wouldn't know what to do with it." He shifted and put his hands in his pockets, then removed them again, as if he had too much energy. Maybe he was on something. "I ain't ever bin farther insystem than Basquenal."

I wondered if he was going to open the gate and come in here to finish what he'd started on station.

"You fight pretty good," he said, finally to the point.

"Had to."

"You expected to actually beat us?"

"Give you a challenge."

"Why?"

"Wasn't that the point?"

"Nah." He smiled again. "Point was for Cap to see if you worth the thought. Know what you shoulda done different?"

"Not run through the shop."

"But we had a clear line of sight on the concourse."

We. Jets. Even though he hadn't been there at the beginning. They all thought the same. "I could've went into the maintenance tunnels. There was an access point near the levs. Do jets know those tunnels?"

The smile broadened. "Probably not as good as someone who's lived in 'em."

"So do I get another chance or am I stuck here forever?" I was only half joking. A couple hours was enough.

"You ain't stuck. You one foot in the door. Now it's up to you not to get it cut off." The brig hatch opened behind Dorr and Captain Azarcon strode in. Dorr didn't turn, but continued to smile at me. "You should know now, Musey . . . there ain't second chances on this ship. *Mac is* the second chance."

"Corporal," Azarcon said. He could've been any jet, in that black uniform and with that young face. But he wasn't. Erret Dorr's back straightened slightly, as if by habit.

"Sir." Dorr nodded to Azarcon, shot a last, mocking glance at me, and left.

Azarcon stood on Dorr's spot and looked in at me. "Cold?"

"Yes, sir." And not all from the temperature.

"I want you to know this isn't necessarily regular procedure," he said. "I only brig the suspicious ones. The ones that have pirates in their pasts."

I kept my breaths regular, watching him and the shadows that cut his face with black bars. I couldn't say anything to that. Anything I said would only make it worse.

He watched my reaction. "So tell me again why you want on my ship."

"I have nothing on station, sir. I've always wanted back on a ship."

"This isn't any ship. This is a deep-space military vessel. And worse yet for you, it's *Macedon*. I'm the god of *Macedon*. I have no qualms about dumping people into the stars if they get on my nerves."

They must have trained arrogance in their academy.

"Yes, sir. But I don't want just any ship, sir." That was truth enough.

"What kind of ship do you want, Joslyn Musey?"

"A fair ship, sir."

"You think you'll find it here?"

"Yes, sir."

"Why do you think you'll find it here?"

"Your jets. In the war. They make a difference, sir. And you command them."

"Musey, the only difference you'll be making for a year is getting my decks clean and my crew fed. Is that going to satisfy your ideals?"

"My ideals are low enough, sir."

He stared at me, long and hard and with undisguised hostility.

"This ship isn't fair, Musey. What goes on is dependent on my moods and my rules. You think that's fair?"

"I know the military isn't a democracy, sir."

"That's a pretty line. I expect that from someone who doesn't know a deep spacer from a damp rag."

I stayed silent. He wanted me to trip over my words, reveal something. His whole demeanor hunted it.

"I know as much of your past that has been recorded anywhere, Mr. Musey. I've talked to your instructors and your caseworker, all of whom just have glowing things to say about you. I'm not so easily impressed. Or gullible. I don't put up with criminals unless they follow orders. You try anything against my ship or my crew and I'll vent you so fast you'll fly to Earth. Copy that?"

I was supposed to gather intelligence on this man and his ship and send it to Niko. He was a pirate in a uniform.

"I copy, sir."

"You still want on?"

My heart gave a slow, painful beat. "Yes, sir."

"Our contracts are for five years minimum, no questions and no exceptions unless you look at me wrong and I toss you off."

"Yes, sir."

"The training and rules manual will be memorized and you will have to repeat any section on demand of any crewmember on this ship, at any time on or off shift. That's how well you will know my rules. You will have no excuses if you break them."

"Yes, sir."

"Recruit training is eight weeks you will never get back. You still want on this ship?"

"Yes, sir." I kept my real answer off my face.

"If there's anything more in your past that you think you've gotten away with, know now that you won't get away with it. Once you sign the contract your loyalties will go to me and my ship, to EarthHub Armed Forces, and to the citizens of EarthHub. In that order. I'm the omnipotent presence in your life now, Musey, and I know my crew. I will know you down to your sleeping habits. You still want on this ship?"

"Yes, sir."

"It'll get worse before it gets better, and then it will be worse." He passed a slate through the bars with a pen attached. "Can you write your name?"

"Yes, sir."

"Then do it."

I wanted to read the contract. As if I had a choice. But he had a manner much like Falcone and I couldn't help it. He saw me hesitate that split second.

"There's nothing in there that I haven't already encapsulated."

I signed my name.

In a few seconds the brig hatch opened, as if on cue, and Madi came in. Not smiling this time.

Azarcon took the slate I offered back. "Private Madison will take you to quarters. RT begins next shift at oh five hundred hours."

"Thank you, sir."

Azarcon turned away, abrupt as a striv. He didn't look back. "Don't thank me, Musey. Wait and see if you're alive in five years."

XII.

So I already knew some things about Captain Cairo Azarcon. He really did take a personal interest in the hiring of his crew, pretty much eliminating the middle men. I was surprised at the amount of contact I'd had with him up to now. If I'd pushed I might have been able to elicit some comments from chatty Madison, but since everything I said probably took a direct route to Azarcon's ears, I held off. I wondered why the captain signed me on so readily, especially since he'd acted so suspicious earlier. He'd seemed unduly interested in my connection to Falcone. I almost wished I could ask him outright what he knew about *Genghis Khan*.

Out of the question, of course.

It was going to be a sparse report to Niko but that didn't matter, since I had no access to a comp yet.

I had eight hours of rest before Recruit Training and I knew I'd need it. Madi walked me back through the narrow, drab corridors. A few jets looked at us as we passed but didn't say anything. We squeezed around other uniforms cleaning the deck or working at the maintenance grates or pipes overhead. The ones scrubbing didn't look happy.

"Punishment," Madison pointed out.

I got it.

He took me to the training deck, which was marked by a small sticker on the hatch that said: SPRIGS WITHIN. WATER DAILY. He put me in quarters, a gray closet of a space packed with six bunks, three at a height with one narrow aisle down the middle. Storage was webbing on the bulkhead beside each bunk. My duffel bag was sitting on the floor when I entered, along with five others. Madi unhooked a scanwand from his hip and made me stand in the center of the quarters while he ran it up and down my body, slow and thorough, checking for tech. He passed the wand over my face and hair as I held my breath. It didn't beep a warning and he grinned at me.

"There's a guard on the door and if he says to jump your only reply should be 'out which airlock.' Got it?"

"Yes, sir." I looked at him with no cheery pretenses.

He laughed and left. I took the lowermost right-hand rack, stowed what little belongings I had, and immediately pocketed a small bottle of salve from my personal kit. I knocked on the hatch and met the jet on guard.

"Where's the head?"

He escorted me down the corridor to the communal washroom and stood outside the door. At the long stainless-steel bank of sinks I waved on one of the taps and cleaned out the salve. I filled the bottle with water, took out the optic receptors, and dropped them in. My eyes felt sore, so I blinked a few times and peered at them in the mirror. They were a little bloodshot.

The jet walked me back to quarters, where another jet now stood at the hatch. She opened it and I passed her, wanting to just fall straight into bed. But my five other roommates had materialized inside. I stopped dead as the hatch shut behind me with a thud and a click.

Three other boys and two girls, looking only a couple years older than me. They eyed me warily, standing as aloof as they could in such a cramped space—except for one boy who'd already appropriated a top bunk. Dark blue battle dress utilities had also appeared on each bunk, along with standard-issue magnum boots and underwear. I moved to my rack. One of the boys stood in my way, not for any other reason than the close quarters. He was brown-haired and smooth-faced, and had the oddest gold-brown eyes I'd ever seen. Maybe they were gene-tampered.

"Kris Rilke," he said casually, with a slight smile.

I really needed to sit but he didn't move. "Jos Musey."

He nodded. The others seemed to take a cue, and introduced themselves. Nathan Jelilian was on the topmost bunk already, smoking a cigret without asking anybody's by your leave, one arm behind his unnaturally blond head. The last boy in the group, skinny and dark-skinned, took the opposite bunk to mine across the aisle and mumbled his name; I only caught "Cleary." One of the girls tossed her pack above him on the middle rack and stuck out her hand to me. I looked at it strangely and she smiled crookedly.

"Oh, yeah, I forgot Austroans don't shake." She took my hand and tugged a bit, releasing it before I could properly react. "Aki Wong-Merton. Aki's fine."

The other girl said shortly, "Iratxe." I heard it, *Ee-rat-chay*.

Jelilian yawned. "Now that we're all acquainted, shut off the damn lights."

I said, "You're not all from Austro."

"No," Aki said. "I'm from Kane."

That was a Spokes colony on the Earthward side of the Rim, a couple leaps from Austro.

Kris Rilke tugged off his sweater and tossed it at the foot of his bunk before swinging up and in. "I'm Austroan, same as you. What module did you belong to?"

"The orphanage."

He looked at me a moment before pulling the blanket over his chest. "Ah."

Jelilian said, "Can we do this show at another time? I need my beauty sleep."

"Won't do you any good," Iratxe said.

"Maybe not for you."

He had an accent I'd never heard; I had to pay attention to understand him. His cigret smoke made my head hurt but I was in no mood to argue with him. I sat on my bunk, hunched over because the one above wasn't high enough that I could sit under it. Resigned, I tilted over onto the pillow, ribs aching worse now that I was forced to pay attention to them.

"They work you over?" Rilke asked. He hadn't taken his eyes from me since I'd entered.

"Yeah. You?"

"A little. When they finally caught me I didn't fight. I've seen gauntlet runs before. If you fight they just kick you worse."

"And you lot wanna join those jets." Jelilian snorted.

"I didn't see any of you before now," I said.

"They kept us in rec," Aki said.

That must've been where the nonsuspicious ones went.

"Lights, zero," Cleary said, and the quarters went abruptly dark.

Now we were disembodied voices in a room full of quiet anxiety.

"Aren't you going to be a jet?" I asked Nathan Jelilian.

"No way. I'm a pilot. I'm already a pilot. This is just a transfer for me."

"But you're still going through RT."

"*Macedon* rules. Everybody's fem no matter what unit you're lookin' to get into or where you been before."

Aki laughed. "We don't wanna know where you been, Lilypad."

"Come yin me yang, Aki-bird. Oh, yeah, right here."

I shut my eyes and blocked out the banter. Their scents filled the small quarters: Jelilian's cigret, someone else's soap or shampoo, day-old clothes, and the lingering spice of another's long-eaten lunch, the smell attached to their skin. From above me came regular breathing, then the silence of bodies settling into oblivion. Even though I couldn't hear all of them breathing I felt they were all asleep.

The sleep of the innocent.

Bunkmates, like I would've had on *Mukudori* when I was old enough to move out of my parents' quarters. Some part of me remembered the smells of these corridors, the sound of the levs when we rode from deck to deck . . . small differences from my homeship, maybe, but not enough to be totally foreign. Human voices everywhere I went, young males and females, harmless insults and peacocking. The rituals of the pack that I'd found so fascinating from an eight-year-old's point of view, an eight-year-old who liked to trail after Evan, his brother Shane, and all their friends. I used to run up and down the corridors trying to catch up. Evan gave me piggyback rides sometimes, or chased me with toy guns and monster masks.

All the little scenes surfaced like dead fish, bobbing just below the touch of daylight.

But daylight didn't exist on deep-space carriers.

XIII.

Reveille sounded at exactly 0500 hours, an incessant staccato buzzing. Then the hatch whipped open and a loud man came in.

"On your feet, children!"

He blew in like a storm wind, immaculately clad in a buttoned-up black BDU with a white T-shirt peeking from under the collar. I tried to roll out of bed, wincing at my bruised, protesting body, and felt a foot brush my shoulder before Nathan Jelilian landed right on the spot I was looking to appropriate in the cramped quarters. I unfolded out beside him, with Iratxe dropping down on my right. Across the narrow aisle, Kris Rilke, Cleary, and Aki Wong-Merton blearily, but hastily, mirrored us.

"Hit the showers!" the man barked, as if we were all deaf. "What're you waiting for? Take your gear and be back here in five!"

We grabbed our gear issue, which most of us had left at the foot of our bunks, and double-timed it. The jet on guard at our hatch escorted us to the facilities. I set my uni, boots, and kit on the bench outside one of the shower stalls and began to strip down. No time to be shy. Everyone else was doing the same, the five from my q as well as others I didn't recognize, who had run in after us from other quarters, I assumed. The shower wasn't much more than a quick turn under the time-released water, a brief soap, and a blast of hot air from the body dryer before we hopped on our dark blue training unis and boots and bolted out of there. Nobody said a word, though I thought of a few very specific ones—in more than one language.

The jet took us back to our quarters where we saw the man handing over all the personal gear we'd brought on board to another jet. She left before we could say anything.

My gut writhed. There went my optic receptors. Who knew if I'd ever get them back. Or if they'd remain undiscovered.

And they had better not "misplace" the ID disk with my parents' image.

The man in the immaculate uniform brushed past us.

"Fall in, recruits!" His voice echoed up and down the corridor in a commanding tone I had not even heard from Captain Azarcon. Other small groups of young men and women lined up as we did, rushing out of other hatches, backs to the bulkhead and eyes forward. At a glance I counted about a hundred of us. Looked like *Macedon* had actively recruited at ports on their way in from deep space.

More jets spilled out of hatches and followed the one who'd taken our gear, disappearing into a caution-striped lev at the end of the corridor.

The man glanced over us, then turned his back. "Two columns, follow me." He started to walk briskly.

We fell in. The recruits on one side of the corridor made their own column to parallel ours. Armed jets flanked the man ahead of us and brought up the rear. Not one of us would ever go unsupervised on this ship, I realized, until we'd completed the training. And perhaps not even then, if we had probation. My days of any semblance of privacy were over, at least for eight weeks.

The sick feeling in my stomach didn't go away.

Our leader marched us up deeply inclined, perforated towersteps, not on the levs, and through a maze of straight

gray corridors, some of which had familiar grub-clad crew
scrubbing and polishing the scored deck and bulkheads. I
tried to memorize where we were going but after ten minutes of walking the route became hazy. Pain lanced from my
midsection to the back of my teeth. I needed another injet of
painkiller. I hoped I'd get some before we began exercises.

Finally we landed up outside the mess. Our leader
stepped aside just within the doors and barked at us again.

"Fifteen mikes, move!"

In a rushed, somewhat orderly line we went to the serving counter, grabbed trays, and shuffled by while the cooks
dumped our breakfast as we passed. I had little appetite
through the pain, despite the fact I couldn't remember the
last time I had eaten anything.

"Better chow down," Kris Rilke muttered as we took our
seats at the benches of the free tables. Crew at the other
tables laughed at us. "We're gonna need it."

Bullying jets. I thought of the knife in my hand and what
I could do with it.

I shoveled in the food, barely chewing, and looked
around from under my brows. The recruits took up five
tables at the door end of the mess, while in the rest of the
wide room other crew sat scattered, talking, laughing, and
occasionally shoving one another playfully. The mess, like
everywhere else on the ship, looked well used but was surprisingly spotless, free of dirt. The walls were uniformly
gray and bare, except for gunmetal trim near the ceiling. The
ceiling itself wasn't very high. It was covered and smooth
except for the banks of white lights.

"Heaven won't help you now," Iratxe said, following my
gaze.

"Only gods we got for eight weeks're our JIs," Nathan
Jelilian said around a mouthful of square eggs. It made him
doubly hard to understand.

"JI?" Aki asked.

"Jet Instructors. Junior and Senior. Hard-ass over there's Junior. Wait 'til you meet our Senior Jet Instructor."

Aki gulped her caff. "Oh, joy."

"Can't be worse than the captain," I muttered.

"You met the captain?" Aki asked incredulously. Their eyes fixed on me.

I shifted. "Didn't you?"

"I met *el capitan*," Jelilian said, as if he were proud of it.

"I didn't," Aki said. "Just that Sergeant Hartman. She told me I'd meet him after I graduated . . . if I graduated. How come you got to meet him?" To me.

"I don't know." My stomach rolled uneasily.

"Maybe he likes only the boys," Iratxe said, showing teeth.

Jelilian looked at her, serious. "I'd keep a lid on that if I were you, birdy. Nobody talks about Azarcon that way."

"Least not on this ship," Kris put in.

"Is it true?" Dread sat hard in my chest.

Jelilian turned his pale brown eyes to me. "No way, you think some of these jets would stay aboard?" He leaned in toward us as if spilling a dark secret. "My old CO said Azarcon's an orphan of the stars himself, he knows all about kids on the wayside of things. Born deep spacer. Admiral Ashrafi adopted him after *Trinity* did her deep-space run. Ashrafi came back with a teenage Cap and the next thing you know he's in the NSC Academy on Earth." The pilot laughed. "And Hubcentral's been rollin' its eyes ever since."

Ashrafi, who was now in the EHJCS, and Niko wanted to know more about him.

"Why'd Ashrafi adopt him? What happened to his family?"

Jelilian shrugged. "Who knows?"

Aki smiled. "Brass are cloned, not born, don't you know?"

"Is that why you want a transfer?" I asked Jelilian. "Azarcon's okay with orphans?"

"I wanna fly for this bad beast 'cause they know how to brand some enemy ass." He grinned and made a sizzle sound.

"Less talk, more eating," Cleary said, eyes darting.

"Recruits, fall in!"

I was beginning to hate that man's voice, though the others besides Jelilian looked borderline scared of it. Nathan Jelilian seemed to know more than the average recruit, off some other EarthHub ship probably. A good source of info.

We stacked our trays and lined up again, all under the impatient eye of the JJI, then followed him out, back down a stairwell and through the cool, drab corridors once more. I longed to see some color in the gray, but the only variety was in the hair, skin, and eyes of the other recruits. Our booted steps echoed on the scuffed deckplates, not quite in unison. The JJI took us through a double set of doors marked TRAINING BAY, into a sprawling room with multiple exits leading elsewhere; no signs indicated anything, like everywhere else on this ship.

The room was occupied by long desks, deck-clamped metal chairs, a drop-down holoarm over a central table, and rows of comps stacked on a shelf against the wall, secured by black webbing.

"Sit," the JJI said.

I gratefully sank down on the nearest seat. Chairs unclicked from their clamps and scraped as everyone found a place, the only sound. Our armed escorts took up positions by the doors and the JJI stood with his hands behind his back at the front of the room, behind the raised and folded holoarm.

"Momentarily you are going to meet your other Jet Instructors and your Training Platoon COs. You will stand and salute when they enter. I'm Sergeant Theron and I will be one of the people responsible for your lives during this training." And responsible for taking our lives too if we stepped out of line—that was the implicit threat. He turned a bit, perfectly on cue as one of the side doors opened and the three other JIs and Training Platoon Officers entered. We all stood and saluted like perfect soljets, then sat when one of the TPOs nodded. The apprehension in the room was thick enough to smell.

The two Senior JIs wore all over black, even their T-shirts, and close-fitting black caps with long brims that shadowed their eyes. They were all mouth and jaw, a man and a woman. When they tilted their heads to regard the training platoon the light cut into that shadow and glanced off their eyes like sun on shrapnel. The other JJI was clad like his counterpart; the only things that differentiated him from the SJIs were his white tee and bare head. The TPOs were dressed like jets but not as casually turned out as Madi or Dorr or the others I'd seen. They were ironed so cleanly I thought their unis might crack if they moved.

The female Senior Jet Instructor walked the width of the Training Bay and looked out over all of us, then stopped dead center, hands behind her back. Her words came at us like rifle report with just the same deadly tone of command.

"This shift will be your last easy shift for the rest of your lives aboard *Macedon*—however long that will be in this war. Nine hours or more ago you signed your futures over to the toughest ship in all of EarthHub, with the toughest crew. We have the highest expectations. Some of you won't make it. Some of you *will* make it only to die by the hand of the enemy."

I thought of Niko. He hung at the corners of my mind like light around the edges of a curtained window.

"Over the next eight weeks it is my job and the job of my comrades to make sure you are as prepared as you can be for what you'll face in this war against the strits and their symp allies. Because I guarantee you now, you will face them.

"The men and women around you are your company, your crew, the equals of your own lives. This is not a competition; there are no prize winners. If you live that is your reward; when you help others to live, that is your duty. Nobody here will tolerate any degree of hotdogging, bravado that leads to careless execution of tasks, or hazing among yourselves. Be assured we hold enough authorization to boot your asses out of this bay and, if necessary, out the airlock.

"It's your duty to convince us that you're worthy to take up space on our deck. Because right now, as I look out at your pitiful faces, you aren't worth the ammo it would take to clean you from this room. Fodder for the strits, maybe, but not *Macedon* crew. A nod from our recruiter or the captain himself is not a ticket onto *Mac*. It's limited cred. It's bought time—time that will run out."

She paused. But it wasn't the end. It was far from the end of this new world.

XIV.

Senior Jet Instructor Laceste had told the truth about the shift being our easiest—and probably about everything else. After our introductions and the orientation speeches that were basically designed to alternately intimidate us and spur us on, half of us were directed to medbay for full physicals while the other half stayed in the Training Bay to write psych and aptitude tests. The JIs and jets also separated with the company; the Training Platoon Officers disappeared back to their holes, I assumed, because they didn't hang about. I wondered that we hadn't been introduced to our company commander, then figured that was probably a good thing. My bunkmates and I and the rest of our loose platoon headed to medical. I wasn't looking forward to Mercurio's presence but I wanted his treatment. Kris edged up behind me in our march.

"You okay?"

"Yeah." I thought I'd been hiding my pain.

Nathan glanced back and whispered, "Ah, perk up, mate. After the prodding we get our heads shrunk!"

"About face, Jelilian!"

In medbay it wasn't Mercurio who looked after me, but a whip of a kid corpsman named Rodriguez. He rolled his chair over to where I sat on one of the examination tables. The edges of a dark tattoo crawled along his neck beneath his pale gray uniform collar. He also had a snake on the back of his right hand and splayed wings on the back of his left. I stared at the intricate work. It almost rivaled a striviirc-na rank tat.

He scanned me with the handheld, the same way Mercurio had done earlier.

"You like?" he asked, following my gaze. He had an open smile and prepped an injet casually. "My own handiwork, y'know."

"Yeah?"

"Yah. If you pass the trainin' I do your wrist." He injetted my arm. "That'll do ya, at least for the pain. It's hurtin' this bad 'cause the healants are workin', anit? Give it an hour more and all the bruises should be gone. Magic." He grinned again.

"Hardly," I said.

"We do you up good so you go back out and get more hurts. That the circle of life, anit?" He laughed.

I imitated his accent. "Anit." The cultures of the galaxy had converged on this ship. Voices flowed around the room like air currents. They spoke the standard language with all the variation of their childhood homes. I hadn't expected that, but it was familiar now, another memory brought to light. The accents were almost musical, though not as pretty as the ones I used to eavesdrop upon, lying on a sun-drenched roof above lower balconies.

Rodriguez liked my imitation of his accent; he laughed and patted my shoulder. It almost made me like him. But then he proceeded to draw my blood and run me through a gamut of tests that left me sore in a number of uncomfortable places. A benign full body scan wasn't enough, evidently.

At least now my ribs were numb. The JIs took us back to the Training Bay and we exchanged places with the other half of the company. The comps stayed activated but on a cleared screen; they were well-used, slightly dented, limited-access comps. Nothing that could reach *Macedon*'s main systems ops.

"Answer all questions," Senior Jet Instructor Schmitt said. Every word out of his mouth was a dictatorial statement, like the other JIs. Most everyone seemed cowed by his tone, like they were at Laceste's, but I was only irritated. Loyalty and willing obedience didn't come through intimidation.

But these were Hub humans.

I scrolled, perusing the questions first. The beginning had standard fill-in-the-blanks: name, gender, birthday, birthplace, etc. Then it went to the typical essay questions: why do you want to serve *Macedon*; what do you think you can contribute to *Macedon* . . . banalities I could tap out with half a brain. The middle sections were basic mathematics and physics questions and some elementary tactical and strategic scenarios. As I scrolled more, the bottom sections grew intense. The psych section asked very pointed questions about your past, your reactions to incidents in your past, your feelings. I dawdled over those. Clearly you could still wash out even at this stage, contract already signed and all. If I told too much, would they think it worth exploring or just file it in records? If I didn't tell enough they might think it suspicious. Certainly they would compare it to what they had already dug up before even letting me on ship.

I stuck to what Niko had briefed me on, just reworded with less professionalism. Pirate attack survivor. Time with Falcone. A little bit about what he'd done with me and then my rescue on Chaos and youth on Austro. Nothing that contradicted anything, fairly open but not too much, in case they thought it too line by line.

I hoped it appeased the captain's eyes. I had a feeling he'd be looking at these personally—or at least at mine.

I saved it all and closed the comp, as I saw others who had finished do. When I glanced to my right I caught Kris Rilke's gaze; he stared at me from the end of the table.

Keeping my face carefully bland, I stared back. After a moment he returned to tapping at his comp.

Had I given him something to be suspicious about, or was he just the curious type? I wanted desperately to go somewhere and be by myself.

The other half of the company filed in some minutes later and found seats, guarded by jets. The SJIs walked about, warning the slow typers they had only a minute more to complete the forms. Then the Junior Instructors gathered up the comps and stacked them on a side table. I started to feel hungry.

SJI Laceste yelled at us again: "Over the rest of this shift you each will be meeting with myself or SJI Schmitt for a personal interview. In the meantime, those remaining will familiarize themselves with the standard LP-150 rifle."

As she spoke, jets came in through one of the unmarked doors carrying the rifles and began placing one in front of each of us on the tables. They weren't loaded—of course. They were missing their pulse charge clips entirely.

"You will be divided into four squads. Alpha Squad here—" She indicated a table. "Bravo here. Training Platoon One. Charlie and Delta there. Training Platoon Two. Take your rifles."

As she read out our names we moved with scrutinized haste. They watched how we carried our weapons, how quickly we got to our places, the expressions on our faces. Me and my five bunkmates made up one-third of Bravo. Then Laceste read out the names of the first two poor souls who had to sit through an interview with her or Schmitt. The victims went into a side room while JJI Theron took up a rifle and stood in Laceste's place.

He showed us how to strip and assemble the rifle and named all the parts. He talked about how it was going to save our lives and how it would kill strits. He said we were going to kill the enemy with this weapon. Strits. Symps. The enemy.

Pirates, I thought at him. You and the *Khan*.

XV.

I pretended I didn't know how any of the guns worked. Mostly they concentrated on the LP-150, which was the basic weapon of all the crew, but especially all the jets. We didn't get to keep any of the weapons except the rifles. They gave us charge clips, but not real ones—sim ones that looked and weighed exactly like the real ones but could be used in the shooting galleries on soft targets (hard targets were for live fire sims). They made us strip and assemble the rifles over and over. I kept pace with the other recruits, even though I could do it with my eyes shut and in under a minute.

The JIs took squads of us out at a time to practice shooting while the others started PT, or physical training, as they called it. I called it running. Bravo Squad went to the range first. The targets were all striviirc-na or symps. You knew they were striviirc-na because they were all white with black eyes and bared little teeth. The tattoos were muddled, the same on the symps. The symps were all ugly, frowning humans. First we practiced with standing holotargets that registered points depending on where you hit the body. The highest points were on all the killzones. Head, heart, neck.

Theron came up to my shoulder. "You trying to read their minds, sprig? Let me assure you, these ones don't think."

I almost glared at him, but stopped myself.

"Well what're you waiting for? There's an enemy in your sight!"

I braced the rifle, aimed, and fired. The shoulder of the striv registered a hit.

"Winged him. He can still come after you."

I pictured Theron's face on that target and shot him through the head.

"Good." He tapped the console in front of me and reset the holo. "Now do it again when it's moving."

No different from what Enas-dan made me do. The targets were fake, it was a game. You just went for the high score.

Except one day it was going to be real.

"Dammit, boy, fire!"

The gallery exploded with sound and harmless, bright pulse flash.

XVI.

"Musey! Rilke!"

I set my gun down on the console, stepped back, and briefly met Kris Rilke's eyes before heading toward the JI who stood by the shooting gallery entrance. The sound of guns and rifles going off was near deafening. Flash from the muzzles lit and went out like lightning up and down the line of recruits. Safe pulses at simulated targets. Theron walked up and down behind the recruits, barking orders or advice. Kris and I followed Junior Jet Instructor Carson back to the Training Bay where he pointed us toward seats to wait.

"You're good," Kris said, "with the weapons."

I couldn't tell if it was admiration or suspicion in his tone.

"Thanks." I hadn't noticed how he'd fared on the range.

"So you grew up on Austro?"

"Yeah." I dug my thumbnail into the brown tabletop where something had already scratched.

"So did I. I was born there."

"Oh." I felt his eyes on me. Was my accent off, did he see through me? "So what do you think about the others? Jelilian, Aki . . ."

"They seem pretty okay. Jelilian might get us into trouble later, though." He smiled.

"Yeah, what's his story? Where's he transferring from?"

"Not sure. He said he flew for a replenishment ship. Now he wants to fly APC. Fly jets around."

"I don't know if I'd trust him to fly me around," I said.

"Apparently he's good to even be considered for *Mac*. Aki's heading into Support Services . . . Medical. Iratxe's soljet like us—I assume you're going for jet status."

"Yeah. What about Cleary?"

"Hell if I know. You heard a word outta him yet?" He laughed.

"No. True."

A door on our right opened and Schmitt stepped out. "Gentlemen."

We stood and I let Kris go first. We entered a short hallway with four doors facing each other, two on each side. Schmitt took Kris into one on the right hand and SJI Laceste stood at a leftward one.

"Recruit Musey, come in and have a seat."

"Yes, sir." I told myself I'd spoken with the Caste Master; this woman was nothing to be nervous about. I sat in an office, smaller than the captain's but just as neat, spare, and square. The sameness of things could drive a person mad, even a merchant kid. Military ships were far more uniform than where I'd been born, and worse because they weren't built with comfort first in mind. I supposed it was just a matter of getting used to it.

A comp lay open facing Laceste as she sat across the desk from me. The room had that ever-present cold metal scent of recycled air. I tried not to be too obvious about looking around.

"Musey, you seem to handle firearms quite well."

"I've had some experience, sir. Plus, I've been told, a certain affinity." Enas-dan had thought so.

"Yes." Laceste clasped her hands on the desk and looked at me, not with hostility, but pure professionalism. Completely unreadable. "Once in a while we are fortunate to obtain that recruit who seems made to be a jet."

I decided I wasn't going to say anything unless

prompted. The more I opened my mouth, the more opportunity they would have to grill me.

"Aside from your firearms ability, you're also an instinctive fighter. I suppose as an orphan you had reason to be."

"Yes, sir, you can say that."

"How did they treat you on Austro?"

These officers lulled you into a false sense of security then struck. I hadn't expected anything else.

" 'They,' sir?"

"The officials. The station itself. How was it, as a place to grow up? Especially for a shipborn youth like you are."

Unwavering eyes. Had I not been used to such stares I would have faltered. Her voice was not particularly aggressive but I had no doubts about the uniform she wore and the man who ultimately commanded her.

"Austro is big and they have good programs, good people. A lot of opportunities, even for orphans or . . . poor people. They try to help you best they can, sir. It wasn't a bad place to grow up. The war doesn't really touch it."

"I'll tell you now, generally we prefer recruits with a shipboard background. They adjust easier to the life of a carrier; they understand certain rules better. Do you remember a lot from your childhood aboard *Mukudori*?"

I scratched the bridge of my nose briefly.

"Honestly, I don't remember a whole lot, sir. Images, mostly. Feelings. Flashes of things. My parents . . . I remember our quarters." I stared at the corner of her desk before I realized I was doing it and dragged my eyes up to her face. If anything the reaction would seem real. In this, I was telling the truth. But I still didn't want to give them any opportunity to run a more intensive psych eval on me.

"Well, you certainly have been through a lot for such a young man. And kept your nose relatively clean."

"Thank you, sir," I said, because something needed to be in that gap of silence.

"How're you getting along with your berthmates?"

"Nothing to complain about, sir."

"Carriers are very communal places, no different in many ways from merchant ships. Or Universalist ships. I can see that you might develop into a good leader. I'd like to help you develop that side of yourself."

I was mildly surprised. I let it show. "Thank you, sir."

"That year you were aboard *Genghis Khan*," she said finally.

"Yes, sir," I said, because she waited for a response.

"How did you cope?"

"Fine. Really. I barely remember the *Khan*."

"One would think it hard to forget."

"I was young."

"You still are," she said. "Your file says you received some counseling on Austro. I've met my share of pirates. Some of them are quite manipulative."

I wanted to shift but she'd note it. "I guess they can be."

"Didn't you find so?"

"I wasn't with them for long. I escaped." I put just enough emphasis on the last word. "I had no intention of building a long-standing relationship with them. The fact they killed my ship kind of soured my impression, sir."

And you can go to hell too.

She looked at me a long time. "Mr. Musey, I'm not asking out of idle interest. It's our duty as well as our prerogative to understand our recruits as best as possible . . . and if there are any lingering issues in their pasts that ought to be dealt with before we put guns in their hands. We have a psychiatric counselor onboard as a matter of course; many of our crew find him helpful. We also have a ship chaplain, should you prefer to speak with her. In any event, being forthright about your past is part of the training. Are we clear on that?"

I blinked halfway. "Crystal clear, sir."

"We'll talk again later, then. Dismissed."

XVII.

As an operative I was off to a rotten start. I would have thought they were just naturally concerned about my year with a pirate, except Azarcon hadn't looked on it with any degree of compassion—even though it was also clear I'd escaped. They couldn't have overlooked that fact, and still they grilled me.

The thought of another interview made my stomach increasingly upset. I didn't know how I was going to last a month on this ship, much less five years. Maybe at my first opportunity I'd ask Niko to pull me out. Maybe at our next port.

Maybe I could leave somehow, get back on Austro, if I could get past the jets.

Coward. Niko needed me here. How could I go back to the *ka'redan-na*, a failure?

I might never see Aaian-na again, if I didn't break for it.

I wasn't going to break for it. Feeling sick wasn't an excuse. Not even homesick.

"So what'd she ask?"

I glanced behind as Kris jogged up to follow me, as I followed the JI back to the shooting gallery.

Conscious of the instructor, I waved a dismissive hand. "The usual. They just want to get to know us."

"I think we're going to start PT once our platoon's done

interviewing. What'd the doc say about you, are you up to it or do you get to sit out?"

"Why are you so interested?"

He gave me a second look; I hadn't disguised my irritation.

"Just conversation, mano." He held up his arms in a casual defensive gesture. "Forget it." He strode ahead to walk abreast of the JI.

These were the people I had to work with; I could see Niko's disapproving face. *Make an effort, Jos.* At least to cast off suspicion.

Still, I didn't say anything.

Kris was right; they had us familiarize with the guns until Training Platoon One had all been through the SJI mill, then they ran us around the ship. By then my ribs were just a dull fire, as Rodriguez had promised, though my surface bruises still ached. The JIs didn't care; I would have to fight in dismal physical conditions probably more than once in my career as a jet, so it was all training.

We took a sweating tour of the training deck, then parts of jetdeck, flight deck, and maindeck. We weren't allowed anywhere near the command deck or engineering without escort. If we were sighted on those levels we'd be shot. And that applied for when we graduated as well. We were going to be on a year's probation, like I'd suspected.

"The Masochist March," SJI Schmitt called it as the squad slowed from a jog to a fast walk on our way back to the training deck. By then my PT uni was soaked with sweat. I took no more notice of the carrier's bulkheads, crew, compartments, or lack of colors. It was a narrow gray world for the most part. When the crew was on duty or on leave, it was a quiet world with the kind of steel emptiness I'd felt when I snuck out of quarters and roamed *Mukudori* on blueshifts. Sounds came from distant corridors in small echoes and when a voice came over the shipwide comm it was like a ghost's message from some netherworld.

SJI Schmitt ran the route with us, considerably less out of breath. I would have fared better if not for my injuries. I'd noticed a few others wincing, some bandaged on arms or showing scrapes on their faces. At least I hadn't been singled out on the gauntlet.

Dinner was a luxurious half hour at 1800 hours before the last segment of the day, which was bookwork in the library. It was a large room with entrances/exits from both jetdeck and training deck—the former forward and the latter aft, with the library between. We were allowed to study there, in the recruit rec center (or RRC; the military had an acronym for everything), or practice more in the shooting gallery during off-hours if we wished. We also had access to the gym but not the sim rooms—both stood between jets and recruits, same as the library. Instead of shadowing us by squad, jets stood on fire watch at the training deck's exits, the extent of our freedom of movement in off-hours.

At 2000 hours we had rec time, one hour of it before lights out. I stayed in the library because it had comps. It also had few recruits, since most of them opted to fool around in the RRC. Niko would have liked this jet training. We had to read and start memorizing the training and rules manual, not to mention *Macedon*'s service history. I found my corner away from any others.

The library had a wide central area with a tactical holo-capable table for working out mission specifics or training simulations. Black embedded comps ran the rim of the table and needed specific authorization codes to activate, which I didn't have. Scattered in intervals around the central area were individual workstations, each equipped with general comps that held files on anything from Earth's weather patterns to the latest disseminated information on the war, some lifted from the Send, others just through EHAF. The comps also had a surprising variety of literary, historical, and artistic files. A few small tables were interspersed between the workstations. Some crewmembers occupied them, talking quietly over their caffs and comps. Nobody paid me much attention.

All the comps on *Macedon* were holoaccess optional but since I didn't have my optic receptors (a nagging worry that didn't get me anywhere) I took a manual tour around the library system files, glancing frequently to make sure nobody looked over my shoulder or even in my direction. I poked into the root nodes. Unfortunately the system files were restricted to ship intranet with no connection to *Mac*'s main systems. Of course. I would need to find myself at a console—perhaps one on flight deck or the jet wardroom—that would have access to *Macedon*'s comm ops.

Which basically meant I'd be incommunicado for at least eight weeks.

The files were useful for one thing, though. I keyed in Falcone's name and did a fast search. A blurt of archive links sprang across the screen. Over a hundred under major categories. *Kali*. Battle of Ghenseti. Court-martial. Kalaallit Nunaat military prison on polar Earth.

Escape.

I poked one of those links. More names sprang up with another list of prison sentences and transcript numbers. Names with Senator, Minister, Justice, and General attached to them.

Somehow that pirate had retained his brass contacts. And they launched a covert mission to free him from the snow and ice of Earth's Northern Hemisphere. They let the bastard go.

Ongoing investigation, one of the articles said. Not all of his allies had been caught yet. And he was still free.

"I give that a ninety percent on the deviant social skills aptitude test." Aki dragged a chair over to my workstation and sat.

I blanked the screen with a fumbled pat. "What?"

Her smile faltered a bit. "Our first day and you're hiding in library instead of blowing off in the RRC."

"I'm not hiding. Did you see the pile of shit they dumped on us to study?"

She shrugged. "I'm too dead tired for my brain to work in any capacity."

She looked it. I looked back at my black screen.

"Anything interesting?" she continued.

"What?"

She laughed and gave me a look I couldn't quite decipher. "To read." She gestured to the comp and said wryly, "It sure looks engrossing."

"I was brushing up on *Macedon* history, but I'm done now."

"Yeah, she's seen a lot of action. You can tell that just from walking the corridors. Some things paint can't hide. Like this." She pointed to smudges on the comp console, then leaned an elbow on the desk. "How old are you, Musey?"

I almost asked why but figured it would be easier just to answer. "Fourteen, Austro years. How old are you?"

"Sixteen. You seem—"

"What?"

She smiled a little. "Half the time older, half the time younger."

I shrugged. "So?"

"Nothing. I'll leave you alone." She got up, set the chair back in its clamps, and headed out. I didn't stop her.

I was the second person back in quarters for lights out.

Nathan Jelilian lay on his bunk reading a *Battlemech Bear* comicprint. He peeked over the pages when I entered.

"Muse."

"Hey. Where'd you get that?" I gestured to the print. I vaguely remembered reading those adventures of the military bear in my school slate on *Mukudori*. Hardcopies of anything were hard to come by and at some cost.

"You can sign it out of library. *Mac*'s got the whole set, mano."

"Serious? Why bother?"

"'Cause jets are fiends for *Battlemech Bear*, mano." He laughed.

"No, I mean, why bother with print? They can just put it in file."

"The cap'n man has a thing for tangibles."

"Tangibles."

"Extras. Perks." The smile grew. "I tell you, if you can survive this ship, it's the sweetest deal around. Azarcon knows how to take care of his own."

"How come you know so much about him?" I leaned an elbow on the edge of his bunk. It was at a level just above my head when I stood.

"Every deep-spacer crew talks about *Mac*. If you ain't a straitlacer and wanna kick some strit butt, this is the place to be. *Angel* and *K-Jack*'re a close second."

I must have looked blank.

"*Archangel* and *Wesakechak*." He laughed. "Mano, you ain't exactly on the up, are you?"

"Your accent confuses me."

"Most find it charming." He grinned. It reminded me of Dorr.

I sat on the bunk, two below Jelilian, pulled off my shirt, and stowed it in my webbing. I lay back in my tank, arms behind my head.

"So tell me about Azarcon," I said to the bottom of the bunk above me. Jelilian gossiped about anything at the least provocation.

"He's a mean mister to cross. I heard he put antagonistic crew off on desolate stations. He gets that corpsman Rodriguez to remove the tat, then he sets you right on station and bye-bye. That's if he don't put you in brig first and forget you're there. But that don't happen a lot with his handpicks. Mostly prisoners. Pirates and symps. Strits when he gets 'em."

"The crew seems loyal."

"It's different from an insystemer. Deep spacers're their own little cities, pretty damn self-sufficient. They gotta be, kinda. The crew knows that. *Mac* grows some of its own food, mano. Azarcon got his own bioengineering team aboard. I swear it pays to have a daddy in the Joint Chiefs."

I certainly hadn't read that, about the food. "The military justifies that cost?"

"Ah, they can boo all they want. When it comes down to it they got no real control of what the deep spacers do out here. Most captains, if not all of 'em, invest in stock on the side, let the crew take shares, and the creds they earn get used to personalize their ships—if you know what I mean."

It made me curious about the parts of the ship we weren't allowed to see.

"Does he have anything . . . specific . . . against pirates?"

Jelilian laughed. "Who don't out here? Those bastards're the lice in the hair of the Hub."

The hatch opened and Aki, Kris, Iratxe, and Cleary shuffled in. Aki and Kris talked lively. Iratxe looked like she'd just had a workout. She grabbed some clean clothes from her bunk and disappeared back out again. Cleary didn't say anything, just dived into his rack facedown and covered up, boots and all.

"Battlemech Bear," Kris said and leaned on Jelilian's bunk. "That the latest issue?"

"Yah, and it's mine. Keep your grubby paws off."

They wrangled verbally. I had to save my questions for later. Aki peered down at me as she undressed, maybe to check if I was asleep. I turned my face to the bulkhead. I might have heard her laugh.

"Put away the bear and cut the lights," she told Nathan.

Jelilian mumbled but eventually ordered the lights out. I lay in the dark listening to them settle. Soon Iratxe hustled in and bumped her way to the bunk above me, climbed up and in. Footsteps sounded outside in the corridor seconds later, loud enough to be heard through the hatch—jets on fire watch, letting us know we had better be in our racks. The entire training deck fell to taps at precisely 2100 hours.

I couldn't sleep, despite physical weariness. One of the others tossed around for a bit. I heard Cleary's soft snores across from me. The darkness was complete. No windows like my room on Aaian-na. But I'd better get used to it, and get used to sharing a living space and breathing recycled air and loving the color gray, because if I didn't get killed first, this was where I was going to be for an indefinite amount of time.

Niko counted on me.

XVIII.

In our two training platoons, which made up a company of recruits, the routine was simple like the best brand of interrogative torture tactics: an early-shift regimen of physical exercise that always included calisthenics and marches; close-order drills; obstacle courses in one of the five simrooms; and bookwork on everything from Earth-Hub Armed Forces battles to specific scenarios jets were likely to face boarding pirate vessels or fighting on stations against invading strivs and symps.

None of this, of course, included the off-shift hazing. With no warning one of the jets on guard demanded a recruit at close range to rattle off the first three *Macedon* Rules of Service: 1. The captain is God. 2. Ship safety is your own safety. 3. A brain is worth more than blind duty, but a mouth means a march out the airlock.

In other words: Smart was good, smart-ass was not.

If you didn't shout it out with conviction the jet felt justified to compel fifty or more push-ups on the spot, usually with a boot on your back. If they felt vindictive they made you recite the entire jet manual. Depending on their mood they stopped you after five or ten minutes. And good luck if you didn't know each and every word, because they corrected you more or less violently, or made you strip and say it to the wall while everyone else watched your bare ass.

I had never been so grateful for Niko's slatework. I had that damn manual memorized in two weeks.

Macedon was still in dock (the captain had family on Austro, Nathan said, a son and a wife), but not everybody got leave, and certainly not all at the same time. "The war ain't on leave," a jet sergeant yelled to his squad, when Schmitt let us peek into a simroom so we could see how the big people played.

The simrooms were equipped to mimic station or on-ship scenarios, since those were the fields in which jets mostly fought. Planets were a rare environment, though not totally unheard of, so one of the rooms was alternately decked out using vid industry-type set dressings in various simulated conditions—desert, forest, mountain, or arctic. Stepping into the other simrooms, however, was like entering Chaos or a smaller ship or an industrial colony. The accuracy of objects was kind of impressive. Some engineer somewhere, not to mention maybe an artist, had taken pains to reproduce the look, smell, and feel of a generic station and ship and mining depot, right down to the bolts in the walls. These three simrooms were by far the largest, cavernous in fact, and must have taken up at least two deck levels on the schematics, somewhere near the center of the ship.

Macedon's jets had a reputation for being the elite of the elite. Holosims weren't enough.

Nathan was right about the deep-space captains funneling nonmilitary funds into personalizing their ships. This was a sophisticated setup that I couldn't imagine EHAF implementing on every carrier, at least not to this extent.

One of the small simrooms was set aside for the recruits, mostly filled with obstacles like steel walls, netted pits as if someone had blown a hole in the deck, wild wire we had to crawl under, and fallen debris we had to negotiate within a certain time index. Somewhere in week six, SJI Schmitt said, we would be introduced to the zero-g chamber.

By week four, after a lengthy training mission brief that encompassed everything from our objectives and safety (they harped on this quite a bit) to boundaries, passwords, and codes, I wondered aloud how the carrier could stay in dock so long.

"You ever seen Cap's wife?" Nathan said, when we gathered in the Training Bay for our pre-mission pep talk. "Major solar flare, mano."

"Yeah, but there's a war on." I found it hard to believe the man was married, or much less had a kid. He didn't seem capable of that kind of emotion. And I tried to put that young face together with a twelve-year-old son, which apparently was the kid's age.

Aki, sitting on my right, leaned into the conversation.

"*Macedon* doesn't hit Austro except once in five years. Give Cap a break."

"I agree with Musey," Iratxe said, sitting behind us with Cleary and Kris. She rested a hand on the back of my seat. I put my elbows on my knees so I wouldn't feel her breath on the back of my hair. "Enough of this sitting around. I want to get out there."

"You're still in diapers," Nathan said. "It ain't like you'll be seein' any action 'til we graduate."

"Don't we have orders?" Kris asked. We as in *Macedon*, he meant.

"Screw orders." Nathan snorted. "This is Cap's ship. They'd have to send some admiral out here to make him move."

Cleary yawned and stretched his arms. "She's getting repairs and a major resupply, anyway. Haven't you guys noticed all the maintenance?"

"I noticed the resupply in galley," Nathan said. "I'm dreamin' of some chocolate ice cream as we speak. But I think Iratxe here ate it all. Those're some hips on you, girl."

"Too bad this isn't a live fire sim," she said back.

Live fire or not, we had to treat it as real.

Apparently there was more striv activity by the Rim than ever before, which the Send attributed to the Warboy's encroaching on Hub space with the intention of taking over some stations, not just disabling them—blatant propaganda on their part, since I knew Niko had no such intention. Trying to maintain a Hub station, in Hub territory—even on the fringes—would be ridiculous considering his already-strained fleet and personnel resources. Of course the Send reporters didn't know a lot about the state of the Warboy's fleet, but even with that ignorance they made a lot of assumptions.

The military reports, which weren't necessarily what the

civilian population got, said the stations were military supply and repair depots. If they were hit, the deep-space carriers couldn't patrol the DMZ for long periods and that gave the striv fleet some breathing room to regroup.

Because of these "breaking" developments in the war—I was so sick of the hyperbole from the meedees—our sims revolved around station defense.

Keg parties, Nathan called them. Crack open the cans.

Our "enemy" in the sims was usually the other platoon. Sometimes we played the enemy. We dressed up in stritstyle robes—not exact, but close enough for effect—and tried to take out the other recruits. My kill points were higher in that scenario than the other. I didn't aim for it, but it was kind of fun sneaking around like an alien or a symp, cleansing "jets." Kris said he was glad I was on their side.

Most of the recruits treated the training seriously, though at the end of the shift a playful attitude came out. We were all still in dress-up and the real enemy was more of a meedee-indoctrinated idea.

Or my fellow recruits were just too naïve, despite the fact most of them were orphans like me. Iratxe thought that once we graduated she would gung-ho herself to a few citations and notoriety as a strit-killer. It wasn't much of a surprise that she thought Corporal Erret Dorr was beyond a solar flare and more like a supernova. Sometimes he dropped in to spy on the training platoons. We saw him standing by the simroom doors, talking to JJI Theron, when we dragged our overworked bodies from the latest training mission. Dressed as good guys this time, our platoon had "won" the objective—the capture of an escaped symp commander. I tugged off my helmet and gingerly pressed a throbbing bruise on my forehead, earned by a piece of falling debris in the station sim.

"I heard Dorr's scoping for drafts," Iratxe said, eyes

bright. "He lost a couple people on his team in their last mission. Think I should campaign?"

"Maybe he shot them," I said. I hadn't forgotten the way he beat me in the gauntlet.

"Sheez, Musey." Aki laughed. "You know," she said to Iratxe, in a tone they sometimes used when they wanted to nauseate the guys in our group, "he is pretty fine. Tall, and a body—"

I increased my stride and caught up with Kris, Nathan, and Cleary.

Nathan was eavesdropping on the girls. "He's outta your league." He sniffed his clothes and muttered, "And I'm outta clean air, aye."

"He's looking our way," Cleary said. "So place your bets."

I glanced at Dorr. He and Theron watched our little procession. I broke ahead of my berthmates toward the exit. The shower was the only place I had any consistent space to myself and it was always better if I got there first and took my time.

But Dorr snagged my sleeve as I passed. "Good run," he said. "Theron's tellin' me you got an eye for sniping too."

You couldn't exactly keep walking when a superior was addressing you. So I said, "Yes, sir," and shifted on my feet. Theron had taken a certain shine to me because I showed rapid improvement in the shooting gallery and he was himself a marksman. JIs liked nothing if not improvement and a steady show of enthusiasm for being where you were. I was adept, by now, at faking both. In reality I could probably compete with any jet easily.

Behind Dorr, but in my line of sight, Nathan stood with the others making fish-kiss faces at me.

These people were all crazy.

"I run a class," Dorr was saying, so I dragged my eyes back to him. "Shotokan. You know it?"

"No, sir."

"Theron says you catch on quick so maybe you can join my class once you graduate. We'd give you a challenge above your fellow sprigs."

I wasn't sure I wanted one, but I said, "Yes, sir."

He laughed. "You oughtta feel privileged. It's invitation only."

I wished he hadn't asked, and wondered if I could say no. He saved me the trouble and just waved me on. By the time I got to the showers, they were all occupied.

"So you got a date with long-blond or what?" Nathan said as I tried to beat him at a flight game in the RRC later that shift. With the holointerface over his eyes like two disks of ruby-tinted glass and his hands like two separate entities, Nathan flew through the false landscapes as if he'd been born in a cockpit. He was equally adept in the simulated vacuum of space as he was on any planet environment; he flew me in circles. I made a horrible pilot.

"It's not that," I said irritably. "Iratxe can have him."

Nathan glanced at me with a raised eyebrow. "He's a throwaway you don't wanna catch back, if you know what I mean."

After the fifth crash and burn I raked off the interface and hung it by its wire straps over the rim of the simstation. I couldn't talk and fly at the same time. "What d'you mean?"

Jelilian laughed and flipped up one of the glass "eyes." He slapped my shoulder, all gracious magnanimity.

"Your reflexes and hand-eye are good but you just dunno how to handle the metal, mano. Must be too much hardware for you." He grinned at his double entendre.

A lot of what jets and recruits alluded to involved sex.

And I was the youngest in the group; with their pack mentality, that meant I was the best one to tease.

"What d'you mean about Dorr?" I wasn't going to be in training forever and the corporal seemed to have me marked.

Nathan poked the game console, resetting it. "Iratxe says—and you know she's *researched*—Dorr's brass balls got him on this ship 'cause he went right up to Cap and asked. Then he got in some jets' faces on purpose and started his own gauntlet run to prove it. And he was fifteen at the time. Can you believe that?"

I did. "What's a throwaway?"

"You don't ever get tired of asking questions, do you?"

"That's why I'm smarter than you." I walked away from the simstation to get a drink from the dispenser. Jelilian followed, laughing to himself.

The RRC had a wide window facing out to the stars, which was a nice touch on a ship so generally claustrophobic. Right now the view was the starboard flank of *Archangel*, which sat in dock beside *Macedon*. Since the rec served the entire training deck it sprawled large, with well-used black couches facing each other and ten round tables scattered like game pieces across the floor. A simstation and vid provided the main entertainment, and a chow dispenser supplied free amounts of salty, sometimes dried snacks and liberal liters of caff in various forms—hot, cold, and fizzy.

I sat at an empty table near the bulkhead and nursed my hot caff. There hadn't been anything like caff on Aaian-na and I'd quickly developed a taste for it here. Nathan plopped down beside me and lit a cigret. His chatty mouth was the only reason I bothered to be with them in rec; if I stayed long enough, useful information usually dropped out.

Pretty soon the others drifted over from other parts of the room, except Cleary. Cleary was deep in conversation with another recruit on the couch, though what could possibly interest him that completely was the entire squad's guess.

"Throwaways," Nathan carried on, eager as always to show me how much I didn't know. "Iratxe, where you from? Where's your family?" He knew; he only asked for my benefit. And they humored him. Or me.

"Meshica Station." That was a Spokes mining colony. "I don't know where my mother is. My father's in a veterans' hospital."

"Aki?"

Aki shrugged a little and shifted. "Dead."

"Kris?"

"My dad died in a terrorist dock bombing a few years ago. Symps." He practically spat the word. "My mom's on Earth."

Nathan looked at me, blowing out a long stream of smoke. "And I'm from the streets of London." I didn't know where that was; Earth, I assumed. "My point is—most of us, and by us I mean we recruits, and probably most of the crew, are throwaways. The kids nobody else wants. Talk to any of us who served on ships before, most woulda heard that Cap takes the hard cases. That's why we try to transfer here. It's a lot less brass to bother with. They wear the stripes but they know where you're comin' from. I dare you to find a rich stitch on this crew, somebody from Austro's elite or some general's son. You'll look long and hard, mano. Ain't that why you came aboard?"

"Not exactly. I kind of just closed my eyes, turned around, and pointed." Humor usually tossed them off the scent. "But why would Azarcon want the troublemakers?" I recalled what Dorr had said when I was in brig, that *Macedon* was the second chance.

"He got his own reasons, prolly." Nathan shrugged. "Maybe 'cause he's an orphan himself."

You'd think Azarcon was a saint from the way some of them talked. "Yeah, an orphan making more orphans. Between him and pirates there's a lot of us to go around in the war."

As soon as I said it I knew better.

"You mean pirates and strits," Kris said.

"The strits go without saying," I said dismissively.

Without warning the shipcomm (or godcomm, as Nathan called it) beeped and Azarcon's voice came through, all around us.

"This is the captain. All nonessential personnel move to quarters. Crew prep for undock. We break in twenty."

People started to get up, chairs scraping, then clicking back into their claws for safety if the ship lost gravity.

"That's us," Nathan said, tossing his cigret in the trash vent. "Nonessential sots."

We tramped to quarters. My thoughts still strayed to Azarcon and the fact all of this intel was going nowhere because I still didn't have access to outgoing-capable comps.

Nathan climbed into his bunk and immediately buried his nose in his comics.

"Wanna play some poker?"

It took me a moment to realize Kris was speaking to me.

"I'm in," Aki said.

"Let's use Musey's bunk," Kris volunteered, and sat on the floor beside my rack before I could say anything, a deck of worn cards in his hands that he flipped and shuffled like a casino dealer.

"How 'bout I sleep," I said, sitting on the blankets on the area they planned to use as a table.

"Aw, c'mon." Aki gave my foot a shove. She kept shoving me until I slouched against the bulkhead by my pillow. She appropriated the foot of my bunk and left a small space in the middle to lay the cards. Iratxe sat beside Kris on the floor and produced a small case of poker chips that she began to dole out. Cleary had long since disappeared beneath his blankets. I looked over enviously.

"This is stupid. Those chips aren't worth anything and we're all broke anyway."

"Consider it credit. When we get on the payroll, then everybody can collect. I'll keep tally." Kris showed me his slate.

"It's lights out in fifteen mikes."

"The jets've buttoned us in and gone to quarters. Nobody stands in the corridors during dock break."

I'd read that in our manual but it was a good reminder for later use. The locks on the hatches throughout the training deck could be easily bypassed with some hotwiring. I'd scoped the control panels already on a march when one of the crew was doing maintenance; all I needed were the tools to pry the panels open.

"Muse, you're about as much fun as a rectal exam." That from Kris.

Nathan's voice drifted down. "Don't knock it 'til you try it, Rilke." He laughed.

"Mano, shut up."

The ship gave three sharp beeps from the godcomm. For a vessel this large, with its crew complement of more than six thousand, I hardly thought we'd feel the unclamping or the drift from Austro unless something went wrong. As Kris dealt the hands I listened. Nothing sounded or happened. We played standard five-card and I won the first round. After a few more rounds with the chips piling on my side of the bunk I became aware of their declining chatter and the probe of their eyes.

"Look at you," Aki said. "Where'd you learn to play like that?"

They didn't know about my link to Falcone and I had no

intention of ever telling them. "Nowhere. You all just play like shit."

"Somebody needs to teach this boy how to smile," Iratxe said. "So serious. This is fun, you know."

"Where d'you think we're headed?" I asked, idly looking over my cards.

Nathan, the eavesdropper, answered from his lofty perch. "Deep space, naturally. Where there be Dragons."

"Oh, all of the Dragons," Kris said blandly, "or just the one small corner of it?"

"Try the area near the strits. Azarcon's a hunter and we're lookin' for some ducks."

As if to emphasize his point, the bulkhead suddenly came alive with sound, a deep thrumming pulse.

"Drives are active," Nathan narrated. "We're headin' to a leap."

Underneath the pulse was a higher, grating whine.

"Goin' faster."

The ship seemed a living thing, louder than Niko's *Turundrlar*, as if it brayed its power out to the galaxy like a war cry. Once *Macedon* reached its intended rate the engines would cut and we'd shoot through the stars on inertia. I knew the rhythm. The noise was a lull, one I'd heard since in the womb. Like falling asleep to a rainstorm smacking your windows or thunderheads booming over your roof. No ship could totally muffle the sound from traveling up through the decks. Kris, Aki, and Iratxe sat still, cards forgotten in their hands, just listening to the harsh symphony reverberating through the bulkhead in muted growls.

After some minutes the higher whine swallowed itself to silence, leaving only the pulse of the drives. The godcomm beeped again, once. An unfamiliar, no-nonsense female voice came through.

"Crew prep for leap. Tee minus ten mikes and counting."

Leaping was mostly a comfortable affair, when things went right. The most you might've felt was some nausea or headache, a kind of hot displacement, as if you had a high fever. The turtle shell shielding and transsteel compound routinely used in ship hull construction effectively insulated the crew from the rougher effects of being shot through spatial shortcuts—the Jordan leap points, the first of which were discovered by some long-dead astrophysicist named Emil Jordan. But one thing he hadn't predicted and nobody could prevent was the memory loss.

Essential personnel got RI, or rapid infeed, from their comp consoles—a dump of information straight into their brains that briefed them on systems status. It could get dangerous if navigators weren't aware of where they were, even for a few minutes, after coming out of a leap. RI was a mind rush, any nav or conn officer could tell you that. Some said it was addictive, but nobody who actually took RI on a regular basis ever confirmed that. Those who didn't infeed, like recruits strapped into their racks so they didn't tumble, had to suffer with complete disorientation and selective amnesia of the few minutes before leaping. As a kid on *Mukudori* it was fun. Now I wondered if too many leaps did more than just short-circuit your short-term memory.

The woman's voice on the godcomm counted down the leap, then the ship shuddered slightly.

Heat rushed from my feet to the top of my head.

I blacked out.

Then I looked up at the bottom of Iratxe's bunk. Somehow I'd gotten the extra webbing strapped over my torso. Everyone lay in their bunks, cards and poker chips absent. I couldn't remember who'd put them away, but obviously someone had. The time on my watch read a half hour later than when I last remembered looking, some time in the middle of our game.

Nathan groaned.

"That was one long fuckin' leap."

It had felt deep. No way to really explain how a body knew that, but the short Jordans were considerably less mind-numbing. I couldn't move for five minutes. My brain just refused to function. On *Mukudori* I'd had no need to move about afterward, but could sleep it off. Now I was just glad we didn't get attacked. Fighting would have been a problem. Apparently the effects got easier to handle the more you did it. That was the theory.

Nathan continued to mutter with his gutter London accent. Cleary was the first of us to slide up, rubbing his eyes.

I lay there for more than five minutes. When I looked at my watch again another half hour had passed. I might have dozed.

A klaxon went off.

"What the hell—?" from Kris.

The godcomm beeped. "General quarters," Captain Azarcon said, with no evident urgency in his voice. "I repeat: general quarters. This is not a drill."

I could picture the man on the bridge, completely calm, ordering deaths.

"We leaped right into a fray," Nathan said eagerly. "Damn, an' I'm stuck in this shit!"

He meant the training deck. Or his webbing. I undid mine and sat up as far as I could with the bunk overhead. I was nowhere near the bridge, I wasn't even a jet yet, but my gut tightened into a hard little ball. "You think they're aliens?"

"Strits or pirates," Nathan answered.

The bulkhead began to whine, then the whole ship started to shudder, as if we lay inside a thunderstorm.

"Those're the cannons!" Jelilian yelled in excitement.

We couldn't exactly hear the blasts, just the machinery, and we felt it.

"C'mon!"

He jumped down from his bunk and headed for the hatch.

"Where're you going?" Aki snapped.

I followed him and didn't care where we were supposed to be. I had to see who *Macedon* was fighting.

Footsteps fell in behind me. They couldn't resist.

Nobody else on training deck had the same idea, or they were too scared. Nathan led us alone into the recruit rec center and straight to the wide window. The ship had slowed considerably from its leap rate but hadn't stopped. *Macedon* roared around us with the thud and scream of its torpedoes and laser cannons. Like the drives, the sound of the giant turrets and loading mechanisms couldn't be muffled, not on a carrier that bristled with weaponry around its thick hide. The battle klaxon had silenced, but the battle had not.

Outside a ship hung some distance off, but I knew the sleek, upswept shape of its aft engines. It was close enough that I could even recognize the large striviirc-na markings on its hull. I could read them. *Havurkar. White Eye.* I counted two torpedoes that had launched from *Macedon*— they matched the gaping, jagged holes in *Havurkar*'s starboard side. The ship sat dead in space, blackened lights and pummeled skin.

Mukudori must have looked like that.

Macedon still fired but not at anything we could see from the port side. Black-shelled hunter-killers streaked by like iridescent dragonflies, targeting *Havurkar*'s engines. The striv ship spun out of sight, but not because it had moved; we had. I put my hand on the window as a second ship shot across our line of vision.

"Not a battleship," Nathan said.

"Looked like a merchant," Iratxe said. "Diamond-class."

One with a lot of gunports. Not a regular merchant. A hunter-killer exploded right in front of us, a brief puff before hull parts sailed out from the center of the blast in a balletic dance. Nathan swore and slammed his hand on the window. *Macedon* wrenched its mammoth body through the vacuum, shooting at the enemy ship like a rabid beast swatting at a rodent on its skin. We saw nothing but benign stars. The battle went on out of our view; only the booming of the cannons told us the merchant hadn't yet fled.

Then as abruptly as it began, everything stopped. The deceptive silence of space bled through the hull once more. The cannons quieted. The ever-present whine of *Macedon*'s drives seemed a whisper by comparison.

The carrier sailed around in its inertial turn until I saw the scattered cold remains of the striviirc-na dreadnought. Like specks of dust in the span of space, the bits and pieces of the destroyed ship spun toward the many stars, toward nothing. My own image bled through, superimposed blur against the black, a ghost with hollow eyes and a hand pressed to its own transparency.

The godcomm beeped and Azarcon's voice rained down all around us.

"Stand down battle stations. Commander Xavier to the bridge."

"It doesn't look like we got that merchant," Kris said.

"Merchant?" Nathan laughed. "Pirate! How much you wanna bet?"

"Well, we got the strit at least," Iratxe said.

In the window reflection I saw them behind me, congratulating one another with high fives and shoves as if they'd had something to do with the battle.

"Dead strit," Nathan said. "How 'bout that for a show? Strit dead, mano!"

No sympathizer dreadnought would have anything to do with a pirate—or an EarthHub merchant. Not Niko. But I couldn't tell them that. I couldn't even ask Niko.

Kris came up behind me and slapped my shoulder, squeezed it. I spun, locked on his grinning face, and forced a smile.

"That was better than a vid." He grinned. "We must've ambushed them."

"We didn't feel it," I said absently. "I guess we wouldn't, really, unless the grav-nodes were knocked off-line."

They agreed.

But I was wrong. I had felt it.

XIX.

I had a final psych interview before graduation, the last one I was likely to receive unless I volunteered to see somebody or showed signs of mental breakdown. Cleary and I sat waiting outside the JI offices. He was folding a piece of colored print into odd shapes.

"Where do you get the paper from?" I asked, to take my mind off the interview.

"My mom sends it out in batches when she can, through the replenishment ships." His deft hands folded and pressed until a blue bird appeared. It was so balanced it stood on its own with spread wings.

"That's amazing." Out of all my berthmates, I liked Cleary best. He knew how to leave you alone and behind his reserve was humble intelligence. He was also going into engineering as a drive technician and would be a good source of information for those parts of *Macedon* I was unlikely to see while on probation. It would be a challenge to make him talk but I had the feeling he would, and could, if it was about something he loved.

"I can teach you." He gestured to the bird. "You can have that too if you want." He smiled shyly.

"Thanks." I took the bird, turned it around in my hands. "Don't take this the wrong way, but you don't seem the type that would want on a ship like *Macedon*."

He shrugged. "My dad served her previous captain. It's kind of tradition."

"Both your parents are alive?"

He nodded. "On Pax Terra."

An oddity in Nathan's theory about throwaways. I would've asked him more except SJIs Laceste and Schmitt appeared in the doorway to the office corridor. "Come on in, gentlemen," Laceste said.

"Yes, sir," we said in unison. Cleary cast me a sympathetic look, then followed Schmitt. I went with Laceste into her office. It didn't look any different from the last time and neither did she.

I couldn't read her face from across that gray desk.

"Since our last conversation, Recruit Musey, much has changed. You've integrated well with your fellow recruits, though we've noticed still a certain preferred isolation. Your scores in the shooting gallery are on top, as well as your performance in the training sims. You're also a competitor in the hand-to-hand fighting and your slate work is impeccable." She folded her hands. "But why, after reading all of this, am I still concerned about you, Recruit Musey?"

I gave her a bland face I'd perfected in jet training. "I don't know, sir."

"Maybe because the library comp system shows an increase in queries regarding Vincenzo Falcone since you've come aboard. Are there things you wish to know that aren't in the public files?" Before I could answer she waved a hand. "Don't worry, we don't purposely set to spy on crew. The system is designed to store queries in that way so the recreation department can gauge what might be in demand. Except your queries didn't involve a particular interest in the marine mammals of Earth, did they?"

Sometimes anger served a purpose. I knew I didn't look scared. "Sir, I don't understand why Falcone's an issue. Yes, I want to know more about him. One day I'd like to kill him. I'm not psychotic about it, but it's not something I'll dismiss either."

"Of course not," she said, in a reasonable tone. "The fact he's still at large and currently in hiding disturbs you."

"Not to the point of distraction, if that's what you mean, sir."

"This is what we're concerned about. Obsessions of this sort can lead to errors."

"I'm not obsessed, sir."

"*Macedon* has a reputation not only for strit killing, but pirate hunting. Is this one of the reasons you chose her?"

"I guess it is, sir." They had me all figured out, I was sure. I kept the sarcasm off my face and out of my voice.

"You realize, Recruit Musey, that the chances of you actually meeting Falcone now, much less killing him, are slim to none?"

This was true. The Hub was big, and I was a nonentity jet on a large ship, tasked for other duties by two different captains. If *Macedon* actually did meet the *Khan*, in some odd stroke of fate, Falcone was the type to either run or die fighting.

One part of me wanted the opportunity to meet him, if only to put a shot in his head. To let him know who was doing it and if he remembered. Memories that were years removed, however close they seemed in quiet moments, were good targets in meditation.

"Musey?" Laceste said, tapping a finger on her desk.

"Yes, sir. I know. As I said, sir, I'm not obsessed."

XX.

The tattoo on my inner right wrist itched maddeningly, as if bot-knitters scurried just beneath my skin. Rodriguez said it would, at first, but that was a small price to pay considering the minimal pain and lack of bandages. *Macedon*'s emblem was a sixteen-point black star overlaid by a blond man's profile. Corporal Erret Dorr told me it was Alexander the Great—an ancient king of the country this ship was named after. The tat spanned about five centimeters in diameter, painstakingly drawn. It was Rodriguez's most holy work and every single one on every crewmember's wrist was a piece of art. If you dishonored it in any way the pain of punishment would be equal to the artistry.

Upon graduation from RT you got three things: your tat, your tags, and your blacks. The first was skin—*Macedon* was now your corps, your body, and your brag. The second was face—the tags held your image, chipped info, and also doubled as short-range comm by tapping the tiny contact pads on the reverse side in code sequence. And they were a key for your assigned quarters lock. The blacks were your uniform: pants, shirt, tank, boots. Other crew wore the blacks, like the command staff, but the uni was most associated with the elite—the anchor, gold starburst, and sweeping black arrows of the Soljet Corps.

I had another patch on my opposite arm—the lion shield of *Macedon*'s Alpha Company, better known as the Ship's Pride. Corporal Dorr was in my company, in fact he was in my platoon as my squad leader. He'd requested me personally for his fire team, along with Kris Rilke. Private First Class Keith Madison rounded it out; he'd been Dorr's teammate since my gauntlet run. Sergeant Odette Hartman commanded three squads, of which ours made up one-third.

Dorr made it clear from the beginning that Alpha Company was the elite.

Now that we were forward on jetdeck I was allowed into the jet wardroom, which had holo-accessible comps with paths to *Macedon*'s outgoing communications. I tread lightly on the new freedom, though, since Sanchez, Bucher, and Ricci—the three jets I'd shot in the gauntlet run—eyed me like barely restrained animals. But I was under Erret Dorr's command. People seemed to walk wide of him and everything he owned. Once I'd strolled by the jet wardroom's open hatch and overheard Dorr warning all and sundry that he didn't want his new ace damaged. That had been a relief until he'd continued: "Any rankin' Muse deserves will come from me."

At least they'd returned our personal belongings. My holopoints were untouched, of course, otherwise I would've been spaced some weeks ago. The image disk was also there, which I wore beneath my uniform shirts, against my chest, and removed only when I took a shower. Other than in the head, I couldn't seem to go anywhere and be alone. Jetdeck was a profusion of uniforms, loud mouths, and nosy, gossiping individuals. Trying to send my first report to Aaian-na took timing I didn't seem to have. The wardroom was open to newly graduated jets, but it was also heavily trafficked. At any given shift people were in there relaxing, reading, or talking idly about the latest reports from some other battle.

It had been nine weeks since leaving *Turundrlar*, less since the battle where that striviirc-na dreadnought had died and the mysterious merchant fled. I knew Dorr, Hartman, and a few others of higher rank were doing some sort of investigation into the merchant, but they didn't share it with their subordinates.

I had my own questions for Niko.

Through trial and error I eventually discovered the best time to hit the wardroom was very early in my duty shift, an hour or so before reveille. It was the tail end of the previous watch, so most of the jets were heading to quarters or already in them. I tried to dress quietly with the lights on a minimum five percent, but Kris, who'd been assigned as my berthmate, rolled over in his bunk and peered at me through the shadows, then squinted at his watch.

"What's going on?"

I had to get stuck with the lightest sleeper on ship. "I'm just going to the head." I stuffed my feet in boots and went to the hatch. He put his face back in the pillow as I left. He never had problems sleeping at the end of shifts, but I couldn't quiet my mind for more than four hours, not since seeing *Havurkar* and that merchant, which everybody said was probably a pirate.

I wished I could talk to Niko face-to-face and ask him about it. Or grab him and shake him. I had dreams about it, yelling without sound, in a room full of people I couldn't get away from even when I shut my eyes.

When I got to the wardroom I didn't have time to open the hatch. It swung in unexpectedly and Erret Dorr stepped back, surprised.

I kept walking, nodding to him absently as if I was actually going somewhere. My heart thudded.

"What you doin' up, Muse?"

"The head," I mumbled, as if I was still half-asleep.

"Come back here when you done. We got a mission."

I stopped. "Sir?"

He looked like he hadn't slept and his temper proved it. "The war don't wait on your beauty rest, Private. Get the hell goin'."

XXI.

"There's a stranded symp out there," Corporal Dorr told our squad, "and we're goin' to help it."

He was lying, of course. He loaded the intel files on our slates as he spoke. The files briefed us on schematics, codes, radio freqs and procedures, enemy strength and weaponry, and our rules of engagement, which, among other things like viable and off-limit targets, also warned us about maltreatment of the enemy. No killing of children, raping, or wanton destruction of the enemy's ship (sometimes they could be salvaged and used). It was all presented frankly, with much detail, as if they weren't people you were talking about.

For this mission we were using a small, salvaged symp runner. A military-employed merchant had picked up a coded distress message, forwarded it to *Macedon* since we were the closest military ship in the vicinity, and *Macedon* had spent a full shift deciphering it—which was quite an accomplishment and something Niko would definitely want to know, so he could revamp the system.

The distress might not have been valid now but Azarcon was going to take that chance. They were still trying to figure out who that merchant had been with *Havurkar*, and getting another sympathizer to question could prove fruitful since the distress originated from the same general coordinates of that battle. Getting any sympathizer would be a boon, no matter what.

Do as you must, Niko had said. His words plummeted to my gut like meteors caught in a grav-well.

Somehow *Macedon* had also got ahold of the symp's IFF code—identify friend or foe—which came from transponders on all the vessels in Niko's fleet, black boxes that traded information with other ships they encountered. EarthHub military vessels had the same things. If the transponders didn't recognize each other, you knew you were facing an enemy. The code changed daily and I wondered who'd acquired a black box, and from whom. What prisoner or traitor had handed one over for *Macedon* to use?

We were going to approach the symp as their relief, board them, and attack them. The bridge crew were immune, but everyone else (minus any children who might be there) were viable targets.

I sat there listening to Dorr, reading my slate, memorizing the schems, and it wasn't until he dismissed us to gear up that Kris leaned in and said, "Our first mission, Jos!"

But it felt like I'd been doing this, reading about what symps were okay to kill, for too long already. I smelled the ship in my clothes and felt its drives in the rush of blood through my system, like an infection.

XXII.

Two squads fit into the symp runner, and that was it. As we headed to our objective some of the jets reviewed the mission specs, others talked loudly about the imminent action (and were equally mocked by the veteran jets in the group), and Corporal Dorr slept. I sat across from him, between Kris and Aki, who was here as our combat medic. I didn't say a word, tried not to think, and hoped that it would be over when I awoke. Some part of me wished it was a bad dream. The rifle in my hands, the million and one pieces of gear distributed on my body from my head to my hips, were heavy hands pushing me into my seat and against the runner's bulkhead.

This wasn't going to be over anytime soon. And I had still been unable to send a message to Niko, to tell him to get me out of here—to ask him why the hell there'd been a strit ship and a Hub merchant peacefully occupying the same space. The question whirled in my head and my gut like a hurricane. I shut my eyes to fight down the nausea.

Fingers touched my knee. I jerked away, glanced at Aki, who pulled her hand back and cast me an apologetic look.

"Sorry. You just seemed unsteady."

"I'm fine." I shifted the rifle between my knees, held the muzzle tightly.

"We're on schedule," Sergeant Hartman said, adjusting the pickup in her ear. She was in contact with the cockpit. "Ready at the lock."

We didn't blow the symp's lock; they got the proper authorization from our stolen ship and opened their end themselves. As soon as the breach appeared the front row of our squad fired on the welcoming crew, mowing them down without any retaliation.

"Go!" Dorr ordered.

Kris and I were fifth in the attack flow. We moved in. Two bodies lay on the deck, riddled with bolt holes. A man and a woman. The woman had a tattoo on her face. The scientist caste.

These were Aaian-na symps. Not like *Cervantes*.

"Musey," Kris snapped, and hit my arm with his elbow.

We could've used paralysis pulses. Except nobody wanted to bother keeping a symp alive unless they were important enough to interrogate, or risk them waking up at our sixes.

"Go!" Dorr shoved my back.

I stepped over the bodies and followed Kris down the corridor. Nothing I could do. Breath stuck in my throat. The edges of my sight grew fuzzy and sweat trickled from my hair, under my helmet and eye shield.

The weapons fire alerted the ship that we weren't

friendlies. Voices barked over comm in a language I knew, but none of the jets did. The symps were going to try to box us in.

Hartman didn't need to know striviirc-na to understand tactics. She separated the teams, spread us out through the small, already-injured ship in a systematic invasion, dropping traps for anyone who dared come up at our heels.

The crew poured out of quarters, thicker and faster the closer we got to the bridge.

I saw Dorr shoot one in the head. On my left flank. He didn't even blink. He didn't even wait for the body to hit the deck before he moved on.

I saw the symps and fired, like I was trained to do. They had guns and they aimed at me because they saw a jet. I killed a man in striviirc-na clothing. The laser pulse went through his face. I'd aimed for his chest but he tried to duck, an instinctive move. I killed three other people, two women and a man, sent a grenade ahead of me that severed limbs from bodies, severed hands from arms. I left pieces of these people in my wake.

But it wasn't me. It was just a body moving. And they were just bodies without names.

We moved fast, but I saw it all slow. One minute was forever breathing in, and the next minute infinity exhaled. Details of red accumulated in my memory like spent pulse packs.

Jet voices reverberated in my head, barking orders, calling clears, a counterpoint melody to the death being played around me, the death that I caused, that I moved through as if it didn't matter and it wasn't a man that I murdered, or a woman, or people that I would've commemorated long ago with a burning paper ship. Here it didn't matter. Here nothing mattered because I was alive and they were dead, and that was it.

I tracked blood on the deck of that sympathizer ship, tracked it from room to room like a pirate.

XXIII.

We lower jets didn't have to debrief, that was left up to higher ranks. I went in silence back to quarters, trailed by Kris. He sat heavily on his bunk and ran a hand through his hair.

"That was serious," he said.

I dumped my gear and started to gather up clean clothes to take to the shower, except I couldn't really see what I grabbed. Shadows spilled from the edges of my sight. "It's war, Kris. What d'you think?" But inside I shook. Inside I hadn't stopped shaking since we got back on *Macedon*.

"I know. I know. And I've seen vids. I'm just—" He couldn't finish it. He didn't know. I was his berthmate. He just wanted me around while he figured out what he was feeling.

I couldn't help him. I didn't know what I was feeling.

So I left him there. I took my kit, went to the showers, and stayed there a long time, blocking out the sound of the others talking above the water spray. Some of them bragged about how successful the mission was, how many people they'd killed, how the symps in brig were going to pay.

I could've reminded the jets how one of them threw up when a grenade exploded and killed a symp, and how another one nearly shot one of us because his hands were shaking so badly.

But I couldn't.

I left without speaking to anybody and almost walked

right on Kris and Aki in the corridor. They stood outside the head, talking quietly.

"Hey, Jos," Aki said, "you all right?"

Their eyes were red, skin a little too pale.

"Fine." I could barely look at them. They looked too sorry and I knew they weren't. They'd do it again tomorrow and they'd call it a victory.

I kept walking.

"Jos—" Aki started, but then I heard Kris say, "Leave him alone. He's like that."

As if he knew me.

At least I got to be alone in quarters.

I tucked my back to the wall on my bunk, cut the lights, and just lay there, thinking of too much until it all became nothing, just a constant hum. My nerves throbbed with each minute. I pretended to be asleep when Kris came in. It felt like hours later. He didn't say anything, but moved quietly in his shift-end routine until he finally settled in his bunk. I heard his breaths until he fell so completely asleep they shallowed out to nothing audible.

I gathered the pillow under my head and pressed my face into the soft, smooth fabric. He was so deeply gone he didn't hear a thing, didn't stir. Nobody heard me, and in the close black of the quarters, I heard nothing else.

XXIV.

Dorr commed us just after reveille sounded. The man never slept, apparently. I got up blearily and hit the deskcomm, since Kris didn't show any interest in moving.

Dorr said *Macedon* was en route to Chaos Station and all the jets from the mission got to have a couple shifts of leave.

Enjoy, he said, as if we hadn't just slaughtered a whole ship.

My eyes were too heavy, but I couldn't lie around. I'd accidentally slept through the hour that I'd told myself to go and send a report. While Kris muttered and rolled over, I gathered my holopoint bottle and cube report for Niko, stuck it in my pocket, and left the q. Maybe I could sneak a few minutes at least to send a heads-up to my prearranged contact on Chaos, for our first meeting.

You just had to put the things behind you that you couldn't help. So by the time I stopped at the head to tap in my holopoints, I'd shoved the shadows from my mind. Do as you must. The wardroom was empty by the time I got there, but there was no guarantee for how long. I slipped behind one of the comps, flicked it on, and dived in. Sending the report would take longer and the priority now was to flag my contact. She might answer my questions, an instant reply. Communication was otherwise one-way, at least over comps. They'd only issue orders to me through my contact, face-to-face.

Niko had handpicked her. It would be as close as I'd get to him.

The message shot toward Chaos, ahead of *Macedon*, snuck under one of the carrier's routine outgoing packets. It was a short construct, the best kind to send, just two coded words:

Meet me.

XXV.

"Ain't it great to be alive," Madison said as our squad tramped down the lockramp onto Chaos Station's dock. Me,

Kris, Aki, Sergeant Hartman, and others who'd been on the mission, all of them loose and excited. Mission forgotten. It was all worth it because it bought us some free time. That was their attitude. Our boots echoed on the ramp. I trailed last.

I hadn't been back to Chaos since I ran from Falcone. Five years ago. He wasn't here now, and even if he was, would he recognize me?

The station looked no different. The walls were still battle-scarred from strit attacks, patched in places by sheets of metal to hide cables of wire and numerous blast holes. Blue paint partially obscured long-ago tunnel kid graffiti. The citizens were still wary, mashed together in colors and shapes you just didn't see on military ships or even pirate ones. Maintenance and polly uniforms melded in the stream of people with civilian drab and office geometrica wear. Late blueshift workers. This wasn't my world. When I saw these many colors and abstractions I thought of Aaian-na, the caste colors, the twining symbols, the vibrancy of a lush landscape under a hard sun. Nothing in space could rival that kind of wide, blue awareness. Stations only falsified the color on their walls.

Like I wore a jet uniform. Unnatural skin.

"Will Corporal Dorr join us?" Kris asked Madison, after some of the others drifted off to their own destinations. Kris was in my team. If I took off by myself for this first time it might look suspicious. Jets tended to travel in packs.

"After he gets done with the prisoners," Madi replied. Whatever that entailed. "So where you sprigs gonna go? This station got shitty selection, mano."

Hartman said, "They should try Junkie's, it ain't bad. Drinks're half-decent, though still on the pissy side."

I said, "I'm going to the Halcyon. I read on the station menu. They said it's got good food." It was a medium-scale bar and den and the place I was supposed to meet my contact. Niko had briefed me on that from the get-go.

"Food." Madison laughed. "We need to get you drunk, Musey."

Aki said, "I'll go with you, Jos."

"Fine, whatever." I took a step toward the concourse to signal her.

"Kris?" she asked.

He grinned. "No, go ahead. Me and Madi got plans."

Aki rolled her eyes. "I pity the females on this station."

Hartman smirked. "Or the pets." She stuck a thumb in her back pocket and strutted off. "See you ladies later."

I took another step away. "Aki, let's go, I'm hungry." She'd be a good alibi, on second thought.

Kris said, "Have fun," in a tone of voice I couldn't read. He smiled at me as if we had a secret.

No point trying to understand them. I headed to the concourse. Aki quickly followed and bumped arms with me. I stiffened and she laughed.

"Relax! We aren't on duty, y'know. Now where's this Halcyon, I've never been here before—oh, there's an imager." She tugged my sleeve to the holoboard and asked it to find the bar. It didn't work.

"I think it's broken. Let's just go, it can't be that hard to find." I headed off.

She caught up, laughing again. "Jos, you're always on a mission, aren't you?"

"What?"

Her grin turned teasing. "You should smile more, you know. You're cute."

I stared at her. "What're you talking about? Maybe I don't smile because I don't feel like it. You forget what we did over on that symp runner?"

Her eyes narrowed in irritation. "No I didn't forget, but

I'd like to. And what did you think we'd be doing on *Macedon*? If you don't want to fight, then why'd you enlist?"

"It seemed like a good idea at the time."

"I don't think you do anything on a whim, Jos."

I didn't know how to answer that, so didn't.

She glanced at me. "We have to learn to get over it, y'know."

I said, "Maybe that's the problem. Everybody just gets over it."

"Well, what else is there?" She looked down the corridor, away from me. As if something were my fault. "Let's just find the bar."

All around us station cits moved, nervous. The sight of jets put people like that on edge, because we brought the war with us.

We were in the den district. It was one long passage, nothing compared to Austro's many levels. Ship crew and station citizens mingled together under pale blue lights. It made Aki's skin sallow and her eyes tired-looking.

I spotted a flashing sign. "There's the Halcyon."

Inside the bar was a gold-lit haze, broken only by the silver reflections from the walls and platinum-colored mushroom tables sprouting from the black floor. We negotiated our way to an empty two-seat in the corner.

"I'll get the drinks," Aki said loudly, gesturing to the bar. I nodded instead of trying to shout through the clanging music. I couldn't just up and disappear with my contact.

As Aki moved off, I glanced around. The bar was moderately occupied. Some people danced halfheartedly on a block of elevated floor. I was underage by two years but I didn't think anybody would care in this place.

A woman leaned on the bartop, watching Aki approach. In the deceiving lights I barely made out her features. Dark-skinned and long multibraided hair. She looked past Aki and locked eyes with me.

I looked away. Not yet.

Eventually Aki came back with two round glasses of amber liquid.

"I don't drink," I shouted at her.

She grinned and lifted her hair off her neck, a quick toss. The air was too warm and dense with cigret smoke. "Don't worry, it's not jacked with anything."

I sniffed at it before I sipped.

She shook her head. "You're so suspicious!"

"I just don't want to get drunk, that's all."

"Why not?"

"I just don't. I don't like it."

"Have you even been drunk before?" Her eyebrows arched.

I shrugged, looked over at the bar again. The braided woman had moved. She drifted closer to our table.

Aki twisted in her seat a little, glancing at me. "What're you looking at?"

"Nothing. Just—these people. They don't seem really into the scene, do they?"

But she wasn't listening. Her gaze diverted to the entrance. "Hey, there's Corporal Dorr!"

I darted a look and almost reached across the table to knock down her waving arm. But I couldn't. And he came over.

"Yo, sprigs," he said, dragging close an empty chair and plopping down. "Anythin' new? What's that piss you drinkin', Muse?"

"I think it's apple juice. Except it's fizzy." He was never going to go away. My contact found a seat nearby. "So what'd the prisoners say?"

Dorr shrugged and lit a cigret. He was in civilian clothes,

a gunmetal-gray shirt and pants, wrinkled, loose. "They were resistant nuts at first, but I cracked 'em a little. Lemme get you a real drink."

"No thanks. Sir."

"Lemme buy you a drink, Muse." He smiled, but it was the face of someone who didn't expect to be denied. "One for you too, Aki. You too young to be sober."

Aki looked like she didn't quite know how to take that.

He was my superior and for some reason decided to find us and not Hartman or Madison. I didn't stop him as he waved at the bartender in a familiar way, held two fingers up in a V, and pointed to me and Aki. Then he turned back with a satisfied smirk.

"Trust me, you need to get drunk, Jos. That sour puss of yours would curdle cheese."

"Sir," I said, instead of reaching across and knocking that expression off his face.

The drinks came. They looked like water.

"On the mission," Dorr said, slouching a little in his seat with one arm hanging over the back. "You stared at those bodies like you wanted to photograph 'em. That ain't healthy."

I picked up the glass and sipped, so I wouldn't have to talk. A spike went through my head, with a simultaneous fire down my throat, followed by a subtle herbal aftertaste. I coughed and sniffed, and Dorr laughed.

In the next glance my contact stood and walked right up to our table. "Hey, cutie." Her eyes locked on me.

Dorr looked her over fast and his smile grew. "Not bad."

She was over twice my age. She grinned at Dorr and leaned a hand on the table, scoped all three of us and lingered on me. "Can you lend him, blondie?"

Aki said, "He's underage."

"Don't ruin the lad's fun now," Dorr said. And to the

woman, "Go 'head, if you can drag him from his seat. He's kinda prim."

"I don't think so," I told the woman, because they expected that.

"Aw, c'mon." She smiled and leaned in close to my ear as if she were flirting. I forced myself not to recoil as her lips brushed my cheek. "Den number nine, in a half hour. Get there." She drew back and gave me a mock face of disappointment.

"Sorry," I said. "You're a little too old for me."

Her smile showed teeth. I didn't think the glare was an act. "Your loss, cutie." She looked at Dorr. "How 'bout you?"

His gaze traveled around, avoiding hers out of disinterest. "Sorry, you ain't my type."

Aki said, "Maybe you should go scope out a twelve-year-old," to the woman. Dorr laughed. The woman drifted off with a noncommittal shrug. Dorr talked on, trying to draw my eyes to some people he deemed "good ambushees," which I ignored until enough time had passed that I could excuse myself to the washrooms.

Dorr said, "Don't fall in."

I threaded through the crowd toward the back of the bar, where a red-striped exit led to the dens. The washrooms were just beside it. A quick glance over my shoulder confirmed that Aki and the corporal couldn't see where I was, so I ducked through the den entrance and fast-walked through the dim, narrow warren of corridors, past people lounging on the floor or in doorways, some of them clearly strung out. Den nine sat in a corner, a scratched, shut door. I knocked, a hand on my sidearm where it was tucked into my waist.

The woman opened it, stepped back so I could enter.

"I don't have a lot of time," I told her as she shut the door.

"*Macedon* jumped a meeting between a strit and a Hub merchant. Can Niko explain that?"

She sat on the rumpled covers of the narrow bed, crossed her legs, and rested an elbow on her knee, looking up at me with dark eyes. The room was a hole, paint peeling. "Siddown, cutie, I don't like how you hover."

I didn't want to touch anything in that room, so just crossed my arms. "Can he explain that?"

"No," she said. She tugged a cigret out of her sleeve cuff, struck the end with her finger lighter. A crease appeared between her brows. "How long ago?"

"Four weeks." I fished out the intel cube from one of my cargo pockets and handed it over. "The coordinates, everything, is in there. The ship was *Havurkar*. The merchant got away and *Macedon*'s on the prowl for it. We just came back from a mission. Attacked a symp—the *Gra'tlir*. It's dead now."

Her gaze lingered on me as she took the cube. "What about general intel about *Macedon*?"

"It's in there." The corners of the room were bare, ripped, furling carpet. "It's all in there. The captain, their policies, all the shit they feed us about what Niko's doing. So you don't know anything about *Havurkar*?"

"No, but I'll relay it to Nikolas."

"Where is he?"

"I can't tell you that." She stood. "Just keep doing what you're doing, Musey. It's still early in the game."

"This is a game?" I stared at her.

"You know what I mean." Her eyes traveled on me. "Symp and strit, you said. They're working you well, aren't they?"

"What does he expect?" I couldn't keep the resentment out of my voice. "When can I come out?"

The crease deepened between her eyes. "Are you in danger?"

"What do you think?"

"Specifically. Urgently."

This woman might've known Niko, but she wasn't going to give a thing. I took a breath of the stale air. "Would he take me back if I wanted to leave now? Could you arrange it?"

"You'd leave in the middle of it? After giving us this report about *Havurkar*? More than ever we could use the intel on what *Macedon* turns up about that merchant."

"The *Gra'tlir* is dead! Don't you care?"

She didn't blink. "Of course we do. All the more reason to discover what's going on. You'd waste their deaths?"

She was a symp, all right. That was a Niko answer.

"I killed them. I don't want to do that again. Can't you tell him that?"

Something in her face softened, but only a little. "Musey, we need you here." She took out a cube from her pocket and went to the small table beside the bed, fished out an old model silver comp. "He sent you something. View it on this, then you better get back to your crew. I'll be in the hall."

She popped the cube in and left me there.

I stared at the comp screen. An icon flashed, waiting for activation. So I sat on the bed and poked it.

Niko's image bloomed, eyes stark against the white head wrap, like the first time I'd ever seen him. He stared at me, but with that odd disconnection that happens when the other person can't actually interact with you, like a first-gen holocharacter. But his voice was the same. He spoke in Ki'hade, a fall of words that poured into me like clear water.

"Jos-na, I believe in you. This is a risk, making this for you, but I want you to know it. I can't speak to you physically but I see you here." He touched his temple. "And here." His heart. "*Ritlua*. Worthy student." A smile drifted through his serious face. "I will see you, *s'yta-na*."

The message shut, then the cube slot made a soft noise. Deleting. No doubt my contact would physically destroy it after I had gone. Efficient and precise, like his words had been. Just enough to remind me what I wanted and couldn't have.

And even knowing that, I wanted it still. I'd only been on *Macedon* for a few weeks. Niko had stayed with me and trained me for over a year. What sacrifices had he made to keep me? What did I have to do to keep him?

I knew what. My heart pounded it out in my ears, like a protest. I'd play his message through my mind for a long time; I already had it memorized.

Ritlua. He'd taught me a new word.

XXVI.

The Charger APC troop bay smelled like gun oil, metal, and the cold sweat of close, nervous bodies. Low yellow light gave everyone a jaundiced complexion and highlighted the dark gray bulkheads like molten metal. Beside me, Kris checked and rechecked the pulse pack on his rifle and fingered his helmet's unfastened chinstrap. Across from me, Erret Dorr sat slouched in his webbing and well-used black plate armor, legs outstretched and eyes half-closed. He cradled his rifle in his arms like a lover, cheek against the muzzle.

After considerable interrogation of the symps in our brig (who were later dumped on Chaos for trial) and investigation into the fleeting sig from the merchant at the battle, Hartman and Dorr identified the ship as Diamond-class

Shiva, a name that rang vaguely familiar, though I couldn't place where. By all accounts it was an upstanding ship, but it had been spotted in the same vicinity as a striviirc-na dreadnought, in apparent camaraderie.

Macedon was too large to approach the merchant without being detected so we had to sneak our way under their scan tech in a stealth-capable Charger, then force a lock and board. After that it was a routine search and seizure. So Dorr said. Jets did this sort of thing a lot.

I flexed my half-gloved fingers around the rifle stock. The pickup in my ear buzzed slightly, then Nathan's voice came over, familiar, moderate, and without the usual joking tone.

"We're under their scan, free and clear. Two mikes and we're sealed."

Lieutenant Stavros signaled Hartman with a brisk hand movement and unstrapped herself. Lieutenant Ballard, commanding the second platoon, motioned the same to his sergeant.

Sergeant Hartman nudged the corporal awake. "Dorr, to the lock."

"Rilke, set the birthday present," Dorr ordered, yawning.

Kris extricated himself from his crash straps and dug into his gear for the shaped charge that we'd prepared on *Macedon*. He held it gingerly and went to our outer airlock. I took up a position behind his elbow, ready to move in, while Dorr and Madison covered the left side of the lock. The rest of the two platoons readied themselves in order of attack flow. Once we got *Shiva*'s lock blown it was going to be thick; by then the merchant crew would know we were there.

Nathan gently bumped and clamped the Charger against *Shiva*'s lock nipple. The light overhead snapped from red to green and the seal flared open. Kris stuck the charge to the middle of the merchant's lock, poked the timer, and stepped back. We slid down our eye shields.

"Fire in the hole!"

We turned our armored shoulders to the seal. The charge beeped five times. A sharp pop and a line of smoke billowed briefly out, then came the heavy clang and thud of the seal falling outward from the explosion, into *Shiva*'s corridor.

Before it hit the other side Kris tossed through a thunder-flash. A deafening boom ricocheted in the air, accompanied by a blinding light. Our eye shields and helmets protected us, but not any enemy on the other side. We laid down fire in continuous, controlled bolts.

"Go!" Dorr commanded, when nothing came back at us.

Kris stepped through, followed by Madi. Dorr and I went after at a measured pace, through the veil of smoke and into a wide white corridor, tinted red by blinking emergency lights. Bodies lay crumpled on the painted deck, cut down and stained. I kept my eyes away so they were no more than dark shadows in my peripherals. The stripes on the deck confirmed we were on maindeck. Kris and Madi fanned the right corridor. Dorr and I followed on their six. The rest of the platoons poured through the lasered seal behind us.

"Deck up." Stavros's voice came through the pickup.

We'd memorized schematics of the Diamond-class merchant ships. Our goal was the bridge.

We spread through the ship like a virus.

"Where's our resistance?" Dorr muttered, once we'd reached the command deck.

The ship sat curiously silent. Only our booted steps along the deckgrille made noise. Overhead the lights flickered red: warning, warning, warning.

"Maybe they're barricaded," Madi said.

"Or evacuated," Hartman said, her voice a tinny relay in my ear. "Jelilian, what you got?"

"No movement in the bays," he came back. "Their outriders ain't peepin'."

"This is shit," Dorr said. He unhooked a singing grenade, poked the settings, then let it go in midair. It shot forward down the corridor with a soft whir and turned the corner, seeking man-sized heat signatures that weren't protected by our coded armor beacons. Dorr flipped the tracker open on his wrist and watched the grenade's route.

None of the other teams reported any contact.

My gut started to coil.

"It's gone to the bridge," Dorr said.

That meant none of the rooms or quarters were occupied between here and the bridge. Kris increased his pace.

"They're lying in wait," I said, just as the grenade exploded against the double-walled bridge hatch.

The ceiling panels slid aside and fire rained down. Two bodies thudded to the deck behind me as I slammed back against a hatch, covered somewhat in the recess, and shot out and upward into the corridor. A blast caught my shoulder armor and I hunkered down in reflex. The laser pulse hadn't penetrated.

"Eyes up!" Dorr yelled through the pickup to the other teams.

A body fell to the deck in front of me from our team's fire. Kris, Madi, and the two teams at our six coughed bolts from their rifles, the report echoing up and down the corridor. No paralysis pulses. Across from me in an identical recessed hatchway the corporal unhooked another grenade and tossed it overhead. I checked fast and fired again where I saw an arm, then again, popping in and out of my cover in stunted cadence when I spied a target. Grunts and swearing came from above and through my pickup. Two more bodies fell at our feet. They were dead before they hit, from our shots.

A silver tube protruded from one pocket.

"They're rigged!"

I slapped the hatch access open and dived through just as the body in the corridor exploded. A wash of red seeped through my sight. Sparks lit behind my eyelids, they were so tightly shut. My breath came ragged.

"Oh, hell," somebody said. Then the sounds of retching.

"We're clear!" Hartman snapped. "Get to the bridge!"

I picked myself up and turned slowly to the corridor.

Dorr stood across the width. His eyes were dark and his armor splattered with blood and things you just weren't meant to see.

He locked my gaze.

"Move out, Musey!"

My body responded to that voice before my mind did. I stepped out. My boot slipped. Dorr shoved my shoulder with the butt of his rifle and I saw Kris on my right, with Madi, wet streaks down his face—sweat, maybe. Blood on his leg armor.

"I said move!"

Kris and Madi covered steadily as Dorr and I jogged forward. The other teams came up in waves. Through the pickup I heard hell raised all through the ship.

"Wire!" Dorr yelled at me.

He swept his rifle around, his back to me, as I pulled the case explosive from my webbing pouch. I used my knife to pry open the bridge hatch's control box, then yanked out the chipboard and wires, attaching them to the proper ports in the case. Behind me the pulse shots started again, loud and alive, stabbing through my mind. The enemy had reinforcements in their ranks. The scent of burned clothing, bodies, and metal swept under my eye shield and up into my head.

I turned my face, held up an arm, and tapped the trigger.

Burned wire added to the melt of scents, then the bridge

hatch grated open automatically, a handspan. I shot through the breach as Dorr, Kris, and Madison came up to pry it wider. Bolts spat out and we jerked back.

"We want one of the officers alive!" Hartman reminded sharply through the pickup in my ear.

"Fuck," Dorr said. He aimed his rifle blind through the crack and sprayed randomly, short spurts to keep the enemy low, then pulled back. "Lay down your weapons or we send in grenades!" he bluffed at the people on the bridge.

"You sure you didn't kill 'em all?" Madi asked wryly.

His answer shot between us in the form of a small thrown grenade. I didn't know how Dorr expected it, but he caught it midair and threw it back.

An explosion burst hollowly through the breach.

"I said alive!" Hartman barked.

Dorr grinned, eyes shining through his smoke-grimed face. "Them or us." He raised his voice. "What'll it be, mates? Hurry it up, I'm missin' my dinner."

I pulled out my small recon optic, flicked it activated, and unhooked it from my armor. I bent the eye to the opening so it scoped the bridge. A ghost image of seven people and some structural damage appeared on my eye shield heads-up display.

"They're behind their seats and armed."

"Stubborn bastards," the corporal said. "We'll just have to convince 'em. You got one marked?" he asked me.

"Yeah."

"Gimme that."

I tossed the optic across to him. It was still primed to my HUD. He held it up to give me a view of the bridge. I gripped my rifle, picked my target, and swung quickly to face the breach. I fired one shot, then pulled back tight as laser rained out.

"One down," Dorr said.

A sharp expletive shot out at us after the laser.

"This'll go quicker an' with less bloodshed if y'all toss down your weapons!" Dorr yelled.

Nathan's voice crackled through. "They launched outriders—and they're armed!"

The Charger sat like a growth against *Shiva*'s side. It had guns but no maneuverability, locked as it was.

"Call 'em off!" Dorr shouted at the bridge. "Muse."

I eyed the HUD of the undecided crew, saw a head bob back behind one of the right-most seats. I swung in again and fired, one shot through the chair, and pulled back. They didn't return fire. I heard the body thud to the deck.

"Call off your fuckin' riders," Dorr said again, in a different tone.

From the pickup it sounded like jets everywhere were taking down crew. Someone inside the bridge gave a command. "They're breaking," Nathan said. Then came the sound of heavy metal hitting deckplates.

"Come out to mid-bridge," Dorr commanded, still braced against the hatch and watching me. I nodded to him when I saw the remaining crew step out from their damaged cover. "Kick your weapons away and get facedown on the deck, hands behind your heads."

I nodded to him again and he signaled Kris and Madi to pry the hatch all the way open. Hartman and the other two fire teams started to come up closer. Reports of all-clear came spattering through my pickup from all over the ship, as well as requests for medics. Dorr and I moved onto the bridge, rifles aimed at the people lying on the deck. Five of them. Two others were dead. We frisked the live ones for other weapons while Sarge and the teams confiscated the tossed guns. Then Dorr stepped on the back of one of the men and shoved his rifle muzzle against the man's head.

"Which one of you's in command?"

"Fuck you, jet."

Dorr pressed the trigger. The body didn't even move. Laser pulse at close range just went right through you. Dorr moved to the next crewmember, a woman with long dark hair.

Sweat stung my eyes. Blood scented the recycled air.

The woman said, "I'm in command."

Dorr stepped back, fixed on her. "Get up slow. Keep your hands on your head."

She rose to her feet, back still to the corporal.

"Walk," Dorr said.

I flanked her with Dorr as the other jets cuffed the rest of the bridge crew. We headed back to the Charger. Up and down the corridors jets escorted restrained prisoners. Some were teenagers. Younger than teenagers.

My boots dragged on the deck.

XXVII.

We maintained a tight circle around the prisoners as we marched them to the brig. A quick head count came up at eighty-seven. There were about fifty casualties on their side, a dozen on ours, five fatal for the jets. We'd taken them by surprise. They seemed to have concentrated on grouping their people off-ship, probably because they knew once jets were aboard, *Macedon* wasn't far behind. Five of their outriders had scattered with who knew how many more crew aboard. Scout ships that size could hold anywhere from thirty to fifty people, depending on how crammed they wanted to be. Nathan had shot two. Even if *Mac* pursued a couple, the others would get away. They either had a sink-hole or they'd eventually starve to death in the Dragons.

Lieutenant Stavros separated the children from the adults and ordered jets to take the kids to training deck, which had a few empty rooms since graduation. The rest of us corralled the *Shiva* crew into the brig cells. They were quiet after the first few rebels were beaten for mouthing off or fighting. None of our medics helped them. Bleeding, bruised, or otherwise in pain, they huddled in the cells and stared out at us as the gates slid shut and locked. Hatred was only one of the emotions in their eyes.

I pulled off my helmet and ran a hand through my damp hair. Kris caught my gaze and without a word we started for the exit.

"Jos!"

My nerves jumped. I stopped and turned. So did Kris. Dorr, Madi, and Hartman looked over while the other jets streamed by us, uninterested.

One of the *Shiva* crew fought his way to the cell gate. "Jos Musey!"

A feral face pressed to the bars. Slate-blue eyes searched for mine, then locked like a missile.

I couldn't move.

"Who the hell're you?" Dorr said, in my silence.

"Evan," I said, from a long distance away. I stepped forward but Dorr grabbed my arm. I tugged at him violently.

"Stand down, Private Musey!" Hartman's voice cut through the sudden dark caul that had fallen over my mind.

I went still. Kris moved up to my other side and held my armored shoulder.

"Who is this?" the sergeant asked me, without tolerance.

"*Mukudori*," I said. All I could say.

"Get me outta here, Jos," Evan pleaded. His voice rose, hysterical. "Get me out!"

"Shut up!" Dorr barked.

I shoved at the corporal and made for the cell. Kris and Dorr both hauled me back.

The prisoners started to yell. One of them grabbed Evan out of sight.

My rifle snapped up. "Let him go!"

"Musey!" Hartman knocked down the muzzle. She strode to the cell, weapon trained. "Bring the kid forward. Now!"

They shoved Evan against the bars. He winced. Bruises stained up and down both his arms.

"Let him out," I said. "Sergeant, let him out."

Hartman glared at me. "Shut the hell up, Musey!" Kris's fingers dug into the inside of my elbow, between my armor. Hartman eyed Evan. "What're you doin' with this lot?"

"They b-bought me. After our ship—" His eyes trailed to me, wet, red, and panicked. "Tell her, Jos. Please—just get me out of here. Please."

Dorr's and Rilke's hands held me fast. The ghost that was Evan didn't take his eyes from me, or me from him. Hartman stared silent for half a minute, then fingered her wirecomm. Then she said, "Captain, we have a situation." She explained it in terse terms, looking at me.

My stomach rolled over and clenched as she paused to listen.

"Yes, sir," she said finally, and signed off. She motioned Madi forward. "Open the gate." She stepped back, weapon up. "The rest of you get to the wall. Now!"

The crew edged away as Evan came up close to the gate. As soon as Madi yanked it back he moved out. Hartman turned him around roughly and cuffed his wrists behind his back. His breath expelled in frightened gasps. I pulled at Dorr's grip.

"Give the corporal your weapons," Hartman ordered. "Then you can approach. Carefully, or I'll shoot you both."

I unstrapped my webbing and dumped it to the deck, then shoved my rifle and sidearm at Dorr. Evan stood motionless, chin lowered, eyes darting up to me and around as I advanced. Then they steadied, two blue sparks from the pallor of his gaunt face. He looked older than his standard age, when he should've seemed younger. *Shiva* was a deep-space merchant.

I remembered those eyes watching the door of the hole Falcone had put us in. I remembered burrowing against his side and listening to his heartbeat in the dark, thinking he could protect us just because he was older. Now he looked at me for protection. His eyes begged. He said, "Get me out of here."

XXVIII.

Sergeant Hartman, on Captain Azarcon's orders, allowed Kris and me to take Evan to an empty q on training deck. I was sure Azarcon wanted this to play out to see what he could get from it—from either Evan or me. Someone from *Shiva* who might be willing to talk was an opportunity. Captains had to think that way.

Hartman told me to talk to Evan (she meant interrogate), then ordered a fresh jet to stand outside as guard. Kris left us alone and I stood awkwardly by one of the bunks while Evan folded his arms against his body and leaned against the bulkhead, as if he was afraid to sit. He shivered and wiped constantly at his hair, which had grown since the last time I'd seen him, like the rest of him—he must have been eighteen now. His hair hung in his eyes, dirty pale. His eyes never settled on anything for long, especially my face.

"You got cigs?" he asked, the first words since leaving brig.

"No, but . . . just a mike." I stepped out of the quarters and asked the jet there for a stick. He fished one out, lit it for me, and I took it back and handed it to Evan.

Evan accepted it without a word and dragged deep.

"You can sit."

He glanced at me and slid down the wall to his haunches, one arm against his stomach.

"I meant on the bunk."

"I'm all right here." He sucked on that cig like it was his last.

I crouched down across from him, then sat, resting my elbows on my knees. The narrow quarters only put us a couple meters apart. He looked at me briefly, wiped his hair back only to have it fall forward, then looked at me again. This time his gaze lingered in a kind of stunned disbelief.

"Shit, Jos. Shit."

"Evan, what happened?"

He shook his head, glanced away, then back at my face. "Look at you. I can't believe it." His eyes filled.

Now I looked to the corner. "I know. I'm alive. You are too. Is anybody else? On *Shiva*?"

"No. No more on *Shiva*."

"Nobody from *Mukudori*—"

"No." He looked toward the hatch.

"Evan."

"What's gonna happen to me?"

I stared for a moment. I was in no position to make promises, and he'd been found on a ship that had shot at a carrier.

"I don't know."

"Don't put me back there. You can't—I'll do anything, Jos, I'll do anything." He shifted forward until I could smell the smoke on his clothes and the sweat on his skin. He gripped my sleeve.

"I'll try and help you, Evan, but—I'm new on this ship, I don't really have a say in much." His breath stank. Up close I saw the blood vessels in his eyes and tiny cuts along his collar and the backs of his hands. He stared into my face now without wavering.

"You're older," he said, flat-toned.

I shifted, trying not to shove him back but wishing he'd let me go. The desperation in his eyes made a hard block of ice form in my stomach.

"I'm almost fifteen," I said, and put my hand on his wrist to disengage his grip.

"Don't trade me again, tell—tell your captain not to trade me."

I got caught in the claws of his gaze. Everything about him was different from what I remembered. Somewhere in that older-than-eighteen face was a vague recollection of the twelve-year-old who had alternately terrorized and played with me. I had looked to him as a lifeline in Falcone's ship.

"Let go, Evan." The fear in his face put me ill at ease.

He released me finally and slid back against the bulkhead. The cigret burned down to a stub.

The hatch swung open without warning and Corporal Dorr stepped in. He looked a lot less fearsome out of battle armor but Evan still shrank back, staring at him guardedly.

Dorr glanced at Evan but otherwise ignored him. "Musey, let's go."

I stood. Evan tucked against himself tighter and barely looked up.

"I'll come back," I said, though I didn't even know that.

Evan nodded slightly as if he didn't really believe me. I followed Dorr out to the corridor. He nodded to the jet who remained behind by the hatch, and headed toward jetdeck.

"Cap wants to see you."

I went cold. Azarcon hadn't seen or said a thing to me since before training.

"He's a mess." The corporal lit a cigret and smoked as we went to the lev and in. Obviously he didn't mean the captain.

"He was on a ship that bought him."

"From who?"

"Falcone. We were both on the *Khan*. Before." I listened to the lev's growling hydraulics as we ascended the decks. Black dirt had crusted in the corners. Scrub duty soon for some poor disobedient crewman.

"So what'd they do with him?" Dorr asked. "He bin there all that time with them pirates?"

I looked at the corporal. He was curious, not concerned. He had to know very well what pirates did to bought crew. Worked them to death or worse.

"Is *Shiva* really a pirate?" I said. "They port legal, don't they?"

"They used to. Not no more they won't."

I remembered then that Falcone had docked legally too, at Chaos. False documentation, false sigs.

Dorr straightened from the gray lev wall as the doors grated open. I followed him out, down the same clean corridor I'd taken with Madi to the captain's office. Not a tube of light flickered here. Dorr hid the cig behind his leg as the hatch opened. He sent me in.

"Thank you, Corporal." Azarcon sat behind his desk, like the first time I'd met him. He gave Dorr two glances as the corporal stepped back to the corridor to wait. "And put out that cigret, you know there's no smoking on open deck."

"Yes, sir." He didn't sound the least bit contrite. In fact he grinned as the hatch shut.

I faced Azarcon. He leaned back in his chair and

motioned briefly for me to take the seat opposite him. This was new. I sat.

"So how is he?" Azarcon said, the last thing I expected from his mouth.

"Scared, sir."

"I don't trust him and neither should you. Feel fortunate that I even let him out of the brig. Do you read me?"

"Yes, sir."

"Corporal Dorr said you did well on the mission."

He jumped from topic to topic and it had to be purposeful. I hadn't had time to think about the mission and I didn't want to now. I just nodded, conscious of the fact I was still in my fatigues, though I'd ditched the armor, and I probably stank.

He looked at me carefully. "Private Musey, *Shiva* is a pirate ship. The fact nobody until now could really confirm it is because she reported directly—and only—to *Genghis Khan*."

I blinked, feeling the weariness that had started to seep into me snap alert.

"She operated legally, as a front, while keeping one foot in bed with Falcone. She was Falcone's second in command."

I had nowhere to look but into his eyes, and I couldn't read them.

"Why're you telling me this, sir?"

"Did you know about her?"

"No, sir." Dread started to shed its skin beneath my own.

"The *Khan* had never rendezvoused with her in the year you were there?"

"It might've, but I didn't know it. He never took me off ship until Chaos and he never told me his operations." I let my voice grow hard. "Sir."

"How long has your friend been on *Shiva*?"

"Since Falcone sold him. He's scared, sir. He's in need of

food and sleep and maybe a hot shower and I just didn't get around to fully interrogating him yet, sir."

I was tired and probably in slight shock, for a number of reasons. Azarcon put a hand on his desk in that casual way he had, though his eyes never left my face.

"You *will* interrogate him and you won't forget that we don't know what he did on that ship. He could be one of their operatives. I want you to find out what's happened to him, what exactly he did after you two were separated—I want details."

He didn't reprimand me for my borderline insubordination. I said calmly, "Yes, sir."

"I want to know everything he knows about *Shiva*'s operations. It might be he knows nothing. It might be he was the bedmate of a captain who talked in her sleep."

"Yes, sir." *Ask the damn* Shiva *captain, then.*

They probably were asking her and I just couldn't hear her screams from jetdeck. If that woman we'd captured was even the captain. More likely the ship brass had fled on the outriders.

"Can I get him cleaned up, sir?" They were allowing the children that luxury.

"Yes, go ahead. Send me reports at the end of every duty shift."

I took that as dismissal and stood.

"And, Private . . ."

"Sir?"

"Write me everything you can remember about Falcone. Everything."

I stared at him, frozen. He would've had a report from Social Services on Austro, a brisk account from the memory of a nine-year-old. Niko had arranged it. And then my own psych form, from training.

"Is there a problem, Private Musey?"

"No, sir."

"Then you're dismissed."

I saluted and left.

XXIX.

Dorr walked me back to jetdeck without asking what the captain had wanted; he probably knew.

"I guess the crew's going to be interrogated," I said. He knew which crew I meant.

"Yah. 'Specially 'bout why they were meetin' a strit ship out in the wide dark yonder. Man, if the strits an' pirates are hookin' up, we'll be in sinking shit."

I had to send another report to Niko. I had to write a detailed report about Falcone almost six years after the fact. And I had to dig at the only other person who remembered *Mukudori* as more than a name on a slate. Everything I did was dirty.

But I wanted to talk to Niko, more now than anytime since I'd been on this ship. My feet moved but I wasn't quite aware of where we were going until Dorr stopped me outside my quarters.

"Ain't I gallant?" He grinned. "Now go sleep. That's an order."

"Evan—"

"Ain't goin' nowhere and you're dead on your peds. I'll have the jet check on him."

"Captain Azarcon said he can clean up."

"Then I'll get somebody to hose him down."

I stared at Dorr. He laughed.

"Crikey, Muse, learn to smile. Alright? Now get lost, I'm

sure Rilke is pacin' the deck waitin' for you." The grin and dimples appeared again.

I longed to hit him. Instead I went inside the q. Kris wasn't pacing, but sitting on his bunk doing nothing. He rose to his feet when I came in.

"What happened?"

"Nothing happened." I went to my bunk and grabbed my pouch of toiletries from the footlocker. The quarters was a double bunk only, our racks against one wall across from each other, with lockers, upright tiny closet space, and a narrow comp desk. It was cleaner than how we'd left it before the mission. Kris must have tidied it up in my absence. I headed back out.

"Musey, wait—what d'you mean nothing happened? What's with that guy—"

"I'm going to take a shower." I said it more to interrupt him than really tell him what I was doing.

"Are you all right?"

He was going to follow me. To the shower. I turned and pushed him back, not gently.

"I'm fine. Just—leave me alone." I glanced into his eyes, not sure of what I saw there, and left. He didn't follow.

The shower was on a timer. After five minutes it shut off and the body dryer cycled. I cut it and cycled the water again and just stood there, letting it come down on my head and steam my vision. Soap scent replaced some of the things that had clung to my skin during and after that mission. But I still smelled *Shiva* lingering through the clean. Images lingered. No amount of water and soap got rid of those.

When I approached my quarters, Kris and Aki were at the opposite end of the corridor, walking away together, their backs to me. She had her hand on his shoulder. I couldn't hear them. They didn't look behind them or see me when they turned the corner. I went inside quarters and shut the hatch before the sound of their bootsteps faded away.

I collapsed on my bunk, put a boot on the mattress and the other on the floor, and stared up at the ceiling. Rows of lights and cold pipes. The ever-present hum of the drives seemed too loud. It grated on my nerves. I rolled over and found myself staring at Kris's bunk. I memorized the wrinkles on his blanket from where he'd sat. Anything to get my mind away from reports and interrogations.

I was still staring when he returned, a couple hours later. I tossed onto my back and he paused in surprise.

"I thought you'd be asleep by now."

"No." I put an arm behind my head and didn't look at him. He fell into his rack.

We lay in silence for a while.

"Jos, what happened to your friend? Who is he?"

Kris came from a station culture. He hadn't grown up with talk or threat of pirate ships and Slavepoint. Sympathizers once upon a time bombed Austro dock and his bad luck put his father on that dockside. But he had the station to take care of him. Pirates killed ships and confiscated crew, then ransomed them or sold them. And the rumors were not as bad as the reality.

"He was my home," I said. "And now he's not."

I felt Kris turn to look at me. I thought he would say something inanely appropriate. But he didn't. I blinked at the lights and said, "We got ourselves a pirate ship."

After a moment he said, "Yeah. Well, we're jets."

And so we were.

XXX.

I awoke an hour before our shift's reveille and stared into the pitch-black of the quarters. Across from me Kris slept heavily for once, the deep expelled breath of somebody who would need a klaxon in order to wake up. Missions did that to him. I slid out from under the blankets and stuffed my feet into the boots I'd left by the bunk and went blind to the hatch. I'd slept in fatigues so I wouldn't have to fumble around.

Everyone was either on duty or in bed, or blowing off steam in the lounge. At the head I tapped in my holopoints and went to the jet wardroom, the only place that wouldn't be suspicious if somebody found me in there. A quick peek inside confirmed it was empty. I opened one of the black comps and sat, keeping an eye to the hatch, blinked a few times, then palmed the comp to holointerface mode. I had to hurry. People tended to interrupt after five minutes. That wasn't enough time to send a code quantum hopping all the way to striv space.

I slid into the main systems ops "city" grid, leaving a banner behind to mark my entry/exit ramp, primed only to my interface code. I soared deeper through the carnival-lit trenches of Operations. Outgoing ship communications was a first tier division in *Macedon*'s complicated network but I had to bypass a thick wall of code to access it, since I didn't have first level authorization. This was where I spent most of my time.

I set my symbol self to an acute awareness, like a tuning fork reverberating to perfect pitch, and concentrated my efforts on dissecting that code, sliding in bogus authorizations that would deke the real scans so they wouldn't send up flags or, worse yet, military polisyms. These were codes I'd spent hours building first on my private comp files, then memorizing in my head as the picture-code the holointerface recognized. I'd had a template from training with Ashdan; once I got to see the customized program tiers on the ship, I'd altered the template accordingly.

The diamond-bright code wall accepted my authorization but you couldn't tell how long that would last. *Macedon*'s own communications officer could be rooting around in here and would recognize an intruder. I flew to the outgoing comm ops, my symself a sharply constructed red dagger, and cut through to the carrier's satellite access. The closest setup was on Chaos, so it would be there I'd bump my sig straight toward striv space, where Niko had placed hidden sats at key pickup points. Blindly I set my holocube into the comp's uplink slot and blinked an undercarrying code. My message would ride under the wire of a normal outgoing comm, or barring that, I'd send it while simultaneously deleting any record of an outgoing from this comp. A quick flicker around the area confirmed that *Macedon* was already sending out comms, like they routinely did unless they were silent running. I tucked my message beneath a particularly thick-coded communiqué and tracked its progress along the satellite link nodes. At Chaos they diverged and I knew mine was on its way on preprogrammed teleportation blinks.

I accessed the second codestring in the holocube and sent it shooting from Chaos to insystem, straight to Austro and another one of my prearranged contacts, a symp who went by the commsig Otter. It was a simple query about Falcone's whereabouts. Otter had more time to dive for the pirate's codes than I ever would on this carrier. A long shot, but since Niko wanted updates I figured I had a right to them too.

I fled the comm ops, whipping back to the entry/exit and dissolving my footprint codes as I went. My eyes burned, sparking black suns, after I shut down the comp and palmed the holocube. The flash of the ops grid still shone in afterimage as I left the wardroom and made my way down the corridor. When I turned the corner I bumped straight into Corporal Dorr. He steadied me. I stepped back before his hand could linger. His gaze flickered.

"Bad sleep?"

I shook my head. "No, sir."

"Your boy's askin' for you. You got him for duty this shift, ahright?"

"Yes, sir." My brain felt heated. I slipped past him and went to the head to take out the optic receptors. Hopefully Ash-dan would pick up my report, or Niko would intercept it himself. It was on a path to Aaian-na but *Turundrlar* could be patrolling in the area. I didn't want another ship to get it, especially one that might meet with pirates. It was in code only Niko and Ash-dan knew, but codes could be broken with the right minds.

By the time I got to Evan's hatch I felt steadier, my vision clear. I had to be clear to deal with him. I handed Private Dumas my sidearm, then knocked on the hatch before motioning the jet to open it. I found Evan huddled in the corner of one of the bunks. A food tray lay scraped empty on the floor. He'd showered and wore badgeless black fatigues. Surplus from supply. It made his skin look paler. His face lit when he saw me, then flattened out to careful suspicion. The jet outside must've given him another cig; the quarters was misty with smoke.

"You're back," he said cautiously.

"I said I would be." I approached the bunk slowly and sat opposite. "How're you feeling?"

"Like shit." His hand shook slightly as he brought the cig to his lips. His other arm lay tight against his stomach.

"Are you cold?"

"Yeah. But the guy outside . . . he said they couldn't do nothin' 'bout that."

"Here. Get under the blankets."

He seemed afraid to move even that much, as if he had no right to mess up the bunk. I tugged at the covers until he worked his legs under them, then pulled them up and around him. His shoulders were thin under the shirt when I patted the end of the blanket there. He watched me with the close intensity of a wary animal. Clean, his hair was pale yellow like I remembered, the same color as Corporal Dorr's, but straight and ragged.

I moved to sit back on the opposite bunk but he caught my sleeve.

"Where did you go? What're they gonna do with me?" His eyes were steadier since the shift before, though far from trusting. Relief, but also resignation.

"I got quarters on board. I'm a jet here. That's where I went."

"A jet. Yeah. That's right." His eyes traveled all over me, looking at the BDU, the emblems and insignias. "They gonna dump me?"

"No." Azarcon hadn't indicated that. At any rate, I wouldn't stand by and let it happen.

"What're they gonna do?"

"You'll stay here for now, where it's safe."

He stared at me, remembered the cig in his hand, and took a long drag. "Nowhere's safe, Jos. Thought you knew that."

I couldn't exactly argue with him. Instead I sat back at the foot of the bunk to give us some room. "Did they send in a medic to look at you?"

"No. Don't want no death doctor pokin' at me."

"What happened on *Shiva*, Evan?"

He darted looks at me, then all around the quarters. His voice was sharp. "What happened on *Genghis Khan*?"

I took a breath. "I was only there a year."

"Huh." He nodded absently and plucked a bit at the blanket, then flicked his ashes in the small cup by his elbow. "I was gone for six on *Shiva*. More than a minute's too long, so why don't you remember?"

"I was only eight."

"And I was only twelve!" he suddenly shouted. My body snapped taut. "Stop askin' me about *Shiva*! I was only fuckin' twelve!"

"All right. All right." I wished I had my sidearm. My nerves twitched.

Evan sniffed and raked back his hair, said with cold calm, "If you're here to grill me then go ahead and be done. It's what you want, right?"

His schiz reactions sent alarms through me. "I don't want anything."

"Yeah you do. Everybody does."

"I just want to help." This was not the person I'd thought would grow into his older brother, handsome and self-assured. Of course he wasn't. My mouth was dry.

"You want to help." He smiled but it wasn't pleasant. One canine tooth was chipped.

"Yeah. Let me help you. If we're the only ones left— Evan, I thought you were dead." The words barely fit around the sudden heaviness in my throat.

"No, guess I'm alive. Cosmic joke, that."

"What d'you mean?"

He didn't answer. Smoke drifted in front of his face. He stared at me through it. "How'd you get on this tanker?"

"I signed on. From Austro."

"Austro?"

"Yeah. Where I grew up."

He squinted at me. "Falcone let you go at Austro? I thought it was Chaos."

I sat still. "He didn't let me go. I ran. How did you know?"

"They talk."

"Who they?"

He waved his hand and shrugged. "You were supposed to be his next thing. He really liked you. You had it sweet."

Somehow I breathed, though it felt as if my lungs contracted and stuck. "Had it sweet."

He shrugged again and smoked.

"Evan. Help me understand. What happened to you after . . . I woke up and you all were gone?"

"I don't wanna talk about it."

Rage simmered just below his fear, equally as thick.

"All right." Azarcon would have to wait. Evan had a right not to talk. I couldn't blame him. "Do you need anything else? I got leave to stay with you, so . . ."

"Stay with me?"

"Yeah."

He was silent for so long I thought he was daydreaming. Then he moved slowly and stubbed out the cig and looked at me from behind ragged ends of hair.

"Is it safe? Here?"

"Yeah, it's safe. If they fed you and clothed you I don't think they're gonna vent you. I won't let 'em, anyway."

He pushed the blankets down and crawled over to me. I shifted back and put one boot on the floor.

"I don't wanna be traded again. Since you know me, they won't trade me, will they? You won't let 'em?"

His shoulder pressed against mine. I moved until I was almost off the bunk. "I told you—I wouldn't."

"Okay. Then I believe you."

His hand found the bottom of my shirt and slipped beneath it.

I stood up hastily, dragging half the blanket with me, almost tripping on it.

"What the hell're you doing?" I stepped back until my legs hit the opposite bunk.

"You said they want you to stay with me. And they won't dump me off or trade me. You said you won't let them."

"Yeah, so?"

"So then . . ." He looked at me carefully. After a moment something shut down behind his eyes and he moved back against the bulkhead. His hands shook.

I had nothing in my head to say. My limbs refused to move.

After a while I realized he was crying. He made no sound, his breathing stayed regular, yet tears made uneven tracks down his face. He didn't even bother to wipe them away.

My voice wasn't at all convincing. "Why don't you—try to sleep."

He didn't move. I wanted to leave. I wanted to reassure him because I kept seeing that twelve-year-old boy in my mind, getting hit when they dragged me away. He bore bruises still. And I wanted to leave.

"Go on," he said finally, without emotion. "Go on before I make you sick."

"You don't . . . you don't make me sick."

"I make myself sick."

I took a hesitant step toward him but he suddenly grabbed the cup of ashes and flung it at me. Gray-white specks flew wild around me, dusted my uniform.

"Go on! Get the fuck out!" He rose to his knees as if to lunge at me.

I stepped back, then back again, toward the hatch. His face was a dry, contorted rage. But not at me. Not at me.

"Get out!"

I fumbled with the hatch but it was locked from the outside. I banged on it until the jet opened it, then shoved past him without a word. Behind me followed only silence.

I walked through the corridors with no idea where I went.

I stopped by some stairs and sat on the cold metal, didn't know for how long, but crew passed and asked me questions and I never answered them.

I started walking again without thought. I circled back to Evan's hatch and retrieved my sidearm from Dumas, then left jetdeck. I took the lev down to the lonely, colder part of the ship, straight into brig where the *Shiva* crew that we'd captured sat huddled in their cells, murmuring to one another. The jet at the security desk ignored them, alternately watching her console and tapping at her comp. I strode by her without a word and stopped by the farthest cell.

"Private?" the jet asked.

I pulled my sidearm and aimed it at an older man. "I'll start with your feet and work up. Unless you answer my questions."

"Private!"

The *Shiva* man stood still, looking at me with stone eyes. His mouth tightened.

"Kid, there ain't anything I know to tell you."

The jet came up beside me. "What're you doing? Private"—she looked at my tags—"Musey?"

"I'm interrogating a prisoner. We got a lot, nobody'll miss this one." I kept my gaze on the man. His carefully set arrogance wilted slightly. The other prisoners had fallen silent, dozens of eyes staring at me. At the gun in my hand.

"Are you authorized?" the jet persisted. "Who's your immediate superior?"

I glanced at her. "Corporal Dorr. So comm him."

She went to do that. I kept my gun trained on the man. "Evan D'Silva. Start there."

He stayed silent.

I thumbed the gun to kill, slow enough that he saw it. "Evan D'Silva, mister."

"Scrub kid. That's all I know."

"Cleaned decks, washed pans, is that it?"

The man shrugged.

I shot at his feet. He jumped back and so did the rest of them in the cell. Some of them shouted at me. I had intentionally missed and I told him so.

"Next time I won't."

"Private Musey," the jet said from behind me. I ignored her. She could come and physically remove me if she wanted.

"I had nothing to do with the kid," the man volunteered. "Some of the others . . . yeah. But not me."

"Which others? And what?"

"Higher ranks. Nobody here."

"Convenient."

Nobody said anything to that.

"What did you do to him?"

The man gave me a long look. "I need to spell it out? He was a nice-looking kid."

I shot that man in the chest.

"Private Musey!"

The jet was fast. She grabbed my arm before I could take aim again. All the cells roused in one yelling match. I shoved at the jet but she was capable and held on. I could have floored her but that would've got me into more trouble.

"Corporal Dorr is on his way. Let go the gun!"

I let it go and stared fiercely into the cell, at the packed prisoners who let the man I'd shot lie there bleeding.

"I wanna know what you did to Evan D'Silva, who had anything to do with him, and where they are!" I wrenched from the jet's hold and strode to the cell gate. "Or I'll end you all the same way."

The brig hatch opened and Dorr walked in. His eyes moved fast. Without a blink he took my gun from the jet's hands and passed it back to me. He smiled everywhere but his eyes.

"You can't go shootin' the pirates willy-nilly, Muse. There's a technique to this sorta thing."

The prisoners fell silent, rather abruptly.

"What you wanna know?" the corporal asked me after looking impassively at the dead man.

"About Evan." I stared hard into the *Shiva* faces. "About Falcone."

I didn't think any of them breathed in that moment.

"We asked 'em about Falcone."

I looked at Dorr. "And?"

Dorr looked right back. "And it ain't your concern right now, Musey."

"It's my concern! It's more my concern than it is yours!"

"Oh? How's that?"

"Let me alone with them, sir. I'm asking you."

"Not yet. You go killin' 'em all, we ain't gonna find out jack. It takes time to pry from pirates. They need to understand the grand opportunity for speeches in this forum. If we're too hasty we just waste good ammo. Got it?"

"Let me alone with them and I'll get anything you need."

Dorr laughed. The prisoners still didn't move. "I'm sure you could. But that ain't my orders and I don't think they're yours. You're supposed to be talkin' to your bud and writin' a report. Am I right?"

Azarcon's agenda. Whatever the hell it was, it kept me on the sidelines.

"Evan's not talking. These bastards will if I encourage them."

"Let me worry 'bout that. You go back to him. He's spooked, strange ship an' all. I got a feeling he was more than some pirate's bedbug." This last he said to the pirates, not to me.

"Why do you say that?"

"Do I need to make my pleasant conversation into an order, Private Musey?"

He strategically pulled rank. And I couldn't fight him.

I holstered my sidearm and strode out. All the questions I'd ever had about Falcone and what he was up to could have been answered right in that brig, if I'd just been given a chance. He was within reach, now that I was in space. And I was older and trained. It would be different.

I looked in the wardroom but three jets were in there, relaxing and talking. I went past the hatch before they saw me.

By the time I got back to quarters some of the heat in my blood had cooled. If I could steal a moment I could always dive into Dorr's report files and find out what they'd discovered about Falcone. Or dive the vid files of the interrogations, since I knew they had optics in the brig walls.

I didn't want to go back to Evan yet. I sat at the limited-access comp Kris and I shared and tried to form coherent thoughts about Falcone. They refused to come.

Kris caught me at it, doing nothing, when he came to dump his training gear before lunch.

"Hey, I didn't expect to find you in here." He shrugged out of his webbing, which was splattered with mud from one of our maintenance sims—as Dorr called it. Maintaining your high level of fitness. Being dirty and still able to function was a requirement.

"Well, these're my orders."

He laughed. "To sit in q looking at a comp screen?"

I turned my seat around and watched him. "You seen those kids? The ones off *Shiva*?"

"Nah. Why?"

They'd be scared. I didn't say anything.

Kris was used to my silences by now. "How's your friend—Evan's his name, right?"

"Messed up, thanks to pirates."

Kris eyed me and I knew he waited for more. He sat on his bunk and worked off his dirty boots.

I said, "What's the captain gonna do with those kids?"

He shrugged. "Take them to Chaos, probably. That's the closest station out here."

"Then what? Social Services?"

"Yeah. Or try to find their parents or some relative, if they're alive. I guess what they did with you."

"Evan's eighteen. He's adult. They're gonna put him in some hospital ward he won't ever stay in. But he's . . ."

"What?"

I shifted. "He's not—he's not socialized for, you know, station life. He's gonna just go the wrong way on a station. Gangs, drugs." Worse, I thought.

"You should talk to Cap, then. Maybe he can work something."

"What could he do?"

"I dunno, Jos, that's why you oughtta talk to him. But I don't think he's the type to just dump somebody like Evan."

I wasn't so sure. Evan was more pirate than me, six years in their custody. I'd only been one and Azarcon looked at me sideways.

"I'm gonna shower, then grab some grub. Wanna join?" He laughed, seeing the look on my face, probably. "The grub, not the shower."

"Maybe. I gotta talk to Evan." I shut down the comp and headed for the hatch.

"Oh, hey. I got something."

I turned back. Kris fished into one of his cargo pockets and tossed me a pack of cigrets and a finger lighter.

"I heard he's been sapping the guards dry. Give those to him."

Kris had to have made a special trip to supply for these and bought them out of his own creds. He didn't smoke. I looked at him and "thanks" didn't even make it past my teeth. He managed to blindside me at the oddest moments.

"Say it's against what I owe you for all those poker games you keep winning." His easy smile appeared.

"He'll appreciate it," I said, then just stood there.

Kris raised his eyebrows, amused. I knew he was laughing at me in some benign way that I didn't quite understand.

XXXI.

Dumas looked at me with raised brows when I appeared again and handed over my gun. But he didn't comment, just opened the hatch. Evan looked up at me but didn't seem surprised either, even when I handed him the cigs. He just slipped the finger lighter over his thumb and forefinger, pulled a stick, and sparked it. He sat against the bulkhead at the corner of the bunk, in a riot of blankets, sheets, and pillows. He'd yanked the others off the opposite bunk for a reason I couldn't fathom. He pulled his knee up and rested an arm against it, smoked and watched me. The wall of his detachment was high and solid. The gloss of *Mukudori*, our only real connection, had dulled.

I just said it, or else we would get nowhere. "Earlier, you know, forget about that."

He'd retrieved the cup he used for an ashtray; it sat secure in an eddy of gray blanket.

"Sure," he said. "So what're you doing here?"

"Just to talk."

He found this funny. "You're still so fuckin' innocent, aren't you. A year with Falcone and you're still this innocent? On a carrier full of jets and you're still this innocent?"

"I'm not innocent."

"How old're you again?" He glanced at the ceiling, counting. "Fourteen?"

Somehow he'd turned things around, when I was the one supposed to ask him questions.

I sat on the stripped, opposite bunk. "What's that got to do with anything?"

"I don't feel like talking to you, Jos. I might offend you." The bitterness could have seared flesh.

"You don't offend me."

"I don't feel like telling you anything about *Shiva*."

"That's okay."

"Fuck you, okay?"

I sat on my hands, watching him. "There's nobody but us, Evan. I looked for anybody that survived *Mukudori* but there're no traceable files."

"I don't give a shit about *Mukudori*."

"I don't believe that. Haven't you ever wondered what it could've been like?" I forced myself to keep looking at him, even through the memories. Him and Shane. His parents. My parents. I needed to get through to him. He couldn't just be this stranger. "Don't you miss them?"

He shot out a breath of smoke and glared at me, burning eyes. "You naïve little snit. Come in here and give me shit about ships and wantin' me to remember. I got no memories. I shit 'em out where they belong."

"Even Shane?"

"I drank and pissed his memory a long time ago. You oughtta try it, maybe then you wouldn't be so hung up. You had one damn year with Falcone and you sit there caught up in it. Yeah, think I can't see it? Can't stand to have someone touch you? Why? What'd he do, Jos?"

My hands were going numb. "You misread me."

"Yeah, sure. Probably you liked it more than you wanna admit now."

"Fuck *you*, Evan."

"Can you?"

I kept sitting on my hands, otherwise I would've gone over there and strangled him to death.

"Austro, was it? Funny 'bout that, Jos, but I'd heard you were plucked off Chaos by a bunch of strits."

I stared, cold.

"Falcone was real pissed about that. Shot at by jets 'cause he was shootin' at you and in the confusion he looks up and his ladybug's gone. None of the jets got you. So *Shiva*'s crew got sent to look for you, oh some kid named Jos Musey, dark hair, blue eyes, ask around. You know him on sight. But no Jos. Strits pulled out of the system and no Jos Musey found on the entire station. So how'd you get from Chaos to Austro? That's a big leap for a kid with no creds."

I wasn't aware of breath. His eyes were bloodshot but behind them sat hard clarity.

My voice broke. "They trained you good, Evan."

His hand shook when he took a drag. So I knew I'd hit my mark.

"Was that what the charade in brig was about, Evan? Make like the helpless prisoner, get me to get you out so you can sit in luxury with regular meals and cigs? Or do you give a damn at all? You wanna leash me along, is that it?"

His face lost some of its nastiness. But I didn't know if I could trust it.

"I'm a jet on this ship. I can kill you now and claim you came after me. You wanna play that game?"

"You won't kill me," he said, steady. "I'm your last memory of our ship."

"Maybe I prefer the one where you're twelve."

He stubbed out the cig and tucked his arms against his body, watching me. "You think I'll tell?"

I didn't blink. "Tell what?"

"About you bein' taken by strits."

"I wasn't taken by strits. I got in good with a lady who took pity on me and she bought my passage to Austro. I was nine and I looked cute."

"That's not what *Shiva* said. Or Falcone."

"How do you know?"

"I got ears."

"And other things, apparently." It was low. I saw it cut deep, despite his attempt to mask it. He knew what he'd become and he knew what I hadn't.

He lit another cigret. "So I guess that means it's back to the brig for me."

"Not necessarily." Some time ago my heart had formed a shell around itself. I looked him in the eyes. "Why don't you tell me all about how you heard things from *Shiva* and Falcone?"

He smiled slightly, but like his other emotions it was steeped in a detached kind of cynicism. "Sure. And then I'll just tap that jet outside the hatch and tell him about you and aliens."

"What you know is shit."

"Yeah? Maybe so. Maybe they'd even believe you over me. But there's always that little bit of doubt. Military ships're paranoid places, 'specially in times of war. You sure this quarters ain't bugged?"

"How do you live?" But my stomach clenched.

He shrugged. "Ask yourself."

"You don't wanna leash me, Evan."

"I want someplace safe. I don't wanna get dumped in some damned hospital and shuffled through some station shit's files. Is this a fair ship?"

"Hell no."

"I like it here. I can stay in this room a long time."

"You're a pirate. Azarcon won't see it any other way."

"And what're you? What you wanna know? I'll tell you, but you gotta do something for me. Yeah, they trained me okay. They taught me you don't get somethin' for nothin'. So I'll put out, I'll bend right over for you, Jos. But you get me on this ship."

"That's not gonna happen. And I got no damn incentive. Your lies're no damn incentive."

"Fine. Good-bye." He leaned back and smoked and watched me with the trained eyes of a baiting, backden whore.

It crossed my mind to kill him. Ash-dan would have done it, even Niko. My position here could be compromised. What he knew could probably be wrangled somehow out of one of the prisoners in brig. Azarcon wouldn't miss him, though he might question my killing a former shipmate, even if I claimed self-defense. The murder would be a whole other mother lode of problems and questions.

And if the q was bugged, no argument of mine would wash.

Looking at him, at his wasted features and suspicious eyes, I just couldn't. He was desperate and didn't trust. So I had to make him trust. And I had to shut him up. He was right; suspicion alone, word from somebody who knew about Chaos, would land me in the interrogation chair.

"Evan, I don't want it to go this way. I know you say you don't give shit about *Mukudori* but I know you do. I know you do. I know you still remember Shane. And your parents.

Don't lose that between us. I brought you out of that brig for only one reason. I don't care if you can't recognize it."

His eyes no longer dodged me like they had earlier. I saw well enough the pirate influence in him.

"I hated it there, Jos. Don't think I liked it."

"I don't think that."

"So help me. I just want a good place. No tricks if you just work that out."

"I want to help. I said that. But you have to give back. I'm not the captain here. I just do what I'm told." Reason. Once you'd calmed them, propose reasonable requests. "So I'll be up front with you. Azarcon wants all that you know about *Shiva*'s operations and her connection to Falcone and the strits—meeting points, munitions depots, other legal ships that're on Falcone's good list. You don't owe them anything, so help us. Captain Azarcon will be more inclined to offer you a position here if you give him those things."

"That crew's still out there. Their outriders escaped." The fear in him was thick enough to see.

"They can't get to you on this ship, Evan."

He was silent, thinking. "And you'll talk to Azarcon for me? I swear you do your end or I'll bring that jet in here."

Eventually he would compromise me. I knew it then. He was far too nervous and desperate.

"I'll talk to Azarcon," I said. "But first you talk to me."

XXXII.

Being with Evan was like being sucked down, forcing my thoughts through the tiny window he allowed. Aaian-na never felt so distant as when I sat with Evan listening to his life since *Mukudori*. And all the things he knew about pirates.

I wanted a shower. I wanted to lie down and never wake up.

I wanted to forget what was in my head.

The shift change beeped when I finally left his q and went a little ways down the corridor, out of sight of Private Dumas. I sat on a stairwell and watched the dust and scuff marks on the deck, forcing my gut to settle. Azarcon expected his reports. Both of them. On Evan and Falcone. Eventually I went back to quarters, ignoring everyone who passed, and commed Kris. I asked him if he could just stay out of q while I wrote my report. He agreed. Maybe he heard something in my voice. Or heard what wasn't in my voice.

I sat at the comp, stared at it a second, then flipped it up. Activated it.

Sat there.

The words came, eventually, like the dragging footsteps of something bleeding.

XXXIII.

I'd just sent the reports to the captain's comp when Kris came in from his off-shift fun in rec. It was late in our shift and one-third of the ship was bedding down for sleep. My eyes stung from staring so hard at the screen. For a long time I sat there, unable to move, fingering the image disk of my parents that Niko had given me. Kris flopped back on his bunk, arms behind his head.

"Me and Iratxe and Aki went to the flight lounge," he said. "And we whipped the wings real good in the star target sim. The Jellybean had *no* face left." He laughed.

I went to my rack and lay stomach down.

"Muse?"

Thorough reports. For Evan's, anyway, I'd been precise. For the one about Falcone I only wrote what I had told Niko those years ago. And in the writing of it, I remembered a bit more. But I didn't write the more. Azarcon didn't have to know everything. He wouldn't know the difference.

"Jos?" I heard Kris shift up on the bunk. "Hey, did you get that report done?"

"Yeah."

"So what'd Evan say—about the strits and his ship? About the pirates?"

I touched a slight dent in the bulkhead and scraped it with the edge of my fingernail. "As far as he knows, some of the ships in Falcone's fleet have been meeting with symps or something. Like regularly for a few years now. He gave dates for future rendezvous."

"Ah, shit! Are they organizing? Allies?"

"Trading partners, he said."

"What're they trading?"

I wished he would shut up. I dug harder at the bulkhead steel, its unforgiving surface. The paint gouged a bit under my thumbnail, but only the surface layer. Underneath lay the same gray.

"Muse, what're they trading?"

"Children and guns."

"What?"

I just wanted to sleep. "The pirates're giving the symps and the strits weapons and tech—and the pirates get to stash their . . . commodities . . . behind the DMZ. Where Earth-Hub can't touch."

"The fuck!"

Strits stole kids. I knew that firsthand. Now they were allowing the other thieves to stash their hostages in territory military carriers were hard-pressed to encroach upon. Very hard-pressed. The Warboy, after all, patrolled there with his ships.

And Niko had said he suspected pirates were pushing into strit space. He knew.

I hauled myself off the bunk and out the quarters. Fast. Straight to the head where I threw up what food I'd had that shift. Footsteps padded up behind me.

"You need a medic?"

I coughed, waved on the water in the sink, and splashed my mouth and face.

"Jos, you okay?"

And I'd sent a report telling Ash and Niko that we'd captured *Shiva* and were interrogating the crew.

Evan had to be lying. Or something. Niko wouldn't.

A hand rested on my shoulder. I jerked and stepped back, casting water droplets all around.

"Easy." Kris stared at me, concerned.

"Slavepoint's real."

His brow furrowed. "Slavepoint?"

"This—this place. This place we knew about, merchant kids. Where pirates took their hostages and other pirates gathered and they bid on them. They bid on the kids and the crew that they don't ransom back to the Merchants Protection Commission."

"Is that what he said?"

"He said strits help them stash us behind the DMZ!"

I heard the "us" echo in the wide, tiled room. I started for the corridor.

"Jos—" He followed. "Jos, they won't be getting away with it anymore now that we know. We'll take down the strits and the pirates."

The idealism of a jet who just got his blacks. Idealism

even after blowing people up. Even after seeing Corporal Dorr shoot that pirate in cold blood.

What was the difference? Niko was an assassin too.

I'd shot a pirate in cold blood. Twice. More than twice.

I sat on my bunk and wiped the wet from my face. The taste of bile still clawed the back of my throat.

"We'll get them, Jos. The pirates, we'll get 'em."

The pirates were only half of it. Sometime Evan was going to expose me. Whether he knew the truth or just insinuation, that wouldn't matter here. Azarcon already paid attention to me because of my link to Falcone. Adding a possible link to the strits would just compound things.

Niko was nowhere that I could ask him, that I could confront him about these claims.

Kris sat beside me and put his hand on my shoulder.

I shoved it off and moved away.

"Jos."

I didn't answer.

His voice got hard. "Get yourself together, mano."

I glared. "You grew up on a safe station, don't *give* me that."

I remembered I was supposed to have grown up on a safe station.

Everywhere on this ship was too close. All I could think about now were the tall mountains of Aaian-na and the wide sea.

And the tattoo on my wrist, in detail and colors unlike any striviirc-na status tat.

I felt Kris's eyes on me, all over me, wondering.

"I wanna sleep, so can you go away?" I gestured to his bunk.

"You know, you've been like this since the start and I just don't get it."

I was standing and didn't know when I had. He still sat on my bunk, almost glaring up at me.

"Get what? I wanna sleep!"

"Being this way. Being this—defensive. Never wanting anyone around. Not even *liking* anybody around. You're way worse than Cleary, at least he doesn't act like he hates people."

"What d'you want from me?"

"You're not like any kid I ever knew growing up on Austro."

His frustration was turning to suspicion. I was screwing up everything. Where was all the training Niko had given me? I could only find enough reserves to keep myself from killing something. Or running. What had Niko taught me if everything he'd ever told me was a lie? If all along he was taking kids from EarthHub and keeping them for pirates? For Falcone.

He made me want Aaian-na and everything that it was, and to think like them—just like Evan thought like a pirate.

I started to notice Kris's eyes, boring into my own.

"Where do you go," he asked, "when you shut down like that?"

"Get off my bunk."

He didn't move. He wanted to test me.

I grabbed his arm to shove him across to his side. He held on instead. We pushed at each other, both on our feet now. My hand shot up toward his chin.

He let go and stumbled, sitting abruptly on the bunk.

I would've broken his neck.

I thought he'd given up. But his leg shot out and tripped me. I slammed to the deck and he pounced on my chest. I twisted to toss him off but he set a knee in my gut, then shoved my arms back, holding my wrists down. He was bigger and I struggled.

"Get off!"

"You would've killed me! You were going to kill me!"

"Get off me!"

"What's wrong with you?"

The lights overhead lanced down like laser pillars.

The deck smelled of cold steel. I felt it under my shoulders, the backs of my calves, the small of my spine. Through my clothes. Behind my skull.

His weight on my hips seemed to multiply. I couldn't breathe.

"Off. Off." The words barely came.

His shadow lay over me, with the light behind it.

He released me. I heard my breath in panicked gasps and felt the tears running down my temples and into my ears. The sound of the drives caved in, suddenly loud. The recycling air whispered through the vents.

Ice settled across my skin. I rolled to my side and pressed my cheek to the deck.

"Are you okay? Look, I'm sorry for jumping you."

A jagged scratch marred the floor, as if someone long ago had raked his fingernails into it. As if he'd clawed with nails as hard as diamonds.

XXXIV.

Kris slept. One-third of the ship slept. I went walking.

I went to the jet wardroom and called up the secondary lights ten percent. Faint blue shone down. Shadows sat at the comps, like they sat all over this ship. They could go anywhere. At a glance, they could be anything.

I opened up one of the comps in the corner. My optics were already in my eyes. They saw a different world.

They caught the message sent by Otter to a general account Niko had set up for me, on Austro. I copied it to my holocube and retreated, yanking up all evidence of my passing as I went. I fell through the self-made exit of *Mac*'s comm ops, and wiped that access too. Maybe the comm officer saw a brief blurt in their numbers. They'd probably assume it was natural interference with the ship's link—a solar flare, a comet. They wouldn't know its origin. They wouldn't trace it to this specific comp.

If EarthHub carriers had vulnerable ware for someone who knew them inside and out, then pirate ships could too.

Genghis Khan was a Komodo-class modified merchant vessel. Niko knew this. Otter knew it. Niko's contacts had links to where some of the pirates bought their ware and weapons. Otter had told me so.

If Falcone was using black market ware to distort his sig so searching ships couldn't track him, then he had to have got it from somewhere.

I popped in the holocube and opened the message Otter had sent. The comp wouldn't keep it in memory if I didn't save it to the main system.

Otter said he'd located Falcone's tech supplier and he'd get back to me. No name. No location.

Dammit.

Maybe Niko sent him word. Maybe my report had made Niko draw back. Because Niko now knew that I knew pirates and symps were bedding down.

I glanced around the room. Too dark to see the walls clearly. Did Azarcon bug his own ship, more than the brig?

I closed down the comp and left, cutting the lights to black.

No, he couldn't. What kind of loyalty would he get from half-rogue crew if they knew or suspected he spied on them? It didn't fit what I'd seen of the man. He was harsh but he wasn't that much of a fascist. If he could trust a jet like Dorr to command a fire team, possess a gun, or even walk these corridors, he wouldn't bug the public places. Maybe more importantly, I doubted a jet like Dorr would be so loyal to someone who went too far on his rights. Dorr and some of the other jets, wild and half-criminal as they were, weren't stupid. They'd know.

But Evan's quarters . . . that I didn't know.

I rubbed my eye with the heel of my hand.

My shift was asleep. The jets I passed in the corridor I barely knew on a personal level. They glanced at me but didn't speak. The harsh white lighting didn't flatter anybody, especially if you needed sleep. Voices from other corridors drifted around corners. The low grate of working levs filtered through the thrum of the drives. Cool air cycled relentlessly. The deck smelled faintly of disinfectant and shone slightly, pale gray and black scars that no amount of scrubbing would ever abolish. Someone had lately been cleaning.

My feet took me aft, to training deck where *Shiva*'s children temporarily lived.

Some of the kids were playing on the floor of the RRC, and at the simstation. Two jets stood at the doors, watching. I stopped between them and looked in.

At a glance there had to be about thirty kids, ages ranging from five to fifteen, though it was hard to be sure—malnourishment and fatigue both stunted and aged a body. Some of them bore the pale complexions of people too long aboard the dark parts of ships. One of the older youths stood by the window just staring out at the black as *Macedon* cut through on her patrol. I took another step in. The jets glanced at my tags but didn't stop me. The younger children, primed to strangers, looked up at me with unsurprised eyes. Nothing more would ever truly surprise them. Even their fear lay so far deep beneath the surface it became only a flatness on their faces. They didn't know me, I could do anything to them, but they didn't care.

I sat at one of the round, black tables. Without hesitation one of the six- or seven-year-olds motored up to me and stood staring. Her coarse black hair frizzed from her head like a brush. Under her eyes were deep lines more deserving on an old woman.

She hit my leg. "You!" she accused.

"What is it?" I asked quietly. I held my hands out, palms up.

But she ran off, back to her group. The adolescents, some of them my age or more, looked my way with wary curiosity. None of them approached. The silence, even in the midst of play, sat hard. They were not used to being boisterous. Some of them did not interact, but sat apart, alone and looking. Just looking around them.

Then they all turned to the entrance like desperate flowers to the sun. I glanced over and saw the captain.

He wore no special insignia, unless you noticed the black stripes on black sleeves, and dressed exactly like the jets that flanked him. But the kids all went still. They knew authority even when it didn't announce itself. They had learned to smell it.

He came in, already attuned to me, and walked over casually. Eyes followed him, as did the utter silence. He didn't seem surprised that I was there.

I forced my hands to unclench.

"Private Musey," he greeted.

I stood. "Captain."

Azarcon pulled a chair loose from its clamps and set it beside mine, facing the children. He sat, gesturing for me to do the same. His towering height, now less imposing, seemed to cue the kids that it was all right to carry on. Quiet play filled the span of the rec center. The older kids still watched the captain.

"Slavepoint exists," he said.

I realized my hands were clenched together again between my knees. I straightened back and let go.

"Yes, sir." He knew about Slavepoint. He wasn't a station kid. Or he knew pirates and their victims.

"With the help of strits and symps."

"Yes, sir." I wished one of the children would interrupt us. "So Evan says."

Azarcon leaned forward on his elbows, hands clasped loosely in front of his knees, watching the children though I knew his focus was on me. His whole manner was considerably less intimidating than when he sat behind a desk—at least on the surface.

"You don't believe him?" he said.

Shiva had been found consorting with a striviirc-na dreadnought. Little doubt in that. "I guess I do, sir. I guess I don't like to think of the implications."

Niko helping pirates. For guns. So he could war more with the Hub.

He was the Warboy.

This couldn't be true.

"Yes, the implications are bad." Azarcon's black eyes slid to me, though he only tilted his head slightly. "It's no wonder Falcone's been so hard to track, if he's got a strit hole to sink into."

I hardly thought the captain of *Macedon* needed to be telling this to one of his jets.

"I read your report about your capture aboard *Genghis Khan*," he said, shifting up to sit straight. He raked his hair back from his forehead, eyes on the children.

"Yes, sir?" Dread reared its head again, traveling from my gut to the back of my throat.

"I suppose you think I rode you hard since you came on board, that the Jet Instructors did too, who were operating under my orders."

As if I would say yes. He didn't wait for a reply.

"The flag on your file about Falcone got my interest. There aren't many that deal with him, for that length of time, and get out to talk about it. You realize this?"

"Yes, sir."

"So I had to ask why. It's a suspicious case. You're old enough that it could be something more than it is."

I waited.

"He hasn't shown his face for years. We suspect he's disguised himself somehow, because he isn't the type to squirrel himself away for very long periods of time. He's vain. He likes to be on the edge. He likes to give EarthHub the finger."

That was Falcone, all right. Taking me by the hand right on a station where deep-space carriers docked.

I looked at the captain. He knew the pirate, maybe even from more than reports. Something in his eyes—even when he looked at me, he wasn't really looking at me.

Azarcon continued. "I know he's been on suspended aging treatments since he was in his early thirties. But from what you describe he must have also had some kind of cellular surgery."

"Yes, sir." Only the bare words came out.

"I know this is hard for you, Musey. I know what you didn't put in your report. Or what you never told SJI Laceste."

I stared hard at the quietly playing children.

"That more than anything has convinced me you're not one of his spies."

I jerked, looked at him. "Sir. No, sir. I'm not!"

"I know." His tone said *calm down*. The children looked over at us, paused.

"Sir, I would kill him if I had him in my sights."

"I know. Let's walk." He stood.

I didn't want to go anywhere with this man who seemed able to look through walls.

But I went with him, left the children. I had no choice. He took me to one of the smaller, secondary levs and up. I watched the light bar blink until the lev grated to a halt and the words "command crew deck" flashed across the panel. As the seconds passed, it became harder to breathe.

He led me out and down the corridor. Occasionally a uniform passed us and they nodded to the captain. We stopped outside a hatch at the end of the corridor. The number read 0001. Azarcon pulled his tags from his uniform and slid one of them into the lock, then went inside.

I stopped on the threshold. This was his quarters.

"Come in and shut the hatch, Private Musey."

I swallowed with effort, stepped in just far enough not to block the hatch, and pulled it in. His quarters was larger than any I'd seen so far, but not luxurious. A small receiving area with a couple of cushioned chairs and a couch, all faux wood and deep blue fabric, occupied most of the main space, with a tiny corner of personal kitchen off to the side. A fastened screen stood to the right, which probably cordoned off his bed and bath facilities. On the walls were abstract paintings, colorful and thematically nongeometric. The effect was not the spartan space I had known in Falcone's quarters.

"Have a seat," he said, gesturing to the couch. He disappeared behind the screen.

I didn't want to sit. I walked to the table in front of the couch, looked down. Objects sat scattered, what looked like miniature replications of ancient Earth structures. A couple pyramids and some sort of lion with a human's face. Off to the side sat an iridescent image cube. Inside one of the six faces was a three-dimensional color pic of a dark-haired youth with rather large blue eyes and a shy smile. Beside him stood the captain, in civilian clothes. They were outside what looked like a restaurant door; slender red neon tubing hung in the wide window in writing I couldn't read, overlaid in ghost patterns by a standard holoprog menu list. The captain's arm hung around the boy's neck in rough affection.

More images were buried in the cube, but I didn't pick it up to look.

"That's my son Ryan. He's twelve years old now, not much younger than you."

I glanced up quickly, clenched my hands behind me as he approached from behind the screen. I forced myself not to step back as he came close enough to hand over a holocube.

"Sir?" I didn't move, to touch it or touch him. He towered over me, taller than Niko. Taller than Falcone. Younger-looking than both of them.

"It's something I thought you might want to see."

The air in the quarters smelled faintly of cooking spices. I glanced at the kitchen space—immaculately clean, all smooth, reflective surfaces—then back at him.

My heart started to run.

"You can use this comp." He gestured to one on the couch's side table.

I took the cube and moved to it. He sat on the couch, rested an arm along the back. I kept him in my peripherals and put the cube in, accessed it.

Mukudori's symbol sprang across the display.

I looked at Azarcon, frozen.

"Dorr told me about the image disk you wear with your tags." He gestured to my chest. "It's all you have left of your parents, isn't it?"

I had to swallow. "Yes, sir."

"Where did you get it?"

"Sir, Mr. Mankar had them made for me." It was uncomfortable to stand when he was sitting, so I eased onto the edge of one of the chairs, glanced at the comp.

"*Mukudori*'s homeport was Siqiniq, right? They had many archived files, including the ship and crew history. You might want to read it."

I didn't know what to say. Those files weren't available to the general public, not even to survivors. They became station property when a ship died. He was a Hub captain so they wouldn't deny him. I didn't think anybody could deny him, not when he wanted something. He had to want something, or why else would he bother?

I knew he was looking at me. I stared at the comp, so tense my head started to pound.

"You can take the holocube and go, Private Musey."

I looked at him. "Sir?"

"You're dismissed."

What was the trick? He didn't move, just gazed at me, calm.

A test. Evaluation, just like in training. "Sir . . . can I ask you something?"

"You just did. But go ahead."

"Why did you get these files for me, sir? What do you know about Falcone?"

"Those are two questions. But good ones. What do I know about Falcone? Altogether too much, and not enough now to get him. Why did I obtain the files? Because a person should have his past, if it's worth having. The part of your history that belongs on *Mukudori* . . . I think that's worth having."

I couldn't see behind his eyes and he knew how not to answer a question. I hadn't expected anything less, but had still hoped for more. Maybe he read that in me. Like Niko, he had the disconcerting ability to strip me with one look or word.

"You should know by now this isn't *Genghis Khan*, Musey."

I leaned over and extracted the cube from the comp. "I know, sir."

"Do you? I admit I was harsh on you in the beginning. But I've followed your progress and been in constant contact with your commanding officers. You're different from most of my crew. I don't quite know why, but I'm sure it has to do with your year on the *Khan*. Falcone has that effect on people."

"Even you, sir?" That fell out of my mouth on instinct. To get something out of him.

His eyes flickered. "Sometimes. But you and I are the lucky ones. Your friend Evan isn't."

Lucky? He knew enough about my past to know it wasn't lucky.

And Evan. I'd almost forgotten. It allowed me to change the topic.

"Sir, Evan wants to sign on ship."

The captain's eyebrows arched. "What does he think he can do here?"

"Sir, he just doesn't want to be left on a station."

"Well, I want him to stay as long as he can help us locate *Shiva*'s outriders. The ones in brig, needless to say, aren't talking much and I'm not inclined to torture them yet."

I might have thought it a joke if I didn't hear the matter-of-fact tone in his voice. Accusations about striviirc-na treatment of POWs were somewhat of an hypocrisy.

Azarcon didn't miss a beat or a blink. "The drop points and caches he turned over will take some time to verify. In the meantime, drag his memory for codes. He didn't mention any of those. Nor did he go into detail about his exact role on the ship. Plaything, obviously, and general errand boy. But I know pirates. He might have been someone's protégé and is still too afraid to signal us. That type of indoctrination doesn't willfully come up."

Half the time he seemed only an arm-length from Falcone's command style. But in so many other things he wasn't anything like Falcone.

Like his tolerance for throwaways. His invitation here and then his distance. As if kindness was something you gave without expectation.

He said, "Between your memory and Evan's late dealings, we have more on Falcone now than we've been able to dig up for years. And I've been digging. So tell him he can stay so long as he's forthcoming."

Azarcon was a strit killer. But he seemed to have a personal vendetta against Falcone, or at least a strong sense of duty to rid the Hub of the pirate.

And the cube. It sat smooth and warm in my hand. Was this why his crew was so loyal? He went out of his way for you, once he trusted you. Or was it set up for something he'd later cash in? Maybe trust had nothing to do with it.

"No more questions, Mr. Musey?"

Many more, but none I could ask him now. He wanted me to leave. I looked at him and he let me know it, a polite dismissal with one stare.

Nothing more.

It didn't comfort me. He commed a senior jet to escort me back to lower decks. When the hatch buzzed I stood, saluted and left his quarters. The man was still a mystery.

XXXV.

On my way back to q I snuck into the jet wardroom to nose around in brig records. The *Shiva* crew interrogations weren't listed or even compartmentalized. It figured. It was just like *Macedon* to question off the record. Any files had probably gone from the brig straight to the captain. I tried diving into Dorr's personal files, but he had a bomb shelter worth of code around his accesses. I'd need an hour at least to decipher them, which was nearly impossible. Jets came in the wardroom and I had to shut down.

In quarters I read the cube. It contained information from *Mukudori*'s initial registration by Captain Kawakami, right to its last scheduled run before the attack. The files held the dates and dossiers on all of the crew, births and deaths and marriages, hires and dismissals and those who'd just simply left.

I couldn't find the breath to speak past the sudden ache in my throat. I manually poked the links, as if I moved under water, weighted by depth. I typed in *Musey*.

A picture came up, with birthdate and biography. A different picture from what was on my image disk, earlier in date. *Musey, Kevin Joslyn*. My father. He didn't look more than twenty. Married to *Wen Young, 2176 EHSD*. I moved the images side by side. Together they were me. I was in my mother's dark hair and my father's dark blue eyes. My mother's nose and mouth, and the shape of my father's jaw. In her cheekbones. In his smile.

They were me.

All of it. Inside me. Flowing through me until it spilled from my eyes and I no longer saw my face in them.

But I didn't want to. They were dead.

XXXVI.

My duty was Evan. I would've preferred to scrub the deck, but when Kris came in to quarters I made Evan the excuse to leave before Kris saw my red eyes. I went to the head and washed my face. Maybe Azarcon's gift of those files hadn't been generosity at all. Maybe he'd wanted me to see what I no longer had and what was left. Maybe this was his way of telling me to forget Falcone. They were all dead, one way or another.

Maybe he'd only wanted me to have it, like Niko had.

Except Azarcon wasn't Niko. Azarcon didn't care about me, not when he had six thousand other people to command. Azarcon cared about his information and his missions and killing strits.

Except Niko wanted to know—was that really all?

I had to discover that by letting the man into my space, when every nerve wanted me out of his quarters, away from him, a stranger to him if I could. He'd taken me there on purpose, knowing what I would think in his presence, knowing my year on the *Khan*. Standing there in his living space while he sat on his couch looking at me, defenseless, I could have killed him if those were my orders; I could've ended his missions against the striviirc-na and the sympathizers, if Niko only said the word. I could've ended it so easily, and he'd never ask me into his space again.

Except Azarcon wanted Falcone too. And he'd let me alone.

Evan had answers. Evan was my duty. So I went there, my thoughts wrapped in a black fog.

One thing at a time.

Once inside, with Evan's cigret smoke crawling into my eyes and down my throat, I took a shallow breath and watched him watching me, the stares of two animals forced to share the same territory.

"You look disturbed," he said, with a bored drag on his cig.

"I told the captain you wanted on ship." I stayed by the hatch.

Evan sat with his feet up as usual, in rumpled fatigues, his nest of blankets all around him. At least he looked like he was showering regularly, though his eyes remained bloodshot. Faint stubble had started to show on his chin and jaw, blond scrub.

"So what'd he say?" he asked.

"He wanted to know why and then he wanted to know what you could offer us for it."

I wanted to know why I suddenly felt dirty for asking. Evan was a pale panic.

"Didn't he get what he wanted? I gave him what you wanted!"

"Codes. Know any?"

His eyes flared. "Yeah. Here's one: strit."

I stared at him. "Evan, my captain wants information. I'm going to give it to him. I'm starting not to give a damn what happens to you or what you could possibly say, which is a bunch of *bullshit.* Are you reading me? Go talk to that jet outside. Do I care? Falcone fuckin' *blew our ship!*"

He flinched. And made for the door.

I grabbed him by the shirt and threw him on the bunk. His fists flailed but I knocked his arm down and seized his other wrist.

He yelled.

The hatch opened. Behind me the jet said, "What's going on?"

"Get out!" I glanced over my shoulder, nudging one knee into Evan's gut to keep him down.

"You aren't supposed to kill him."

"I'm interrogating him. On the *captain*'s orders. Now get out."

The jet wasn't a fool. He knew I was there at Azarcon's behest. He knew I talked to Azarcon on more than one occasion. He knew Dorr was my squad leader.

The hatch shut.

I looked down at Evan. He was breathing so hard he barely had strength to struggle. "I want him, Evan. I want your boss's head on a platter. I'll go through you to get it."

"He's not my boss, Musey!"

"Then what? Tell me everything."

He began to cry. It was a strangled sound. My anger shrank back at the sight of it. I released him, moved back to the opposite bunk, and sat on my hands. They shook. His face flushed red, high on his cheeks and all down his throat. He wiped his face furiously with his sleeve but it didn't do much good.

"I'm not protecting the pirates, Jos. I remember when they blew the ship. I saw them shoot my parents. And Shane. I saw them shoot yours."

My voice broke. "Codes, Evan."

But he wasn't listening. "I went to engineering. I don't remember why. I was bugging Shane. Then the ship was attacked. And things happened so fast. Your parents came in with guns. Shane put me up on the rampart, you remember that place? We used to fly down airplanes when Jules let us, on off-hours."

"It's over, Evan."

"The pirates came to engineering first. Our parents were supposed to help protect it. But they couldn't." He brushed his face again with a sleeve but it stayed slick, red, rubbed raw. "I saw them die, all of them—"

"I don't wanna hear it, Evan!"

"You should! You wanna know about me and pirates. I hate them, Jos. How can you think otherwise? How can you even ask me? I don't know any codes! I don't know anything more! I need to stay here, Jos. You're here. I don't know anywhere else but on their side."

"How do I know you're not on their side? How do I know you're not just trying to make me trust you—with this talk about our ship—"

"I know what they did to make you think that way," he said.

"I don't think any which way. I think you were six years with them and learned a few things."

He didn't answer that. But for a moment the twelve-year-old swallowed the eighteen-year-old, and it was the face from the *Khan* staring back at me, when I'd been hauled from the room that first time and taken to Falcone.

He hadn't wanted to let go of me.

"I need someone here, Jos. Please."

I couldn't move.

"Please."

My heart thudded like a frantic drummer. "No."

This didn't need to be part of it. I was here because of Azarcon, who just wanted information. I was here because of Niko, who might've known about symps and pirates bedding down, but until I knew for sure; I was here for him too, and Evan didn't know anything. Evan couldn't tell Azarcon.

Evan wouldn't tell Azarcon if I gave him reason not to.

I was here alone and Evan wasn't going to protect me. He never had. He wanted things from me, like everyone else. But those things were never just what people said with words. Everything about it, instead, was meant to manipulate you to feel something you wouldn't otherwise feel, and screw up your steady, rational thoughts. You didn't just offer your body like that unless you expected some return. Some kind of insurance.

But that wasn't my voice in my head, like it wasn't my body that felt the heat of Evan's stare. My hands were numb, yet I pushed myself from the bunk and out of the quarters, like an animal in retreat.

XXXVII.

I sent what I hoped would be my final report to Captain Azarcon about Evan, the fact Evan claimed to know nothing more. I was sure Azarcon would still persevere with the *Shiva* crew in brig, and it would be up to him whether Evan was going to stay aboard or not.

It was out of my hands. Gladly.

The duty roster at the next shift showed my name on guard duty of the *Shiva* prisoners. That had to be the corporal's idea of a joke, considering my last visit to the brig. I checked my personal messages and sure enough, Dorr had sent me a small note: *Don't kill any of them—yet*. And, *See you in shotokan class*.

They remembered me. The cells were unusually quiet for the duration. Sometimes I escorted one of them out, cuffed, to a separate room nearby where Dorr and another jet usually waited. When the time came I escorted the prisoner back to the brig. They never looked quite the same.

This went on for a week.

Azarcon let Evan walk to mess for meals now, under guard. Evan started to lose some of his nervousness and pallor. He'd been the *Shiva* captain's favorite, the decoration on her arm, her status doll and her trainee. He'd kept his eyes and ears open and kept his mouth shut. And waited. Betrayal was nothing to him now that he knew Azarcon wouldn't dump him. If he could've, I knew he would have offered another kind of favor to the captain. That was how he translated gratitude. I avoided him when I could. When he wanted to talk he went straight to the captain.

It gave me time to do other things. Like work out in the gym at the end of shift, which I could do alone and with concentration that nobody thought to interrupt. Except Sanchez, who hadn't forgotten that damn gauntlet run. He and his cronies Ricci and Bucher sidled up to me as I kicked at an exercise bag.

"Your little buddy's sure racking up points with Cap lately," Sanchez said.

"He's not my buddy." I kicked the bag hard enough that Bucher had to step back.

"Out of all the pirates we got, he's the only one walking with a captain's pardon."

"With a guard."

Ricci said, "We're watching you, mano. You and your fellow pirate prince. We don't care what Cap says, or how many breaks he gives."

"Or how many times you go to his quarters," Bucher put in.

I stopped kicking, looked at him. So they had eyes on command deck. "Why don't you take that to Azarcon? Let him hear you."

"Because Bucher's a coward," Kris said, walking up behind the other jet from the gym entrance. We traded glances. Kris kept out of Bucher's line of sight.

"Shut up, Rilke," Sanchez said. "The only reason you don't bitch about D'Silva is 'cause you're already tradin' sweat with squeaky Mouse here."

I launched at Sanchez and knocked him onto his back before he had time to react. His head smacked the floor. I went for his throat but a hand grabbed my tank and hauled me back. I drove my elbow into somebody's face, heard a muffled cry. The hand released me and I spun.

Kris had Bucher on the floor, a knee in his back and a fist in his hair. Ricci was holding his nose and swearing at me.

Then Corporal Dorr appeared in the hatchway, a black shadow. "What the hell's goin' on?"

I knew better than to move, hearing that tone. Kris released Bucher and stood slowly.

"I asked a question," Dorr said.

Sanchez got to his feet, a little dazed but spitting fire. "Your bitch is in heat."

The corporal strode in, right up to Sanchez without pause, and backhanded him, lightning fast. Sanchez staggered, swore.

Dorr gazed at him levelly. "What was that, mano?"

They were of equal rank. But Sanchez stared only a second before backing up, raising a hand. "Forget it."

Dorr glared at him, then gave equal attention to Bucher and Ricci. "I don't think I will. Keep away from my team or I'll remember I got a gun at my disposal." His eyes cut to me and Kris. "As for you two—get your butts to the wardroom. We got a mission."

XXXVIII.

The laser bolt thudded by my ear. The flash of it nearly blinded me. I dodged in reflex, a desperate dive to the station deck, my world suddenly, deafeningly quiet from my entire right side outward. I breathed harsh, the sound echoing through my skull, and squinted up against the sparking, smoke-obscured lights of the dock far above. Kris stood over me, yelling something and firing into the enemy. Tiny flashes of light burst from his pulse pack as shot after shot spewed from his rifle. Corporal Dorr appeared in my view, his hair-tail whipping around his shoulders as he barked at one of our team. I saw his mouth move and his rifle jerk as he lay fire, but the sound remained muted.

Kris dragged me by my webbing behind one of the fallen girders. I struggled to sit up, orient myself. Kris slapped my cheek lightly to get my attention. His sweat-flushed face appeared in view, hair stuck to his cheek beneath the helmet and eye shield.

"Are you hit?" he yelled.

I shook my head. I pressed a hand to my right ear, then adjusted the helmet. The pain lanced all the way to my brain.

"Close one," he said with a relieved grin, then rose slightly from his crouch. I heard him lay down an arc of fire at the pirates across the dock. They were barricaded against the inner doors. We'd been trying to remove them for the last five minutes. Five minutes? Longer, maybe. Their numbers depleted rapidly but they still held to their position. They knew the moment we broke that barricade the station would be ours.

I struggled to my knees and peered over the girder. The battle sounds were reduced to distant cracks and thuds, intermittent now as the pirates' ammo ran out and they waited to choose their targets. All across the wide dock jets crouched behind insect-shaped loaders, tossed containers and supply bins. A few jets lay in the open, dead or too injured to move. Inside the small station core were the weapons. Mountable howitzers, crates of LP-150s and modified LF-89s—hull-breachable cutters with flame capability. Jets called them Jaws.

The load was meant for the symps and strits, who were supposed to rendezvous here. Evan had fingered the cache

and the schedule; his information panned out. In his head
was a veritable timetable of pirate activity in the sector. Our
sister ship *Archangel* took care of other leads near the DMZ,
by Ghenseti's sector. Right now I wanted a strit or a symp to
question.

I transferred the pickup to my left ear where I could actually hear the teams. In space the Chargers, hunter-
bombers, and hunter-killers swept by the station bays to
make sure nobody cut and run. *Macedon* was tangling with
a striv assault runner, out of short-range comm. The runner
had come for the cache. We had to assume *Macedon* would
win or else we were stranded with the Chargers.

"Dorr, on the right flank," Hartman said through the
pickup. I watched as fire team two's grenade barrage created
a hole in the barricade of metal and plastic junk the pirates
had erected.

Dorr barked an order and Kris and I dashed forward toward that hole as our people spat cover fire into the enemy.
Footsteps followed behind us as the other jets came up in
waves. I knew it was Dorr and Madi at my six without having to look.

The inner doors cracked open and the few remaining pirates fled through them, the bite of our bolts against their
heels. Our backs hit against the doors. I checked in fast for
retaliation. Nothing rained out. I dodged in, weapon sweeping the right hand of the murky corridor as Kris covered my
left flank. They'd shot out the lights or cut them from the
mains. The backups glowed dully overhead, sickly yellow. I
glance-flicked my eye shield HUD to swap over to night
scope. Sharp green glow washed through my sight, illumi-
nating wall angles and the narrow emptiness of the run-
down corridor. I advanced cautiously.

"Check for heat sigs," Dorr's quiet voice came through
my pickup.

I glanced that command and another layer of color swept down over my eye shield. The faint yellow of residual body heat passing through the cool station air filled my sensor scope. I followed the quickly fading signatures, stopped at a corner, and dodged a peek. My shield flashed into fiery color. The sound of kill bolts echoed through me. I pressed my shoulder to the wall, snaked my rifle around the corner, and shot blind to break up the enemy's barrage. Footsteps pounded in retreat. I checked quickly again, then ran out in pursuit. Kris raced beside me, a sharply cut shape on my left. We fired in tandem into the retreating backs of the pirates, then dodged into doorways when they returned shots.

Our steady advance brought us to a four-way. The enemy fled down the twelve and nine directions. Out the corners of my eyes I saw a shape flash by on my right. I turned and caught a faintly illuminated figure running across the corridor into one of the rooms. Something about the way it moved told me it wasn't a pirate. I ran down the corridor after it. Most of the jets behind me dispersed after the pirates, footsteps echoing.

"Musey!" Kris yelled.

I slapped the door release. It opened abruptly and I lay fire in before moving farther. A door on the opposite side of the room was just slamming shut. I avoided the green-bordered forms of sparse furniture in the darkness, through that door just in time to catch a pair of legs dangling from a maintenance shaft overhead. I thumbed to stun and fired. The legs went still but the torso still moved, arms heaving the now dead lower weight farther into the shaft. I jumped up and grabbed the body by its waist belt and yanked.

It tumbled down. I stepped back quickly and snapped my rifle to aim as it fell in a heap to the floor. Through the glow of night vision I saw the twining tattoo on the face and the dark spread of hair. Puddles of shadow showed where the eyes would be if the room had been lit normally.

Not a strit. Human features shone hazily up at me. A symp.

His hands twitched, going for weapons in one of the many folds of his coat. I shot them.

"Who ordered you here?" I snapped, in Ki'hade.

His eyes widened.

I stepped on his chest and shoved the rifle muzzle against his cheek. "Who ordered you here!"

"Kia'redan bae," he rasped, glaring up at me. *"Ki-a'redan bae."*

Niko.

"You're lying!"

"Het kia'redan-na hamma de kan. De kan, ki sraga!" The one without comparison sent me here. He sent me, you fuck.

"What's he saying?"

I swung. Kris stood in the doorway, weapon trained.

I took a breath. "How the fuck should I know?"

"You said he was lying."

Through the night vision I saw the hard contours of my teammate's face. Suddenly he fired.

I hit the deck, tumult and heartbeat in my ears. But I hadn't been shot. I wrenched a look over my shoulder, rolling to my side. The symp lay still with a black wound in his chest and a blade in his motionless hand. I started to scramble to my feet, looked up at Kris. Not breathing.

Behind him materialized a shadow.

"Get down!" I swung my rifle around but he suddenly jerked where he stood, then crumpled to his knees. I shot past him into the shadow at the same time it shot at me. Laser lanced my shoulder armor. I rolled and fired again, over Kris's head. And fired again at another shape that appeared behind the first one. Kris sank onto his chest and rolled in pain just as both targets fell.

I palmed my wirecomm, fingers feeling too large and numb to hit the connection properly.

"I need a medic here!" I scrambled over and put a hand on him. The enemies I'd shot lay motionless, tattooed. Dark figures with caste symbols I recognized. One of them held a dagger.

I wrenched the gun from the other's hand and shot them both point blank to make sure they stayed down.

I bent close to Kris to feel his breath.

It came barely. Raggedly. Loudly, in the sudden silence in my mind.

"Medic, damn you! Somebody!" I started to loosen his armor. The dim lights and green glow on everything made nothing clear. Yet Kris's warmth spread across my vision in false color, leaking out so the eye shield sensors zeroed on it as it encroached upon the darkness of the floor. I edged my hand around his side to his lower back. Thick, sticky liquid. The symp had stabbed up under his armor, like we were trained to do.

"Kris. Kris, look at me." I fumbled in my thigh cargo pocket for the standard field medkit.

"Symp," he murmured.

I ripped open the stim packet and pressed the patch to his neck. I started to roll him onto his chest so I could spray and clamp the wound. The door opened. My rifle snapped up but it was Aki and Dorr and Madi. I hadn't been paying attention to the voices on my pickup. I realized now the corporal had been yelling in my ear that they were tracking my tags sig and to stay put.

Aki ran up and shoved away my hands, opening her kit. Dorr waved Madi to assist her, then hauled me up by the scruff of my neck.

"Sir—!" I still fixed on Kris but Dorr turned me around and hit me one blow with the back of his fist.

"He's your fault, you little shit! Running off—the area wasn't clear, you bastard!" His anger blasted against me. He shoved me into a chair and hit me again.

My head reeled from the blows. I gripped the hard edge of the table beside me so I wouldn't topple over. The voices in my pickup slowly began to make sense. The jets were locking down the station, corralling pirates, calling all-clears. My gaze started to focus on the dead symps. Somebody got the main lights up again, blinding me.

I yanked off my helmet and eye shield, blinking fire spots from my sight. A pool of blood lay around Kris like a red eye.

"Is he gonna live?" My mouth felt dry, the words hard-pressed.

"Let's get him on the Charger," Aki said, ignoring me and nodding to Madison.

"Aki—"

"Shut up and let her do her job," Dorr snapped. As Madison and Aki lifted Kris onto the unfolded stretcher, Dorr wandered over to one of the symps and toed the body. "Well, well."

I remembered Kris's eyes, asking how I understood the alien language.

I levered up unsteadily and went to the stretcher, took Aki's end unasked. Dorr didn't stop me but I felt his gaze on the back of my head, drilling.

XXXIX.

The hangar bay was filled by medics, flight crews, equipment-toting techs, and jets staggering in from the mission. Commander Hunsou stood in the center of it, barking orders, her small dark form almost lost among the traffic. Vented air from the Chargers and hunters misted my sight. The launch arms hung from the high ceiling like huge steel dragons, ready to clamp the small ships in their jaws until another opportunity arose to spit them into space. Fuel lines snaked along the sealed deck. Parts of the deck doubled as two of the four bay doors. I watched where I stepped so I wouldn't pitch Kris's stretcher to the floor. Madi and I followed Aki's brisk strides toward the exit. The noise made it difficult to hear any one thing. Nathan had to grab my shoulder to get my attention.

"Kris?" he yelled to me, walking along.

"Knife wound."

His face was steady and blank, but pale. He held it in, slapped my shoulder, and squeezed, then got called away by his copilot.

Evan met us at the inner bay doors. Maybe it was his way of confirming I was still alive. I supposed I should've been thankful for that kind of concern. He broke away just far enough from his jet guard to intercept me.

"What happened?"

"What does it look like?"

He trailed me. "Ah, Jos, I'm sorry."

My head buzzed from Dorr's punches and my own skittering thoughts. The stretcher was stained in places by Kris's blood, despite the hasty sealant and clamp Aki had ministered. Dorr had taken the blade the symp had used; it was serrated and more than a hand-length.

I stared hard at Madi's back as we marched swiftly to medbay. Kris was unconscious, despite the stim and blood transing Aki had managed to hook up to him on the Charger. Anything done in the field was always just enough to keep them alive until we got back to ship. We were lucky we had a ship to come back to. On our return ride Nathan reported that *Mac* had taken a beating. But the striv assault runner was history.

Evan shadowed me, with his own jet shadow, all the way to medbay and inside. The trauma section was packed and hectic. Aki called to the other staff on duty. Most of them were busy with other casualties brought in. The wide room was a swarm of bodies, the cool air filled by the thick scent of blood and the vague rubbery smell of med sealant. Once Madi and I got Kris settled on a table I went to one of the medics and grabbed his arm, shoving him to Kris's side.

"Go help him."

"Musey!" Aki shot me a look and elbowed me back. Madi tugged me away so they could work. I jerked from his hold, bumping into someone behind me.

I pivoted, expecting to find Evan, but saw Corporal Dorr. He stood close enough I felt his breath.

"Get to quarters," he said. "And don't damn well move from it."

"Sir, I'd like to stay."

"I don't give a shit what you'd like, Musey. Get out!"

I backed up and turned. My eyes stung. I would have crashed into a medic if Evan hadn't hauled on my arm to get me out of the way.

"Stop *following* me! Dammit!"

His mouth tightened. "Come on. You're all over blood."

"Are you deaf? I said leave me the hell alone!" I unslung my rifle and waved it at him. He stepped away, arms folding protectively. His jet guard watched, eyes trying to capture my own for some sympathy or warning or something, but I shoved past both of them and hurried through the crowded corridors. They were occupied by zombie bodies moving in a steady line from the hangar deck to maindeck. Jets dragged in from the mission, went to see comrades in medbay, or headed to the lev to go down to jetdeck. I got all the way to quarters and inside, threw my weapons on the bunk, then realized the hatch hadn't shut behind me when I'd pushed it.

Evan stood in the way.

"Get out!" I shoved at his shoulder.

With surprising force he pushed me back. "Quit it, Jos!"

"What're you doing here? Why're you still around me?"

Something flickered in his eyes. An expression I remembered from long ago. "You look like you need it, dumbass."

"Get the hell out of my quarters!"

"You're crying."

That stopped me. I brushed roughly at my face; it was true. I stank of smoke and blood and sweat. No getting rid of it. No getting rid of the image of those dead symps. Or the fact I'd shot them in the heads. Or the voice speaking that language I understood, even months removed.

No getting rid of what he'd said. *Kia'redan bae.* Niko had issued the orders to get those weapons.

I struggled to get out of my armor but the clasps at my ribs were cracked and they stuck. I wrenched at one to no avail.

"Fuck!"

Evan stepped in farther, glancing over his shoulder at the jet outside the hatch. The jet shut it. Evan came toward me and grabbed my arm to hold me still.

I yanked back. "What're you doing?"

"You're being stupid. That'll never come off in a tantrum." The cold clarity on his face said well enough how he hadn't suicided all those years on *Shiva.*

He'd settled all right into his new life on this ship, the pirate turned informer. He talked to his escorts now, bummed cigrets off them, played cards and sims in the rec lounge. Everybody knew he'd been the *Shiva* captain's whore, but

that didn't bother him as much as I'd thought it would, now
that he had his place. Some of the crew eyed him openly.
They played the games people played before they bedded
each other. Maybe he thought it made him tighter on this ship
because he was the latest fascination. Maybe it didn't occur to
him they were using him just like *Shiva* had, except in a nicer
way. They gave him food and protection and clothing—he
was a cheap date. They didn't need to give much back. They
didn't whisper secrets in his ear that he could use later if he
decided to turn traitor here. With his new status, with the privilege of remaining on board when the rest of the pirates had
been dumped into the system for trial on station, Evan no
longer talked of blackmail. He didn't ask me about aliens. He
spoke to me as if we were equal. As if *Mukudori* tied us together. As if anybody from our dead homeship would recognize either of us now.

"Stay still and I'll work it loose," he said, reaching for the
clasps on my chest armor.

I stared right into his face. "Get out, Evan."

A week ago he would've immediately dodged my eyes.
Now he looked at me for a long minute before glancing
down.

"Why d'you hate me so much?"

"I'm tired. While you're here baring ass for everything in
uniform, we go out there and bring in your old friends!"

He jumped at me. I sidestepped quickly and shoved him
to the bunk. He landed on my weapons and tossed over fast,
pushing himself to sit up. We looked at each other as his
hand touched the rifle.

Stupid, stupid.

But he got to his feet, left the weapons where they were,
and just walked up to me. I stood my ground, but my hands
curled tight.

He said slowly, "I'm doing what I can. I ain't crawlin' into a hole like they had me do. This time it's my choice."

"Yeah, you adapt real well."

"I had to. Didn't you?"

I wanted to shut my eyes.

My tags beeped. I turned my shoulder and fingered them. "Musey."

Corporal Dorr's voice came through, emotionless. "Come to medical."

My heart flickered, then increased beats to the edge of bursting. Somehow I ended up in medbay though I didn't recall getting there. Aki stood by Kris's table with her head bowed. He lay covered to his chin with a stark white sheet. Where was all the blood? Dorr stood beside her. Madison. One glance and I also saw Nathan and his copilot Gitta Hamrlik. Iratxe still in her dirty battle gear. Like I was.

Cleary, silent. Where had he come from?

I couldn't take another step.

Dorr approached. I backed up. He was going to hit me again. He had that dead fury in his eyes, like he wanted to kill something.

"Musey," he said in an oddly calm voice. He didn't reach for me, not with his hands.

"No," I said.

"There was poison on the blade," he said. "The docs tried."

A stone fell through me. It dragged me down to the deck. It made me rattle like a hollow thing.

XL.

I still couldn't get the armor off; it became an afterthought. Corporal Dorr escorted me to the captain's office.

The walk was brisk, with no wait outside of the hatch. As soon as we approached it opened. Dorr had palmed his tags to let Azarcon know.

He left me in the office without a word or glance. The hatch shut with a hollow thud and clang.

The captain didn't invite me to sit this time.

"What the *hell* went on out there?"

My mind jumped like a scared animal, then hid.

I was sure he knew. I was sure Dorr had filled him in right after Kris's death and before I'd made it to medbay.

"Musey!" He got to his feet and leaned his fists on the desk.

"Sir, I saw the enemy. I went to take him out, sir." It wasn't my voice. It wasn't me. I stood somewhere against the bulkhead, under a gun, watching the bolt fly. I saw my body, so rigid the muscles began to ache like the pain in my head.

"You left your team. Without warning."

The words broke. "Yes, sir. I screwed up, sir."

"No, Private. You didn't screw up."

I dared a glance into his eyes, surprised. He waited there to snare me.

"You *fucked up*. Now Kris Rilke is dead."

I blinked and felt the tears rise, but they didn't fall.

Azarcon sat and looked up at me, his face pale, expressionless. Controlled. Very controlled, the way it could get when it was one second from explosion.

"Private Musey, you're confined to quarters until dock. The reprimand will go on record, as will a month's forfeit of pay. I want a detailed report of your actions in my comp within the hour, after which I'll decide if you ought to be brought up on formal charges. In addition, you will assist Commander Mercurio in preparing the body for send-off. Dismissed."

The last was the punishment. Everything else was necessity.

XLI.

Somehow I wrote that report. My fingers moved over the keypad on a will of their own, forced to because I couldn't make my voice work enough to verbally input.

After, I went to medbay. It didn't look any different from any other time I'd been in there after a mission. Jets lay in beds, injured and asleep or awake and griping. Just normal reactions. A normal sight. Mercurio approached from his glass-walled office.

"Private Musey, your armor—" He gestured to it. It was still stuck.

I stared at him.

After a small silence he led me to one of the rooms I'd never been in. It was bare except for a large sink and counter against the far wall. And a metal table in the center of the room with a drainage basin below. Kris's body lay on it, covered to the chin in a white sheet.

Everything was clean. Straight. Respectful. Sound didn't bleed through here. It was where you went when churches weren't available.

"Put your hands here." Mercurio motioned me to a disinfectant grille. His eyes grazed over my face.

I pressed my hands on the grille, suffered the slight sting of the blue sterility beam, then went to the table.

Mercurio removed the sheet. He instructed me on how to wash the body for storage until it was time to burn. Kris had been no particular religion that made cremation out of the question. Even in that, the bodies were always washed and

stored. Then on the shift of the ceremony they arrayed the
body in full dress uniform and either set it to burn or placed
it in a tube for careful jettison, somewhere out of the routes
of other ships.

Practicality, even in death.

I lifted his stiffening arms and set them back, passed the
water and the soap over every part of him that I had never
touched in life. I noticed his hands, which looked older than
the rest of him. I noticed a scar on his arm. It was paler than
the rest of his skin. He could've had it fixed, wiped it away.
But maybe he'd liked the reminder. I had never thought to
ask him about it.

At the end of it his face was bare and pale, even his lips.
His hair lay wiped back, close to his skull, as if he'd just got
out of the shower. He never combed it like that. Thin blue
veins made marble art on his lids. I saw the individual eye-
lashes as they lay against his skin. Long and dark, each of
them perfectly settled.

When people died, they became murderers of the living.

Mercurio kept looking my way, maybe to see if I would
break.

But it was a stranger's face. And I was nowhere there, in
that grim duty, in that weak ritual of apology. I was standing
outside of myself. We were both strangers here, where we
weren't meant to be, looking at each other with our eyes
shut.

XLII.

They trotted in and out of my quarters. Maybe I was
Kris's nearest surviving relative to them. Aki was a
squeezed sponge of tears. It wasn't but three hours since

he'd died. I sat in quarters in my stubborn armor while she sat across from me, on Kris's bunk, crying.

"Don't sit there," I said, when I noticed.

"What?" She wiped at her eyes, stared at me as if I'd spoken another language.

"I said don't sit there."

"Jos." She came over to me and settled close. "Let me— let me help you with this." She reached for the armor clasps. Some of Kris's blood was still on it, where I'd wiped my hands.

"I'm fine." I moved away.

She wanted to be held. She wanted to hold me. But I couldn't tolerate her crying. I sent her to Nathan or Cleary or Iratxe, who were all in the mess drinking themselves into consolation like soldiers were supposed to do. I felt nothing at the hurt and hatred in her eyes. My fault. And if it wasn't my fault, then it was my fault that I couldn't connect long enough to mourn him properly.

In the quiet, on my bunk with his empty one across from me, I thought how he would never tell Corporal Dorr or the captain about my talking to that symp.

I lay in my armor. The same damn thing had happened after the last mission . . . the mission before this one. Kris had to work at the clasps for a good ten minutes, though most of that time was spent laughing at me. He said it suited me and maybe I ought to start a new fashion. Battle gear chic. He said if I grew a few more centimeters I could even model it on the TrendSend. Trying to be funny.

Now I raked at the clasps but they were jammed shut. My fingers pinched, the nails cracked. The small pain brought tears. It was okay to cry over this.

It felt soldered to my skin, right through my uniform.

The hatch opened. I hadn't bothered locking it after Aki left. I couldn't seem to get off the bunk and walk the two

strides it took to do that. Evan came in. I sat up. He shut the
hatch behind him and came to me and began working on the
clasps. I didn't have the volition to dodge him now. He said
not a word of how sorry he was about Kris. Maybe because
he couldn't really feel sorry. He hadn't known Kris. Kris had
given him a pack of cigrets once. That was nothing to cry
over.

He moved my arms so he could slip off the chest armor.
The webbing came off perforce. Underneath was damp,
wrinkled uniform. My second skin. The air swept against the
sweat, chilling me. I looked into his face, where he crouched
in front of me. The person who I'd thought dead, now alive.
We were the only ones. Maybe somewhere someone else
was alive, but we were the only ones here. He remembered
the shift when Falcone had boarded us. I saw him remembering it, as if he were watching a vid in my eyes. It played
between us.

He started to undo my dirty uniform, and I let him.

My hands were made of stones, numb and hard by my
sides. I sat in a dark sea. I was sinking straight to the bottom
and the water stood between touch and feeling.

He pulled the T-shirt over my head and felt lightly along
my shoulders and down my arms, caresses meant to comfort.

If I remembered anything at all, it drowned in the thought
of death.

Before Niko, before pirates, I had followed Evan around
the decks. Evan liked to hold toys above my head. Or steal
my desserts. Or wrestle me into a complete tousle and let me
pull his hair. Or he took me on station with his brother Shane
and paid for games in the cybetoriums. He lifted me upside
down and tickled me senseless.

Niko was working with pirates. And Kris was dead.

Evan didn't tousle me. He pulled off my boots and set

them carefully aside. He sat beside me and held me against his chest, like he'd done in Falcone's ship. He rested his cheek against my hair and I listened to his heartbeat. It was alive.

On this ship, we were alive.

XLIII.

I awoke surrounded by a body.

I struggled and sat up. Evan lay wedged against the webbing on the wall, rumpled in his badgeless uniform. He blinked blearily from my movement. My cheek still felt the fabric of his shirt. My back felt the warmth of his hand. I was naked from the waist up.

I worked my way furiously out of the coiled blanket and stood barefoot on the cold deckplates, off balance. I sat on the empty bunk. Perfectly made up, just the way Kris had left it before the mission.

"Jos," Evan said, levering up to his elbow.

I shook my head.

"What?" His lip curled in vague irritation. He rubbed his eye, then the side of his hair. "Nothin' *happened*. So you needed not to be alone for once. What's wrong with bein' with someone for no other reason but just bein' there?"

I looked for my shirt, reached to the floor to get it.

"Jos."

"No, Kris."

I hadn't said that. Except his silence said a different thing.

I held the shirt, sinking back on the bunk. I bunched it in my hands.

"Jos."

"Just go, Evan."

"If I say no?"

I stared at him. "What d'you want? You're on this ship! You got what you want!"

"They trained you good too."

I pelted the shirt at him. "Get out!"

He batted it away. "Or what?"

My throat closed on any words. My mind spun in a funnel of black. Something painful stabbed at my ears. It was me. My own deep breaths. The room was so small it cast the sound back to me in a torrent.

Evan came over and tried to hold me. I struggled away and got to my feet, dragging up my shirt from the floor. My fingers and feet were going numb.

"I'm fine. I'm fine. He's dead, that's all. It's my fault."

"How's it your fault?"

"Corporal Dorr said it's my fault and it is." Because I'm a symp. And I ran off when I should've stayed with my teammate.

Evan's worry reverberated around me. I wiped furiously at my eyes. I looked for my kit to take to the shower. It was my shift again and I had to shower.

"Jos."

"I think you should go now. I have to . . . I have to clean out his locker."

"You don't have to do that now."

"I have to do it!"

He slid up and grabbed me by the shoulders, so hard it shocked me. He shook me just as hard.

His voice cracked. "I don't wanna be alone on this ship, Jos. So you'll damn well hold together."

Did he still think I'd been taken by strits? Did it matter anymore?

He turned me briskly toward the hatch. "Shower and dress. Then come back."

It was a slow thing. My body was out of sync from the rest of the ship. Under the cycle of water I let it all fill my head like the steam from the shower. Lies had attached to my skin like bot-knitters on broken bone, but instead of mending they tore apart. What was sure? What had been sure since my homeship had died? Absolutely nothing. Where was my place? Not on Aaian-na. In that Niko had been right. Not on Aaian-na when my past was still in space.

I couldn't take the word of a symp. If Niko was really screwing with me, I wanted to know it face-to-face. And then I'd go to Azarcon and spill the whole damn thing.

I must have stood there for five cycles, burning in the steam. Just burning it all.

XLIV.

I chased Evan out of quarters, told his jet escort to keep him away. I was confined under the captain's orders. I shouldn't be allowed visitors.

I slept for twenty-four hours. The blankets smelled like Evan's cigrets, so halfway through I kicked them off the bunk and dragged over Kris's. My dreams burned.

Sometime during my sleep the ship docked. I awoke to silence from the drives and darkness in the quarters. Neither of them insulated me against an immediate memory. I was alone. A voice murmured from the walls through the god-comm. It said we were at Chaos Station.

I got dressed and went to the head. Everyone gave me cautious looks, but nobody said a thing. Corporal Dorr met me outside in the corridor.

"Cap wants to talk to you," he said calmly. No trace of the anger that had fueled his punches. He walked me to the captain's office and inside. And stood beside me, just behind my peripheral vision.

That scared me more than meeting the captain alone.

Azarcon looked into my face for a long moment. I didn't know how I looked. But I stared back.

"In your report you said you ran off because you thought you saw a symp. Why was a symp such a compelling reason to break orders?"

Brain functioned down habitual tracks. Even though my body felt like curling up and never opening again.

"Sir, I saw the enemy and I didn't think, I just went after him."

"Without a word to your team."

"Sir, I admit it was a fatal lapse."

Understatement.

"Are you sure you didn't go after that symp for any personal reasons?" Azarcon sat so still I didn't even see him breathe. That restrained anger was far worse than anything I'd ever felt from Ash-dan.

I sweated and I knew it showed.

"Private Musey, I asked you a question."

"Sir, pirates destroyed my homeship." My voice broke. My hands shook at my sides. No reason for that. This was old news. "Pirates and symps—strits—working together to transport orphans. Strits with illegal guns and condoning Slavepoint. I want them, sir. I just want them all dead."

I wanted the truth. If Niko betrayed me, then this man would know it. I would tell him. I made that decision. My eyes filled. I had no control and Azarcon's gaze was a drill, digging me out.

Then Dorr surprised me. "Sir, Private Musey made a fatal error out of vengeance. I don't believe he meant to put Private Rilke in danger." He paused. "Besides, I think Rilke's death is enough punishment, sir."

Tears snaked out and I couldn't stop them. But I kept my face still.

Azarcon watched me cry. His eyes were black stones.

"I don't like errors, Corporal Dorr."

"Yes, sir," Dorr said.

Azarcon sat back, one hand on the arm of his chair. "Formal charges won't be lodged, otherwise you'd find yourself facing prison. But the incident will be on your record, Private Musey. I strongly suggest you get your shit together when you're on duty. I don't care if Falcone himself walks on your ass. You don't hie off like a lone gunman and leave your team unaware. Am I clear, Private Musey?"

"Yessir."

"You're a privileged individual, Private. Corporal Dorr here has spoken on your behalf. Sergeant Hartman has spoken on your behalf. They all just have a high opinion of you. They understand that maybe you've had it a bit harder than most. I might even sympathize, but it won't stop me from tossing your ass out the airlock. You're allowed this kind of thing only once. The next time it happens you're off my ship. I won't bother to charge you. Do you understand me?"

"Yessir."

"Corporal Dorr, he's under your supervision. Do with him what you will."

Dorr said, "Yes, Captain."

"Dismissed."

We saluted and left. I shook. I couldn't make it to the lev without stopping.

I had no chances. And only more attention on my actions.

Dorr lit a cigret and waited. "What's with you and Falcone?"

The lev took its own damn time. I stared at the doors.

"He killed my ship."

"No he didn't."

I looked at the corporal. His eyes were flat and tired, but everything about him made your nerves taut. You could never drop your guard.

"He didn't kill your ship, Musey. *Macedon* is your ship now. You wearin' her tat. Don't you know what that means? *Mukudori* is dead and gone. Get that straight and we won't have problems."

I had no words. His eyes didn't let me go. I didn't know why he spoke up for me. He didn't act like he had a soul otherwise.

"So Falcone fucked with you," he continued. "Big deal. He fucked with a lot of people. He even fucked with the captain."

"What?"

He said, "Falcone and Cap got a past. Admiral Ashrafi was huntin' Falcone when he found Cap way back when. If it goes further than us I'll kill you dead. Got it?"

I didn't say anything. He knew I wouldn't talk.

Dorr said, "Falcone was a Hub captain like a million years ago. He went too far with some strits out by Ghenseti—"

"I know all that."

"Shut up and listen. I ain't gonna say it twice. Falcone was court-martialed but escaped, thanks to his brass ties in the Hub. Admiral Ashrafi's had it in for Falcone even before Cap. 'Cause Birdman made the pirates into a fuckin' franchise with all he knows 'bout Hub ships an' shit. And he came out here terrorizin' colonies and ships and one day attacked the Meridia mines. Cap was twelve. Falcone took him."

I stared at Dorr. Nathan wasn't the one I should've been grilling.

"Like I said." He smiled grimly. "Say anything an' I'll

know who to shoot. Cap don't broadcast it, not even the
Send knows. Ashrafi rescued Cap when Cap was eighteen or
somethin', but he never told nobody from where, and
Ashrafi's crew was a top bunch. They take secrets to their
graves. So y'see, the fact Falcone killed your little ship ain't
all that grand in the grand scheme of things. It ain't like you
got dibs on the bloke."

The lev finally grated to a stop. The doors opened and
Dorr stepped in. I followed him, numb. He leaned against
the wall and smoked, watching me.

I said, "How do you know this?"

He smiled. "That's a bedside story for another time.
Meanwhile, get your head in perspective about this damn pirate."

I wondered if anything bothered him, if he was ever
scared.

"It won't happen again," I said. "I mean—about Kris."

"Damn right. Your ass is mine."

I looked at him. He wasn't smiling.

"But later," he said. "First we pay tribute to a damn good
jet. Cap has his rituals. We got ours."

XLV.

I told Dorr I wanted to change clothes, so he left me alone
with a time to meet. It wasn't something I could get out of,
I saw it in his eyes. I owed him, anyway. I was going to owe
him for the rest of my life.

After going to quarters and the head, I detoured to the
wardroom. Now that we were docked, nobody cared to hang
around here. I dived a quick message to my contact—*Niko*

in league with pirates? I quoted the symp I'd killed. It was
dangerous if it were true and they now realized I knew.

But it couldn't be true.

I took my gun to the airlock, tucked under my shirt. They
were waiting for me there, a guard of mourners, in the way
soldiers mourned. Stoic if not drunk. Hartman, Madison,
Nathan and his copilot Hamrlik, Iratxe, Cleary—

Evan was there.

"Sir." I looked at Dorr.

"Oh, give him a break," the corporal said. "He wanted to
come and he won't run off, he knows we'll shoot him."

He was showered and dressed. Amazing how well he'd
adapted to his new life. But I guessed adaptation was part of
what they taught him. Or part of what we were.

He tried to catch my gaze but I ignored it.

Dorr said, "C'mon, I need a drink." He led the way.

Nathan came up to my left, glanced briefly at Evan, then
tousled my hair lightly.

I dodged my head. "Can we go to the Halcyon?"

She'd have seen *Macedon* come in, and she'd wait.

It was well into station blueshift when we got to the bar.
Other crew were already there but we took our own tables
by the wall and gathered around. Drinks flowed in. Pretty
soon we were making as much noise as the music coming
from the walls. The heavy bass punctuated every sip. I
watched and didn't drink. Beside me Evan gulped like the
beer was water.

Kris hadn't been the only one. Dorr loudly joked about
any number of other jets; they were no longer here to defend
themselves but I knew it was his way of remembering them
under a good star. I stared across the bar, watching the
smoked-glass entrance. Civilians scattered in and out under
tricky lighting, blue and purple and dynamic shadows. The
decorative strips of chrome running along the black walls

reflected the noisy colors of gyrating bodies on the dance floor. Smoke hung from the ceiling in a perpetual cloud. My eyes burned.

Hartman asked Evan to dance, having to shout. Madi and Dorr whistled, and earned solid punches on their arms from the sarge.

Evan went. I didn't think he knew how to say no. Starvation chic, the *Shiva* captain had called the look of her wasted protégé. It made people want to coddle you and fondle you. Evan had told me with a damaged grin.

The jets hooted when Hartman and Evan headed to the floor. Dorr said, "The sarge is kinda cute when she ain't givin' orders."

It all just went on.

Hartman knew how to dance. Out of uniform and without a rifle in her hands (though I knew she was armed, like all of us, under her clothes), she lost what distance might have been there between her and Evan-the-former-pirate. Evan knew how to dance too. Probably something they'd taught on *Shiva*, for those business contacts. Falcone had liked to set tables for me with sparkling cutlery he'd stolen off some dead merchant ship. The people you could fool, the rich ones who could afford you, who liked the way you looked and liked to watch you move. You could take them for a ride, he'd said. In a lot of senses. In every sense.

Evan and Sergeant Hartman moved against each other in waves.

Dorr snapped his fingers in front of my eyes. When I turned to him he was grinning. He sipped his beer.

"He bin a big help, don't y'think?" Dorr had a way of talking through his teeth that made every word an insinuation.

"He shouldn't even be on station."

Dorr laughed, well on his way to a good hangover. "What pirate's gonna attack a bunch of jets in plain sight?"

"Bunch of drunk jets," I said.

"Death warrant," Nathan said, and he wasn't even a jet.

"Some of them aren't too bright," I said. *Or some of you.*

"What?" Dorr tilted his head at me, shouting above the music.

"Forget it!"

He grinned. "You know, I think Musey's jealous of the sarge."

"Shut up!" I stood and slapped the drink out of his hand. "Just go to hell, *sir!*"

All around the tables the music blared, but the crew fell silent.

Dorr slowly wiped his beer-splattered hand on his pants. "I'm gonna excuse that."

"Yeah, go ahead. Sit there, all of you, joking about it when the bodies're being prepped for send-off."

Dorr's eyes locked on mine, dark in the inconstant bar lights. "Sit the hell down, Musey."

"Why? So I can get blind drunk and wake up to remember it all at the funeral? Fuck this. Fuck all of this." I strode to the doors.

Evan got himself off the dance floor to intercept me. "Hey!"

"Jettison yourself, D'Silva."

"You gonna keep tossin' tantrums? This won't do you any good!"

I turned on him. "What d'you know about it? You don't know me."

"I know you're grieving."

"You don't know shit! Pointing fingers for Azarcon and dropping a sob story in his lap so you can get in good on the ship doesn't mean you know a damn thing!"

"I know a lot. I know you don't wanna admit you cared about him. Did Falcone train that out of you in a year? Or was it something else?"

Someone cut between us to get to the bar. I didn't move. Neither did Evan. The lights played across his face like fingers.

The music drowned everything but the most pointed words.

I stepped closer. "What're you doing, Evan?"

"Taking advantage of where I am. Maybe you should too. *Macedon*'s a good place to be."

"You'd know about taking advantage. Did you take advantage on that shift? When I was asleep maybe? You perverted piece of shit!"

He reacted like I'd struck him. I left him stunned, left the bar and lost myself in the crowd on the concourse.

I'd walked the same corridors, once, with my hand in Falcone's.

Alone on a station deck, in a jet uniform, while carriers raided pirate outposts up and down and sideways wasn't the brightest thing to do.

I found a bench by one of the walls and sank down. I didn't know how long I sat there, looking at nothing, but when I moved to stand, to go back to the ship, a dark-skinned woman veered from the uneven lines of people and sat beside me.

"Got a light?" she asked, fishing out a cigret from her jacket pocket. Her hair was short now beneath a tight cap.

My hand brushed my sidearm in reflex. But I recognized her. "No, sorry."

"No matter." Her eyes cased the crowd, the line of eateries across the wide concourse, flocked about by hungry soldiers and Chaos citizens. "Niko says hello."

I sat back. "Yeah, I bet."

She looked at me. "You want to hear this or not?"

Our last meeting had been mostly *Keep doing what you're doing*. I'd given her *Macedon*'s schematics, what I knew from walking the ship and talking to Cleary. I'd told her my impressions about Azarcon.

That was before a symp told me Niko had given orders to trade with pirates. Before that it had just been Evan's word, Evan who'd spent six years with pirates. And one encounter in the deep, one strit ship and *Shiva*. Maybe Niko was ignorant of it.

"Yeah, I want to hear it."

I kept my hand on my sidearm.

She tugged me up and slipped her arm around my shoulders, familiar. More than familiar. "Come on, cutie."

I walked even as I realized it might be a trap.

She led me to a low-scale den at the edge of the barstrip. A long way down from the Halcyon. It was dark as we threaded our way through the bar crowd, to the back doors and into a shadow-ridden corridor full of dross people drunk or high or both. Nobody would notice us here, not even my uniform.

She ushered me into a stale-smelling room and locked the door. It took a few tries before it beeped red. I remained standing in the middle of the space, one eye to her and the other to the small bathroom door on my right. Someone could've been in there, though I didn't hear anything.

"Siddown," she said, "this might take a while."

"Where's Niko?"

She sat on the unmade bed, reached in the side table and pulled out a finger lighter for her cig, which she still carried. After flicking it and taking a drag she pulled off her cap and scraped at her hair briefly.

"He's close by. You know I can't tell you exactly where. I been shadowing you since you came off *Mac*."

"I know."

A stream of smoke blew up toward the ceiling and hung there in a dissipating spread. "He ain't the one in league with the pirates, Musey."

I searched her face. But I didn't know her that well and she was capable. If she was lying I wouldn't know it. "Then who? A symp we caught named him."

"The symp lied, obviously," she said flatly. "As for who—you been sending your messages to him."

I squinted. "Messages . . . *Ash-dan?*" That was almost as incredulous as Niko being involved.

She raised an eyebrow and dragged on her cig.

"That doesn't make any sense! Why would Ash—he *hates* pirates, anybody this side of the DMZ." And me, I thought. Something I had never been able to really figure out. Long after Niko and even Enas had accepted me, he had not.

"Let's just say his opinion about how Niko is running this war . . . differs."

"He respects his brother."

"Look." She tapped her ashes away and stared up at me, the tired eyes of somebody too used to hiding. "Niko had suspicions about his brother. He didn't tell you. Now he is. Now that you've confirmed that some faction of the sympathizers and the strivs is in league with Falcone and others like him."

"But to what end? It makes no sense."

"You know why you're on that ship, cutie?"

I looked at her hard. "Information gathering. About Azarcon. About *Macedon*. He must have told you."

"To what end?"

I recited some of my mission objectives. "Niko thinks a peace treaty might go via Azarcon, if anybody. Azarcon's foster father is in the admiralty, a good uplink. And from everything I've seen, Azarcon does his own thing and the Hub be damned. Niko knows this now. Azarcon's also the top striv hunter in the fleet. Getting him to stop can only help us, right?"

"Azarcon's also less of a warmonger and more of a . . . how is it you said in your report? Patron to throwaways." She actually smiled.

"You still haven't answered my question."

"Ash," she said, tapping her cig, "doesn't want a treaty with the Hub."

"But that's stupid. Why wouldn't he? We've been fighting for so long, they've been keeping the strivs on Aaian-na for years. The planet can barely afford the war as it is."

"Well, exactly. Niko thinks Ash would rather go on an offensive for one fell swoop. That's why the alliance with the pirates. You said they're trading for guns and other weapons."

I sat on the edge of the bed. Of course Niko would never go on the offensive if it meant dealing with pirates to get enough firepower. He'd had his opportunity—even Markalan had, in his day—to raise the level of the war. Right now he wore down the Hub fleet by strike attacks on convoys, munitions depots, and military Rimstations. It kept the Hub fleet far back from the space that the Hub had allotted the strivs since the Battle of Plymouth Moon. As it stood now, if Hubcentral had its wish it would govern all the way to Aaian-na and bring the symps up on criminal charges. Niko was the only thing stopping them.

"But Ash is letting pirates stow people behind the DMZ. We still have no idea where, either." I hadn't thought even Ash was so rotten to the core.

"What else could a symp guerrilla offer a pirate like Falcone, except safe storage of people who bring in ransom creds and black market funds?"

"But he's betraying his own brother."

She didn't answer that. Maybe she'd read about the caste wars. This sort of thing had precedent on Aaian-na. A junior member of the caste didn't necessarily see eye to eye with a senior member, and in the way of strivs, the solution came on the sly. All the details came to light only after everything had fallen to its conclusion. And then . . . either the junior member was victorious in his plan, or he was assassinated by the one he'd betrayed.

"What does he want me to do?"

"Just what you're doing. He'll handle Ash. He needs solid proof before he can take action. This isn't some fisherman's debate, it's high up in the caste and blows wide on all sympathizers. Right now the links don't go all the way back to Aaian-na. Yet. Ash made it look like only a few rogue ships are working crosswise of Niko's orders. Ash is the expert on comps, right? Nontraceable comms. So you let Niko work that end. You—you keep your eyes on Azarcon. Feel him out. He seems to have turned his attention on the pirates and less on patrolling us." She eyed me. "That kid from your old ship. He's been helping, you said."

"Yeah. And the captain's asked me about Falcone."

"Good." She nodded. "Good."

"I want to know more about Falcone. I've been in contact with Otter. Can you dig for me and leave me the information at my Austro link?"

She sucked in the smoke and squinted at me. "We're already hunting Falcone, cutie."

"I want in the full loop. Dammit, Azarcon wants that pirate. He has a vendetta. A history. It could help my position with him. Tell Niko, make it strong with him."

I didn't mention that I needed all the help I could get, dealing with the captain. I wasn't going to tell her that Evan suspected me either.

She stubbed out the cig. "I'll see what I can do."

The relief at Niko's noninvolvement in the pirate alliance made me somehow weary. I wasn't going to see him for years, if at all. That realization hit like a high-beam paralysis pulse. When I'd left him I knew that possibility, but some part of me had always believed I would return to Aaian-na before long. It was home, after all.

But it wasn't.

My hands throbbed numb.

"So what should I tell him about how you're doing?" the woman asked. "You look well enough."

I nodded, but it wasn't my answer. "Tell him someone died. Tell him I hate it. But tell him I'm still doing my job."

I tried to remember why I was doing it.

I thought of casting paper ships off balconies and the flame light dancing toward the sea.

Little meteors for the fallen dead.

XLVI.

I go back to *Macedon* with things in my head I have no language for. They are just hoarse sounds in a hollow drum of silence.

PART IV

I.

Falcone isn't in hiding any longer, that's what his allies say. Once again Iratxe and I escort our latest batch of criminals to brig, with Madison and Dorr and other teams, and the pirates brag at us about Falcone. The pirates shout at us the same old shit. They're growing, they say, and we're never going to defeat them and jets are nothing but colored sugar on the good-ship lollipop.

That one's new.

Dorr bashes that pirate on the back of the head with the butt of his rifle before kicking him into the cell.

"You'll know what jets are by the end of this shift, I guarantee."

We lock the cells. One of the pirates presses his face to the gate and leers at Iratxe. She spits her gum at him.

"Forget it," I tell her. "Waste of a projectile."

"It was stale anyway."

Dorr taps my back. "Get to medical and check that wound."

"Yes, sir."

Bloody pirate caught me in my shoulder with a bolt. It was from a 790 and it penetrated my armor. Iratxe peers at it as we walk out. She would've shot the pirate before but another one kept her busy. Pirates try to do that because they know jets watch each other's backs.

"Clean through your shell. Those mothers're bitches, mano!"

"Hurts like a bitch." I can't move the shoulder.

A year ago, after Kris's death, Dorr got Iratxe transferred to our team from Sanchez's unit (boy did he whine). Somehow she never seems to get a scratch on her. She says she's too pretty to get shot. Dorr says bolts are just too scared of her. They see her face, turn the other way, and hit me instead.

"You should use that face of yours to direct those bolts toward the enemy," I tell her now. An old joke.

She laughs and walks me to medical. As usual, Aki's radar finds me right away and she propels me up onto one of the examination tables.

"What're you doing to him, Chay?"

Iratxe slings her rifle and holds up her hands. "Not me, mano. This boy finds it all on his lonesome."

"I don't go looking," I mutter. The teasing, like some missions, has gotten pretty routine.

Aki gives me a glance like, Right. She works my torso armor off, and the shoulders. Now it really starts to hurt.

"I hope the pirate who did this to you is dead."

"He is." I clench my teeth as she cuts my shirt and peels it back from the wound, then starts her work. It may eventually heal from her ministrations, but the advance procedures always seem to make it worse. The spray bites cold, little teeth straight through the wound to my bones.

"Dirty lot," Iratxe says. "I miss the good ol' days of killing strits."

Comments like that remind me who I am.

"Those days aren't over," I tell her. "It's not like we're in treaty."

"I wish they'd hurry it up," Aki says while she examines the wound, her face close to my shoulder with the handheld scanner. There's been some chatter about a peace treaty on some parts of the Send, but nothing that isn't shouted down by diatribes.

"Chicky, are you serious?" Iratxe hops up beside me on the table.

Aki's voice is slightly muffled as she works. "Of course I'm serious. Aren't you reading the reports? The Rimstations and the ones in the Dragons're having a real hard time and we're running around between pirates and aliens, thanks to this Falcone jerk. It'd be a lot easier if we could get the pirates without worrying about our backs facing the DMZ."

She doesn't know that the guerrilla strikes are sapping Niko's fleet as well, not to mention his planet support. He decreased his attacks on Hub space, though didn't eliminate them entirely, and the only thing stopping the warmongers in Hubcentral from invading Aaian-na space is the increased pirate activity. Which, I know, is partly thanks to Ash. Falcone came out of hiding, it seems, to work the new alliance.

The irony.

Deep-space carriers do all the running around out here. Azarcon isn't in a good mood lately about it. He thinks the pirates and all of the strits and symps are in alliance. Of course my say-so about Niko's good character would land me out an airlock, so I say nothing. Not to Azarcon and not here.

"Everybody's talking about Falcone like he's the president of the pirates," Iratxe scoffs. "He's not the only enemy out here. Did we all forget the Warboy? They're *working* together."

"If they are," Aki says, poking me some more in the name of treatment. I wince. "If they are, how come strit fleet action's waned in the last year?"

"Too busy shacking with the enemy," Iratxe says bluntly.

At that precise moment, Evan walks in.

"Speaking of which . . ." she continues.

"Shut up," I tell her. I feel Aki look at me but she doesn't comment. They think I'm bedding him. A ridiculous lie. Just because he hangs around me, meets me after missions, visits me in medbay. I don't encourage it but he isn't put off. Crew Recreation and Morale Department, that's where Azarcon placed him. The captain's got a dark sense of humor. Evan helps choose what entertainment to bring on ship, when once he was the entertainment on another ship. It's his ticket here and he doesn't complain. Not all of the jets harass him. He cleaned up well.

So they think I think so too.

I have nowhere to go as he approaches.

"Are you okay?"

"I'm fine. Aki, are you done yet?"

"Almost. Sit still."

My shoulder is numb now and the painkiller's starting to make me drowsy.

"What happened?" Evan asks, looking at me, then Iratxe.

She stares at him. "It's not my fault, boy."

"Those pirates." I interrupt them. "We got the last of *Shiva*'s survivor ships. The ones we didn't kill are in the brig now."

"Might want to pay them a visit," Iratxe says to Evan. "You know, reacquaint yourself."

"I'm not with them anymore," he tells her, glaring. "If the captain thinks so, why don't you?"

"I have a right to my own opinions."

"Does that count when you bed Sanchez?"

She gets off the table, fast. I grab her arm.

"Stop it!"

Aki looks between us, holding an injet. "All of you stop it or I'll use this on your asses."

I look at Evan. "You better go."

He never listens to me. "Just because you jets can't seem

to do anything but stop a shipment here and there, while Slavepoint's still undiscovered—"

"Evan." I let go of Iratxe, slide off the table, and shove his shoulder toward the hatch.

"Don't blame me for it!"

"Why not?" Iratxe says loudly. "You put out every which way except where it matters."

We've attracted the attention of other wounded jets and their visitors. And Doc Mercurio, who likes to give reports to the captain. He strolls over from the biolab.

"Problem?"

Evan yanks his arm from me and walks out.

"No, sir," I say. Just because it's easier than listing them all.

II.

When Aki finishes with me I tramp to quarters alone, sore and half-asleep from the drugs. I hope Iratxe will spend some time with Sanchez or Nathan so I can have a few moments of peace.

Iratxe isn't there, but Evan's leaning on the bulkhead outside my hatch.

I'm too tired to act nice. I yank out my tags and run them through the lock. "Go away, Evan. If she comes back and you get in a fight, I might let her kill you."

"Do you know where Slavepoint is?"

I stand there, holding the hatch open, and stare at him. "What?"

"This whole last year," he says, eyes tight and fixed on me, "in the Send—don't you read? Merchants and passenger lines getting hit by pirates. And you know when crew's never

found where they go. And the strits in treaty with pirates—
Slavepoint's out there and I want to know if you know where
it is. Or if you know somebody who knows where it is. Because I'm tired of getting blamed on this ship like I should
have all the answers to what pirates do!"

"Shut up and get inside." I shove him in, keep shoving him
with my one good arm, right onto my bunk. I stand over him.
"You're not bringing this shit up again, are you? Because *I'm*
tired of it."

"I don't care if you are in contact with the strits—"

"I don't know any! I keep telling you how I got to Austro
but all these leaps must've wiped that section of your memory."

He looks up at me, doesn't bother to argue. He's had the
thought in his head since the first and there's no dissuading
him. He just doesn't say anything because I got him on the
ship and he wants me.

He wants me and he'd blackmail me if he could, except he
knows I'd kill him before I ever bedded him, threats be
damned.

Sometimes it's hard to believe we share memories of
Mukudori. I've offered to show him the files Captain Azarcon
got for me from Siqiniq, but Evan always refuses. He'd rather
forget, he says.

Sometimes I wonder if we would've got along this way on
our homeship.

Useless thoughts.

"Jos," he says now, "I just want to know if you know. I'd
tell Azarcon myself and say it came from me. I'd make something up just so we can find that damn place."

"I don't know where Slavepoint is. Now get out so I can
sleep."

Ash must know, but my contacts say that none of the sympathizers or striviirc-na crew Niko captured ever fingered Ash

as the head behind the pirate alliance or said anything about Falcone's whereabouts. In the way of things, he can't exactly ask Ash since he has no grounds for action. Accusation without proof puts the accuser under suspicion, in striviirc-na law, and Niko says that sort of suspicion does no good for sympathizers on Aaian-na. In fact, the entire striv-pirate alliance is under wraps, something Ash and Niko both agree on, though probably for different reasons.

Evan hasn't left yet. He's trying to read my mind. The silence congeals between us.

"Feel free," I say finally as I start to work off my boots, "to sit in here until Iratxe gets back."

"I'm not scared of her. And I wish you'd stop using her as a shield."

I stand lopsided, one boot off. "What?"

He gets up from the bunk, forcing me to step back or we'd touch.

"That," he says, pulling out a cig from his pocket and lighting it. "Keep stepping back 'til you fall off the ship, Jos."

He purposely brushes by me, making contact in the narrow space, before slamming the hatch shut behind him.

III.

I won't be going on any missions until my shoulder heals. A couple weeks, Aki said, before I get to put myself in the way of laser bolts again. The circle of life, I remember Rodriguez saying. Patch you up and propel you back out. The circle of death.

A week into it and I have to do something while my teammates assault pirate caches, so I take my sketchbook to the lounge and make pictures from the battles I see through the window.

It's this distant sometimes. I can draw things from any part of the ship and be the observer, not the observed. Even watching a skirmish streak by my view—you can put yourself away from it and pretend it doesn't matter, in the grand scheme. You're a year removed from where you were, six years from things you can barely remember, so if you wait long enough it all becomes habit. Life is a habit.

A jet's life is a vice.

Bunk-hopping, drunks on layovers, denial of deaths you see happen in front of you, or cause yourself. My skin soaked it up until I can't get the scent off me. This ship is my exoskeleton and I only remove it when I burndive. The dislocation I feel coming out of the comp world and back into the real one only gets larger every time I do it, until I walk around on shift with the grid patterns emblazoned behind my eyes and codes that refuse to leave my head. Codes and information I send to Niko—they walk with me through the corridors of this ship.

But then they fade, and it's just the ship. It's all the noise and the chaos and the intrusion of faces you've grown accustomed to, even in quarters. Iratxe is more of a jet than she is a woman, so it doesn't matter that we share a space, like it didn't matter with Kris. We stay out of each other's ways and when we're in battle, we watch each other's backs.

And when I get hurt, Aki or Rodriguez or some doctor here fixes me up. When we go out, Nathan and Hamrlik take us, or some other pilot team we know, and when we get in trouble they come to get us and bring us back. There's nothing like the buzz in your pickup and the voice of your ride telling you he's here, you can get out of the drama of enemies shooting to kill and be safe. *Macedon* never leaves her jets behind.

Never. Azarcon will hunt for his people before he takes orders from the Hub to run after another enemy.

The skirmish breaks before me. The pirate runners are in retreat. Small-ship debris floats around in a macabre, inertial dance, as well as parts from the blown cache, which was no more than a double-lock ministation in space. How many enemy did we kill this time, and will we take any prisoners? How many of ours won't make it back?

I fold up my sketchbook and head to the hangar deck. Each step is a clanging "what if." It's not easy to adjust to a new teammate, even when you've fought with them before, or trained with them. It's just not simple.

I try to remember if Aki said she was on this mission. I stand behind the inner bay doors and watch the jets disembark from the Chargers. In a few minutes a familiar blond saunters down the ramp, rifle slung on his shoulder, with another tall blond beside him. The corporal and Madi. Scuffed but alive. Behind them Lieutenant Hartman walks with her new Sergeant McCrae. Dorr didn't get promoted, not with his station antics and breaks in the rules of engagement.

Iratxe appears with Nathan and Gitta Hamrlik. Looks like she prefers the pilot this month. Too bad for Sanchez.

Then Aki emerges, weighed down by kit and helping PFC Dumas onto a stretcher brought up by the medical crew that always meets returning jets. I hit the door release, go through the small passage that serves as an airlock in case the bay is damaged and a deadly vacuum created, and stand to the side as the jets pass.

"Sir, how was it?" I ask Dorr.

He waves a hand. "Borin'. The cache ain't worth shit, looked more like some pirate's dumpin' bowl. I'm gonna kill our bozo intel."

"Waste of time," Madi agrees.

Frustration can kill a crew. I see it in the corporal's eyes.

"Cap seems hard-pressed to get any decent leads on Falcone," I venture. He's not the only one. The problem with trying to get any intelligence on somebody like Falcone, who was a captain with ties to Hubcentral, is it takes a patience-trying amount of time to accumulate to something useful.

"That's 'cause Falcone's got help," Dorr says. "If I ever come upon one of them Hubcentral brass-caps, I'll shoot 'em dead." Then as usual he jumps to another topic. His mind is like that. "I gotta get me outta these stinky clothes."

"I'm sure you'll find some help for that," Madi says wryly.

I move off before Dorr decides to draft me for that detail.

IV.

At the end of the second week since my injury, I go for my checkup in medbay. Things have been quiet lately, no missions, and the wide trauma room stands mostly empty now. I spy Aki carrying a tray of medical instruments to one of the back rooms. I don't have to hover for long before she sees me and comes over.

"How're you feeling?"

"A little stiff, but it's good. The knitters're itching me like crazy." I know the routine and hop up onto one of the tables.

"Take off your shirt," she says professionally, and readies one of the at-hand scanners.

I do that and she inspects the now-healed wound. "It looks good. The bot-knitters are crawling out." She sets the scanner down and slowly peels back my bandage and sprays an accelerant to encourage the bots along. She has a light touch unless she's pissed at you.

I look around the room, otherwise I'll get stuck looking

into her face. And she's necessarily standing close. I smell the mix of shampoo and sterile air around her.

She dabs at the ashes of bots on my shoulder, says absently, "Evan was in here earlier."

"Yeah?" I don't try to hide my disinterest. Everybody seems to think I want to know what he does every shift.

"He was hurt," she says.

I look at her. A second goes by before she meets my eyes. "How?"

She shrugs. "He said he fell down the steps. But you can't convince a medic of that. I recognize a beating when I see one."

"He didn't say who did it? Do you *know* who did it?"

Teasing is one thing. Even nasty insinuation is one thing altogether different.

"I don't know who did it." She motions me to put my shirt back on now that she's done. "But I figured you can ask him if you want."

"Thanks." I slide down. A few suspects already come to mind.

She snags my sleeve before I go. "Jos."

"Yeah?"

For a moment she just looks at me, somber, as if she's suddenly lost the knowledge of language. Then she waves a hand briefly and sets it on her hip. "Nothing. Don't worry, he's going to be fine."

"I'm not worried."

I leave medbay and head straight to Sanchez's quarters. I just get to jetdeck when my tags beep.

"Dammit." I swipe at them. "Musey."

"Private, come to my office, please."

The captain.

I stop in my tracks. "Yessir."

He breaks the connection and I head slowly to the lev.

Sudden calls from your CO are never good. Maybe it has to do with Evan. A part of me wishes it does, because if it has to do with me I don't think it will be anything good. After the conversation in Azarcon's quarters he never called me back for a one on one. He probably still monitors me through Dorr or Hartman, but all my interactions with him in the last year were casual, unpremeditated incidences—at funerals for fellow jets, in the corridors, or even in the gym. He always seemed preoccupied.

No surprise.

My speculations about what he wants make my gut fold in origami shapes for the entire lev ride up to the command deck. The hum of the active drives is always louder on this deck, because it's so quiet here compared to jetdeck. There's something lonely about being that consciously encompassed by the ship; there is no escaping it. You hear *Macedon*'s size when you listen to her drives. On the command deck, you feel doubly small.

I take a long, slow breath before I buzz his hatch. The lock lights green and I go in and stand at attention.

"Have a seat," he says. I notice he does this when he's predisposed to be patient, but his voice now is anything but friendly.

I sit, hands on the chair arms, and look at him expectantly. Carefully blank-faced.

His comp sits open and turned toward him. The vaguely blue-tinged lighting casts slivers of pale neon reflection on his short, jet-black hair. He is so pallid against the dark eyes and hair that you'd think it a side effect of suspended aging treatments. But I know it isn't. The younger-than-chronological forty-something years of faint lines between his brows and beneath his eyes come from a life spent far away from Hub-central and never in one stationary place for long. Biologically he's in his late twenties. But that isn't indicative of his experience—or his memories—in deep space.

Not in any way.

"Lieutenant Commander Firsken," Azarcon says temperately, pointedly, and my gut sinks into a void.

Firsken is the ship's senior communications officer.

"Last shift she noticed an anomaly in one of our outgoing comms to the Chaos sat."

I keep my breaths regular. "Yes, sir?"

"It went through under a reverse Send transmission update, pretty sophisticated considering the news Send is usually one-way coded to the receiver. Lieutenant Hartman says that you are quite adept in satellite communications tech."

"Sir, only what was taught in jet training."

"You have an affinity for that sort of thing. Like with weapons."

"Sir, I'm maybe more intelligent than the average person, but it's just a matter of brain application with the tech." Jets are expected to be arrogant. And he likes it when you're forthright.

His finger slowly traces a short line on the black desk, then stops. His eyes don't move from my face. "We were able to acquire some new ware from the Guard at our last port to Rimstation 30. You didn't know this of course; it's not something that would interest any jet. With this new ware, however, Lieutenant Commander Firsken was able to trace the reverse code to a comp in the jet wardroom. Time index: oh-five-oh-five hours last shift."

Oh, shit.

"Corporal Sanchez also says that he saw you leave the wardroom at oh-five-twenty hours last shift. Alone."

My hands are below his line of sight, gripping the chair arms. I let it all flow down to my fingertips before I open my mouth.

"Sir, it's no secret the corporal has had it in for me since day one when I tripped him up in the gauntlet."

"I'm aware of that. I strongly advised him against slander. He stuck by his claim."

Damn that prowling son of a bitch.

I let my voice grow hard. Indignant. "He's lying, sir."

Azarcon stares at me. In the silence I hear my own words.

Oh, fuck. That's all that goes through my head. A mantra of idiotic profanity.

"I like you, Musey. I don't necessarily like everyone in my crew, personally, but I like you. You're an orphan and you've had it bad with Falcone, but despite all that you've managed to serve admirably here, in the main. I respect how you've turned out."

I remember Dorr's words. If he's right, the captain was with Falcone for at least five years. Will this help me?

There's no reading him. I have never found a way to really read all of his contradictions and purposeful words.

"But," he says, "I strongly suggest you be forthcoming. If you're hiding something and it's left up to me to discover it without your help, I'll dump you at the nearest pirate cache. Am I clear?"

I allow a breath. When he asks that question it is not an idle threat. "Yes, sir. Very clear."

Our shared past with Falcone will not help me. He's far removed from it and I screwed up once already, with Kris.

It makes his eyes doubly hard to meet.

"So what do you have to say for yourself, Private Musey?"

"Sir, I've been corresponding with burndivers."

His face shows no reaction. "Why?"

"Sir, I've been working with some of them to try and find out Falcone's whereabouts and ship codes. I didn't say anything because, well, it's illegal. Burndiving the way we—they—we do it. Because of Falcone's Hub ties we—I—

suspect he's been hiding a lot behind legitimate ships. Just like he did with *Shiva*, sir."

"This isn't news."

"Sir, my contacts discovered his tech supplier. But they're still trying to trace the equipment specifically. And they think they might have the name of someone in Falcone's crew who is willing to roll."

It's all going to be out on the table now. But better this than the other reason I send comms on the sly.

I don't know if any of this information has the least effect on him.

"Private Musey, in order for you to burndive you have to have optic holopoint receptors."

"Yessir."

"You're not authorized to have those on this ship."

"I know, sir. But I want Falcone, sir."

"Like you wanted him when you took off after that symp and got Kris Rilke killed? I don't like renegades in my crew unless they work for me. But you're not working for me, in this, since you've been keeping it a secret."

"Sir, I don't want to go renegade."

"Indeed?"

"This is just me, sir. Me and some contacts I made on Austro and elsewhere through the satlines. It's not going against any of our missions."

"Burndiving into unauthorized systems using a Hub carrier link. You don't see a discrepancy here?"

I can't answer that. Any answer would just put me in deeper shit.

"Mr. Musey, I thought we had this conversation over a year ago." His voice is hard. His eyes bore into mine now, no longer impassive. "When you took it upon yourself to chase down symps you put your teammates in jeopardy. Now you are corresponding with burndivers—criminals, for all I know—using carrier lines. Do you recall my admonition after Rilke's death, Mr. Musey?"

"Yessir."

"Do you? Because I see now that your memory is rather short and quite convenient. You are on a deep-space carrier. You are a jet. You're my jet, on my carrier. While I don't discourage a certain independent spirit, I don't like my crew doing things under my nose, especially things that threaten the security of my ship or its personnel—and that *includes* linking up with unauthorized contacts to investigate pirates. *Do you understand that, Mr. Musey?*"

"Yessir."

"I don't think you do. I don't think you truly understand the sheer stupidity of your actions. If it weren't for the fact you might have discovered some things about Falcone hitherto unknown, I might vent you out the port side airlock."

"Yes, sir."

"Shut your mouth, Musey. Now. You're going to write a full report of everything you know. That means the names and comm numbers of all your contacts and what information you've gathered so far. You're going to be detailed and thorough. I'm going to give you some privacy to do it too. You're going to the brig."

It's better than out an airlock, I guess. Though not by much.

He comms Sanchez to take me. He wants me to hurt.

I have to sit, looking at him, while we wait for Sanchez to show up. He stares at me.

"Sir," I venture.

"What?"

"Sir, my contacts won't like it that I reveal their comm codes. I can lose them, sir."

Not to mention most of them are symps.

"And how will they know that I have them, Mr. Musey? Are you going to tell them?"

"No, sir."

"Then they won't know, will they. You'll keep in touch with them, never fear. Only this time you'll work for me, *with* my knowledge, and with Firsken riding your ass in the comps. Since you seem to have this diving skill, you can share what you know with her. I am excited to see you use it."

His face says otherwise. His face says I better be agreeable or he'll forget where he put me.

"Your belongings will be searched. If I don't find those holopoints you will direct me to them. From now on your comp codes will be blocked from all systems unless you receive Corporal Dorr's authorization. That goes for duty reports too. He will sign off on all your comp usage. That will doubtless piss him right off. You can explain to him why this will be—after you get out of the brig, of course. If you get out of the brig. I haven't yet decided if I want you roaming my decks."

Sanchez buzzes the hatch. The captain lets him in.

I stand and salute. I manage not to shake.

Azarcon doesn't notice. He looks at his comp. He has already dismissed me.

V.

At the end of the shift, Evan sneaks in to see me. I don't have a guard, just the optics somewhere in the bulkheads. I'm one person in a vast quiet, and the sound of the hatch opening makes me jump. He turns up the lights, only twenty percent, but I still see the cuts and bruises on his face and knuckles when he limps to the cell gate.

I remember other things. "What happened to you?"

"I should ask you the same thing. Sanchez was bloody gloating that he'd got you, after he touched base with Firsken, the bitch. I tried to stop him from telling Cap."

"You?"

"Yes, me. Don't act so shocked. You forget who used to chase your little ass up and down deck?"

I want to hit him. "Are you stupid to take on Sanchez?"

"Sheez, Jos. A simple thanks would go a long way."

I stand and go to the bars. "Thanks for what? You're swollen purple and I'm still in here."

"Yeah. You are. And when that bastard came to tell me *specifically* that he was going to take you down, I didn't have to think about trying to make him stop, I just clobbered the shit. 'Cause I don't care 'bout what you don't tell me, Jos. I'll still try to help you." He wraps his fingers through the gate.

"You're crazy."

For some reason that makes him smile. His chipped tooth shows.

"You better get out of here before somebody finds you."

He watches me, then threads his other fingers through to pluck at my sleeve. "Just get yourself out somehow. Okay?"

"Well I don't plan on starting a colony here."

In one flash, through the cell door, we look at each other as if we're both young. But it's only a moment, and a second later he hobbles to the brig hatch and cuts the lights, leaving me the way he found me.

VI.

The shift in the brig stretches out to a week, then a month. I've become accustomed to the total darkness in my sleepshift, the cold, and the thoughts. Sometimes I dream, and I've become accustomed to that too. It's not like I've never been in darkness before.

I have a slate where I write everything as I remember it. Dorr comes in to take it from me after every shift, so he can give the information to the captain. The first time he came he yelled at me, opened the gate, and hit me. I guess I deserved that. The jets go out on missions after pirates and strits. I don't.

Firsken comes in every three shifts with holopoints—a set for me and a set for her. She follows me in the dives, like Ash did when he trained me, watching me drop my codes to Otter and pick up the info packets from him—all of which she screens first. I haven't sent a message to Niko in a month. Otter will tell him I'm still alive, but I don't mention sympathizer stuff to Otter, only about Falcone. I dropped a duress code in one packet, a prearranged, seemingly innocent greeting that he'll know means I'm being watched in the dives. So Otter never mentions symp stuff and that part is safe from Firsken's adept eyes.

I think Azarcon will never let me out.

He's got his own resources of information, but too much never hurts when it comes to pirate hunting. At least the stuff I give him has nothing to do with Niko or the striviirc-na. Niko's still uncompromised.

It's only me that is compromised. And in that brig, I'm unreachable. Niko couldn't get me out even if he wanted. I don't even know if he wants to. Maybe I'm still useful where I'm at. I've been useful for over a year. Alive, at least.

One shift Aki brings me food instead of the regular jet, and turns the lights up. I get off the bunk and go to the gate. I know I must look like shit. I think I need a haircut and I can't take showers because there's no shower, only a sink that I have to dunk my head in. I usually splash my body with water and wipe off with a small towel. The water is always cold.

She slides the tray through the slot. It smells wonderful. Not the usual dry food. There's hot caff and soup and toast and synth eggs with pepper on them.

"Thanks." I smile at her.

"Sure," she says, looking at me with a physician's eyes. "How are you?"

"Good." I sit on the bunk and eat.

She puts her fingers through the bars and slides her gaze around the cell, then back to me. "Jos, what are you doing?"

"I'm eating."

"Not that." She frowns. Her hair is down and it's grown past her shoulders, straight. Her eyes are darker than Niko's. "I mean, what're you doing? Sending illegal comms, talking to burndivers? You don't do things behind Cap's back, Jos. Not illegal things like that. Not things that bear on missions. You should've at least told Cap what you found out about Falcone."

"It wasn't much. I was waiting until it was something conclusive."

"You could've at least told Dorr."

I look at her and laugh. "And admit I had the holopoints?"

"You know Erret is a rulebreaker. He could've spoke up for you before Cap found out on his own."

"You mean before Sanchez spied on me."

"Whatever. But you could've told somebody."

Told her, she means.

"You said it yourself, I was doing something illegal. I'm not going to tell people."

"Some of us wouldn't rat on you." She pauses. "Did Evan know?"

"Not 'til Sanchez had to rub it in."

She would like to own me too.

I think if I ever get out of here and the ship docks at a station, I will quit.

She usually looks like there's always something more she wants to say, but never bothers. Maybe she thinks I ought to be attracted to her or want her like she thinks I want Evan, or how Evan wants me. But she doesn't get it. Evan doesn't get it. I don't want anything. Except to get out of this damn brig.

"I wish you were outta here," she says. To fill the silence, I think.

"Yeah, well," I say, "wishes don't count for much."

The brig hatch opens as I say it and Corporal Dorr strolls in.

"Oh, yah?" he says. "Well rub this genie's tummy. You're free at last."

Aki looks at me for a reaction.

"Yeah?" I don't accept it at face value. "What, are we going to take a promenade to the airlock?"

"Nah, worse," Dorr says, with an evil little grin. "To Cap's office."

VII.

"Have we learned our lesson, Mr. Musey?"

His office is warm. It makes me sleepy. I think I've played this scenario so long in my head, for the past month, that numbness pervades every reaction.

"Yes, sir."

"You've been diligent with your reports. I appreciate that. It's helped us tremendously. One step at a time, that's how you catch pirates."

He's in a good mood. I'm so glad. I'm so glad he can sit there behind his desk and smile at me in that way adults get when they know they have successfully disciplined a kid. Behind me Erret Dorr stands silent. Sometimes he's my advocate, other times he hits me.

"Are you ready to return to full active duty, Private Musey?"

I blink. "Yes, sir."

"Good. There will still be restrictions, however. No unauthorized main access comp usage. Corporal Dorr will keep signing off on you. You don't get your holopoints back, needless to say, except for when you dive for me—supervised of course. This talent of yours is quite handy."

I'm sure.

"Erret, that'll be all for now."

My back straightens a little as Erret sirs him and leaves. Azarcon looks up at me.

"You can sit."

I do. He seems pleasant enough, not like the last time I spoke with him. He's had a month to temper. He watches me for a long minute.

"Jos, have we moved on now?"

"I don't know what you mean, sir."

He leans forward, hands folded on his black desk. "I mean, are you past the point of rebellion? Do you trust me?"

I don't forget that this man screens his crew. He knows how to read them. He might even be as skilled as Niko at reading me.

"I trust you, sir."

"Jos, I don't want to hear what you think I want to hear. I want honesty and I want you to look me in the eyes."

I drag my eyes from the wall to his face.

"Can you see it from my standpoint, Jos? You came aboard with a file that says you had a year with Falcone. You escaped him. This told me you're a survivor. You found yourself on Austro, in an orphanage—and I know how those places are.

You ran with a questionable crowd. Not surprising and not exclusive. Quite a few of your comrades come from similar backgrounds. Except you had a year with Falcone. I know the man. I know his tactics. I know what he does and what he leaves in people. I had to wonder if this wasn't some sort of elaborate setup on his part to get somebody from his camp onto my ship. Because I know he tries."

I can't take my eyes away now.

"So I gave you a hard time. I tested you. You didn't disappoint me—for a while. I know you're insular. I know you don't trust easily. But I've given you chances, Jos, so many that I'm starting to really wonder if I was right about you. Am I right in thinking you're not trying to screw me?"

If I tell him everything now, what will happen?

"I would never do anything to harm this ship, sir."

Except tell the enemy all about it. But it's an enemy you can trust, I promise.

I'm used to looking people in the eyes. And I learned to lie to faces, beginning with Falcone.

I lie to Captain Azarcon. With my face and my words, I lie to him.

"*Macedon* is my ship too, sir. I'm not trying to screw you."

"I believe you," he says. "Maybe I'm a fool. But someone took a chance on me once—more than once—and I guess I can take a chance on you. Let's not repeat the brig episode again. Deal?"

At some point he's going to make me pay this all back, all this generosity. The files from Siqiniq and now this.

"It's a deal, sir." He hadn't brigged me since that first shift before training, until now. "I never meant harm. I never meant for Kris to die."

I don't know where that's coming from.

But he says simply, "I know."

VIII.

The news comes over the Send when we're in the mess—
Dorr, Hartman, Madi, me, and Iratxe. The unit on the wall
blares the story. On New Year's Day, 2197 EHSD—the year
of my seventeenth biological birthday—one of our sister
ships is destroyed. Completely. *Wesakechak*, a deep spacer I
remember from my first arrival on Austro and a few joint
training missions after, was attacked by *Genghis Khan* and a
symp marauder near the Gjoa asteroid belt, one long leap
from Chaos Station and three from the DMZ. No survivors, at
least none when the rescue ships got there.

We're in the Dragons, heading toward a resupply base in
the old Meridia mines. The Hub converted the dusty moon
Rim colony six months ago to a military depot. Rumor has it
we're also going to meet a couple of battleships sent by
Ashrafi himself, some sort of powwow for the captain with
officers directly loyal to the admiral.

"This war is getting too fucking long," Dorr says, a certain
distance in his voice.

"Which war is that?" Hartman asks. "Seems we're fighting two and that's the problem."

"We ain't," Erret snaps. "And that's the problem. It's one
big bloody one now."

It's going to be another year of deaths. You start to mark
time that way, not by birthdays or good news. Instead you say,
That was when Kris died. That was when *Wesakechak* blew.
Every death I cause on a mission, and every one I hear about,
seems to stack in the space between me and Aaian-na, until
there's no way to see over them to the place I think I need to
be. Home, which is just a word I don't believe in anymore.

A whole ship. A carrier the size of *Macedon*.

We sit there with untouched food, numb. It's going to be
impossible to look my Chaos contact in the face when next

we dock. A symp helped on this one and Niko still hasn't arrested Ash.

I don't know why Niko just doesn't coerce Ash into space somehow, and shoot him. Azarcon would do it, in the same position. It's the expedient course and what's some planet government ten leaps away going to do about it?

My contact's been telling me for the past couple years that Ash's tracks are so well hidden that it will take time to build a case against him. Like with Falcone. I wish I can hear that from Niko himself. I wish I can hear anything from Niko himself, something more than short messages meant to comfort and encourage me. I don't need encouragement. I'm here already.

I haven't sent an unsupervised outgoing comm since my release from brig. My code to even activate any main access comps is flagged immediately by the bridge. I've spent the last year trying to steal someone else's access code, but Corporal Dorr has been my diligent watchdog. I'm never alone for more than ten minutes, except in the head, and there are no comps in the head.

Having to admit to my contact that I lost my outgoing communications ability wasn't pretty. But what can you do.

Dorr pokes at his syrup-laden pancakes. "Maybe we oughtta toss these at the pirates."

I'm just about to leave the table when Evan comes in and beelines toward me. "Did you hear?" he says, and sits down with us.

Iratxe frowns. "About *K-Jack*? Just now."

"No, about *Caliban*. She's been sent out here to take *K-Jack*'s place."

"They don't waste time," Madi says.

"Can't afford to," Erret says, stuffing his mouth with pancake. "Gap in the ranks means a big freeway for the local criminal element."

The item scrolls up on the Send display. I look at Evan. "Where'd you hear so quick?"

"I was just talking to Nathan. I thought you'd want to know."

Jelilian the gossip. Somehow information takes detours to his ears, then disseminates to the rest of us.

"*Caliban*'s an insystem carrier," Erret says, frowning. "Just what we need, a converted junker. Those blokes chase their own tails more than they do pirates."

The godcomm beeps, then Commander Northam, the XO, booms through the ship. The man has no quiet voice.

"We are now orbiting the Meridia moon. Personnel assigned to resupply duty, please ready at the bays."

"That ain't us, thankfully," Dorr says. "I ain't in the mood to work."

"When are you ever," Hartman says. "But just so you don't get too fat, how 'bout you get your tail to training and take your pups with you."

"Yah yah," Dorr says, getting up. I stand with him.

Macedon has to stop in order to load supplies of new weaponry, small-ships, or food. The drives whine to a halt, blanketing the ship in the thick kind of silence you get when you aren't on the move. The Send seems unduly loud now, everyone's voices in the mess too stark and empty.

Evan says, "See you later, Jos," just as the deck at our feet suddenly shakes. And again, so violently I grab the table to keep upright.

Shock waves from below. Below this deck are the hangars.

Lieutenant Hartman's tags beep just as she reaches to make contact. Commander Xavier's voice comes through, loud enough that we all hear it, even as the ship's battle klaxon erupts.

"Get to gear, we're under attack! Missile barrage on our sensors—"

We run from the mess in a stream of crew. The corridors are alive with uniforms, most of them black.

"—and hangar bays. Expect boarding parties—"

"Not if they blow the bays!" Iratxe yells.

Priority is to arm ourselves and link on the tacfeed.

"They'll come in through the escape pods," Dorr barks.

Which are located all over the ship, even near the drive room and the bridge—which would be the enemy's goal. A multiple point attack.

It's an orderly scramble to get our gear, assisted by whoever has the extra hands—from cooks and laundry people to the ship chaplain and shrink. Evan materializes at my elbow to help me with the armor. He's armed himself with a rifle. Once the pickup's in my ear, all the bad news starts to pour in.

The missiles came from around the dark side of the moon. They travel faster than ships, but even if we detected them early, *Mac*'s at a full stop for the resupply. Ashrafi's battleships haven't shown up yet. Our long-range sensors are blown, along with three-quarters of the hangars. The inner bay doors are locked down or that whole deck will depressurize. We lost people.

And two Komodo-class pirate ships just slingshotted around the moon and have already launched outriders toward our escape pods—just as Corporal Dorr predicted.

"They're prepping to disable the clamps and scuttle the pods," Xavier says over the feed, and that's all I hear as more explosions boom throughout the ship, echoing right down to jetdeck.

Dorr yells at us to get to engineering and start securing the perimeter with small-charge concussion grenades and claymores. We don't wait for the levs, but pour down the steps in haste, brushing elbows with more crew. Smoke vomits through the vents in gusts, then squeezes to a mere line as the air flaps shut.

Our team gets to the drive room in one piece. Cleary and the other techs shout to one another in terms I can barely understand but amount to the fact they're trying to get *Macedon*'s drives online. Their comps are alive with reports, little flashing lights on the schematic displays, some parts glowing with 3-D holo representation. Commander Pasqual's on comm with the bridge. It's all a muddle of voices laid over the ship's wailing defense.

Iratxe and I set to booby-trapping the perimeter, far enough away from anything vital, but close enough to give proper protection. If pirates try to enter the drive room they will leave limbless.

From here on in it's a deck-by-deck fight.

You don't spend time thinking.

You turn a corner and there's a body in clothes you don't recognize, and you shoot.

You can't see their faces because they wear black helmets, protection against any chemical gases the ship might release into isolated corridors. Smart bastards. But it doesn't matter. They die the same, faceless or not. Rifle pulses penetrate even helmets.

It's a race to own compartments. You move room to room, corridor to corridor, setting traps that will bite the heels of anyone who follows you. Bleed them to death in your wake. The noise deafens you—shouts in your ear from all parts of the ship, shouts by your elbows from the crew beside you, fighting beside you. In the intersections behind you explosions go off from delayed switches. You're clear to advance, to keep moving ahead, corridor by corridor and death by death.

The enemies pour in from another makeshift airlock—where the escape pods used to be, back near the mess hall. They've used the blown hole to lock their own ships to, and they come out firing.

A splatter of red bursts on my sight, but I feel no pain, not even in delay.

It's not me who's hit. It's Iratxe.

She's at my feet as I crouch in a hatchway, shooting around the frame. She's dead.

Dorr tosses a grenade, waits for the crack of fire on impact, then moves ahead. I follow, step over her body, and keep going. Just keep going. It's all you can do. Somebody treads behind me and I assume it's another jet.

Soon we're at medbay. Another escape hatch pops in and enemies rain out.

We exchange fire, bright pulses. The medics are armed, shooting from their position just inside the doors. I look quickly behind me, feeling someone's breath.

Evan, who's followed me for how long, I don't know. I see a glimpse of wide eyes before yanking him back into a recessed hatchway, grazed by bolts.

Then a voice through my pickup says Ashrafi's battleships have finally arrived.

Someone must be telling the pirates the same thing. One of them shouts to his comrades to retreat.

Then he tosses a thunderflash toward us. I cover my head but the boom shakes me to my marrow, tilts me into the corridor. Time enough for somebody to grab me up and haul me off my feet. I can barely see, but fight, seeing streaks of armor, then ceiling lights, then helmets. Something knocks me across the head. The world is a painful, throbbing silence, then my rifle's ripped from my hands.

Sound and sight and awareness eventually bleed in. Low lights and voices talking about insurance. "They won't shoot with their own jets on board." And, "Our mothers will keep 'em busy 'til we're home."

I blink through the fog, the scent of my own sweat and

somebody's blood, the sound of swearing and the sight of a dozen unfamiliar faces.

I'm inside a pirate outrider and it smells like *Genghis Khan*.

IX.

My arms are numb, pulled behind me and cuffed. I can barely see, but it's not my eyes. The inside of the rider is dim. We're all sitting on the grease-stained deck. No benches, just nonslip flooring that bores hard through my uniform. Evan and Erret are crammed on either side of me. Evan's head is bowed. Erret sits up, glaring across the narrow space between jets and our captors.

I glance down the row. Our squad is here. Madi, Aki, Hartman, Venice McCrae, Rodriguez. We were covering the same corridor. Eight of us, and now we're here. Insurance.

Erret fidgets. I feel the movement of his arms against me. He tests the cuffs.

I don't move. I know what it earns you.

The pirates are a line of blank, smudged faces. Some of them young like us, a couple of them much older. None I recognize. Of course. But I know them anyway, I've seen them before. Just masks of hardness with death behind their eyes.

Despite the bodies beside me, I'm cold.

"Your ship's too easy," one of the pirates says, taunting. "Takin' it's easier'n takin' a shit."

"That why you in retreat?" Erret says.

I want to know how they knew we were going to be there. Carriers don't broadcast their resupply schedules on the Send.

"We ain't in retreat," the pirate says, "we just got bored."

"Yah, it does get borin' when two battleships come up on your ass," the corporal says blandly.

Luckily for him at that moment the outrider jostles us around, going into dock. Through the bulkheads we hear the deep, heavy sound of bay doors shutting.

We're inside one of the ships.

The back ramp whines down. Light pours in. I squint. Evan shifts beside me. My arms and shoulders throb from numb to extreme pain.

A pirate comes up and hauls me to my feet. Each of them takes a jet. The movement makes my head black out. I stumble and he hits me, as if that will orient me better.

Our weapons are gone, of course, and our utility belts, armor, webbing, anything that can help us. We're left just in our black BDUs and boots. And our tags. They searched us thoroughly.

They march us down the ramp and onto the cold deck of their hangar bay. It isn't as large as *Macedon*'s, only half the size with space enough to house about ten APCs. Or twelve outriders.

They walk us out of the hangar, guns at our backs.

The gritty bulkheads arch up over my head like gray, badly lit specters. I remember these corridors; years on Aaian-na could not burn them from my mind. Every few meters the smooth exoskeletal support beams jut out like the ribs of some large beast, a design inherent only in Komodo-class ships and especially favored by heavily armed merchants and pirates.

Painted deck directions in red and yellow are mostly scraped away or smudged over by years of collected grime and laser burns from old fights. No amount of scrubbing can get rid of those scars. And Falcone likes it uncomfortable, he likes these reminders of injury. There is that pervading smell: cold steel, cigrets, the faint distant odor of cloud drugs. Blood.

It's in the walls and through the vents, years of submission and violence.

Behind me in the line as we walk, Evan breathes deeply. He's afraid. I want to turn around and look at him, at least look him in the eyes, but I can't. The guard propels me forward. My head throbs with each echoing step we take to their brig.

It's not as formal a place as the one on *Macedon*. There are only three cells, caged on every side, dim lighting, and no security station. The bulkheads are damaged skin: pockmarked, scarred, and stained by who knows what. The cold, stagnant smell is worse here. Chains are affixed to the walls in each cell and high steel bars run along the ceiling.

A bolted chair sits empty in one of the cells.

They stuff us into one of the cages, one without the chair. I bump between Madison and Aki, then land up beside Evan. I meet his gaze finally.

He is twelve and I am eight. There's no dodging it.

I edge to the cage wall between the two cells and Evan does the same. I keep my eyes on the two guards that the ringleader pirate leaves behind, the mouthy one from the rider. The two are as impassive and focused on their prisoners as jets would be. After a moment I feel Evan touch my sleeve and hold on.

"Well, this is just dandy," Dorr says, plopping himself down on the single cot in the cell.

"Be quiet," Hartman says.

This brig is probably embedded with optics. We won't give a show to whoever watches. And our tagcomms are useless, too short range.

Silence weaves through us. Aki keeps looking at me; maybe she sees the same fear in my face as I do in hers. I try to avoid her eyes but there is not a lot to look at. We all wait for the same thing and within the hour it arrives.

Evan straightens beside me, rigid.

I slouch back behind Aki and catch glimpses over her shoulder.

Falcone's appearance has changed, like I thought. His hair hangs past his ears, a dull blond, not the spiked silver I remember. His face is stubbled and thin. It makes his nose and large eyes more pronounced. Lines arch down from the corners of his nose to the corners of his mouth. He's dressed in dusk black and deep blue fatigues, the colors of bruises.

He seems smaller than I remember, physically. Older, of course, but not as old in appearance as he should be.

If I only had a gun. Or my hands around his throat.

Everybody keeps perfectly still. Not out of fear, for them. But rage. Indignation. Restrained rebellion. Jet reactions.

With slow deliberation Falcone lights a cigret and looks into the cell, the same unblinking stare, the same hard, almost bored expression I remember.

"Everybody toss out your tags, here." He points to the deck in front of him.

Same voice, all smooth like someone who grew up privileged. Same smell. And something inside me tucks into itself, a tight little ball.

Our tags with our names and faces on them, that's what he wants.

Evan shakes his head slightly at me. I don't want to either. Ours are names he might recognize. Our faces too, even though we're older.

But we toss them out with everybody else's; they fall musically at Falcone's feet.

He riffles through them.

Evan shakes. I touch his sleeve. My hands are cold.

Falcone stops sifting. He holds one of the tags up to his eyes, the cigret burning between his teeth.

"Private First Class Musey," he says. "Step forward."

Aki's gaze reaches out to hold me back, but it is only her gaze, and I go.

A hand lands on my shoulder and pulls me back before I reach the gate. Madison steps in front of me casually, to block Falcone's line of sight in case he decides to pull a gun. Dorr keeps hold of my shoulder.

They know my past. They're actually trying to protect me from it.

Falcone steps to the side, as if Madison is no more than a door he wants to see around. He stares into my face.

Don't let me go, I think at Dorr.

"Joslyn Aaron Musey," Falcone says, and something lights in his eyes. Not pleasure or even anything as vibrant as surprise. Something else. "Joslyn Musey. Front and center."

No. I can't say it but I think it, and my feet don't move.

Dorr says, "Why don't you come in here an' get him, Birdy."

Erret will get himself killed and it will be my fault.

I tug out of the corporal's grasp but he's quick and grabs the back of my shirt.

Falcone pulls a gun from his back waist, in no apparent hurry.

"I'll kill the mouthy jet, or any jet. Front and center. Now."

"He doesn't bluff," I mutter to Dorr, and step forward. The jets make room for me, but not too much.

I stop on the opposite side of the cage door. And there he is, up close. I find myself locked on his face. If he just steps closer I can grab him through the food tray slot and ram his nose into the bars.

We look at each other, Falcone and me, through the cage bars and across eight years.

I stand still as his eyes rake me over, head to toe and back up again. My eyes don't leave his face. I'm not a child anymore. We're almost of a height. And Nikolas S'tlian trained me. *Macedon* trained me.

If I don't breathe I will black out. I try not to make any sound as I draw in the stale air.

His eyes, like welding flames, finally settle on my face. His lips curl like thin sheets of burning metal, in a heated smile.

"You are a curious bastard," he says in the tone of voice you use to compliment somebody.

My throat locks. I blink halfway.

The smile grows sharper. In one brisk movement he gestures one of his guards to open the gate. The other one stands with his rifle aimed, doubtlessly on a wide beam spread.

He's going to take me away from the jets and there's nothing they can do about it. Nothing I can do about it. I hear commotion behind me and to my left, glance and see Evan fighting his way forward to grasp the cell bars. Fear, plain on his face. Fear and worry. Aki comes up behind me and touches my arm. But I can't look at her directly. If I do it will be the end of it.

The guard opens the gate. I walk out under Falcone's gun, on leaden feet.

There is one moment of opportunity with the gate still open and the guard within kicking distance. One half of a second.

I don't take it. The second guard, standing out of lunge distance, would take all of us down with one widespread shot before I could even reach Falcone.

The gate shuts behind me with a clang. The lock buzzes. There are three guns on me now. You just don't take chances with jets. Falcone would know as well as any EarthHub captain.

"You and I are going to get reacquainted," Falcone says. "Privately."

My thoughts plod doggedly down trained routes. One guard will likely stay behind. Two of them covering me as we walk would not be enough. They don't know who trained me. I can handle two, even armed.

But Falcone doesn't motion me to walk. He smiles and shoots me himself.

X.

Getting shot at point-blank range with a paralysis pulse puts you down for a couple hours, but it always feels like days. Nausea permeates every cell in your body when you finally awaken. I take deep, slow breaths to combat it but my mouth still waters, the saliva tasting sour. Blur recedes into sharply drawn shapes and numbness bleeds into painful clarity. I sit wire-cuffed to a bolted metal chair, ankles bound to the chair legs and arms behind me, in a small cold room. There's another chair opposite, empty.

A guard stands by the heavy, paint-chipped hatch. She watches me with dark, alert eyes and a hand on her gun. The yellow lights flicker slightly in distracting rhythm. Breath pulls icicles into my lungs, and exhales in clouds.

I'm still clothed, at least, though my wrists already feel raw.

The guard says into her wirecomm. "He's awake."

It's a long wait. I know enough that it's purposeful. I try to get myself into a distant, numbing state, but there's the inescapable fact of where I am. And I am small under the guard's glare, small under the lights and in this cold room, waiting with my gaze in the corner.

I think of Niko. Focus point, like he taught me. I allow my eyelids to droop.

The hatch clangs open and Falcone steps in. Clouds of breath bloom in front of my eyes. Focus scrambles away.

"You can go," he tells the woman.

I clench my fists where they are bound behind me. Pain to fight the block of ice in my chest. He sits across from me. I force myself to look at him, not to bow my head.

"Joslyn," he says, smiling in a way that has nothing to do with me. "I remember you so well."

I don't reply.

"Don't you remember me?"

He's going to make me say it. So it's begun. So I just say it. "Yeah, I remember you."

"I'm pleased. I really am. Because now I won't have to tell you what can happen if you aren't forthright with me."

His chair isn't bolted or clamped to the deck. He drags it closer until his knees almost touch mine.

"Let me get a good look at you." He holds my jaw with callused fingers and tilts my head back, peering close at my face. I see every line and pore on his skin and the gradient browns and yellows of his hair. He smells like his cigrets and that sharp soap. It clouds my mind with memories. He smiles. "You turned out as well as I'd thought you would. So tell me where you've been."

"I'm a jet."

He frowns, vague disappointment. "Jos. Let's not do that."

"You asked."

"You know what I mean. You forget how well I know you. I don't think eight years changed you that much. You said you remember me, so you must know there are better methods than beating someone nearly to death to get what I want. So tell me where you've been."

He uses his voice like a hand. I say, quietly, because it doesn't matter, "Austro."

"How did you get from Chaos to Austro?"

It's nearly impossible to keep my eyes on his face. I can feel his breath. "Woman took pity on me."

"Really? Then how is it that I saw a strit pick you up off the deck and behind their lines, after I shot you? How is it that I know you were taken to the strit world?"

Ash must have told him everything. That brings up the anger. But I don't say anything that will confirm his words.

"I knew who took you from the start." His voice grows steadily harder. "A lot of commotion then. Jets. Strits. I nearly got caught myself, except the strits were pretty efficient in blasting that dock. They must've had help from some symps." He pauses just long enough to make me hear that word. "You don't remember, do you?"

"You shot me."

"Yes, that's right." His face takes on mock regret. Parody. Insult. "I hated doing it. You know how much I enjoyed you. You're bright, beautiful. A beautiful child. Still a beautiful youth."

It comes out of his mouth like profanity.

He touches my leg, above the knee. I can't stop it, and flinch. He pretends not to notice. "So tell me what really happened after that strit took you."

"You shot me. I blacked out. I woke up and this woman took me to Austro. I don't know about any strit."

His eyes darken. His fingers grip. "Is that what you told Azarcon?"

"Ask him yourself."

"I might, after all. You're mine again. This time I'll make sure you don't run away. And I hear he comes after his jets."

There's something in his eyes like a challenge. And pride. Like before, this has nothing to do with emotion. Not his emotion.

He looks like all common sense, like he's giving me a

chance, doing me a favor. "Jos, we don't have to go this way if you stop lying to me."

"I'm not lying."

"You know, I really did miss you." He starts undoing my belt.

I struggle but the wires cut.

"I saw that strit take you. The strit took you, didn't he?" He pulls the belt from around my waist, slow. He stands over me and tosses the belt to the floor, then puts a hand on my shoulder.

I spit in his face.

I expect a backhand, just from reflex. Anything to get him to stop what he's doing. But he's restrained. Cold and deliberate. Nothing's changed. He just wipes off the saliva and stares down at me.

"You think about how I had you, Jos. Do you want me to take you again?"

I'm not aware my eyes shut until the darkness starts to spark. If I open them he will ask another question. Or do things I don't want to see. This isn't what is supposed to happen. Niko trained me to focus. *Macedon* trained me to focus. I have to focus.

It's impossible to focus.

His hands are on my shoulders. "Did that strit take you off Chaos?"

"No."

His fingers tighten, then relax. They start to stroke my neck and along my jaw. His hand slides inside my collar and along my collarbone and a finger hooks around the ID chain with my parents' faces on it. His other hand reaches down in front of me.

There are words, then there are no words, for things such as this.

"Did that strit take you off Chaos?"

"No."

"Did that strit send you to Austro? Did you grow up in an orphanage?"

"I grew up in an orphanage."

There's silence. I make myself look up into his face, to let him see the hatred in mine.

"You're lying," he says. "I know you're lying."

"Then you don't need to ask."

He hits me. My head snaps back. Blood bubbles in my nose and I cough, try to bend over, but he grabs my hair and yanks my head up.

"Do you see how it can go?"

I spit blood on his chest. He hits me again. And again. Then I lose count. That's fine. Anything but what he wants to really do.

The room tilts.

He leaves me there alone. It is all tactics.

The cold air and flickering lights surround me like a spirit adrift from its body.

XI.

The drives hum, healthy. I memorize the deck beneath my feet. Scuff marks and where my blood dripped. He comes back with a glass of water and sets it on the floor near my chair, and sits back in his own seat.

"*Macedon* can put up a fight," he says. "I've always admired that about Cairo."

"Where is *Mac*?" I ask, for the hell of it. "Where are we going?"

"Can't you guess?" He smiles and leans back, lacing his fingers across his middle and stretching out his legs. His eyes settle on my face and stay. "I'm so curious about you, Jos. I have to admit. Look at you. Do you still avoid mirrors?"

I tried getting in a meditative state when I was alone. But it didn't work. Instead I am just numb.

There is really nothing different, except the chronological fact of our ages.

"You just spout the same old shit," I tell him in the gap of silence he leaves for me. "And you still get off on helpless kids."

The smiling mask dies. "You're no kid anymore, Joslyn. And you know getting off was never my motive, don't you? I wonder, really, how much you do remember."

"Enough."

"I recognize Evan D'Silva. Serrano's pick. Maybe you know how it could've been for you if I'd sold you to *Shiva*."

"Yeah, the same."

"No no, think back. Think back, Jos. Do you suppose I would set all that time training you just so you could be everybody's whore? Or slave? Cleaning and running errands until the skin on your hands and feet is raw? What would be worse?"

There are razors in my throat.

"You were mine." He leans close and touches the side of my hair, gripping when I try to dodge my head. "I took you in personally, and did anyone else ever touch you?"

I give him my thoughts through my eyes.

"None of my people touched you. Was D'Silva so lucky, was his captain so watchful?"

He has another target, if I don't cooperate.

"If you hadn't run, Jos . . ." He releases me but doesn't lean back. "If you hadn't run, you would've climbed high in my crew. You had that fight."

"I would've killed you sooner or later. If you think otherwise you're more deluded than I thought."

"I don't think so." That arrogant smile. "You're attached to me now, even with eight years between us. Think of how much more attached you'd be if I'd had you all those years."

"Untie my hands and I'll show you how attached."

He laughs.

"You fucking coward!"

"Jos." He picks up the glass of water and sips. "Jos, wouldn't you rather be my whore than the whore of a symp?" He waits only a moment, but long enough that I hear the silence. "How is the Warboy, Jos?"

"How should I know?"

"I thought you would. All those years spent on Aaian with him. All those years in training with him. Is he good, Jos? As good as I am?"

Ash-dan. In league with pirates. Falcone must have known all along where I was, who had me, and why.

For two years I knew they were working together. But it doesn't sink through me until now.

He says, "Maybe I ought to remind you how good I am. And how loyal you should be to people on this side of the DMZ."

My own voice makes me cringe. It's not my voice. "I'm not loyal to pirates, 'specially to ones who screw kids."

He leans over me, one move, toppling his chair in the process. He grabs the back of my hair.

"But you're not a kid anymore, are you. And this isn't about training, what I would do to you. It wouldn't be about making a bond between us far greater than if I beat you into submission. It wouldn't be about that, would it."

They are not questions.

"I would do it for knowledge, now. Think of that, Jos, while you consider what I want. I just want to know all about the Warboy, Jos. I want to know all about *Macedon* and Cairo Azarcon's plans."

Artifice is completely stripped away. Now I see only what he wants, drilled deep into his face. I see what he will do to get it.

My skull feels ripped from the hold on my hair. "I'm a private first class. The captain of *Macedon* doesn't tell me his plans."

"Then maybe I'll ask one of the jets. Maybe I'll make you watch as I ask her. You should know by now not to be coy with me. The strits took you off Chaos. And took you to Aaian. And trained you to be one of them. Didn't they?"

Words will kill me. So I say nothing.

"These are things I already know. You need only say yes."

He wants to hear it. He needs to hear it.

I won't say it.

He starts to unbutton my uniform, one handed, while his fingers dig into my scalp.

But I won't say it.

He yanks my shirt down my arms, between my back and the chair. He takes out the blade from his boot that I remember, that hasn't changed, it's so strange how much has not changed. All the reactions are there as if no time has passed.

He grabs the front of my T-shirt and slices it from neck to bottom.

I can't say it. His questions flee my mind.

So he reminds me. "I don't think D'Silva would hold out very long. And jets, despite their bravado, are still flesh. I can let my people at them, one by one." He fingers the ID chain. "Oh, and what's this?"

He rips it off. He looks at it. He smiles at my parents' faces. Then he tosses it into a corner.

The cold air claws against my chest. My heartbeat fills the room.

"First, the Warboy. Tell me about him. Where is he?"

If I just close my eyes, I can think that the cold comes from the mountain peaks on Aaian-na. The balconies and the rooftops in winter, when you lie on your back and just breathe.

But Aaian-na doesn't smell like Falcone. He's all around. And Niko is absent. Niko's been absent. Everything is absent.

His hands rake down my skin and back up again, close around my jaw.

Sometimes you don't quite feel it.

"Of course I'm going to start with you." His voice is conversational. "Did you think I would bother beginning with a jet I've never seen? You can help them, Jos. Just answer my questions. You and I know each other. You know I reward obedience. This doesn't have to be so unpleasant. It's just information, information I will get one way or another. Through this. Through this and drugs, maybe. It's up to you if I get it the hard or easy way. It's up to you if it will hurt or . . . not hurt."

His hands speak the same as his voice. My skin is not my own.

"You're controlling how this goes, Jos."

Words will make him stop. It's a lie. But they fall out of my mouth like baby teeth.

"I don't—know where he is. I don't know."

"The Warboy?"

"I don't know where he is!"

"When was your last contact?"

Behind my eyelids I see black. Fire. And black.

"When was your last contact with the Warboy?"

"I'm not in contact with him."

"What is your code string to contact him?"

He explores.

"Go to hell!"

He hits me. Three blows that dim the world. I reel, taste

blood, then feel the deck against my cheek. My legs are free but I can't move. I can't think. I don't want to see a thing.

He familiarizes himself with what he lost eight years ago. All over again. All over and again.

The room heats, and the noise is terrible. I think it's me.

"Give me your code string, strit-lover."

He kicks me over. His pupils are wide black holes in the center of flame blue. All the rest of him is violence. The lights flicker behind his head, far above like stars.

My wrists bleed. Blood comes out of me and what else. What else. Words and salt and life he wants to own.

He tries to buy it all with his hands.

My body meets the cold when he releases me. It's all raw and rotten. He grabs my face. His fingers are damp. Or maybe it's my own skin.

"You rethink about keeping quiet, Jos. I want those code strings."

But there's only darkness. There has always been only darkness.

XII.

The leaps come hard. I'm in black already and my memory doesn't fade. When I open my eyes I see myself and there is evidence enough to make memory all the truth you never want. There's no thinking that I'm older now. Time has no place on a ship that travels this deep.

Wherever we're going, we're going there fast. While everything else in me spins backward.

XIII.

I don't know when, but sometime later the drives go silent. The low grating thrum of the air vents working somewhere in the arteries of the ship seeps into the room. Sometimes voices carry muffled through the hatch. Footsteps go back and forth, sometimes in a hurry. The lights keep flickering until one blows briefly and goes black. Shadows crawl up the walls.

They don't bring food or water or anything. He put me back in the chair and tied my ankles again. I sit forgotten, trying to remember myself. To prepare myself for when he comes back. I know he's going to come back.

But he doesn't. Instead come two guards, big pirates who know how to handle jets. They each carry slung rifles, more for swinging than shooting at this close range. They unravel my ankle cuffs and haul me to my feet. It's been so long unmoving that I can barely walk. Stiff muscles protest in fiery contractions as they drag me from the room, through the twisting corridors, my wrists still bound behind me. My clothes still undone and cut. They pull me by the arms and hold the waist of my dirty fatigues to keep me on my feet.

They take me back to the brig. There are more people in the cells, more prisoners. From other outriders. Vaguely I see and hear the jets rush to the bars.

"Jos," Evan says.

The pirates bang the cells, drive them back. Dorr swears at the pirates.

They throw me into the third, empty cell, facedown on the bunk, and leave. At least they leave.

I roll over, pain so acute up my arms and shoulders I want to scream. But screaming does no good, it just gets you hoarse and gives them satisfaction. At least the lights here don't flicker, though they are stark white and hurt even when you don't look up directly. I lie on my side with my cheek against the rough, scratchy blanket on the bunk. Familiar smell. Familiar texture. Unpleasant.

He's going to want more. Bastards like him always want more, so much more they disembowel you to get it. They reach into places you never knew existed in yourself, and touch everything that is untouched, until there is nothing in you that hasn't been stained by fingerprints.

Body divers. That's what they are.

"Jos," someone says.

"Muse. Hey."

I'm in secondhand skin.

I struggle to sit up, because he can't find me on my face, waiting. I won't let him.

"Jos, just stay still."

The hatch opens. I hear footsteps. The lock on my cell buzzes. I look over, through the pain, through the vision that threatens to narrow into tiny points.

Falcone comes in, ignoring the hurl of insults and profanity from the jets. He grabs me up and shoves me into the empty chair in the middle of the cell.

In front of the jets. He's going to do this in front of the jets.

"Now we're going to talk," he says, impatient.

I kick toward his groin. But he's fast and knocks my head back. Explosions go off behind my eyes. His fingers dig into my scalp. He hits me again. Voices shout, but not my own. He moves my feet and ankles. I feel the bite of wire cuffs. I try to kick him again but he slugs my stomach and my face. I wheeze and tilt. He binds my feet to the chair. My arms are still behind me and I can't move.

He grabs my face in his hand.

"Do you hear your fellow jets? Here, look at them."

He turns my head. I blink, sweating, bleeding. Sight blurs but I see their faces from the other cells, staring, watching. Mad. For me.

He takes out his gun.

"If you don't answer my questions, I'll shoot one of them."

"Don't tell him nothin'," Dorr says. "Don't worry 'bout us."

"I can do worse than shoot them," Falcone says. "I'll begin with D'Silva."

Evan's face, bruised, all of his hair cut off. Adalia crying. Four-year-old Adalia. They fill my sight.

It can't happen again.

Not to them. Not like this. Not again.

I say around the blood in my mouth, "What do you want to know?"

Evan says, "No, Jos."

He knows. He knows as soon as you let one thing go, everything else follows.

"You know what I want to know. I want to know about the Warboy and your captain."

They're far away but I'm here. Evan's here. Aki and Erret and Iratxe—is dead—

Kris. My fault.

Falcone walks out toward the other cell.

"No!" I strain forward against the cuffs. "No—"

The guards stand taut. Falcone aims into Evan's cell, toward Evan, toward anyone who tries to get in front of him.

"He don't know the Warboy, you bastard!" Dorr yells. "You daft or what?"

Falcone smiles. "Well, Jos, you sure have them fooled. So what will it be? The truth or Evan's life?"

Their eyes lock on me.

"Don't believe him," Dorr says. "Fuckin' pirate, what d'you know? You put a gun on a guy's bud and he'll damn well cluck like a chicken!"

Falcone ignores it all. His gun is set to kill and it's pointed at Evan. The guards are statues, on edge, waiting for one command.

Evan isn't breathing. But he shakes his head at me, slow. I can read his eyes. *Don't give in.*

My vision blurs.

Not these people and not by my word. They won't die. I won't let it.

I can't watch it.

The first thing you do is stay alive.

My father puts me in the secret compartment and my mother kisses my hair. You can be safe and so can they.

So I say, "I don't know where the Warboy is. I swear it."

Falcone walks back into my cell.

The jets are silent.

"When's the last time you sent a message to him?"

The guards move closer to the cells, rifles aimed.

My eyes clear, but I feel the tracks down my cheeks, mingled with blood. Red edges at the corners of my sight.

"Months ago. I can't remember."

Falcone smiles.

Erret shoves his way to the side of his cell, staring at me. But he doesn't say a word.

None of them do.

But it's only the beginning for me.

XIV.

Falcone asks about Niko. Luckily I don't have much to tell him. I haven't spoken to Niko directly in years. I never know where he is. My contacts never told me, maybe for this exact reason. But I answer what I know because Niko can take care of himself. He isn't here, he isn't facing this, and he will never be in this place, watching his friends in front of Falcone's gun.

Not just any pirate. But this one, who knows exactly where to cut.

Falcone can know everything on Niko. But Falcone has to find him first to get him. Not even Ash will get him that far. So I tell him what he wants to know about my stay on Aaian-na and my mission on *Macedon*. The jets hear it. That's all a part of it. Falcone wants them to hear it. I feel their shock, doubt, then hate. But I tell Falcone what I know about Niko so he doesn't kill them. Niko can take care of himself. But I'm supposed to watch their backs. Even here. Even now.

It's all warm-up to what he wants to know about Azarcon. He knows once he gets me to betray Niko, I will betray the captain.

I was loyal to Niko first. I am loyal to the captain at the last.

Somewhere in the back of my mind are images of Azarcon and his son, standing in front of restaurant neon. Surely he'll understand these things I say, these words about one ship in a fleet of ships. They're just words and they can be lies, but the people in the cells next to mine are real. And true.

They're the truths in my heart that make it run. They are my vices.

When he leaves me alone they talk to me.

"You're not lying, are you," Aki says.

I don't answer.

Dorr's words are a roll of profanity and threats. It doesn't stop. Madi chimes in. Hartman. But the ones who don't speak are the ones I can't look at. Aki. Evan.

I'm sure time passes but I don't know it.

Then the ship's battle klaxon starts to wail.

I look up, look at the others. They're all on their feet, watching the hatch.

"It would seriously suck if *Mac* blows us up," Erret says.

Heavy footsteps run by outside. Someone has finally caught up with Falcone.

I stare at the hatch, willing it to open. I don't want to die on this ship.

Genghis Khan gives everything she's got. The bolts in the bulkheads shudder it out. The ship itself shudders and tilts. I'm cuffed to the chair and can't move, but the jarring goes all the way to my teeth. The jets hold on to the cell bars.

Then the hatch opens. A figure dressed in white and gray coiled clothing scopes in, rifle aiming. She sees three cells filled by jets and turns to leave, saying something to someone outside the brig.

"*Ka'redan!*" I shout. Assassin-priest.

The face turns back. A human face, but tattooed. Guarded.

"*Oa-nadan ngali Jos Musey-dan.*" My name is Jos Musey-dan. It's choked. It's desperation. I don't try to hide it. I can barely remember the words but they surface in my memory like beacons on water. "*Oa-nadan ngali Jos Musey-dan!*"

The battle sounds filter through the open hatch and the bulkheads, but inside the cells is dead silence.

The hatch opens wider and eight assassins move in. Four symps and four striviirc-na.

"Bloody hell!" Erret says.

One of the sympathizers comes to my cell and shoots it open with her rifle. She says, "You better not be lying," in Ki'hade.

"I'm not," I answer, the same. "Just take me—"

"We will," she says, pulling a blade from somewhere in her clothing. She slices through my wire cuffs as if they are made of string.

They ignore the jets.

"Release them, *ka'redan*. Please."

"We don't have time. They'll fight."

"They won't. You can't leave them here."

She drags on my arm. My legs cramp so she yanks me out.

"*Ka'redan*, please. Release them, they won't fight." I look at the jets and switch out of Ki'hade, even as she propels me to the exit. "They're going to let you out but don't fight them. They'll kill you. Just come on—"

"Hurry!" one of the striviirc-na says, guarding the hatch with three others.

The female symp motions briskly to the cells. The three humans shoot the locks open.

The jets pour out, but on guard. They don't fight. They know it would be pointless here.

"Give us guns," Erret says.

The symps ignore him. The aliens look at the jets like they would at targets. They motion with their rifles. The jets must go first.

"Move or we shoot you," the female symp says.

The jets go, but not before a few pointed looks my way.

They duck out the hatch and run.

I stumble after the symps. The strivs keep pace with the jets, firing at pirates who cross our path. The corridors swarm with assassins. I lean into a hatchway to breathe when the group stops to clear an extended passage on our left.

A hand slips under my arm. I look up, expecting to see the female symp.

It's Evan.

He doesn't say anything, just helps me along after the jets and the symps.

None of the others help. They would prefer to see me dead. Even Aki.

Erret grabs a rifle from a dead pirate in the corridor. He might shoot at us.

He doesn't. He helps lay waste to the ship, on our way to the main airlock. He must know there's only one way off this ship and it isn't through *Macedon*. All the invading uniforms are alien.

I can't do anything but huddle into hatchways when the fire becomes too thick and we have to stop. Or run behind the assassins, with more of them behind us, and use them for shields because I'm barely on my feet. The smoke burns my eyes. There's blood on the deck, bodies, the scent of charred flesh and singed clothing. Blurs of sound and sight that amount only to death. It throbs through the veins in my temples, underscores the scars Falcone gave me, the bruises and cuts and the debilitating pain in my ankles and wrists. But I move. I run. If Evan didn't hold my arm I would run in circles and never stop.

The airlock yawns open. The strivs herd the jets through, with guns at their backs. Evan pulls me in. Cold air hits me in the face, then slightly warmer air inside the striviirc-na APC. Benches line the walls, not unlike inside a Charger. Except it's cleaner. It's warmer. It smells like Niko's ship.

"Sit!" the female symp shouts.

"Give that—" Dorr starts, but a striv wrests the rifle from his hands and takes a swipe at the corporal's head with the butt of his gun.

The jets push against their captors. Some of them are armed, stolen weapons from dead pirates.

I see disaster in two seconds.

"Erret, no! Lieutenant Hartman—stop it! They won't hurt you if you just sit—"

"Maybe for you, strit!" the corporal says.

The sympathizers don't have patience. One shoots the corporal on stun and moves with intent toward the others. But the others don't move. They're outnumbered. Dorr lies in a heap on the deck.

"Sit," the female symp says again. "Or we vent you."

The strivs collect the guns.

The jets sit reluctantly, watching the assassins. Evan eases me over to a seat. I sit harder than I mean to.

"Disengage," the symp says through her pickup, to the pilot.

The APC shakes and jerks violently.

We are free.

XV.

I know it's *Turundrlar* the moment we step out of the APC. The hangar bay, about the size of *Macedon*'s, has the faint spice smell that I associate with Aaian-na and Niko. The striv symbols decorate the bulkheads. I read *Deathstrike* high up near the ceiling and lights. The design specs of the striv ships all come from EarthHub sources. It isn't that strange. There are a couple dozen striv fighters and APCs on the deck, and aliens everywhere. The jets need prodding to move down the ramp. They know the ship's reputation.

I catch the female symp's arm. "Take me to Nikolas-dan. Please."

"I will ask him." She shakes off my hand.

I grab it again, hard. "You'll take me now."

Her eyes widen, affronted. She's young and probably wasn't a crewmember when Niko handed me off to *Cervantes*.

A tall striv walks up. "I will take him," she says.

It's Yli aon Ter'tlo. My former classmate. I stare at her white face, her long white hair, the caste tattoos on her cheeks and forehead.

"I will take you, Jos-na," she repeats, because I don't move.

All the jets stare at me. It stuns them when I speak

Ki'hade. To see me talking with the enemy. It stuns them that this enemy knows me.

I don't have time for it now. I walk off with Ter'tlo.

"Jos!" Evan says, behind me.

"Don't hurt them," I say to Ter'tlo-dan.

She signals the other assassin-priests. "We won't. They'll go to the brig for now."

They are jets. It's the only place they belong on this ship.

Ter'tlo doesn't help me in the long walk through *Turundrlar*'s familiar painted corridors, even though she has to slow down to match my hobbling steps. My feet and ankles are swollen in my boots; I don't know that I'll ever get them free. My hands are numb, the wrists crusted by rings of blood.

She leads me to the threshold of the bridge hatch and I see Niko's back.

"Kia'redan bae," Ter'tlo says.

Niko turns away from his navigator and stops, seeing me. But it isn't the fact of my standing there that surprises him; I'm sure the symp commed ahead. I think it's my appearance that gives him pause. Bloody and bruised.

"Where is *Genghis Khan*?" I ask, against that silence between him and me. The bridge itself is not silent. The ship is not silent. Ships are firing at one another. The bridge is alive with the data of it.

But Niko won't make a scene in front of his people. "The *Khan* is behind my brother's ship," he says.

"Ash is here?" I move forward toward the scan.

"I tracked him." Niko holds my arm. Maybe I look like I will fall over. I don't really feel it now. "He left Aaian-na a couple weeks ago. Apparently to set up another communications satellite. I suspected he might be going to meet his pirate contacts. It so happened it was to meet Falcone himself."

"Why would he risk it now?"

Niko nods to the scan data, scrolling on the console. "A

very large shipment of weapons. *Genghis Khan* was off-loading when I jumped them."

Lines of light travel across the screen. Niko brought three other striv marauders with him, a standard attack group. Against us is Ash's ship, and the *Khan*, and another blip on the screen that isn't friendly. Another pirate. Maybe the same one that attacked *Macedon*.

A blurt of numbers and symbols appear in holo in front of the scan operator. Niko lets go of my arm.

"Another ship has leaped in," the striv at the post says, as Niko leans over her shoulder. "Signature—EarthHub vessel. *Macedon*."

I don't need to hear it. I see clear enough that they fire—not only at the *Khan*, but at *Turundrlar*.

"Evasive," Niko orders. "Tell the others not to fire on *Macedon*!"

The grav-nodes stay online. *Turundrlar* rolls to avoid the shot. I don't feel it. But I see it on the display.

The blips on the screen start to break apart, avoiding torpedoes. *Macedon* is all the distraction they need. One of the blips suddenly darts off scope.

"Ash is heading out of the system," one of the strivs reports.

"Pursue him," Niko orders.

"No," I say. "Niko, that'll leave *Macedon* with the two pirates."

"They are not my concern. I'm sure reinforcements will follow them."

"Until they do, *Mac* is open to the pirates. She's injured, she was boarded—" I can barely breathe. "Falcone is on that pirate. If we leave he'll run."

Niko stares at me, one deep, quick second. Then he waves his arm, briefly.

"Belay that. Return fire to the pirates. Tell *In'tatliar* to follow Ash."

"Yes, *bae*. Returning fire. *In'tatliar* is in pursuit."

Three striv ships now. And two pirates and *Macedon*. Azarcon must see *Turundrlar* fire on the *Khan*. The pirates attempt to break but the other two striv marauders block them. The holo readouts above the scan station billow sudden light, a flash. But the striv there reads it like she's mapping stars.

"*Beowulf* is down," she says.

Comm says, "We have incoming from *Macedon*."

Not a missile. A message.

Niko goes to his command chair and sits. I find a place on the extra bench at the side of the bridge. The pain floods up my legs. Blood pulses in my head.

"Link us," he orders the comm officer.

Captain Azarcon's voice comes through. It's calm, as if he's speaking from across his desk.

"*Turundrlar*, this is *Macedon*."

"*Macedon*, *Turundrlar*. I am reading you," Niko answers in accented words. "I have *Genghis Khan* in my fire line."

"Do not fire. I want that ship alive." There is no negotiation in his tone; there isn't even a question. Even though he is a Hub ship in facedown with three strivs.

But they haven't fired on him.

"I have boarded her," Niko says. "They *began* their self-destruct. The search is incomplete, but I believe Falcone is not on board."

"Was he on the other pirate?"

"No. I believe he is on my brother's ship. It has fled."

Silence.

"Captain, please wait on the link," Azarcon says, and breaks his end of the connection. Niko turns slightly to his scan officer.

"Where is Ash?"

"He's outbound toward Hub space, *bae. In'tatliar* won't pursue alone."

"No, they can't. Comm, tell them to hold position inside the DMZ. But continue to track him."

"Yes, *bae*."

Scan: "*Bae, Macedon* is firing on *Genghis Khan*."

The holo blooms again, briefly.

I can't move. The *Khan* is dead.

Scan again: "*Bae*, there are two battleships inbound. Earth-Hub signatures . . . *Trinity* and *Arabia*."

"Those were sent by Admiral Ashrafi," I say.

It is like all of EarthHub, right in those three ships.

"They are tracked to fire on us," scan continues.

"Azarcon will tell them not to," I say, hoping.

"He'd better," Niko says. "Hold position. Hold guns."

"Captain," Azarcon's voice comes through again. "Are you there?"

"I am here, *Macedon*. Please tell your comrades to stay out of my way."

Nobody's gunports are closed.

"They won't move without my order," Azarcon says. "Falcone wasn't on *Genghis Khan*, according to his late crew. Now what is this about your brother's ship?"

"He is now in Hub space," Niko says. "Escort my battle group through and you can find out. I have delayed pursuit to guard you."

An EarthHub carrier escort the Warboy?

"Before the *Khan* died, the pirates said you had my jets," Azarcon says.

"I do."

"I'd like them back. In one piece."

"Captain, they are safe. My brother gets farther away. Soon he will be out of scan range."

"Niko," I say.

He holds up a hand to me. Shut up.

Azarcon says, "I want my jets, Captain. I want to know why you're chasing down one of your own. I want to know that whatever the *Khan* was transporting hasn't landed up on your ship—or on the one that got away. Did it skip payment to you? The pirates I captured on my ship said they were going to meet some strits at Slavepoint, behind the DMZ. And here you are. I want answers before anybody goes farther."

"Captain, your ship is injured. Ours are not."

I know how Azarcon will interpret that.

"Captain," Azarcon says, still calm. "That status can be readily changed."

"Niko, let me talk to him."

He looks at me. He's doubtful. I convinced him to stay and now there are three Hub ships against him and Ash farther out of reach. But he motions me forward.

The jets in brig know. Now so will my captain.

I limp to Niko's comm and lean on the chair arm.

"Captain Azarcon, it's Private Musey."

Dead silence. Brief but pointed. Then he asks: "Are you okay?"

He thinks I'm a prisoner. He thinks this is the Warboy's show of good faith. He's waiting for my duress code, so he'll know I'm being coerced.

I don't give it. My fingers dig into the arm of Niko's chair. "Yes, sir, I'm fine. Please, stand down your battle stations. Captain S'tlian doesn't want a fight with you. His brother, Ash, has been the one in trade alliance with Falcone and the other pirates. Captain S'tlian has been tracking his brother all this time, to arrest him."

"And you know this how?" Dangerously temperate.

"Sir, I think you know." I swallow and taste something sour. "Sir, the jets are safe. But Ash will run into a sinkhole in Hub space, with Falcone, if we don't move."

"I have no reason to believe a traitor. I want my jets back. Now. This is not negotiable."

Damned suspicious people. The fact Niko doesn't fire on *Macedon* isn't answer enough?

"He'll return the jets. If you escort the battle group through Hub space. Captain, he did stay on my suggestion until the battleships arrived."

"I'm going to send over a Charger to pick up my crew. I advise you not to fire on it."

The link breaks.

Niko looks at me. "You know this man. Is he agreeable?"

My grip on the chair sends shaking pain up through my arms. "I don't know. But, *kia'redan bae*, if you fire on them this war won't be over anytime soon. Return the jets and take what he offers. If you shoot them now in order to pursue Ash, the long-range outcome will destroy Aaian-na. Admiral Ashrafi will see to that." I look him in the eyes. "You were right. Azarcon has a lot of rein in the Hub. If you work it with him, the rest might follow."

"He seems disagreeable," Niko says. "I haven't shot at him once. If I intended to kill him, he would be dead."

"He wants his crew back. That will convince him."

Because *Turundrlar* never returned prisoners of war before.

Niko taps his comm. "Tkata, escort the jets to airlock two."

"I want to go," I say. "To see them off."

I can't go back with them. He looks at me. He nods, but doesn't get up to take me. This is his bridge and he can't leave it now.

So I go alone.

XVI.

The jets and pilots say nothing. It's all in their eyes. Except for Evan, who stands a bit apart, looking at the deck. They mill in front the airlock, surrounded by armed strivs and symps. And me. Waiting.

Finally Aki looks at me. "Did you kill Kris?"

I meet her eyes. "No."

Dorr snorts and looks at the ceiling. His smile has sharp edges.

Aki wants to believe me. But her doubt is thick. Like their derision. Like my guilt.

Like my guilt.

"That tat's gonna come off," Dorr says. "If I gotta hunt you six ways from the sun. You don't wear *Mac*'s tat on your traitor skin."

I breathe out. "I'll remove it, sir."

"Don't sir me, you bastard!"

It's the truth burrowing into every expression, like the pain of an old wound.

"What'd you tell Birdman, huh?" Dorr continues. He's started and he won't stop. "When he took you out, did you spill about Cap?"

"No. I didn't tell him anything."

"Yah. Yah, 'cept how you whored for the Warboy on our ship."

I am speechless.

"What you tell the Warboy? You tell him all 'bout *Mac* and her armament? What's it take, Muse? He do a little sign language in your pants? That all it takes to get you to roll on somebody, Musey? Damn if you ain't the whore's whore. Loyalty as long as you get your piece of ass."

"You don't know what you're talking about!"

"Yah? You didn't feed info to the strits about us and our routes? About our missions?"

The strivs shift. Most of them might not understand the corporal, but they know the rage.

"Niko has no intention of hurting *Macedon*."

"Who's Niko?"

"The Warboy. The Warboy—he has no intention of doing anything to *Mac*. He put me on her to scope out a peace—"

"You sick bastard. You're on a first-name basis with him."

"Peace through spying?" Hartman asks. "That's novel."

I can't explain. There's no point. Their hatred just builds.

Aki's eyes are hard and shining.

"He saved me from Falcone," I tell her.

But she doesn't answer.

Dorr says, in a tone I can't decipher, "So that justifies you?"

All my words are withered.

One of the strivs gets a comm. He says, "They're ready," and motions to another. We hear the clang and grate of the Charger locking on. The strivs motion the jets to face the airlock.

Evan stares at me.

He doesn't want to go. I see it in his eyes and I can't believe it. He would stay on an alien ship. He asks it, with his eyes, as the lock cycles open and a gust of cold air surrounds us.

But this isn't his place. He didn't survive *Mukudori* and *Shiva* to end up on an alien ship.

I shake my head at him, one movement of denial.

My vision blurs. Maybe it's better that way. I just watch his back, all of them in their black uniforms, as they walk from *Turundrlar* to the Charger. Evan looks back but I can't see his face clearly.

All of them blur and then they are gone.

XVII.

I sit on the deck, in the corridor, because I don't know where to go. Maybe back to the bridge, except it's a long way and my legs don't work. One of the strivs stays, but only one. The rest leave. The striv doesn't talk to me. I want to sleep, but it's so urgent to sleep that I don't think even if I could lie down that I would. I'm too tired to sleep.

I don't know how long I'm there, but the deck gets warm where I sit.

Then footsteps approach. Soft, padding footsteps. The shadow of the striv goes away and another replaces it. I look up against the lights and Niko is there, tall and clean in those white, coiled strips. He holds out his hand to help me stand.

I still have Falcone's scent on my skin. Not even the cold can take it away.

I let Niko grip my hand and pull me up.

On my feet I try to balance. But he doesn't let me. He tugs me into his arms and holds me. A long time. He is warm and I feel his heart, even through the layers of clothing.

There isn't a word in my head to say.

I remember he's human. I feel his arms around me, crushing me breathless. I close my eyes against what I see. I try to make it all black. But I can't and be this close.

I realize my arms are still at my sides. He realizes it too.

"Jos-na." Finally he lets me go. Then he holds my face in his hands, staring into me. I can't say anything. I can't feel anything. He's a face from a dream that I forget when I wake.

He looks down, picking up one of my hands, gently. He runs his finger along the crusted blood around my wrists, where the cuffs bit. "This needs help," he says.

I can't breathe. It rolls in me like nausea. But it's something else.

I step back, almost stumble, but he holds my arm, anchoring me. He cups a hand under my chin. My world dissolves and he catches it all, everything that pours out of me that I can't control anymore.

XVIII.

I fall asleep in his quarters out of sheer exhaustion, in clean clothes like the loose black garments I used to wear on Aaianna. He made me change after he treated my cuts. He put me on his pallet. He cut the lights and let me lie there, alone, because he has to be on the bridge.

The darkness is filled by his scent. I drift and awaken and drift again. More than once I wake up shouting, but nobody hears me.

So I lie there and the sound of the drives is not *Macedon*'s sound.

He comes back. I don't know how long it's been. He brings food and sets it down by the pallet, and sits beside me. For a moment it's almost like no time has passed, and I could be back in my room on Aaian-na.

But it's only a moment.

"What's happened?" I ask him. I can't touch the food. My stomach refuses to unroll.

"*Macedon* is escorting us through Hub space."

I look at him. "Then it's all right?"

He steals some of the cold vegetables. "No. But they are escorting us. I think he's waiting for a wrong move so he has an excuse to shoot at us."

"Has he said anything—asked anything?" *About me?*

"No, Jos-na. I think he's too angry for that."

He eats in silence for a while. I just sit.

"You'll want to debrief me," I say eventually.

He hesitates. His eyes haven't left my face. "Not now. You need rest."

"Now, Niko." It's strange saying his name like that. It's strange to be speaking this language. It feels like an extra skin over my words. "Give me a slate. I'll write it."

His hesitation goes a beat too long. But he finally rises and goes to his desk in the corner. It's a small quarters, bare compared to Azarcon's. Just the pallet and a desk and a washing place, obscured by a curtain. He comes back and hands me the slate. He pauses, caught looking at me. As if I'm a face he's trying to remember. Or memorize.

The deskcomm beeps. He goes to it, answers. His co-captain Tkata aon Tul says they are in attack distance from Ash. He taps off and goes to the hatch.

"Stay here, Jos-na."

He doesn't want me underfoot. Not when he has to capture his brother.

"Are you going over there?" I know how assassins think.

"He is my brother."

"I want to go with you, Niko. Falcone is there."

"You're unwell."

"I'm well enough."

"No."

I stare at him. He let me go for three years on an EarthHub carrier. But he won't let me go two meters onto his brother's ship.

He leaves. I know it's just his way, but for some reason it stings.

I look at the slate. It's faulty. The screen blurs and the image shakes. It's impossible to write. There's nowhere to put my thoughts. They all just collide and break in my mind.

XIX.

I walk around the ship while the attack wears on. The aliens look at me with their black eyes and bold faces, colorful, tattooed faces that I haven't seen in the past three years except at the end of my rifle sight. But those were different strivs. Those were Ash's partisans. The symps I killed were his symps, not like Niko. Not like me.

Except those times *Macedon* caught strivs near stations or depots and attacked, and pirates were probably not involved, they were just strivs and just symps. Like Niko and like me. Maybe some of them that I killed were related to the ones that pass me in the corridors. It's hard to say. The caste colors and tattoos obscure features. And they don't speak to me. I'm a ghost in their way, moving through the Warboy's place.

Tkata aon Tul announces on shipwide that Niko is on his way back. I go to the hangar bay. It's cold and deep and nobody stops me here either. Nobody speaks to me. Ter'tlo isn't around; she probably went with Niko. It's oddly quiet, not like the ruckus in a bay filled by jets and pilots. Equipment moves here, fuel lines lock and scrape across the deckplates, but the people are well tempered, dutiful, purposeful. I stand behind protective plexpane as the APCs lower into the bay on lit platforms. When the lights start to blink green I head down to the deck.

Niko emerges first, holding Ash's arm. Ash is cuffed and there are two strivs behind him with guns aimed. His face is blank.

Behind Niko come more strivs and symps, with others under guard. Streams of them.

One of them is Mra o Hadu. Under gun. He is older, like I am, with the white cold face of an assassin-priest. I remember our spars in the *inidrla-na*. I almost step forward but it is a line of assassins and they are all silent. No taunts, no coercion

n violence. The prisoners can't fight or they will die running
ike game. I stay where I am, off to the side near the bulkhead.
Watching.

No Falcone.

Niko's face does not invite questions. He doesn't see me.
He walks past with Ash, straight out of the bay.

I follow them.

They don't go to the brig. Instead Niko takes Ash into a
wide, clear room. Like a gymnasium, except there is no
equipment. Just clean flooring. Like the *inidrla-na*. Except
here are no windows and no swords on the walls.

It's just as cold here as in the hangar bay.

"Line them up," Niko orders.

His crew positions the prisoners in a line side by side in the
middle of the room, with Ash at the head of them.

I catch Mra o Hadu's black eyes. He stares through me as
f he doesn't recognize me. Maybe he doesn't. It's been years.
We are two different people. Two different beings.

Niko's crew stands behind him, a mirror line to the prisoners, all of them symps and strivs, similarly clothed, simi-
arly colored and tattooed. All of them expressionless. They
might not even be breathing, they are so still.

Niko says, "Begin recording."

The striv nearest to him hooks an optic around her ear and
ilts the eye toward the line of prisoners. A small red light
urns on near the eye.

"Recording, *kia'redan bae*," she says.

Niko says into his brother's face, standing directly in front
of him and only a hand apart: "Speak."

"I have nothing to say," Ash says.

"You have something to say to me. You choose not to. You
choose instead to say it to pirates."

"What can I say that will make a difference to the *kia'
redan bae*?" His voice is the same weary mockery. "*Eja*, you

will make treaty with the captains who have killed our people, our *father*, and look to persecute our mother if given the opportunity. They speak of protectorates in the halls of their government, even as we stand here. Do you think a peace will last, or mean anything?"

"I don't know," Niko says. "Because nobody has yet tried. And don't speak of our mother. This will hurt her more than anything EarthHub can do."

"What do you want me to say, Niko? I'm not sorry."

I see it. I see that Niko is more sorry. I see his profile, how unmoving it is and how carefully he keeps his hands at his sides.

He takes one stride and stops in front of Mra o Hadu.

"You slept in our house," he says to the striv.

Hadu doesn't blink. "*Kii'redan* Ash-dan is my teacher," he says.

"*Ki'redan-na* D'antan o Anil is your leader."

Hadu doesn't answer. But Ash-dan looks at his student and there is pride in his eyes.

"You failed," Niko says.

The blade is in his hand. He stabs Mra o Hadu where the striv heart is, in the center of his chest. He pulls the blade before Hadu crumples to the deck.

The transparent, diamond-specked wings flutter just a little, settling last on the deck. Deep amber blood begins to stain them, spreading out from under his chest.

Ash breathes heavily, staring at his brother. His entire body takes in those breaths and expels them, like he is trying to get rid of something inside that refuses to go. Hadu's blood touches his boots. But he doesn't look down. I don't breathe. I want to stop it. But there's no stopping it. Niko steps back to Ash.

"I curse you," Ash says. Suddenly there are tears in his

eyes and his voice is unsteady. "I curse you for what you're doing."

"It's already begun," Niko says. "You carried it too long, Ash. You became it. And sacrificed children."

"Because this war won't end any other way," Ash says. "You're fooling yourself." He settles. I can't hear his breaths. I can't see his eyes or what they look at. Only Niko sees.

Once Ash was my teacher too.

Niko says, "I do what I have to do."

He raises the knife. He doesn't hesitate. And yet it's not so quick that I don't see the blade. I see it. It's in his hand and it comes down.

XX.

Niko leaves the rest of the prisoners. He holds that knife and walks toward the doors. He doesn't see me. I walk beside him. My booted steps are heavy compared to his light stride.

But his face is hard.

"Niko."

The corridors change as we leave them and enter others. But his eyes don't change, fixed on a point ahead of him. Far ahead of him.

Maybe he's a stranger now. But I grab his arm.

He whirls on me. I step back.

"Go away, Jos-na."

"If you didn't want to do it—"

"Go away, Jos-na!"

"Why? Why did you do it if you didn't want to?"

"Stop asking questions. I'm not your teacher now."

No, he isn't. He is an assassin and I never truly realized it until now.

But I say quietly, "You'll always be my teacher, Nikolas-dan."

Even when we no longer understand each other.

The dark stones of his eyes turn to me. They shine like they have been smoothed and polished by hundreds of years of rivers.

"He betrayed me," he says. "He betrayed himself."

I take the knife from him and he lets me. I take his hand and he doesn't stop me. Then I drop the knife and take his face in my hands. I touch the dark tattoo around his eye, trace it with my fingers. It's everything he is, a complicated knot of meaning, perfect in its intricacy. Alien and immediate. His skin is warm under my hands.

But then he removes my touch, turns, and walks away.

My heart seems to curl. I can't quite reach him in this world, this ship, his place. And I don't know whether he has moved, or I have.

XXI.

Niko wasn't the only one to board Ash's ship. *Macedon* insisted on being part of the raid, since the weapons Ash was trading for were Hub tech and Hub stolen. Niko got Ash and the jets took Falcone. The pirate is on *Macedon*.

Both ships are injured, the carrier more than the striv. Ash shot Niko's ship in the attack but it's exterior damage only. Yet *Macedon* invites *Turundrlar* to dock at Chaos Station for repairs and resupply. It's a long leap back to Aaian-na space.

Niko, on the bridge, agrees. I sit by the bulkhead, in shock.

"I didn't shoot any of his jets," Niko says, as if that explains it. "Maybe he trusts me now."

"Or maybe it's a trap," I have to admit.

"I will risk it," Niko says. He doesn't smile. It will be a long time, I think, before he smiles again.

I try not to feel extraneous. But there's nothing for me to do and Niko seems to think I'm all right just to sit.

Turundrlar docks alongside *Macedon*, at Chaos Station, with two battleships and three striviirc-na marauders hanging offside in space, watching. Not quite trusting. They aren't inured enough to require docking and they all rather keep their eyes on one another. Just in case.

I can imagine the conversation between Captain Azarcon and the Chaos stationmaster. Niko says a few brief words to confirm his good intentions. I doubt anybody really believes him.

"What're they going to do with Falcone?"

Niko glances at me. He turns to his comm. "*Macedon*, here is a crewman aboard my ship. He inquires after your prisoner."

There's a brief pause. Then Azarcon himself answers. "He will be transferred to station authorities, to be extradited to Earth for trial."

I rise and go to the comm. "Sir, may I be in the escort party? In the transfer?"

"No you may not."

"Sir, I—"

"Captain S'tlian, I want to assure you that this is a safe station for you to make your repairs. If you are in need of supplies, simply comm *Macedon* and we will arrange for the materials to be sent, under guard, to your ship. This is in appreciation for your help in apprehending Falcone and stopping that contraband shipment. As soon as you're equipped and spaceworthy, you may peacefully depart from Hub territory and return to your planet."

Thank you and please leave.

"Acknowledged," Niko says. "And appreciated."

I wonder if he understands the nuance.

I leave the bridge.

"Jos-na—"

I slam the hatch shut behind me. Falcone escaped a Hub prison before. *Genghis Khan* may be dead but there are others in his fleet. I'm sure he has allies in the Hub, all the way up in the governments. He was a carrier captain. He thinks he was wronged by his superiors. He thinks he is right to do what he does, because it's war. He probably thinks he will get away with it.

Captain Azarcon should kill him. I don't know how he can have the pirate in his brig and not kill him. Not after he spent time with the man, however long ago that was.

I go to Niko's quarters, where he's letting me stay. I look for weapons.

The hatch opens behind me.

"Jos-na, what are you doing?"

"I'm going to *escort* Falcone."

"You can't do that."

"I've earned it."

He turns me around. "You can't do that. It might make it worse."

He means the war.

I stare into his face. "Falcone got me on his ship. And I couldn't do anything." My voice breaks, a betrayal.

The silence lasts a breath. He knows what I mean. But he's adamant. "If you kill him, then what? EarthHub says you took their rightful prisoner. You, a traitor. A symp. You took the law out of their hands and put it into your own. This isn't their way."

"It's my way. It's my right!"

"It's out of our hands."

"You put me on that ship, Niko. I was three years on that ship and then I got caught again by him. If you'd kept me—"

I can't finish it. I can't even really blame him. Because I betrayed him too.

I try to sit. Or walk out. But he doesn't let me. He holds my arms. It's him and I know it but I see the captain and Erret, Aki and Nathan and Evan following me around the deck.

Kris, dead and gone.

I pull from his hold. "I have to just see them, Niko."

"They will kill you."

I look into his face. I say with no animosity, just as a matter of fact, "My life's been in danger before, with them."

And I got out of it. Without you.

Maybe the thought passes between us. His jaw clenches and he goes to his cabinet and retrieves a striviirc-na designed laser-pulse rifle. It's lighter than the standard LP-150. He tosses it to me. It's his own rifle. I see the battle scars beneath the polished black casing.

He pulls one of his own blades from a forearm sheath and slides it into the side of the rifle stock, where there's a designed place. One quick movement away from where your finger rests on the trigger.

"Go to your jets," he says. "But remind them you are mine."

He would kill them, now, if they hurt me.

"Niko," I tell him, "I'm not yours."

He takes a step toward me, words snared in his throat. I see the thoughts trapped behind his eyes.

It's a tangled silence I can unravel if I stay.

But I open the hatch without looking back.

XXII.

Niko doesn't follow me through his ship's corridors. I don't expect him to. A feeling creeps into my heart like smoke under a door—I don't want him to.

XXIII.

As I step from *Turundrlar*'s ramp I see the dock boards, high above near the maintenance gantries, over the doors leading to the inner station and the concourse. *Caliban* is here, just arrived from insystem. Beside their name says RESUPPLY. Already?

Insystem carriers, Dorr would say, with a smirk. I guess he's right.

By a great show of trust, or perhaps the complete opposite, *Macedon* docked beside the Warboy's ship. There are two jets guarding the carrier's ramp and airlock, armed to the nines. They recognize me and scowl.

"What d'you want, strit-lover?"

"Nothing." I stop at the bottom of the ramp to wait.

"Get lost, Musey."

"I'm not doing anything. I won't do anything."

"You got a weapon. We don't want symps with weapons near our lock. So move it." The jet, Pyper, levels his rifle at me.

I back away. But shadows appear behind the jets. A group of them. One with bright blond hair.

"Well well," Erret Dorr says. He strides down the ramp, in jet uni and his weapons. Behind him come more jets: Hartman. Madi. Dumas. Sanchez.

Falcone in the midst of them, cuffed and bruised.

Captain Azarcon, last, with a gun in his hand.

"Come to bury Caesar?" Dorr asks me.

All of them notice my rifle.

"This isn't wise of you," Azarcon says.

I feel Falcone's eyes on me. I'm not in jet uniform. My clothes are sympathizer clothes, alien clothes, coiled white with hidden knives.

"Are you going to shoot me?" I ask Azarcon.

"Not yet," he says. "Right now I'm busy."

"Hey," Madi says. "There's some of *Caliban*. A day late and a donut short, as usual. We coulda used them at Meridia."

Station Marines are already on their way around the docking ring from the inner offices, come to take the pirate off everybody's hands. I see them in my periphery, a wall of blue uniforms.

The *Macedon* jets stand around Falcone in a guarded circle. He can't run and his hands are tied. They lead him down the ramp.

But I see his smile. I see his eyes go over my shoulder, toward the incoming *Caliban* crew.

I turn, rifle up.

"Musey!"

One of the *Caliban* jets already has a gun in his hand, half-hidden behind his leg. I shoot him first.

The others scatter and return fire.

"Get down!" somebody yells behind me.

I dodge behind the ramp. The dock lights up with laser streamers.

Erret shoves Falcone's face in the deck, half kneeling on his back. "Insystem bastards!"

It looks like *Caliban*'s entire jet complement has swarmed the deck. The station Marines take up positions behind us. *Macedon* can't dispatch jets from the lock, it will put them right in the line of fire.

Turundrlar's lock flanks the *Caliban* jets, on their left.

"Give me your wirecomm," I say to Sanchez, on my right.

Sanchez glares at me. "Why?"

"So I can comm Niko. He'll help us!"

"Do it," Erret tells him, as more laser pulses whiz over our heads.

Sanchez hands over the wire. I slip the pickup in my ear and tap the contacts. But not fast enough.

"Incoming!" Hartman shouts.

Singing grenades fly toward us.

"Move move move!" Dorr yells.

I don't think. I grab Falcone, Erret at his other side, and haul him back. But he fights, kicking though his hands are bound. I hit him with a fist. Dorr tugs the other side.

Captain Azarcon propels all three of us into the station bulkhead with his shoulder as the grenades explode the ramp.

Laser follows the grenades. Going both ways, from their side and ours. It's a mad light show.

I knock the captain down and land over him, feeling the heat sear over my head.

"Strits!" someone yells.

I didn't have to comm them. They heard anyway.

I look up, past the debris of the destroyed ramp. Beyond it, on *Caliban*'s flank, swift bodies descend, firing.

It's a swarm of white into jet blacks. Decimating them.

The captain nudges me off and pushes himself up, looks over at the aliens. In his eyes are good degrees of caution and disbelief.

Falcone slides himself up the bulkhead, in my periphery.

Before the captain says anything, or moves, and before the jets can stop me, I yank the knife from the sheath on Niko's rifle. In one move I throw it through the air.

It sings like a lament.

XXIV.

Falcone tries to get up. I'd hit his chest but not fatally. I pull another blade from my forearm sheath and step on his stomach to keep him down. The knife swings down.

He has no idea until the blade sinks through. I miss his heart purposely and get his shoulder. The bone resists but the knife is sharp and not easy to break. Striviirc-na steel. His blood comes out over my fingers as I feel the weapon tip exit his shoulder through the other side. It doesn't make my grip slide. There are grooves in the hilt. He gasps and struggles, even this injured. Desperation engulfs his eyes, the lines on his face. It makes his cuts and bruises shine. He must feel my weight and see my blade with his blood on it up to the hilt. I stab again into the other shoulder.

The dark centers of his eyes start to expand and freeze.

I'm kneeling in blood on a scuffed deck.

I clamp my free hand over his face, shoving his features into themselves. His skin is hot. The bones of his skull resist.

He says through gritted teeth, "Joslyn."

Before he speaks again I stab his jugular with Niko's knife.

There's a warm flood, and the station is quiet. Space is silent and without a breath. It's like a birth.

But then there's nothing.

XXV.

Their eyes are fixed on me. There's a distance between the jets and myself. I rise to my feet above the body, careful not to slip on the blood. Red streaks snake long patterns up my hands to my wrists. Blood covers unevenly over the tight white coils of my clothing. I wipe the blade on my thigh to clean it.

Aki is there with her medkit, kneeling beside an injured Sanchez. But she isn't doing anything. She looks up at me, like all of them are looking at me, and there's something between horror and tenderness there. I don't know why she would care. Or any of them.

The captain's eyes don't move from me.

A crowd has suddenly formed. Citizens and merchants, all forcibly hanging back but looking at the destroyed dockside. Station security gray, Marine blues. Jet blacks with *Macedon* patches. All the *Caliban* jets are dead or facedown on the deck, guarded by jets and strivs standing side by side. A squad of suits pushes through the crowd. Some of them wear Earth-Hub governmental pins on their lapels. One of them asks sharply, "Who killed the prisoner?"

Erret says flatly, "Why do you care?"

Azarcon looks away from me and stands beside Dorr, addresses the suit who spoke. "Who are you?"

The captain looks like any jet who has been through a firefight. He still holds his gun.

The suit says, as if he's speaking to just a jet, "Harrison Ventura, Chaos Liaison Officer for EarthHub. Who are you?"

The captain says, "Azarcon."

Ventura looks twice. But he's too embarrassed to apologize. His eyes fall on me, my face, my clothing. He blinks a few times. But he's a professional and he turns to the captain.

"Isn't he a symp? You realize this act was unlawful? It was murder."

He actually says that on this dockside, littered by traitors. He says other things, about due process and indictment orders.

I don't know what I'm doing but I'm not going to stand

over that body like I'm paying it respect. I pick up Niko's rifle and start to walk away. I don't know where I'm going.

Aki stands and holds my arm, not hard. But she says, "Stay. Wait."

They talk behind me.

Ventura wants me to stand in the Hub for taking away their due process. He doesn't know yet what I did on *Macedon*. I have half a mind to show them what a sympathizer is up close, but I figure they've already seen it. He says there are lawyers who have come all the way from Earth to collect the prisoner.

Dorr's voice rises above Ventura's, with the authority and arrogance of a soljet of *Macedon*.

"He ain't goin' nowhere with you lot. He belongs to us."

That stops Ventura cold.

Azarcon says, just as cold, "There is no debate. Your prisoner is dead and so are those traitors who tried to free him."

"The symp's alive," Ventura says.

"His guardian is the Warboy," the captain says. "Would you like to contest it?"

"I thought we were contesting it already," the man says dryly. "We're at war, are we not?"

"You might have noticed," Captain Azarcon says, "that the Warboy's ship is currently in dock. So I suggest you talk to Admiral Ashrafi. He's just appointed Chaos Station as the location of our negotiations."

This stuns everyone into silence. I don't know if Azarcon just made that up or if it really has been arranged. I'm acutely aware of meedees with optics vying for a clear view but the Marines and jets aren't having it. Azarcon pretends not to notice and looks at me.

"Corporal Dorr will take you aboard to clean up. When Captain S'tlian arrives you'll be remanded into his custody."

Niko is already on dockside. I see him walking toward us,

flanked by three striviirc-na. But he pauses before he gets here. He hears the captain's words. Nobody recognizes him.

"Sir," I say. "Captain."

Azarcon's eyes look over my shoulder at what's on the deck. He looks into my face. There might be gratitude there. Or compassion. I'm not sure. It's not something I am used to seeing.

Maybe I should apologize, for what that might be worth, but for some reason instead I tell him, "My ship is dead."

Mukudori. For a long time. *Macedon*. I don't deserve her.

Maybe I'm the only one to see it, but the captain's face relaxes slightly.

"Not both," he says. "When you're ready, one will be there."

XXVI.

I find myself in medbay with Aki spraying sealant on my wounds. I don't even remember getting them, but lasers must have brushed me. The crew looks at me but their hostility is muted. Because of the blood on my hands? I don't know, but jets respect that sort of thing. Maybe the captain said something. Maybe the fact he didn't shoot me on sight is something. Maybe Niko's alliance in getting the pirates and the other traitors . . . I'm too weary to ask about it, as Erret hovers and Aki works in silence.

Evan comes in and straight toward me. I think he's going to embrace me but he stops and just puts a hand on the examination table beside me, as if he needs the support in order to stand.

"I thought you were lost again on that other ship," he says. His voice shakes, but not from fear. From memory.

I want to wash the blood from my hands before I touch him. But that might be never and he tried to protect me.

He's always tried to protect me.

So I just rest my hand over his, on the table.

XXVII.

Erret lets me stay in his quarters after my shower. He has to keep an eye on me, he says. For once he makes no innuendo.

"Why are you doing this?" I ask. *Forgiving me.*

"I got orders," he says. But he's lying.

Maybe I'll never really know. He isn't predictable.

There are pictures stuck to his bulkheads, of stations he's visited and crew once or still alive. I look at them all. I recognize a dark blond jet with an *Archangel* patch. Pictures of Hartman and Nathan, Stavros and Madi. There is a small one of a young man and a woman, both fair-haired. An older picture, frayed at the edges, tacked right above his pillow. He resembles them.

There's one of me and Kris and him that is so untouched I see a fine layer of dust. A newer one of me and Evan and Aki, in some sim game drama I can't remember, in the jet lounge. There's one of Iratxe in battle gear.

I sink into Dorr's pillow. It smells like him, like guns and candy. His presence is more comfort than obstruction.

Even the sounds of him packing away his weapons do not grab me from the fingers of sleep.

It's a long, hard unconsciousness.

XXVIII.

The captain comes to see me. It's been a shift, maybe. He's cleaned up, in spotless fatigues, like I am. He leans against Dorr's desk, holding the edge.

"I'm not going to kill you," he says, "or turn you over to the Hub."

I don't know how I look, but something makes his voice gentle.

"Why?" is all I can think to ask.

"You killed him," he says.

"That's not worth anything," I say. "You could've killed him. Why didn't you kill him?"

If Falcone were dead before *Macedon* docked at Chaos, *Caliban* never would have attacked.

"I thought I could," he says. He doesn't look away from me. But I see how difficult the words are for him. Yet he's here, as if he owes me something. "I planned it for years, maybe for too long. When it came down to it I looked at the man—saw nothing but a pathetic old manipulator. Death was too quick for all the years he's made people suffer and I didn't have enough—immediate hatred to do it, anyway. I *couldn't* do what you did, when it came down to it. Do you understand?"

"Because you were afraid?"

He shakes his head. "No. Because I *wasn't*. But that does-n't mean I'm not glad he's dead. I think it's right that you did it. I think you needed to do it more than me, or anybody."

In his own way, he is thanking me.

The captain of *Macedon* is thanking me. For something we have both wanted to do since we were children.

XXIX.

They give me jet BDUs, so crisp and black that Erret says I look like burnt toast. Sprig, he jokes. We stand at the airlock waiting for the captain. It's three shifts later and Niko awaits us. I haven't talked to him. Erret's been my shadow through funerals and long walks, where some of the crew scowled, others looked away, and yet others didn't seem to see a difference. Maybe because *Macedon* is the second chance and maybe we're all on that number. Or maybe just because Erret shadows me.

EarthHub still wants me, but they aren't willing to argue with Niko over it. In a strange way they're less willing to confront Captain Azarcon about it. Maybe because they know who rules deep space and who really controls their borders. Maybe Admiral Ashrafi has a hand in it. Dorr laughs about the fact I have so much brass on my side.

But they aren't really on my side. Only Azarcon and Ashrafi, who have a use for me. Like Dorr does for me, whatever it is. Or like Evan. Maybe it's just in the way people need each other. I don't know. But the rest of EarthHub and the rest of *Macedon* aren't that forgiving. Or practical.

Word went ahead on coded communications that Captain Azarcon is going to begin peace talks. EarthHub either has to support it or fall on their faces in shame when stations and merchants who are tired of the war wonder why the govies aren't online with the deep spacers. The Hub could wrangle it out, Cap said, with his father the admiral. He's just going to have some caff with a sympathizer.

He said, "I already gave one a gun, so why not share a drink."

The humor of this crew.

"Your Warboy ain't all that hot up close," Erret says, lighting a cigret as we wait.

"You haven't gotten close enough."

"I was plenty close. I could smell the strit on him." He grins.

I don't. Some things will take more than a signed agreement to change.

Cap strides up in dress uniform, frowning. Erret and I are decked as jets. I have no clothes but what they give me and they don't seem to mind I am in a uniform that no longer applies. Erret hasn't even mentioned the tattoo on my wrist. Lieutenant Hartman follows the captain. We are the only escort. Erret's appointed himself my guard for the duration so we're a comfortable striviirc-na number of four. Like the principal forms of *na*. Niko agreed to the same.

"Put that out," Cap absently orders Dorr.

"Sorry, sir," Erret says, not really meaning it. He squashes his cig on the deckplates, which makes Cap frown more.

The captain tugs at his collar and heads down the ramp. We fall in behind him.

Niko walks across the short distance between airlocks, perfectly timed. *Turundrlar* is moored beside *Macedon*, doubtless to the extreme nervousness of both crews. But you can't see it in the faces of their captains.

They greet each other with nods. Marines and jets line the dockside, straight out the doors and to the upper level conference room where it will all take place. It's more parade than a show of force, but it's both. Three striviirc-na dreadnoughts hang off stationside, in space. There is an admiral on his way to the deep from Hubcentral. Nobody is fooled that this is absolute friendship.

Captain Azarcon looks Niko in the eyes. Even if the stare isn't habit for him, I told him what strivs and sympathizers expect.

"I have one of your spies," he says, gesturing to me. "I figure we might as well put him to use for both of us, just to make sure there are no misunderstandings. Especially in anything we may write down."

A treaty, he means. It's in his deadpan face, his dark humor.

"You are looking to write something down?" Niko asks, accented words and without a hint of humor. Of course that's just his way.

I glance at Azarcon. He might not understand.

But Azarcon says, "One or two things. Maybe. We'll see how it goes."

Niko looks once at me, but he isn't talking to me. "Do you trust him?"

The captain says, "He saved my life."

I remember that I did. But I couldn't save Kris. Or Iratxe. Or my parents and *Mukudori*.

Maybe they see it in my face. They both look. Niko gestures for me to walk ahead of him. He doesn't know the inner parts of this station, but I can show him.

There will be opportunity in the future, I suppose, for sometime going to a balcony, on a world, with a paper ship in hand to watch it soar and burn.

But it's not now and that's not my place. This is my place. This is where I'm standing, on a station between worlds.

ABOUT THE AUTHOR

KARIN LOWACHEE was born in Guyana, South America, and grew up in Ontario, Canada. She holds a creative writing and English degree from York University in Toronto and taught adult education for nine months in Canada's tundra community of Rankin Inlet, Nunavut.

CRITICALLY ACCLAIMED SCIENCE FICTION
from MAXINE MCARTHUR

"McARTHUR HAS ARRIVED ON THE SF SCENE . . . [WITH] A RICH PROSE
AND OBJECTIVE EYE ON THE INTRICACIES OF HUMAN NATURE."
—Peter F. Hamilton, author of *The Reality Dysfunction*

TIME FUTURE
(0-446-60963-3)

Halley, commander of the deep space station Jocasta, is desperate. Her station is blockaded by hostile creatures, communications and key systems are failing, rations are low, and tension between humans and aliens is at the flashpoint. Then a foreign trader is killed—apparently by an extinct monster. The murder is impossible and the clues make no sense. But Halley must now solve the mystery of a locked room in closed space—before Jocasta erupts in an explosion of terror and death.

TIME PAST
(0-446-60964-1)

Jocasta is awaiting the outcome of a historic neutrality vote to win freedom from the Confederacy. Then the vote's reluctant instigator, Commander Halley, vanishes when an experiment with a captured jump drive leaves her trapped in Earth's past. But as she desperately tries to find a way back to her present, Halley uncovers a conspiracy that threatens history itself and will destroy the Confederacy. Her only hope to avert disaster is to make first contact with the enigmatic aliens who invented time travel—if she can survive long enough.

AVAILABLE FROM WARNER ASPECT WHEREVER BOOKS ARE SOLD

A STUNNING NEW TOUR-DE-FORCE NOVEL
FROM
PETER F. HAMILTON

Author of the Night's Dawn Trilogy

FALLEN DRAGON
(0-446-52708-4)

By the twenty-fifth century, the brilliant notion of a star-trading civilization linking Earth to its interstellar colonies has petered out—the victim of stock market manipulation and cost-benefit analysis. Trade has been replaced by a business-friendly policy of "asset realization" . . . which some might call piracy.

Corporate starships of the Zantiu-Braun 3rd Fleet deploy to colonies, disgorging hordes of invulnerable soldiers called Skins. Enforcing their dictates with both orbital weapons and civilian hostages, the Skins loot whole planets, leaving only poverty, misery, and an industrial infrastructure—so that a few years later, Z-B can harvest again.

But on the bucolic world of Thallspring, Z-B's plans are about to go badly awry, all because of Sgt. Lawrence Newton, Denise Ebourn, and Simon Roderick.

As the players' machinations unfold, none of them suspect that their private war will explode into unimaginable quests for personal grace . . . or galactic domination.

AVAILABLE AT BOOKSTORES EVERYWHERE
FROM WARNER ASPECT